To Karen
Thank you for
your Christian
witness. Enjoy this
as I enjoyed
writing it!
Darla McCann

Debbie Sutton   11-19

Endorsement

When you again awaken from your recurring nightmare only to discover, to your horror, it is all happening to you right here and right now—and that right here is somewhere in the Western Canadian Wilderness, and all you have to save your life is a few years of selling Girl Scout Cookies, it is surprising how your survival instincts can kick start an amazing chain of events, which ultimately results in a life changing decision, which eventually brings you the true peace, contentment and happiness you had always long for.

Darla McCammon has woven a survival adventure love story into a page turning drama, which will keep you pinned to your seat! So buckle up and enjoy the ride.

Lane Anderson, CEO, Intercomm, Inc.,
Specialists in World Wide AVangelism

Diamond Bait

(A North Woods Adventure)

Darla McCammon

WestBow Press
A DIVISION OF THOMAS NELSON
& ZONDERVAN

Copyright © 2015 Darla McCammon.

All rights reserved. No part of this book may be used or reproduced by any means, graphic, electronic, or mechanical, including photocopying, recording, taping or by any information storage retrieval system without the written permission of the author except in the case of brief quotations embodied in critical articles and reviews.

Revised Standard Version of the Bible, copyright ©1952 [2nd edition, 1971] by the Division of Christian Education of the National Council of the Churches of Christ in the United States of America. Used by permission. All rights reserved.

WestBow Press books may be ordered through booksellers or by contacting:

WestBow Press
A Division of Thomas Nelson & Zondervan
1663 Liberty Drive
Bloomington, IN 47403
www.westbowpress.com
1 (866) 928-1240

Because of the dynamic nature of the Internet, any web addresses or links contained in this book may have changed since publication and may no longer be valid. The views expressed in this work are solely those of the author and do not necessarily reflect the views of the publisher, and the publisher hereby disclaims any responsibility for them.

Any people depicted in stock imagery provided by Thinkstock are models, and such images are being used for illustrative purposes only.
Certain stock imagery © Thinkstock.

ISBN: 978-1-5127-1571-2 (sc)
ISBN: 978-1-5127-1572-9 (hc)
ISBN: 978-1-5127-1570-5 (e)

Library of Congress Control Number: 2015916693

Print information available on the last page.

WestBow Press rev. date: 10/22/2015

With much thanks to Adjunct Professor Dee
Anna Muraski for the first editing review
And Dan at West Bow for the developmental editing review

With love to my four beautiful, sparkling daughters
Michele
Darlene
Marlo
Dee Anna
And love to my own diamond in the rough: my husband, John

Chapter 1

June 6, 1994

I woke slowly, much like I remembered from my teenage years when I was sluggish in arising from bed, but the similarity ended when needle-piercing pain from an agonizing headache wrenched my eyes open. Light entered my pupils and intensified the pins pricking my eyes, then morphed them into daggers, almost blinding me. Nausea kicked me like a beach volleyball that had been launched hard at my stomach. I sat up quickly and was immediately sorry. Dizziness and pain throbbed in my head. I felt as if I would be sick to my stomach any moment.

I was correct. I heaved, retched, and gasped. I looked around with blurred vision, but I could see well enough to tell that I appeared to be alone. My stomach became my own enemy as it continued to empty. Soon I felt certain there could be nothing left to empty. I tried to look around a little more, but I felt weak—disoriented. I ached. There was misery in every muscle I owned. My body felt like elastic that had been stretched to the limit and would never recover resiliency. The glare from the sun seemed so bright—was it reflecting off water? *Where am I?*

I could see large shapes moving above me. As I blinked, I saw there were trees towering overhead. They resembled a canopy, waving gently from a soft wind. The sun angled through openings between the branches and sent spears of light to sear my eyes. A vague memory tried to surface. I turned my head slowly and propped myself up on one elbow.

I very carefully looked at my surroundings, but each movement I made produced jarring, searing agony.

I was somewhere outdoors—alone. I could hear water lapping and managed to turn my head to the left. I puzzled over the rocks protruding from the earth like huge pebbles strewn by a giant's hand. They looked familiar, but why? I thought I remembered food—a picnic? I remembered wine or was it champagne? More memories returned. I had been on a lovely picnic with someone—Joel.

Where is Joel? I tried to call his name, but a wave of sickness came over me, and I fell backward. Blackness came again and called me back into unconsciousness. I fought off the blackness. Was this all a dream or was it real? I let the memories flow as I tried to orient my thoughts. Another event in my life surfaced for some reason. While I struggled to stay conscious, I allowed the experience to come back to me ...

I was about eight years old and on a fishing trip with my father in northern Minnesota. We had our boat pulled up and tied to a fallen tree at the edge of the water. We were looking for firewood so we could have a shore lunch featuring the good-sized walleye fish we had pulled in from the large lake where we had rented a cabin.

We had fished all morning. When we clambered out of the boat, my father said, "I'd guess we are about ten miles from our cabin, Mattie." He stroked my long, blonde hair affectionately. I felt like a much admired Rapunzel. He continued, "We are going to have to try to memorize this location. The fishing has been great hasn't it?"

I smiled and nodded and savored one of the rare moments I had alone with my dad. "Let's gather some wood so I can make a fire, and we can eat our great catch," he encouraged me.

We both began gathering twigs and small pieces of downed wood. I found some nice chips left by a beaver around a felled tree. I looked ahead, and deeper in the woods I saw another possible source of beaver chips so I wandered into the forest. The odor of the area was musky with a mossy dampness but heightened with the wonderful scent of evergreen. The day was warm and the sun shining through the trees felt benevolent. I found more chips to put in the bag I was carrying for the wooden treasures I was collecting, and I continued deeper into the forest.

In the distance I saw a beautiful, brilliant red flower, and then I spotted several more in a small clearing just beyond my first discovery. I made my way through the woods to get a closer look. The head of each flower looked like a small red cross on a slender green stem. I was entranced and began picking a few of the flowers as I followed their random distribution throughout the clearing and the area just beyond that.

I completely forgot my wood-gathering mission in my distraction with the flowers. I continued to wander and pick flowers, and when there was quite a nice bouquet, I finally thought about going back to offer my wood chips. I turned around to start back to the boat so I could show my prizes to my father.

I hesitated. Something was wrong. I could not see the boat, or my father, or which direction I should take to get to him. I had wandered much further than I realized. The woods around me, which had looked so warm and wonderful just moments before while I was picking the flowers, had now turned into a formidable barrier. All I could see were more trees and dense underbrush and no sign of how I had arrived at this place. Within a moment, I realized I was hopelessly lost. I felt like a heavy concrete statue, and I could not make myself move. I was frozen in place and frightened.

Finally, I gathered my courage. I turned all the way around and looked in every direction and began to call for my father. "Daddy!" I called out, but my voice sounded small and squeaky. I tried again more forcefully: "Dad!" I was greeted with silence except for the sound of a breeze rippling the tree branches over my head. I heard a noise and scrambled toward the sound, but it was only a squirrel high on a branch dropping a nut to the ground.

The unknown territory and enormous trees loomed around me and became my undoing. The eerie silence following the dropped-nut sound created a fear that welled up in my next panicked call for my father. "Daddeeeee!" my shrill voice echoed through the forest. Still I heard no response and was totally confused about which direction I should take. I was so frightened, tears poured out to blur my vision on their path down my face.

I could feel my nose begin to sniffle and run. I brushed my face with the arm of my sweatshirt and continued to sob. Never had I been so lost and alone. I yelled again and could not tell if a tree branch was scraping another or if there was a distant sound. I tried to listen alertly in spite of my panicked breathing and noisy sobs, but the sound did not repeat itself. Looking around in terror, I wondered what to do. I could not think—could not move.

I heard a loud noise approaching through the underbrush—it was coming toward me quickly. It was easy to imagine that a wolf was breaking through and coming after me. Once again I called for my father, "Daddy, help!" I screamed in fear.

Before I could run away, I heard my father's strong voice call from a distance, "Don't move, Mattie! Stay where you are!"

I obeyed instantly, but continued to watch for the wolf in terror. A few moments later, my father's voice was against my ear, and his big hands held me, soothed me. "It's all right, Mattie," he said while he stroked my head and shoulders gently.

I clenched his strong body in desperation and gratitude. "Oh Daddy, Oh Daddy, I was so scared," I cried into his flannel shirt. "I got lost."

"Yes." His voice held concern and relief. "I know that you got lost."

"I didn't know which way to go."

"I'm glad you didn't move, Mattie. It made it easier for me to find you." He took a big bandana out of his pocket and used it to wipe my face, eyes, and nose.

"It did?"

"Yes, it did. From now on we are going to work on learning some things to help you in case this ever happens again, okay?"

"Okay," I said, "but it's not gonna."

"Not gonna what?" He smiled down at me.

"Not gonna happen again," I said sternly.

"You are right about that."

We made a fire and ate our shore lunch, but almost immediately my father began teaching me things about surviving in a wilderness. "I'm going to show you how to know, without a compass, which direction you are going," my dad said while I listened intently. Then he always gave me a test. "Okay, Mattie, which way is north from here?"

I pointed.

"Good girl!" he praised me.

I learned more under his tutelage. He instructed me carefully. "Here's how to build a fire from very little beginnings, and how to always mark your trail so you can retrace your steps. Do you understand this?"

I did understand and absorbed the knowledge. More lessons were interspersed over my formative years, including summer scout camps with friends. My father and I were always close, but after this incident, we seemed to have an additional bond that strengthened over time.

Why was I remembering that old fishing incident? I was jolted back to the present—an unpleasant place right now. But where was I? How did I get here? I was still disoriented, and I did not like the feeling. Nausea shook me again with violence. When it had subsided, I tried with renewed effort to gather myself together and look at my surroundings. Things started to come back to me—the food, the picnic. I was sprawled on the warm, wool picnic blanket we had retrieved from our boat.

Fragments of memory shot through my mind. Joel had been here with me. It had been just the two of us, and I remembered it being a happy time. I had gulped down too much champagne and then fallen asleep in the lure of the sun's beams atop the cozy blanket. But where was Joel? Why was I feeling so ill? What was wrong?

Something seemed terribly wrong, but I couldn't organize my thoughts into a cohesive union. Vague memories floated in and out of my mind, but I couldn't concentrate. My head and limbs felt like they weighed five times their normal weight, and it took monumental effort to try to move.

I felt lethargic—almost liquid. My vision was blurry, and I had trouble bringing things into focus. Was Joel ill too? I must get up to help him—must try to find him. I tried to move, to get up, but I grew dizzy immediately. I felt weakness coming over me, and I felt myself falling back on the blanket. What had prompted me to remember that old fishing trip? Perhaps it was seeing all the trees overhead much as I had seen them when I was a lost child. Perhaps it was concern over the possibility that Joel was as lost as I had been then.

Although I tried to remember, only snatches of my life were coming back to me since I had awakened. Scanning my surroundings again, I was less concerned about my own safety and whereabouts than fear for Joel. But as I turned my head and searched the rocks, water, and forest, I could not see any sign of Joel. I called him, much like I had called my dad as a youngster: "Joel!" The only sound that returned to me was the lapping water and the rustling trees.

I realized that this time I was lost, and my father was not here to rescue either myself or Joel. I had a crazy thought: *Would Daddy even want to rescue Joel?* That direction of my thoughts led me back to the first time Joel and my father had met each other.

Chapter 2

I was twenty-two years old on the day I brought Joel home and introduced him to my father. Joel was six years older than me. "Dad, I want you to meet Joel," I said, beaming at my father.

"How do you do, sir?" Joel smiled that smile that mesmerized me. It did not seem to be having the same effect on my dad.

"Nice to meet you, Joel." My father's voice was cordial but measured as he shook Joel's hand. "You can call me Mitch."

"Yes sir, uh, Mitch. You sure have a nice house here. I really like those sculptures over there. Are they by Russell?" I made a mental note to give Joel a plus for art knowledge. I had no idea he would be able to recognize original art. Dad did not seem impressed.

"Remington," he corrected.

"Those paintings behind that couch are very nice too."

"Thank you." My father always dismissed comments about his art collection except when he was with special friends with similar tastes. He avoided further questions about his valuable sculptures and paintings by asking a question of his own. "I understand that you work over at our country club?"

"Yes, that's how I met your daughter. She's really something." Joel complimented me, and I smiled at him. This meeting meant a great deal to me, and Joel knew it.

"You're not from around here?" my dad stated, and it was not a question.

"No, but I like it here—a lot." Joel looked pointedly at me again.

Ignoring the looks darting between Joel and me, my dad continued, "Is this your plan for a career then? Working in a country club?" The notion that my father disapproved of this vocation for his only daughter's social circle was not lost on Joel.

"Oh no, sir, not at all. I expect to move into a business marketing position soon. This is just temporary."

"It is?" My father looked as surprised as I was at this revelation. "What college did you attend? Do you have a business degree?"

"Uh, it's a small college in … uh … Pennsylvania. Not many people have heard of it." Joel changed the subject and asked "Do you play golf, sir? I don't believe I've seen you out at the club much since I've been there."

I interjected, "Dad's a great golfer, Joel, but he gets pretty busy sometimes. Dad, I guess I haven't seen you out there much this spring either."

"Well," my dad responded to both of us, "we will have to fix that very soon won't we?" He smiled at both of us, then turned to Joel and asked, "What is your golf handicap?"

"I'm usually around a 9 or 10." Joel smiled proudly.

"You may have to spot me a few before I make any wagers then." Dad nodded. "How did you learn to play so well? Your dad?"

"No, my dad died a long time ago, uh, back in Pennsylvania. I used to hang around a golf course when I was a kid, and they kind of took me under their wing and began to show me the ropes—and the game. When I got older, they hired me to work there."

"So you had references for this job?" Dad said thoughtfully. "How did you fit in college and work before then?"

"I had references, but I doubt if they checked them since I usually demonstrate professionalism from the start," Joel said somewhat smugly. "As to college, I managed to do both by working part-time and attending classes part-time. It was a lot of hard work." Joel seemed to be attempting to enlist sympathy for his former life and struggles, but he did not know my father. I would suggest he tone it down next time they met. My father set the standard for hard work. I should know.

"Why didn't you go straight into business marketing instead of this job?" I was now wondering the same thing and why Joel had not told me he had a business degree. This certainly seemed to be several steps down and a waste of his education. Joel did not answer immediately, and this also surprised me because he was usually very quick-witted.

"Well," he paused and I could almost see his brain organizing his answer, "there were some family issues when I got out of college. One of my professors who became somewhat of a mentor for me, suggested that I not try to step into a high-pressure job for a while, that it would be good to take a hiatus from all the school and work and stress. He suggested a move—a fresh start—and he said learning how businesses work from the ground up, like this country club, could actually be a good plus in my résumé for the future, and it would benefit me in the long run with experience that others would not have."

"Hmmm. Help you understand more of the life of someone on staff in case you had to supervise a staff someday?" my dad offered. I was learning surprising things about Joel and felt a little hurt that he had not shared any of this with me. I looked across the room and saw his expression change—was that relief?

Joel jumped on this lifeline offered by my dad. "Yes, that's it exactly!"

My dad had that measuring look again and said to Joel, "Do you know Sam and Barry Hanks? They are usually regulars out at the club. I happened to have lunch with them last week. They talked about one of the new employees in the pro shop. I wondered if it might be you since Mattie has been giving me vivid descriptions about your appearance." He looked at me fondly. "I believe she is correct in your resemblance to her favorite movie star."

Joel smiled at me across the room at this comment. I was embarrassed. Dad continued, "At any rate, Barry was talking about an experience he had in the pro shop. It seems there was some incident involving a golf shirt?"

"Oh, that." Joel looked discomfited for a moment, then said, "It was all a misunderstanding. It could happen to anyone," he said as he tried to dismiss it.

I was surprised by Joel's hesitant answer. He was usually so confident. I was also surprised that Joel had not told me about any incident since we had grown very close lately. We were now in an exclusive dating relationship that, at Joel's request, we were keeping secret for the time being. I was complying, but with reluctance. I wanted to brag to my friends about our affection for each other. I wanted my father to approve of my choice in Joel.

"What happened, Joel?" I asked him, wanting to be sure my father didn't get a wrong impression. I really wanted him to like Joel. "What was the misunderstanding?"

"I was working in the pro shop," Joel explained, "and Barry came in with his monthly bill. You know how we allow members to charge things each month and then send them the amount they owe for the previous month?" He looked at me, not my father.

I nodded. "So?"

"Well, Barry claimed that a golf shirt I had sold him last month had been charged at sixty dollars rather than forty dollars. He claimed I had not given him a receipt, but I am usually very careful about things like that, so at first I told him the charges had to be right; however, when he got argumentative, I just took it off his bill."

"*Barry* got argumentative?" my father interrupted and looked mystified. We both knew mild-mannered Barry, and this did not fit his character.

"Y ... yes, I know, he's generally a nice guy," Joel stammered as if he recognized a mistake, "but he did get a bit nasty with me. It surprised me too."

"Well, you did correct the billing didn't you?" I defended Joel. "I should think Barry would thank you for fixing what had to be a mistake." I looked pointedly at my father, who did not look convinced, but we changed the subject, and I saw to it that the rest of the evening passed pleasantly. Joel roundly beat me at our pool table, and I laughingly accused him of being a pool shark.

He just laughed, looked around to be sure we were alone, and then hugged me.

Shortly after that introduction to Joel, my dad began appearing at the club more often. It might be a round of golf one day, meeting friends for dinner there the next. I frequently saw him watching Joel as well as talking with him as I continued to date Joel and fell deeper in love with him.

My one disagreement with Joel was over keeping the depth of our relationship secret. I chafed at this because I wanted all my friends, many of whom were also enamored with Joel, to know I was the one Joel had chosen. I especially wanted to share this news with my best friend Josie. I told Joel this one evening when he and I were together.

"I don't understand why you do not want to broadcast this to everyone," I pleaded. "I want my friends to know you love me," I wheedled.

"I know, but I want to be sure your father approves of me first." He remained unconvinced. "So I think we need to go slowly, Mattie. Please bear with me, sweetie." I didn't like this situation, but Joel was firm and I wanted to please him, so I followed his lead.

I invited my friend Josie to the club one day to help me volunteer for a charity golf outing. We were positioned with a golf cart and coolers of different beverages in back for the golfers' convenience. It was a fundraiser for the local animal shelter, and we also had some of their staff back at the clubhouse with pets available for adoption.

It was a scramble tournament, and we had been selling our ice-cold beverages like crazy in the hot weather. The foursome with Joel included in their team boisterously rounded the curve and came up to where we were sitting in a space between the fourth and the sixth tees. Joel looked so handsome in his slacks and golf shirt as he said, "Hello, you beautiful ladies." Joel swept off his golf cap like a buccaneer and bowed at us.

I did not recognize the other three, but one of them snickered and asked, "Yeah, you offering refreshments? My lap is available."

Josie held up the drink sign. "This is *all* we are offering," she emphasized. They all laughed, including Joel.

Joel walked over near me and reached in the cooler for his drink. He leaned over, touched my cheek, and winked at me. "How is your team doing?" I asked.

"We're four under par so far," He smiled at me and looked around before he quietly added, "and that prize money is going to be very nice!" Within minutes, the four men jumped back in their two golf carts and took off for the next tee.

Josie looked at me oddly. "Did Joel bring in some ringers? I've never seen those guys around here before."

"Why would you ask that?" I became defensive, but also wondered who those other three golfers were and how Joel had teamed up with them.

"Nobody in this club, even in a scramble, ever gets four under par in the first four holes." Josie looked skeptical, and I knew she had overheard Joel tell me he was planning to win.

"I know," I answered her, "but I am sure it was just a coincidence. Maybe some friends he knew from his old course in Ohio dropped in. I'll ask Joel about it later."

"He also did not pay for his drink." Josie looked at me pointedly.

"Who?" I questioned her.

"Joel."

"Oh, I am sure that was just an oversight. We were busy talking."

"I could see that. I could also see he thinks he has you wrapped around his finger."

"Here, I'll pay for his drink. He can pay me back later." I ignored Josie's "finger" remark and added, "I'm sure he forgot about paying for his drink because we were talking, and he had to hurry and catch up with the others." I dug into my purse and put the money in our little dog bank that was for collecting the funds. Josie was my best friend. She had to know I wanted her to like Joel. She made no further references to the incident, and I decided to ignore it.

A while later, we sold out of our supply of drinks and headed back to the clubhouse. I walked over to look at the pets from the humane shelter. One little dog, a mix of wirehaired fox terrier and mutt, was precious—and smart. His tannish-red fur sprung out in the most adorable places, giving him a mischievous air.

"Sit," Josie commanded. He sat. His tail was unfettered in the process, so it wagged very happily, swishing the ground behind him.

"I wonder what the adoption fee is?" I smiled at Josie and petted the dog I had already mentally named Fred.

"I wouldn't care if it meant he found a good home," Josie said.

"I'm going to check—" was all I said when Fred suddenly stiffened and began to growl—but not at me.

"What kind of flea-bitten mutt is that?" I heard Joel's voice say derisively as he came up behind us. Fred growled more, and I picked him up to quiet him. He continued to look at Joel warily.

"He's a certified mutt," Josie said indignantly, "and they're the best kind."

"Huh?" Joel scoffed. "That thing looks like a ragtag jumble of bones and hair."

"But he's so sweet—" I began.

"She's thinking about adopting him," Josie spoke out defiantly. Joel's stance changed immediately.

"I think this is something you might want to wait on, right now, Mattie." Joel changed his voice to a softer tone and seemed to realize how much I liked Fred. "There will be other opportunities, but for *right now*," he emphasized, his eyes full of meaning, "don't you think it would be better to wait on a decision like this?" His voice was cajoling. Josie was alert, her eyes full of unanswered questions. Fred continued to squirm.

"I suppose it could wait …" I looked down at those big brown, doggy eyes and felt another tug at my heart. I handed Fred to Josie and said, "How about if I pay the adoption fee and let you adopt him, with me having visitation rights?"

"You're kidding, right?" Josie looked at me in surprise. "I already have Buster plus my two cats, Sinbad and Sheba. Did you forget? I am not sure Buster would welcome another dog in the house."

"Tell you what," Joel said with a smile, "if the dog does not get adopted by the first of next week, I'll go down with you and we'll work something out together. How does that sound?" Relief coursed through me at this chance we could do something for this wonderful dog. "That's wonderful, Joel! Thank you!" I beamed. I gave Fred a final pat, and Josie and I returned him to his crate. I couldn't hear what Josie mumbled under her breath, but I did not think it was complimentary toward Joel.

Joel and I were very busy for the next week, and I never did find the time to get back out to the shelter to check on Fred's welfare. I did worry about him, so I went online to their Web page and saw a big "adopted" banner across Fred's photo. I felt sad for me, but happy he had found a home. And Joel was right—the timing was not the best.

One day about a month after the golf outing, I arrived earlier than usual at the club. As I climbed out of my convertible, I saw my father and Joel in a conversation in another section of the parking lot. Both looked somber. Joel gestured several times with a surprisingly defensive posture, and my father carried that stern look I had seen a few too many times in my childhood when I was being reprimanded.

Once they saw me, they stopped talking, and I thought they almost looked guilty. But they changed posture immediately, smiled and waved at me, and then disappeared to go their separate ways. I wondered what that was about, but I waited to see if either of them would bring it up. Some time passed before I was able to find a small clue.

"Your dad doesn't like me," Joel stated flatly one evening when we were down by the amazing St. Louis arch overlooking the Mississippi.

"What makes you say that?" I asked and avoided the *I'm beginning to think the same thing* thought that floated into my mind. Things had been turning awkward when the three of us were together, or when Joel came to our house for a swim in the pool with me.

"Your dad hardly acknowledges me when I come over," Joel complained. "In fact, last Thursday when I went into the kitchen to get you a soda, he looked at me like I was going to steal everything in the refrigerator."

I had to admit Dad had been bordering on rudeness to Joel a few times, so it was hard for me to defend my parent, but I tried. "Dad has been under a lot of stress lately," I said weakly. "I'm sure it has nothing to do with you, Joel."

"I'm not so sure about that." Joel turned to face me. "In fact, whenever we are in the same place, I can feel tension from your dad like static electricity about to spark. He really doesn't like me, and I can't imagine why." Joel's voice carried the complaint that if I didn't know better, I could have interpreted as a whine. Along with this, I felt a sense of guilt that surprised me by leaving me with resentment toward my own father. I thought about the situation for a few moments before I responded.

"You said you want to marry me, Joel. Did you really mean it?"

"Of course I mean it. Would you like to elope tomorrow?"

"No. You know very well I have always dreamed of a marriage like my dad and mom had. I have photos of her at their wedding when she was still so healthy and pretty. I want to wear that same gown when I marry you."

"Well, your dad is not going to approve of a wedding, I can tell you that. That's why I have cautioned you not to push him just yet." Joel was careful not to show his own animosity toward my dad, but it came out in subtle ways.

The same loathing—perhaps stronger—emanated from my father. They maintained a courtesy for my sake, but there it was: my father and the man I loved and now hoped to marry only tolerated each other because of me. I loved them both, and they abhorred each other!

"I think we are going about this the wrong way," I said thoughtfully. "Why don't I just have an open conversation with my dad and try to bring him around? I don't want to keep silent about our love any longer, and I think the best thing is for me to talk to him."

"I don't think that is going to work. He has made up his mind about me, and I don't think even *you* can change it. I still think you should consider eloping with me—and soon."

It took a while, but I finally convinced Joel how badly I wanted that beautiful wedding and how I felt my father would relent in the end. We agreed I would approach my dad for a talk.

How vividly I remember the clashing conversation with my father on the fateful day I told him I wished to marry Joel.

"So you want my blessings for this fiasco," he hissed, his face red from controlled temper.

"Joel loves me, and I love him," I replied, not deterred by my father's gruffness. I knew there was a gentle person underneath the rough facade he presented to the rest of the world.

"Mattie, you know so little about love—" he began, but I interrupted.

"I know you're remembering my mother and the love you had. I know how you have been both dad and mom to me since I was five. I loved her too, you know, and I saw the love the two of you had. Wouldn't you want me to have that same wonderful experience?"

"Mattie," he said slowly, trying to switch his tone, "yes, I want you to know that kind of love, but can't you see this isn't the same?"

"I remember my mother and your love more than you realize, Dad. I can still see her. She would scoop me up in her arms and wrap them around me in a big hug. I remember how you used to smile, like a benediction on both of us. Great love like that is exactly what I want. And that is how I feel when I am with Joel."

"Love?" he repeated. "Love?" he almost spat at me. "Love means much more than the infatuation you are feeling for Joel." His voice softened, "I'm sorry Mattie, but you know so little about what constitutes love and marriage." I knew he was remembering her—my mother.

"I remember her too, Daddy." I frowned at him. "I remember how suddenly my beautiful mother turned sick when I was only five years old. I watched the cancer take her away from us for the next two years. I know you loved her, but I loved her too, Dad."

He didn't answer me right away, but I could see my own thoughts reflected in his face. My mother's illness had been a harsh and severe time. My laughing, playful, joyful mother faded into a shrunken skeleton.

"We didn't mean to push you aside Mattie, but the point I was trying to make is how marriage also means a commitment to struggle through very harsh times. And sometimes there are casualties while we learn. I know you were bewildered by her illness and then losing her."

"She tried to help me, Daddy. She told me to take care of you and to help Blanche take care of both of us."

"Yes, dear Blanche." He smiled sadly. "Not many people have a housekeeper who becomes such a part of the family. She was able to help you when I ignored you."

"When mama died, it was Blanche who came and found me where I was hiding."

"She found me too," he added ruefully, "and chastised me for forgetting about my little girl's needs in the middle of this disaster in our lives. That's when I came and found you."

"I thought maybe Mama didn't love us anymore, or that I was too naughty and that made her leave."

"We were both devastated. Seeing your pain helped me forget my own and realize I had a beautiful little girl I needed to console. Do you remember what I told you?"

"Yes, you said she was gone from our lives and nothing could bring her back. You said it wasn't anybody's fault; it just happens sometimes. That she would have stayed here with us if she could. Then you told me that we only had each other from now on."

"I left out Blanche. She has been our family too, hasn't she?" Dad reminded me.

"Yes, Blanche is the grandma I never had ... and Dad?"

"Yes?"

"I have talked to Blanche about Joel. She thinks he is charming."

"That doesn't mean she thinks he's good for you, Mattie." My father was revealing more of his attitude about Joel.

"You may remember your mother, Mattie, but you are inexperienced in love," he told me, his voice harsh again. "What you feel for Joel is infatuation—not genuine love."

"It's love," I replied, not giving an inch.

"Mattie, do you remember the shirt incident at the club, when Barry was overcharged?"

"Yes, what does that have to do with anything?"

"Barry is not the only patron who has complained about erroneous charges on their bill."

"So? Mistakes happen."

"Yes, mistakes happen, but they have consistently increased since Joel started working in the pro shop. It would be very easy for someone to pocket the difference between the inflated charge and the actual charge wouldn't it?"

"Not if they had the receipt."

"Quite a few patrons say their receipt was not put in the bag."

"Can you prove this was Joel?" I could not believe my father was pointing out something so petty, especially since I had quizzed Joel about this and was assured that he had not been the one making the error. Joel had informed me he did not say anything to my father about it at the time he had questioned Joel because he did not want to implicate Jeremy. Joel said he suspected Jeremy, the other worker who was hired on at about the same time as Joel. I couldn't help but admire Joel for protecting Jeremy until something could be proven.

"No. At this time there exists no solid evidence, but the circumstances look very suspicious, and I think you should consider the character of this young man before you think about getting married to him." The argument was not to end there, and I continued to resist my father's no-nonsense business mien that had made him so successful.

Being my father's daughter, I could also be stubborn when I chose, as Blanche often reminded me during those times. "He's not the only one," she pointed out when I complained about my father's unyielding spirit. "You inherited a bit of that strong will yourself. Remember how you learned about firm business dealings at your daddy's knee?"

After my mother's death, Daddy, the owner of a large telecommunications company, took me on many of his business travels, especially in the summer when I was out of school. He made me feel important and useful. "You must be my personal assistant," my handsome parent would coach me as he helped me dress for the occasion.

On would go my "business" outfit, a little vested suit tailored in my small size. The jacket, a miniature version of his, all the way down to the edge of a white handkerchief peeking from the breast pocket, was pinstriped; the skirt and vest custom fitted to match. My blindingly white starched blouse—a testament to Blanche's care—would be expertly set off with a natty looking scarf tied round my neck in imitation of Daddy's ties.

"There are some gentlemen coming to our hotel suite," he would tell me as I fastened my black patent leather shoes and pulled up my favorite white stockings—the ones with the lacy frill around the top.

"Will we get to play some games?" I asked, while my tummy tightened in excitement like it did right before one of my birthday parties.

"Yes, but they will be very grown-up games." He smiled. "You will not get to participate until you are older." He saw my frown and quickly added, "But you will learn as you watch what happens." I still remained puzzled, and he could read my face very well. "This is important to me, Mattie. I am depending on you. These men won't be accustomed to children in a business meeting, so you must be on your best behavior. You must prove to them it was not a mistake for you to be here, understand?"

"Yes, Daddy." I nodded solemnly. I did not want to do anything that would disappoint my father.

"Now," he said with a smile, "when I ask you for The First Federal Papers, you must bring me these." He pointed to a folder with a blue tab.

"Okay, Daddy." I almost strutted, excited to feel so important and part of his business dealings.

"Then, when you hear me say, 'Monroe Street Construction Plans,' this—" he picked up a folder with a green tab, "is the folder I want you to bring to me." He looked at me, his brown eyes serious. "Mattie, if you do these things correctly, I will be able to give you more responsibility next time. Do you think you can handle the job?"

"I can do it," I said, standing as straight as I knew how and ready to take on this special challenge.

"I know you can, sugar. I'm counting on it." He nodded with a fond, yet smug look.

At these meetings, the gentlemen would arrive in their dark suits and shining black business shoes, their muted ties of burgundy or navy tones very properly knotted under the stiff collars of their bleached white shirts.

I often wondered if they had a "Blanche" at home, but I was careful never to ask such a question. My father would have considered it out of bounds. I was very careful to be helpful yet inconspicuous. If it bothered the businessmen to have a schoolgirl in their midst, they never mentioned it in my father's presence. I would execute my duties without flaw under the benign watchfulness of my father, and each time he would increase my exposure to his business procedures.

"You're good for my business, Mattie," my father laughed and confided in me after a particularly successful negotiation. He hugged me to him as we snuggled down in a big wing chair in the hotel suite living area after the meeting. We were waiting on room service to deliver our meal. "You gave me the little edge I needed today." He smiled. "No one else has a Mattie to soften them up." I snuggled closer and enjoyed my sense of importance.

As I grew older, it seemed natural that I become more and more involved in those business dealings. I began to understand and learn in more depth what went on in those hotel rooms, those conference rooms, even—as I later matured—those board rooms.

We became a team in many ways, and our wealth multiplied under my father's sage management. I learned much about telecommunications, my father's primary field of expertise and investment. I understood the importance of transatlantic cables for expanding global markets and could communicate this information with ease to others. I was taught the magic of how a telephone could carry my voice across a street, across a continent, and across the sea.

With my father, I visited central offices before they converted to electronic technologies, and I would look up at the racks and bays of colorful cables, mingled like brightly hued spaghetti strands that stretched endlessly into the overhead void. Vertical sections joined the cables and connected them at juncture boxes that had brilliantly colored flashing lights indicating the continuity of signals traveling through all the cables.

The technicians would point out a blue wire and a blue novelty wire that indicated it had an alternate colored stripe wound around it like a peppermint stick. I was amazed at the constant chattering sound of the relays overhead as they processed each call. Each pulse dialed caused a chain reaction, duplicated by a thousand other pulses a thousand times an hour.

I used to imagine some of the conversations taking place as I watched the technicians with their test sets that monitored for troubles on the lines. My childhood imagination was vivid during those times. I imagined this line carried a call from a wealthy foreign prince to his forbidden love: a peasant waitress he met here in the States. That line over there would be another call from a group of evil men who were planning a flamboyant bank robbery. Yet, another call would be a young woman—thwarted from her true love by her family—talking with her love about their plans to elope at midnight.

My fantastic dreams knew no restrictions, but the reality I knew, was much more mundane. "George, would you bring home a loaf of bread?" or "Geraldine, have you heard the latest about Marge?" or more frequently commerce phone calls, "We need to order supplies for our office."

However, my childhood was not all work and business with my father. We took these business trips, but we also took vacations. I went to wonderful Girl Scout camps each summer held on various lakes in the hill country of Missouri. I learned much from those outdoor activities about safety and survival. Sometimes friends, like Josie, went with me.

The Ozark Mountains were a wonderful place to learn about the outdoors and how to appreciate both its natural beauty and its potential hazards. I also had opportunities to take what I had learned and teach it to other younger Scouts and even Brownie Scouts. I loved how they looked at me with adoring eyes as I explained some new secret of tying knots or catching rainwater to drink.

In addition to the Scout outings, there were also wonderful trips that broadened my view of the world. My favorite jaunts were trips in the summer to northern Wisconsin and Minnesota for fishing. Daddy would plan his fishing excursions far in advance. We would make a list of all the paraphernalia we would need: the nets, the various poles, reels, and lines. We included the tackle box, crammed full of lures; some were old favorites, some new hopefuls.

We would take an assortment of clothing on the optimistic chance we would have warm weather and others for the more realistic possibilities of chilly, cold, and wet. Chilly, cold, and wet often happened, but it didn't matter to me. I was with the one person I adored above all others, and I had him all to myself for a full week! We rented cabins and boats to try various lakes. We caught bass and panfish, mostly the flat, disk-shaped bluegills or golden striped perch.

We ate much of our catch and froze a portion to take home for Blanche—she especially liked the flavor of the northern walleye, so we always made an effort to take home our limit. When we were out in the boat fishing on the lake, I enjoyed teasing and tempting the northern pike out of their hiding places in the weed beds that lined the shore.

Occasionally, one of us would experience a thrill when we hooked into the more rare muskellunge or "muskie" fish known for its ability to fight back and extricate itself from the hook. These were exciting moments in an attempt to land a big fish. Yes, those were magical times for me.

It was on one of those enchanting fantastic fishing trips that we devised our secret code word. My father had been particularly thoughtful that day as our time on the lake was nearing an end. He was pensively watching me, his eyes glowing with an intense fondness. I felt basked in warmth and love. In a few seconds, however, his demeanor suddenly shifted and his eyes took on a look I had never seen there before. Was it fear? Was it possibly concern? There had been breaking news before we left home about a young man from a wealthy family who had been kidnapped. We had talked about how I should never talk to strangers.

"Mattie." He reverted to the carriage he usually exhibited around me and smiled. I had just hooked a small northern pike and was grappling with it, but I managed to smile back while he continued. "How would you like to have a secret code word, just between us? It will be our little mystery—our little secret."

This sounded very exciting to me, so I quickly wrestled the fish (that was too small to keep) back into the water where it thrashed its tail at me and darted away under the boat. I turned my full attention to my father. "What do you mean, 'secret code word,' Daddy?"

"I mean a special word that only you and I know. Let's say, for example, someone came to your school saying I'd sent them for you," he paused thoughtfully as if searching for the right words. "You could ask them, 'What's the secret code word?'"

"Oh yes!" I giggled. "And if they didn't know it, I would know I shouldn't go with them, right, Daddy?" I was fascinated by the idea. It sounded like an exciting spy mystery, and as I was about to enter my teen years I had become enamored of books about spies. This new idea met my fanciful dreams perfectly.

"Absolutely right, sugar!" My father gave me a lopsided grin. "We have not talked about it much, but not only have I been very successful financially, you also were left quite a legacy—which means a lot of money—by your mother's family. This will protect both you and your inheritance."

"Oh. Okay. That'll be fun! What's the word gonna be, Daddy?" I flung my lure back toward some lily pads and reeds to let it slowly start to sink before I jerked it and reeled quickly to simulate baitfish that might attract another northern pike. My attention was only halfheartedly on the fish because I was enthralled with the idea of a secret word.

"Hmmm, I don't know—do you have any ideas?" His comical, sideways grimace as he pretended to struggle to think, made me laugh. I stared at my fishing pole and thought about a secret word. My young mind loved puzzles and challenges.

"How about where we are—Wisconsin?" I suggested.

"Hmmm, yes, that's good. But a secret code word should be a puzzle don't you think? A lot of people might know the word *Wisconsin*." He paused.

"I know! I know! How about 'Wisconsin' spelled backward?" I said excitedly.

He cocked his head, "Let's see if that would work. That would be n-i-s ..." he hesitated.

"N-o-c," I added halting between each syllable. Thinking backward was a challenge.

"But s-i-w?" he interjected with a frown. "That's a bit awkward."

"Let's make it nis-noc-si, without the *W*, Daddy," I proposed as I pronounced it with an accent on the middle syllable, "Nis-*noc*-see."

"Sugar, that's great! Nis-noc-si it is. Let's shake on it."

"Do we need to take a blood oath or something?" My Girl Scout days of reliving Indian lore came to the forefront.

"No, I think we can just cross hands, like this, and remember it forever." He took my hands in a cross-handed shake that looked like a giant X.

We shook our special handshake, and then he reached across the boat and hugged me. In a few minutes, he helped me unhook a nice, big fish and store it in the live well. When the pike was safely swimming with our other captive fish, my father looked across at me once more and winked as he said, "Now, don't forget our special secret code word, nis-noc-si."

"I won't forget, Daddy." I winked back, glad to have another bond with my father. From that time on I would receive an occasional note or call from him that was a little different.

"Secret password?" he'd ask, waiting for my response.

"Nis-noc-si." I'd jump with the response, glad he'd remembered, and glad we had this special secret between us.

School had just started in September when I was called to the front office by the receptionist. "This lady is here to pick you up today." She smiled. I looked at an older lady who looked pleasant enough.

"Yes, dear, I am here to take you home early because your dad has been called out of town, and you have a dental checkup," she explained.

"I do?" I didn't remember any dental appointment. I decided this was a good time to try out my secret code word. "What is the secret code word?" I asked her.

"Secret code word?" She looked puzzled.

"Yes, my dad and I have a secret code word. If you don't know it, I can't go with you."

The receptionist now stood and looked concerned. "You don't know this lady?" she asked me.

"No, and if she doesn't know the secret code word, she was *not* sent by my daddy to get me."

"Well, Natalie." The lady looked upset. "I am very sorry, but I am supposed to pick you up, and I do not know of any secret code word."

"My name's not Natalie." I looked at the receptionist, who in turn, looked at the lady.

"Oh dear, I thought you said 'Mattie' when you came to the desk." The receptionist had a frightened look on her face. "I think I had better call our principal, Mr. Phillips."

When Mr. Phillips arrived, I overheard parts of the conversation. "I did not say 'Mattie Huntington.' I very clearly said 'Natalie Hunterton.'" The lady now began to sound indignant.

My father and Natalie's family were both contacted, and once everything was straightened out and corrected, I was loudly praised, especially by my father. The secret code word worked. Natalie's family found out about the idea and decided to use one with their daughter in the future as well.

So, our lives went on and my relationship with my father grew strong—even surviving a stepmother when I was nearing my teen years. Eleanor was glamorously beautiful when she came to live with us. She had a warm smile, which was a mile wide and showed teeth that had no evidence of ever needing the awful braces I had endured. And she had soft, intelligent hazel eyes, shining with a need to be loved.

I was indifferent to her. Eleanor was pleasant to me—in fact, more than pleasant. She was extremely nice and extended herself to me in many ways. I was courteous to her, but there was a wall, mostly erected by me, that remained between us that we could not seem to breach. Each of us waited, I suppose, for the other to tear it down. Perhaps in time we might have reached out to each other, but it was not meant to happen that way.

They returned, my father and Eleanor, from their honeymoon. Dark haired, perfectly featured Eleanor was dewy-eyed, my father fondly indulgent. Our lives settled into a routine. Father quickly went back to his normal schedule with his work being his all. I was accustomed to this and did not feel isolated since he still often included me in his business transactions, and I had many opportunities to learn about the business. This left Eleanor disconnected from us, because, for some inexplicable reason, my father did not invite her to join us in our business ventures. Therefore, she was left to her own devices in our big house.

It wasn't long before she wandered into housekeeping territory and asked to be of help. Blanche looked like a poodle on a mission with her frizzy perm and tinted hair when she shooed Eleanor out of the kitchen. Blanche's Kentucky heritage rang out when she gently reprimanded Eleanor, "No, no, honey-lamb, this is myah job. Don't y'all mess your purty little hands!" I still remember the slump in Eleanor's shoulders as she went back to her *Parent* magazine.

I would often come home from school to find Eleanor sitting in the living room. She might be thumbing through a magazine, her expression bored. She would look up eagerly when I came in the door, but I would simply smile, wave, and disappear to my room where I spent hours on the phone with my friends in an effort to avoid the changes Eleanor threatened to bring to my world.

Sometimes, I would bring friends home, but we would, again, disappear to my room, excluding Eleanor from our girlish, giggly conversations. Eleanor offered me all kinds of opportunities to confide in her and to become her friend, but I remained aloof. I made myself stay loyal to the blonde, blue-eyed angel of my memories, and—in this instance—conveniently forgot her sage advice to go forward with life.

I was also busy with my Scout troop, and as one of the older girls (now a twelve-year-old), I loved the experiences I had in working with the young Brownie girls. I developed a great fondness for leading them in crafts and teaching them all kinds of important things to help them through life. I even considered becoming a teacher and talked about this possibility with my Scout leaders. So I was not available for much of the time to do things with Eleanor.

One evening I overheard Eleanor talk to my father. I was in a corner of the living room doing my homework. It was after dinner when my father, as usual, sat in his favorite recliner. He was engrossed, his dark brown head buried in the newspaper business section.

"Mitchell," Eleanor said, "I need something to do. Your house is so well run, no one here *needs* me." She paused, as if she hoped this opening would prompt a response, but there was only silence and then a noncommittal grunt from my father. Eleanor's voice finally continued after a pause. With a resigned sigh, she said, "Mitch, I think I'm going back to my old job."

"Whatever you want, sweetheart," he mumbled over the top of the evening paper without raising his brown eyes from what he was reading. "Might be good for you to get out of the house."

I looked up from my school papers in time to catch the expressive look of disappointment on Eleanor's face when she heard my father's answer. She paused, then seemed to droop with resignation. "All right then, I'll call Jones & Snyder in the morning and see if I can come back." The decision was made, but somehow I didn't believe Eleanor was happy with it.

Not long after that, I noticed that Eleanor and my father were living in separate bedrooms. I could tell there was an emotional need that wasn't being met for her. My father was not cruel to her in any way, but like me, he kept a part of himself in reserve. He remained friendly, but lukewarm as if he were not ready to risk the hurt that giving all his love might bring.

There seemed to be a wall for him, too, and again, like me, he was reluctant to remove it. I could tell Eleanor wanted—no, *needed* more than that from both of us. I could see the disappointment in her eyes, and though I felt sorry for her, even liked her, I couldn't bring myself to take that first step across the chasm yawning between us. My father was the same.

Chapter 3

"Irreconcilable differences," the attorney told my father. I tossed the words around in my mind when I overheard this conversation. I made my way to Blanche, who disapproved of these "goins-on." I could tell she condemned what was happening. Her square jaw jutted out on her aging face, and her eyes darkened when I told her. She pursed her mouth into a thin line, and she muttered, "Land sakes, how ah hate divorce. T'ain't right!" But she would not talk with me about her feelings. Another time I was in the kitchen watching her bake cookies, and I made the comment, "Eleanor's lawyer was here today."

"That right?" She looked at me over the top of her glasses, her words noncommittal, but her back stiffened. Suddenly the rolling pin she grasped in her fists doubled its speed as she pressed it back and forth across the dough.

"Yes. He wanted to talk to Daddy about the divorce. I couldn't hear them say what the settlement for a marriage that only lasted four years would be."

"Such goins-on, an' in front of a child too!" The cookie dough was taking a beating.

"I'm not such a child anymore," I said looking at my sleek legs. "Besides, they didn't know I was listening. I was doing homework on my desk, which is right beside the floor vent, and I could hear their voices from my dad's office." Blanche looked up with disapproval, so I added, "It's right below my room, you know."

"Little pitchers have big ears," Blanche snorted and resorted to one of her colloquial sayings which, in this case, said nothing I didn't already know.

"But I have a question, Blanche," I wheedled. "Eleanor's lawyer said she didn't want any settlement, but Daddy got mad and said he wanted her to have something—so, I think I have a good idea, but what exactly is your opinion of a settlement anyway?"

Blanche smiled grimly, her full lips twisted to one side. "So, she won't take nothin' huh? Good for her! Make him stick that in his craw for a while! No, no, this is not right an' they both know it! He can love again, but he's clingin' to a dream. Now you scoot on outta here little miss mischief an' no more eavesdroppin' y'hear?"

I was able to verify my knowledge about a settlement later. But it wasn't long after this discussion that the lovely, sad Eleanor disappeared from our lives. She and my father remained friends, but that was the extent of it. Surprising myself, I missed Eleanor and felt guilty that I had not made more effort with her. Blanche missed her too, I could tell. But we prided ourselves on being survivors, so we endured and life went on.

My father finally sat down with me to talk about Eleanor's leaving.

"I made a mistake, sugar," he told me. "I thought I could find a mother for you and a companion for me. Eleanor seemed to fill the bill. She was a wonderful lady. Still is. We've agreed to remain friends, you know. But there was something missing for me from the beginning, and for a marriage to succeed, you must have that missing ingredient. Marriage is difficult enough as it is, and without the love or passion for each other, it becomes even more difficult. I wasn't being fair to Eleanor and I know it. She knew it too. She deserved far better."

"A love like you loved my mother?" I solemnly questioned him.

"Yes, like I loved your mother," he said wistfully. Then he hugged me protectively. "When you grow up, Mattie, make very, very sure you have that love before you marry."

I remembered that comment when I grew older and had to face my father and remind him of it. It was six years later. And now that I'd found my love, my father was shaking his head in refusal. Here I was, twenty-two years old, a fresh graduate with a business degree, and he could still make me squirm.

As I stood there in his office, I felt like a misbehaving child. Back and forth went his glossy, impeccably sheared, crown of silvering hair as if by shaking his head, he could will me to change my mind. His strong fist was tightly clenched around a paperweight on his desk. I could see the veins bulging in his hand from the pressure he was applying. I expected the glass paperweight to suddenly shatter into a thousand fragments and scatter across the desktop.

When I stubbornly said nothing, he became vehement. "Mattie, I can't in good conscience give you my blessing for this marriage. This man has accomplished nothing of worth in his entire life with the possible exception of snaring you. Can't you see he's a fortune hunter? I know his type. He's not right for you. You deserve better."

I stood up to him but continued to call him the name I had yet to outgrow—Daddy. "Why do you dislike him so, Daddy? He's done nothing to earn such an attitude from you. Just because he hasn't earned millions by the time he was twenty-nine years old like you did, does that mean he's worthless? He's had a rough time of it, holding a job, I'll grant you that, but if you knew the way he's been treated by people because of his background, you'd understand why he felt he had to quit all those jobs. His job working at our country club and helping on the golf course is only temporary until he can find something better. He just needs someone to give him a chance at a better job, one more suited to his qualifications, then he'll do fine."

"Harumph" and a glare was the only response he gave me. He wasn't budging from his opinion. And I wasn't budging from mine.

I talked with my best friend Josie. I was certain she would agree with me. Instead, I found her hesitant. Her pixie face looked pensive.

"Don't you like Joel?" I asked her in surprise.

Again, I could sense that thoughtfulness while she considered her words carefully, "It isn't a matter of 'like' Mattie," Josie answered slowly and shook her round chickadee cap of black hair. "It's a matter of compatibility. Yes, they say opposites attract, but Mattie, his background is so very different from yours. You don't know that much about him—"

"I know all I need to know," I interrupted stubbornly.

Josie smiled sadly; she knew that stubborn set of my chin meant arguing was futile. "Mattie, I wish you would wait a while longer before taking the step of marriage, but you know I will always support your decision. I care about what happens to you."

Thus, I discovered my best friend also had reservations about my marriage plans. My father was more vocal and adamant. We had never disagreed to this extent before.

We continued in this vein for quite a long time—weeks, with neither of us changing our stance. I proved to be my father's daughter, equally as stubborn and strong-willed. I was determined to convert him to my way of thinking about Joel, but it never happened. I was to learn over time that my father had gone so far as to hire a detective agency to investigate Joel's background. They had been unable to unearth much of anything except a glitch in Joel's story about having a college degree. It was as if he had never existed before coming to our city—St. Louis.

I looked for an ally. I found Blanche in her familiar role, making dinner in our large kitchen. Hot broth was simmering on the stove and sending out appealing aromas. A pie baking competed for the nose with a compelling apple and cinnamon fragrance wafting across the room.

I watched Blanche at work for a few moments and then asked her, "Why is Daddy being so stubborn?"

The years were beginning to show on the motherly face she turned toward me. She paused over the noodle dough she was making, set the rolling pin aside, and wiped her floury hands on her apron. She looked me straight in the eye and said severely, "He's not the only stubb'rn one 'round here, missy!"

She then returned her stocky figure back to her work and made no further comment. So, I knew and understood that Blanche agreed with my father about Joel. There was something about him that caused them concern. I would not find the ally I was seeking in Blanche.

But they had not seen the side of Joel I knew so well. He was attractive, a fact that was easy to prove with the way women and girls clustered around him at the golf club. Joel had a charming smile with a big, sideways grin that gave him the look of a mischievous boy. He wore his light brown hair brushed rakishly to the side, adding to the youthful yet slightly naughty appearance that drew females like water over falls.

His eyes could fluctuate with his mood or his choice of clothing from almost light blue to the dark green of a breaking wave on a cloudy day. His nose was smooth and nicely proportioned to fit his face. His ears neatly stayed close to his head with no protrusions. Joel could very easily have become a model or an actor. Everything about him was well-proportioned, including his trim body. But that wasn't all that appealed to me.

One evening after Joel and I had taken a dip in our pool and after the fourth or fifth interruption from my father with refreshments and a few not-very-well-disguised attempts to find out more about Joel's past, Joel watched my father disappear back into the house. "Your father is suspicious of me for some reason," Joel looked at me with his pleading soft green eyes watching for my reaction. I laughed and said, "He has always been protective of me."

Joel hesitated and replied, "Well, Mattie, if he starts digging, he may find out my family history is not the best."

"What do you mean by that?" My curiosity was aroused.

Joel looked at me and then at the door as if my father might come bursting back through. "I will tell you the whole story when we go out for dinner this evening. Will that work?"

I didn't miss his concern about my father, and I understood and was somewhat embarrassed by my father's actions of late. "Yes, it can wait. I'm looking forward to dinner with just the two of us." I smiled.

"Just the two of us," he agreed.

That evening Joel explained. "I feel I have to share some of my past with you, Mattie, simply because I don't want your father finding out something and making a judgment with only pieces of my story. It is a difficult story for me to share with you, so please bear with me."

I was flattered that Joel would trust me with information he felt could be used against him, and at the same time I was very curious about his family and why he never mentioned them. Wasn't his willingness to be honest with me a good sign?

"I can't believe my father would have you investigated Joel, but I am ready to hear about your family." I sipped iced tea and nibbled on an appetizer as I waited for Joel to begin.

"Your father is right to be careful about your friends and companions. I hope I will be able to change his mind about me, but—and Mattie, this is important—I have never shared this with anyone here in this community and I need you to keep all this confidential, even from your father. I need to win him over on my own. Do you understand?"

At that moment I was swept away by admiration and love and yes, a strong desire to know more about Joel's past. "Yes, I understand. I will not tell anyone—even my father," I agreed.

Joel swallowed his last bite of appetizer and began his tale. "My father was an alcoholic—a nasty, mean alcoholic." His face grew bitter, "So much money was spent on his alcohol there was very little left for a home or food or any of the other things little boys need."

"Where was your mother? Didn't she help you and make sure you had food?" I interrupted.

A twisted grin flicked across Joel's face. "Not much. She enjoyed alcohol too. She partied with my father, and they both went bar-hopping all the time. I stayed home in a small apartment, alone most of the time. I remember many nights going to bed hungry."

"Oh no, I'm so sorry, Joel." My sympathies were instantly engaged for this struggling little boy. "Didn't someone call family services? Did you know the neighbors? Why didn't one of them call social services to get you some help?" I was indignant.

"We moved too often to make acquaintances with neighbors," he explained. "And I was constantly warned not to talk to the neighbors. My only friends were my books. My teachers at school gave me books."

"I can't imagine my father holding any of this against you, Joel. You were just a child," I said.

"There's more. One night my parents came home so drunk they could barely walk. Did I mention that my dad had a violent temper?"

I shook my head no at this piece of information. "Did he hurt you?" I guessed.

"No, he did not hurt me this time. When I heard them arguing, I hid in the closet. Dad was jealous because my mother had been flirting with several customers at the bar. She yelled back at him, and when I opened the door a crack, I saw her swing a skillet and hit him. This enraged him even more, and I was so terrified I shut the door and crawled as far back in the corner as I could get. I heard pounding and shoving and scraping noises, more yelling, and then more odd noises; then all was silent."

"Oh how horrible for you," I sympathized, shocked at behavior so alien to my own pleasant life. "What happened next?"

At this time, the waitress delivered the rest of our order, but I found it hard to dredge up an appetite. Joel seemed to be having the same problem and waited for her to leave before he stabbed at one piece of his shrimp Alfredo, then put down his fork and continued his story.

"Eventually that night I crept out of the dark closet and went to the kitchen where they had been fighting. I found my mother's lifeless body, but I also found my father dead. He had beaten my mother to death and then killed himself by slashing his wrists. I did not even wonder about the fact that I felt no sorrow over the loss of either of them."

"Joel, this was a terrible tragedy, but why would my father hold this against you?"

"Because, I just wanted to escape any association with them, so I robbed both my dead parents' bodies of any money or valuables, then I searched our apartment to get everything of value, including my birth certificate and any papers that looked important. I did not report anything I had witnessed or heard that night. I gathered up everything that might help me, and I slipped out when I was sure no one would see me. I left the state."

"I looked older than I was at the time, so I was able to find jobs and support myself at places where they paid cash or did not ask too many questions. Eventually I was able to get a social security number and find better jobs. It was tough, but I never went back. For all I know I could be wanted for murder. I know I've thought about it often enough." His eyes held a haunted expression that made me feel protective.

"But why not clear this up—" I began, but he reached across and touched my hand.

"You promised," he reminded me. "Mattie, I need to deal with this my own way. I am determined to do better with my life, and I will never go back to that old life. I will never allow myself to be like my father," he told me in a stern voice. "I can control my drinking. I know when to quit." I felt an overwhelming sympathy for Joel, which only added to my feelings of love and strengthened my resolve to marry him.

I did not reveal Joel's past, but I did offer some stories about small hardships Joel had told me he would allow me to share about his childhood. But none of these stories, when I shared them, affected my father's opinion. He felt Joel used his past as a crutch and an excuse for not performing. "He hasn't used these experiences to better himself," he pointed out. He talked about Joel's failures, while I continued to defend him and explain them away.

In one conversation, I became more assertive. "Daddy," I strove to be self-controlled, to win his approval, "no one has ever really given Joel a chance to prove himself. I think if we hired him at one of our companies, you would see him shine."

"Mattie, he's had plenty of chances. Joel needs to prove himself in every job he takes, no matter how mundane it is. I don't see him doing that—or trying to work his way up. Even Larry, the pro out at the golf course, who's as easygoing as they come, complains that he wastes too much time flirting in the clubhouse. He also says Joel is not dependable."

"Oh Daddy, that's my fault! He just wants to spend as much time as possible with me." I hesitated, and then plunged on, "Also Daddy, we think Larry is simply jealous of Joel. You know Larry had a crush on me when we were in high school."

"Mattie, if it were only one occasion, I could give him the benefit of the doubt, but Joel has had numerous opportunities to show his stripes, and he hasn't acted on those opportunities."

"Name one, Daddy." I demanded proof.

"I can name two *others*. What about the car sales job he had before coming to the golf club?"

"You can't count that against Joel, Daddy! You're not being fair! Everyone in town knows the guy who runs that agency is as mean and nasty as they come! He makes absolutely no allowances. Just because Joel was late to work a couple of times, he fired him! I can't understand how people can be so unreasonable. Joel actually went to work feeling ill, and instead of appreciating his dedication, the guy fires him for being late!"

"Funny how people in business expect you to show up for work, isn't it?" Daddy wasn't giving an inch. "And what about his nighttime job at the school? I suppose there's another good reason for quitting that job as well? Or did he get fired there too?"

"That wasn't Joel's fault either." I found myself on the defensive again. "The cleaning company lost their contract with the school because the students complained that things came up missing out of their lockers. So the cleaning company fired everyone who worked on the night crew rather than challenging the school. It was probably other students who were stealing the stuff, but there was no way to prove it. Joel happened to be on that night crew and so, through no fault of his own, he lost that job. Surely you don't hold that against him! Surely you can see he's had some bad breaks, Daddy, can't you?"

"Yes, if everything is as he says, he's had some bad breaks. But Mattie, your character shows up in how you deal with adversity. Don't you think some of his excuses are rather weak?"

"No, I just think he needs someone, like me, to believe in him." I was able to give my father an explanation for every failure to which he pointed. I begged for some humanity and understanding, but he remained unconvinced.

Not long after this conversation, my father asked me to meet him at our attorney's office to "sign some boring papers," he said. Our attorney, George, was also a lifelong friend of my father's and had always treated me like an uncle.

I shamefully used that opportunity to gain my wishes. I had despaired of ever bringing my father around to my way of thinking, so when I went into the firm to sign the papers for my father, I barely glanced at them. Our family friend and attorney, George, said some of them had to do with the trust I inherited from my mother's family, "to make it more safeguarded," he told me. I signed where George pointed and then brushed the papers aside.

Instead of paying much attention to that little piece of business, I asked my father in front of his dear friend, "Don't you want me to be happy, Daddy? Don't you love me? Can't you give this marriage to Joel your approval?"

"Yes, I want you to be happy" my father replied, "and that is why I object to Joel. I do not feel he is a good match for you at all. Even his story about a business degree is bogus—" My father broke off as if he had said too much.

I looked at him in amazement, "What do you mean by bogus? Is that what you were about to say?" I put my hands on my hips and glared at my father. "Have you been checking him out?" I was furious.

My father exchanged an uncomfortable glance with George. "I was waiting for a good time to tell you, Mattie. His employment application at the club mentioned his degree and a college. I simply called the college to see if I could buy a transcript of his grades. Turns out it is only a two-year, junior college, but he did earn a certificate in business."

"And those two years are often accepted at four-year institutions when someone pursues a degree." I glared.

"And no four-year institution I've contacted has him listed as a student. So, not only is that probably fictitious, but he was not entirely accurate on his employment application either," my father retorted, not budging an inch.

"There could be all kinds of explanations for that," I said. "You are always assuming the negative about Joel. I am really disappointed you did this, Daddy." My father had the grace to look embarrassed.

"It's only because I love you and want to protect you," he began. George coughed.

"If you love me, you will recognize I am old enough to make this decision," I interrupted.

I looked at George and repeated the tactic I had tried earlier with my father. "George, can't you help my father see this means the world to me?" George had known me for years, and I saw the two men exchange meaningful glances.

My father then dropped his bombshell. "Some of those papers you just signed, Mattie, will also need to be signed by Joel. It's a prenuptial agreement to protect you in case things don't work out. It prevents him from walking away with any of what you had before you met, and it shows his assets versus your assets."

"What?" The looks between these two men I loved dearly now made sense, but I was devastated they had resorted to this ruse to get me to sign it. "Dad," I tried to maintain control of my voice and emotions, but I was trembling when I said, "if you so much as *hint* about this document to Joel, I will never speak to you again! I want you to tear it up!"

"Mattie, please think about this and hear me out," my parent pleaded.

"No! You've done enough! I trust Joel. I know you don't trust him, but you don't know him like I do. He will not be asked to sign a prenuptial agreement. To me it's as if we are assuming from the beginning that there is a possibility of divorce. I do not ever want a divorce to happen! Joel doesn't either. You have so misjudged him, Daddy, and it breaks my heart!"

"Mattie, your father is trying to protect you," George interjected. "You have a lot to lose if a marriage to Joel does not work out. Most people have no idea of the inheritance from your mother's family, and that huge foundation and trust fund that is now in your name, not to mention the wealth your father has amassed and has willed to you."

"I don't want my father's protection," I said with a scowl, "I want his love."

"You know you have my love, Mattie," Dad said sadly.

"Then give this marriage your approval and show me," I challenged. I would not relent. I finally managed to obtain the surrender and approval I wanted from both men, and the wedding plans began over their strong objections.

The one blot on my wedding day was the image seared in my brain of how ashen and unhappy my father looked as he prepared to walk me down the aisle. I was so gloriously happy that day in my white Cinderella wedding gown that little could mar it; however, I was momentarily struck with a feeling of remorse at how aged my father suddenly seemed to be. He had become older so gradually I had not noticed the wrinkles, grayness at the temples, the more hesitant walk. I noticed it now—on my wedding day.

I hugged and kissed my father fervently. "It will be just fine, Daddy. You'll see," I said reassuringly. His look told me he was not convinced, but he hugged and kissed me back, his despondent voice almost cracked when he replied, "I hope so for both our sakes, sugar. Just be happy, it's all I want—and by the way, Mattie …"

"Yes, Daddy?"

"Your mother would have been very proud of you today. You're beautiful in every way."

Chapter 4

We spent our honeymoon touring Europe. Joel had shared with me how little opportunity he'd had to travel in his life and how someday he was going to have the money to go first class everywhere, so the honeymoon was my wedding gift to him. We took our time. Nearly two months passed while we visited Barcelona, Paris, Rome, London, and Venice; all places I'd been with my father.

How much fun I found it to share my experiences with someone new. I felt very important, playing the role of the tour guide while I introduced this part of the world to Joel. We visited the Louvre and stared up at the famous Venus de Milo statue I found so breathtaking. "But she is cold marble." Joel smiled. "I like my live, warm version much better." His eyes caressed my face. I was smitten all over again.

I showed him the Mona Lisa and Winged Victory. I would have spent all day at the Louvre. I loved all the art and sculpture and history, but Joel became very bored and impatient. He wanted to head for the Moulin Rouge and the bright lights of Pigalle. We left the Louvre and made our way to that area of Paris and stayed out till the wee hours.

Later the next day, while still in Paris, we went to the top of the Eiffel Tower and looked down at the miniature world scurrying around like tiny insects below us. I looked over at Joel. How handsome he was! Almost six feet tall, his ocean green eyes and light brown hair coupled with his trim moustache gave him a rakish appearance, similar to the look of a Hollywood star—a boyish, rebel type whose brooding demeanor had women swooning.

I adored how he looked, and I smiled smugly when women stared at him. But now, as we stood in the breeze at the top of the tower, Joel appeared pensive. "What are you thinking?" I asked him. "Are you unhappy about something?" I tucked my arm in his.

"All those people down there," he said slowly. "I've watched them, scurrying around like little worker bees. I don't want to be a worker bee, Mattie. I want to be in *charge* of the bees. I'm not going to end up like my parents!" His voice was charged with an emotion I couldn't identify. He paused as if he'd embarrassed himself with this admission—as if he had said more than he wished.

After Paris, we took a train to Barcelona. We cheered when we watched the bullfights, and Joel enjoyed them immensely. For him, I tolerated the events surrounding the killing of the bulls, though I personally found the whole thing rather unpleasant and distasteful. We moved on to Italy, beginning in Rome. We both enjoyed touring the ruins and the old buildings and vineyards in Italy, and I savored the romantic canal ride in Venice—while Joel complained about the filthy water. I wanted him to have a wonderful time, but I found myself giving up many of my own preferences for things Joel wanted to do. I endured more nightlife and bars and less museums and historic sites in order to please Joel.

He will try to reciprocate and do some things that please me, I thought, and was surprised when he continued to insist on visiting what I considered less desirable places. Rather than chide him about it, however, I chose to be generous. *It's my gift*, I decided. *It makes up for all he has missed.* But I did feel a slight disenchantment at how easily Joel accepted my gift of self-sacrifice. I also felt a pang at remembering how solicitous my father had always been when traveling. I buried that comparison and chastised myself for being disloyal to Joel.

When we returned from our honeymoon, Joel was given a wonderful position in one of my father's companies. I was so grateful to my father for this act of generosity, and I noticed that it was a job that I knew would suit Joel very well. We were both very happy that first year of our marriage, and I often found myself wanting to tell my father how wrong he had been about my choice in a husband.

We set up housekeeping and had fun finding just the right furniture for our condo. I used some of the money from the trust I had inherited from my mother in order to purchase most of our belongings, "just till your job gets you back on your feet," I told Joel when I sensed he was going to object.

I was correct. "Mattie, your father already thinks I am a no-good poacher who married you for your money. This will just confirm that in his mind."

"He doesn't have to know," I argued back. "It's for a good reason. We can't keep sitting on these packing boxes. Besides, it is a loan, not charity. I know you'll earn it back soon."

"You're probably right," he finally agreed with me as he stroked my hair. Then he turned to utilize his great acting skills by imitating a soft Scottish burr, "an' that money's just lyin' around in a nasty ol' bank doing nothing when we could be using it as a verra comfortable couch!" We laughed together, and that was the end of Joel's objections to the spending of my money.

In fact, I was extremely pleased when he suggested that I "lend" him enough to get a new car. "Because," he joked, "that old bomb of mine is about to fall apart, and the janitor at work drives a nicer vehicle!" I enjoyed doing things for Joel, and for quite some time I was busy and content. I had my own job helping to run projects in father's original telecommunications company, National Telecommunications Services (NTS).

Father was one of the pioneers in the field of telecommunications. After Judge Green had set up the ruling that caused the divestiture of AT&T, father had the foresight to take all his funds, leave his job at "Ma Bell," and start up a competitive company in the long-distance business. NTS was spectacularly profitable, and I grew up with knowledge about microwave towers, switching systems, fiber optic cables, and dial tones far beyond that of the average child.

I particularly enjoyed managing large multilocation data networks for our customers. I had been doing this type of work about a year as an intern during my last year of college. I was a natural, they told me. In reality, my endeavors on the job were very successful owing mostly to my years of informal training at my father's knee. It was a job that gave me a great feeling of accomplishment.

Only occasionally did I wonder if I had ever been given a chance to determine if other careers or other directions might bring me more satisfaction in life. Occasionally I remembered my little Brownies, and I wistfully recalled my teaching experiences with them. But those memories passed, and I was content with my position at NTS. It had been assumed that I would advance to full-time employment after my summer vacation and honeymoon. I knew my dad was looking forward to having me on board.

Joel's new position was in one of the companies my father had purchased after his initial success with NTS. This acquisition happened when Daddy decided diversifying his holdings would be a good idea. "Don't want all our eggs in one basket," he had said with a wink when I'd questioned him. He had then purchased FEI, Future Electronics Incorporated.

Daddy very generously put Joel to work as the assistant to the director in charge of a well-established and successful sales force. This team had been extraordinarily profitable in selling the office equipment manufactured by an arm of Future Electronics. I remembered the "worker bees" discussion and was grateful my father had given Joel such an important and supervisory position. This was clearly an already successful position. All Joel needed to do was maintain, and hopefully improve upon, that success. His salary would be based on his improved sales.

We were able to set up housekeeping in a nice condo in one of St. Louis's newer developments not far from either of our offices; the first year's lease was already paid as a gift from my father. I was grateful to my father for his continued generosity, but Joel, it seemed to me, would have preferred not to feel so indebted. He didn't like being in the position to need my father's help. In fact, rather than learning to like each other, they seemed to grow ever more alienated from one another as time progressed. I was the only thing upon which they both agreed—and both loved me.

To keep the peace, I simply began to arrange to see my father at times when Joel was not around, and vice versa. The fewer contacts the two had, the better they both seemed to like it. We had plenty of other social contacts and activities. Joel had always enjoyed going to the many parties of the country club set, and though I felt some of the people there were rather shallow, I had plenty of lifelong friends who were not so shallow with whom I could mingle.

The country club was where I had first met Joel. I had been paired with him in a golf scramble tournament, and that beginning was the introduction to many rounds of golf and tennis we played together. I later learned that since Joel was working at the club, he was in charge of arranging the pairings. So, as he had informed me, it was no coincidence that we wound up together. I was flattered that he had gone to that much trouble to be with me.

"I have a confession to make." He smiled at me the day of that first pairing.

"A confession?" I looked at the attractive man named Joel with whom I had been paired for a golf outing. He had a wide smile and an air of confidence.

"Yes. Zis pairing vas no accident." He jokingly used a French accent and stroked an imaginary moustache with a leering posture. He was charming. I was intrigued.

"So," I slipped into a poor imitation of someone from France, "Zis vas no toss of ze coin?"

"Aha! I 'ave been revealed by la mademoiselle!" he laughed and added, "and now ve must 'ave ze clandestine meeting at ze pool after ve vin this round!" What an audacious invitation. Of course I accepted it.

After that first meeting, we had spent numerous deliciously lazy afternoons around the pool. He had a way of making me feel as if I were the only female at the pool even though I could see many gorgeous, bikini-clad members scattered on lounge chairs within eyesight. He paid attention to what I said and acted as if I were the wittiest and most profound person he had ever met.

I could say, "Dave and Carol won the tennis doubles match today," and he would say, "Really? Who were their competitors?" and we would evolve into the nuances of the game and famous people in tennis, and I would feel every word I said was significant. He also made great efforts to make sure I had lotion, towels, drinks, and of course, his company.

At that time, I was out of school for the summer, and Joel worked at the club "just till I can get back on my feet," he told me, so it was quite natural for us to have a large amount of time together. My friends at the club, especially the females, clustered around Joel as if he were the magnetic North Pole, and they were helpless pieces of metal. I couldn't become too critical however, as I felt exactly the same way. He had one of those personalities that intrigued and attracted people—including me. He knew how to make people feel they were important. He used that knowledge very well and was popular.

Our first year of marriage saw us at first increasing and then cutting back a bit on our social outings. The latter caused Joel to become somewhat disgruntled. He missed the adulation and attention he received at the club. We had made friends with two new singles who had hit it off with Joel especially well. Their names were Necia and Freddie. I first met them one evening at the club restaurant where we were having dinner. Joel saw them come in and motioned them over to our table.

"Mattie, I want you to meet our two newest members. This is Necia." He pointed to a beautiful woman with a pouting posture and very red lips.

Necia analyzed me with an up-and-down gaze that was almost but not quite contemptuous. "Hello. Mattie is it? Nice to meet you." A hint of insincerity was in her voice that I did not miss. She turned to the suave man beside her and said, "This is my friend Freddie."

Freddie stretched out his hand, but his handshake was lacking firmness. I nodded at both and said politely, "Hello, Necia. Nice to meet you, Freddie." I was curious about them and wondered why Joel had singled them out.

"Why don't you join us?" Joel encouraged. "We have room at our table and a pretty good view for the entertainment coming in this evening."

Once seated, the two newcomers seemed to relax and became much more jovial, especially after a couple of cocktails before the meal. I reserved judgment, and the four of us joked and had a fairly fun and relaxing evening.

This was the first of many such evenings out with Freddie and Necia, and for a while things seemed to be moving along well and everyone was happy. But as often happens in life, circumstances change. Our increasingly busy schedule both in our personal life and our jobs meant we didn't see them as often as they—and Joel—would have preferred.

I was not as disturbed by this as Joel because they were not ones I would normally have picked for friends. I tolerated them because Joel definitely liked them both. Over time, they both revealed character flaws that bothered me. I had heard comments that gave me the impression there was a furtiveness or dishonesty about them.

I could not put a finger on it, but my intuition was alert. I thought about speaking out against them and wanted to encourage different friends, but then I remembered Joel's harsh beginnings in life and pushed aside my misgivings about Freddie's cold, cruel-looking eyes, and Necia's barbed sarcasm.

At one of our first evenings out, Necia asked me, "How does it feel to have a real rich daddy instead of having to resort to a sugar daddy?" I was speechless and gave a weak smile. Joel and Freddie laughed uproariously, and I tried to join in, but there was a twinge of hurt inside at being the butt of Necia's joke, and the lack of defense from my husband.

Necia's poor taste in conversation was not only reserved to me. My friend Josie with her cute cap of black hair and elfin face happened to be visiting once when Necia dropped in. Instead of, "Hello, nice to meet you, Josie," Necia said, "Well, no one would take you two for sisters. Mattie is very thin." Then she turned to me and said, "You two could go out on Halloween as a beanpole and a pumpkin!" and erupted into a harsh laugh. I learned her biting wit was usually expressed at someone else's expense.

"I like her just as she is," I said firmly and hugged Josie.

Freddie with his thick, dark hair had a brooding appearance. He wore the bright white shorts and the colorful polo shirts that fit the tennis club look, but I never remembered seeing him play tennis at the club. His eyes were deep, obsidian black that conveyed a cruel appearance, and they were overshadowed by dark arched brows. His nose was long and thin, adding to the sharpness that became his face. His smile, from small, narrow lips often carried a mocking twist to one side.

He was attractive in a mysterious way. He was a relatively small man physically, but he carried himself proudly when he walked. Freddie could be charming, as he was when Necia tried to carve Josie into a pumpkin. He came to her rescue and introduced himself with, "Don't pay any attention to Necia. You, Josie, have an adorable face and a very nice smile." But there was a lack of honesty behind his manipulative charm, and his efforts were lost on me.

I could not figure out how he and Necia had become friends. They almost acted at times like a relationship was in place between them, yet at other times, they behaved as if each was single. I didn't ask, and I deliberately avoided each of them when possible.

I also became more busy and involved at work, so I consoled myself with the fact that due to our busy work schedules, we would not be able to see either Freddie or Necia as frequently as had been happening. I felt the problem would resolve itself, and I would eventually be able to migrate with Joel to a different social circle where we would meet friends with whom I also felt comfortable.

Necia's choice of attire often produced comments from some of my longtime friends when she wore clothing they described to me as sleazy and inappropriate. I spoke to Joel about it.

"Joel, many of my friends are concerned about how Necia dresses and comports herself. They asked me if I had any influence on her. Should I say something or try to give her some guidance? I think I can be very tactful." I assumed Joel would be proud of me for trying to help her and that he would agree with me about her failing reputation.

Instead Joel bristled. "What a bunch of high society snobs!" he ranted. "I hope you are not planning to try to convert Necia, Mattie. I never dreamed you would be so judgmental. All the other women at the club are jealous of her. Are you getting jealous too?"

Joel paced back and forth as his ire continued to build. He directed his anger at me. "I can't believe this, Mattie! You don't like her do you? Just because she's a voluptuous woman with gorgeous long, black hair, you think she's a tramp."

"No, Joel, it's not like that at all." I tried to defend myself. "Look at it this way," I suggested. "What if I were to show up at the club in that short, tight, low-cut red dress she wore last Friday? Would you want me to go there looking like that?"

"You could use a little more of her style," he said, which shocked me. "You tend to be a little dowdy sometimes." His words felt like shards of glass cutting my soul. I had always been assured of my careful grooming and professional style. Now I wondered why my looks were not pleasing to my husband. It hurt to learn his real feelings. I couldn't help myself—I struck back.

"I have to admit that Necia is beautiful in a voluptuous way. She has that long, black hair that shines seductively when she switches her head around. I have noticed how she allows her hair to slither from side to side. But would you really want me flirting so outrageously with all the men at the club like Necia does?"

"I like other men to envy me the woman I have on my arm," Joel responded as he shattered an illusion I had cherished. He seemed defensive of Necia but careless of my own sensitive feelings and not concerned about my need to be admired by my husband. "You have to admit she has flair," he shot back. "Those women complaining to you are obviously jealous."

"I will only admit Necia is shapely and displays her attributes more than is tasteful." I was wounded and struck out. I was close to tears.

"Like I said, all jealous—including you." His eyes held a hint of cruelty.

I also felt his criticism of me was unjustified. I remembered a lunch with Necia, Josie, and another friend, Helen. Necia had shown up ten minutes late—to make her grand entrance, I supposed. Her tight black leggings hugged her curvaceous legs. A silky, low-cut top draped down just to her hips. Her long, red fingernails were impeccably polished to match her deep crimson lips.

She had dark brown, almost black, eyes with shapely dark, carefully defined brows. Her high cheekbones indicated a possible Native American heritage and accented her long, elegant nose. Her face was always intricately made up with a multitude of cosmetics, and she frequently had her compact and mirror out to correct any potential blemish while she admired her reflection.

I stood when she arrived to let her scoot into the booth we were sharing. I felt gangly and tall next to her petite five and a half feet. Her height was helped a little by her arrival that day in the highest heels that could be obtained to help increase her elevation. Her walk was much like the rest of her. She had a flaunt in her step and a "dare me" attitude that challenged the women and attracted the men.

"Sorry I'm late," Necia said in a breathless tone that did not sound sorry at all.

"That's okay," said Helen. "Let's get our orders in so we can start work on this benefit for the hospital while we wait for our food." We placed our orders without incident, and Helen handed each of us a list from our last meeting. The list detailed our responsibilities as the committee to carry off this charity effort to raise funds for the children's wing of the local hospital.

"Hey, you have me down for soliciting stuff for the silent auction," Necia complained. "I'm not going to be able to do that!"

"Why not?" said Josie. "We don't need you to do it all. Just approach eight to ten merchants and ask them to donate. It's easy."

"Then *you* do it. I can't." Necia was adamant.

"We all share in this, Necia. We split the work so it is not too much for anyone. Each of us will contact eight to ten merchants for donations. Most of the merchants know this event is important, and they will be easy to ask. They get these visits from us every year, so they'll be expecting us," Helen explained.

"Well, I'm just no good at asking, so you will have to find someone else! I thought I could greet everybody at the front door as they came in. I would be a hoot at that!" Necia stated.

"We already have special children assigned to greet the guests, Necia, but I suppose you could help the children. Each one has been helped by this hospital program in some way," Helen temporized.

"No, that won't work either. I can't stand kids!" Necia blurted.

Helen tried again. "We really need your help with the silent auction. You will get to organize the gifts into beautiful baskets as we assemble all the donations. Won't you enjoy that?" Helen cajoled.

"No! That will ruin my fingernails! This is not what I thought I was signing up for at all! Just take my name off your lousy list, and I won't even come that night, but Joel and Freddie won't be happy to hear this."

All heads turned toward me at this little piece of blackmail. I took a deep breath and said, "Wait, Necia. We can work this out. You can go with me, and we will double our list and work on it together. Then, after we've visited all our merchants—yours and mine—I will be sure you get organizing jobs on our assembly line that don't harm your fingernails, okay?"

I looked around the table in time to see Josie roll her eyes. Helen, usually unflappable, looked very uncomfortable. I could tell both were embarrassed and annoyed at Necia's behavior.

"So I have to go with you to twenty businesses and listen to you beg for a donation?" Necia grumbled.

"Yes, that's about it." I tried to smile. "Remember it really is for a good cause, and I think you will be surprised that you have a flair for this you didn't know about," I tried to say as diplomatically as possible.

"I doubt it, but I think this will work for me." Necia gave in grudgingly.

I did not expect nor receive a thank-you. The meal ended peacefully, but I continued to receive complaints, mostly from the women at the club, about Necia. I was now sorry I had brought up the subject of her inappropriate behavior and dress, because my own husband was expecting me to be more like this distasteful person.

At this point I did not even try to point out to Joel how I had offered to do a good part of Necia's work and help her on the fund-raiser. I wondered why Joel was so determined to foster a friendship with Necia and the equally difficult Freddie. I had heard disturbing rumors about the group associating with Freddie and Necia; rumors that included worrisome information about activities such as alcohol abuse and drug addictions. I listened to the rumors and tried to be objective, but no one ever had real proof something was going on with them in those areas.

Although I did not care for the two of them, I certainly had never seen anything that would indicate any illegal activities. Because Joel adored them both, I chose to dismiss the rumors as more clubhouse gossip, the type that goes on all the time and usually has more fiction involved than actual substance.

After this turn of events in which Joel was adamant we were all jealous of Necia, I tried to continue to be objective, but it was difficult for me, especially with the hurtful comparison Joel had made about me. I battled myself every time I thought about how I had agreed to do most of Necia's work on our club fund-raiser so she would not harm her fingernails. I tried to tell myself that maybe he was right. Should I consider if I was jealous? I had never been a jealous type person before, so why now? It was a conundrum I could not solve.

Fortunately around this same time I was saved from more involvement with Freddie and Necia when our busy lives and especially our jobs became even more hectic. Additionally, I tried to involve Joel in more of my work at distributing funds from the foundation money I had inherited from my mother's side of the family. I loved being able to make a difference in the lives of people who were struggling.

I thought this would unify us as a couple and bring us closer together, but just the opposite happened. Joel grumbled or complained about each grant request we reviewed. "These people are just taking advantage of you, Mattie," he would say and then imply some devious way they were after the money but not the help.

So, for a while, these and other activities cut into our time with the couple Josie referred to as "The Gruesome Twosome." We saw them less often than usual, but my friends at the country club let me know they were continuing to be disruptive—just never quite enough to be ejected. Gossip filtered to me, especially through Josie, who kept me informed.

We did still meet them for dinner at the club or the occasional nightclub. Necia often complained in a petulant voice that "it seems as if the owner's daughter and son-in-law ought to have the right to some time off." Freddie wasn't far behind in supporting Necia's comments. "If you are running things right, your staff ought to be able to take care of things when you need a little playtime," he told us. They continued to needle us about joining them more often.

It wasn't too long after these comments by Necia and Freddie that things seemed to change. Joel seemed affected by their view of our work and often added his voice to theirs. I tried to get them to talk with us about their own jobs so I could get Joel to see there might be a difference, but they were both very vague when questioned about where they acquired the money they used for their membership and how they supported themselves.

"Uh, I dabble in a little of this and a little of that ... mostly sales," Necia would say.

Freddie would respond to questions about his career with answers like, "Oh, I am an investor and an entrepreneur. It keeps me on my toes." Neither was forthcoming with more details about specific companies or places they worked. However, I found both were extremely informed about every detail of my life, and I assumed this information had come through my husband. It left me disgruntled that they knew so much about me, and I knew so little about them.

Both Necia and Freddie seemed to be on a campaign to force us to spend more time with them. They continued to point out how Joel and I should have more privileges at work because of our relationships and my father's position. In reality, my father had always expected more, not less, from me, and I knew he felt the same about Joel.

I was proud of how my dad had found the job that seemed as if it were the best fit for Joel's personality, and at first, Joel appeared to enjoy it and even thrive at the experience he was gaining. Not long after this pressure from his friends began, Necia and Freddie showed up at our house one evening. Joel and I had been working on some reports for Joel's staff.

"Hey," Necia said as I let them in the door, "there's a new place in town called Redwood Grill. Have you heard about it?"

"Yeah," Freddie chimed in. "It's really hot and popular right now. Best ribs in town. C'mon both of you. Grab your jackets and let's go!"

Joel looked at me, "Mattie? Sounds like fun. Why don't we take off and join them? I'm ready for a night off."

"Yes," I said, "it does sound great. I heard about it from someone at work. But really Joel, we both have reports we promised ourselves we would get done before we went back to work tomorrow, remember sweetie?"

Joel looked disappointed, but he turned to the couple and said, "She's right. I did promise to get this done, but I sure will miss you guys. Can we try again this weekend?"

"Sure," said Necia, "but this weekend may not work. They're getting booked up, and I think they are going to go with reservations only. If you're lucky, it'll be available." She looked at Freddie and added, "Let's go. Maybe Christine and Harry can go tonight. They don't have much pull at work, but they are always ready to party!" She swung around with an air of dismissal and barged out the door, leaving us with no question she was angry with us. Freddie quickly followed.

Joel looked unhappy, but he went back to his desk and started working. I tried to work on my own report, but I kept hearing mumbles from his direction. Then I heard a sheet being ripped from the pad. I looked up and Joel had started on a new page. I tried to concentrate on my own work, but in a few more minutes he tore up the page he had started and crumbled it into a mutilated shape. He forcefully pitched this into the wastebasket. "I don't know why we didn't go with them!" he grumbled out loud.

"Because we had work to do, and sometimes work is more important than play." I tried to sound reasonable.

"Oh, now it's my fault that I want to play!" he retorted with some heat. "I'm just a playboy, is that it?"

"I did not say that," I sighed. "I simply meant that we made a commitment to our work, and I think that should come first."

"Did you ever hear the saying 'all work and no play makes Jack a dull boy'?" His voice carried a stinging rebuke.

"Joel, there is plenty of time to play after we get the work done," I responded. "I don't see why this seems to be bothering you. We can go out next weekend." I tried to placate him.

"You heard Necia say it might not be available then," he sneered. "So I don't see why we have to be so stuffy and miss out on the fun all the time."

"I didn't know we were stuffy," I said stiffly. "I thought we were responsible and getting enjoyment from a job well done."

"There you go again!" Joel exploded. "You're trying to make me feel guilty! I'm really getting sick of it! Here, you think you know so much about creating these reports—you do it!" He left his work scattered on the desk and marched out of the room. I heard him getting in the refrigerator, and soon I heard the TV going in the spare bedroom.

I was not sure how to handle the explosion or the undone work. I finished the report for him but went to bed troubled and unhappy. He did not hug me later when I felt him slip into bed.

Not long after that explosion, Joel began expressing his discontent with his new job. He was shaving one morning, and I popped in to hug him with my usual, "Good morning, sweetheart."

"What's good about it?" he grumbled and continued to shave.

"The sun is shining, we have good jobs, we love each other," I encouraged.

"My job stinks." His tone of voice surprised me with its negativity.

"What is wrong with your job?" I said in surprise.

"I don't want to talk about it. You wouldn't understand anyway." His voice held accusation.

I left for work concerned about what might be going on with Joel at work and yet not wanting to sound judgmental or nosy. As I was driving, I thought about how my father had managed to find a job that seemingly fit Joel's personality and talents. Joel had seemed impressed with the opportunity in the beginning. I had even considered the job myself at one time and thought it would be a very rewarding thing to do, but even more so for Joel. So his change of attitude surprised me.

After this, other things began to change very subtly. It was imperceptible at first, a little like a small spot of poison ivy that unnoticed causes a small itch, but once it is scratched begins to spread everywhere and multiply the blisters. Joel's personality, usually upbeat, began to seem more morose as time went on—especially after we had spent time with Necia and Freddie. He seemed on edge, and his testiness seemed to be directly related to his new job and coincidentally with meetings involving Freddie and Necia.

One day I thought I would surprise Joel and show up to have lunch with him. I made my way to his office just as he was hanging up the phone. "Hi, honey!" I smiled.

"What brings you out here?" He smiled back.

"I thought maybe we could have lunch," I suggested.

Brent, one of the top salespeople, knocked on the office door. Joel motioned him in. "Sorry to interrupt" Brent smiled at me but turned to Joel. "Joel, this can't wait. McGruder and company called, and they need your decision now or they said they will have to go somewhere else," he explained. Joel looked disconcerted.

"What a pompous …" he caught himself from finishing the sentence and instead turned to Brent and said, "Brent, I am going to leave that decision to you. Call McGruder back and try to seal the deal at the price he offered."

"But Joel, the team evaluated his offer, like you asked, and the price point he wants is going to hurt us. I thought we were all in agreement to pass up his offer and hope he would reconsider." Brent looked puzzled.

Joel began to fidget. "I said take care of it!" he almost snarled at Brent, who gave a curt nod and left the office.

I was silent at this exchange, but I hoped this was not a common occurrence. Joel must be having a tough day. He looked at me challengingly. "Now you see what I have to deal with," he complained. "I am not treated with the respect due to the son-in-law of the owner of this business. You would think they could make decisions without me having to babysit them all the time!"

"But Brent wasn't …" I faltered helplessly. I did not want to tell Joel how to handle his job, but this was not the best way to treat your staff, in my opinion. I felt like I was walking across a room full of balloons in my metal-spiked golf shoes and could not cause any of them to burst under my feet.

"Oh, I'm sure you'll take Brent's side, Mattie. Must follow Daddy's methods, mustn't we? But you don't know what it's like. I get no respect because this job was just handed to me. I didn't work my way up like the others! I am getting very sick of this place and this job. Let's get out of here and go have that lunch! You may not allow me to go to the Redwood Grill, but lunch is okay, isn't it?" His voice mocked me. He did not allow me to respond, but held the door and then marched me out to the car without speaking. I could tell he was upset.

By the time we got to the little café, Joel had calmed down, but I was not so sure I recognized him any longer. At times he acted as if his new position were beneath him; at other times his bearing befuddled me. Gradually, Joel's attitude grew progressively worse, and it seemed to me he was constantly complaining about his work.

I still did not recognize those spreading blisters for what they were, so I kept trying to encourage him and tell him how important it was to get along with everyone at work, but he would say that I didn't understand all the pressures he was under and how hard the job was.

One evening, Joel and I had our first really big argument, and I had to face the poison that was spreading into our marriage. We were eating dinner when I became irritated at something Joel said, and rather than placate him and encourage him as I had been trying to do now for quite a while, I finally spoke up. It was just the two of us discussing what kind of day we both had.

We didn't talk long about my day as I was not doing anything in my work that Joel found important or interesting to him. He soon grew tired of discussions about LANS, networks, frame relay, or D4 versus ESF or voice over IP conversations. I could never seem to gain his interest in these subjects I found interesting—even fascinating. So, as often happened in such situations, we discussed Joel's new job rather than mine.

"How are your sales results doing lately, Joel? Did that McGruder deal help things out like you hoped?"

"Uh, I don't know if I want to stay in this position at the Future Electronics and Office Products Company." He dropped the bombshell. "This job was never a good match for me and the staff is so jealous of me that I can't get any cooperation from them."

"Joel, this staff was doing an excellent job when you took over." I tried not to sound judgmental. "What happened? Have sales fallen off or something?"

"I don't want to talk about it, but yes, Brent and the staff have really slacked off, and I know I will have to take the blame for their laziness! It isn't fair."

"Joel, maybe I can help—"

"No! That's the worst thing you can do. They already hate me. All I need is the boss's daughter stepping in to make it worse! I don't want to talk about it, Mattie."

It was now apparent to me that sales were more than "slightly" off from when Joel had first started. I wanted to pursue this topic, but Joel, it seemed, wanted to avoid it. As we talked, Joel became more keyed up and edgy, which had become a common mood for him nowadays—one I couldn't understand.

"People are sabotaging me." He began rambling about missing boxes of paper clips and people blaming him for not rinsing out his coffee cup. Then he ranted about the executive secretary and her claim that reams of paper and printer ink were coming up missing. "They think I stole that stuff," he ranted. "I can see the accusation in their eyes when I go to work."

"Those are rather trifling things compared to loss of sales, Joel. Wouldn't you agree?" When he just stared at me, I thought I had gained agreement and went on, "Seriously, Joel, why don't you let me come in this weekend when no one is around and have a look and see if we can improve your sales somehow? We really need to spend time working on improving your sales figures and not worrying about a few lousy reams of paper."

Joel's silence was not the agreement I had imagined. He became eerily silent and then looked at me in a way I had never seen before. I could only describe it as a haunting, vacant, almost venomous, glare. There was a moment's pause, and then he took his fist and pounded the table so hard I heard all the dishes rattle. This startled me into silence. Next, Joel blurted out in a nasty voice I'd never heard from him before, and in a harsh tone that totally alienated me.

He yelled, "Yes it's easy for you to ignore little things, isn't it, Mattie? You've always had everything you've ever wanted. You've never had to scrape for each cent and wonder where the next meal might come from. If you had, you would know that you have to fight for every step and stay on top of every issue. If you don't, someone is just waiting to take it all away from you!"

Then completely off the subject, in a sing-song voice he chanted, "Daddy and Mattie, Mattie and Daddy, two peas in a pod. You and your father can pass judgment on me all you want, but I can tell you this. You both make me sick!"

Dumbfounded, I watched the man I loved metamorphose into a stranger. In the process of watching this venom boil out of Joel, my darling husband became a wild, unrecognizable caricature of the husband I had known for over a year now. He was a distorted stranger. It was frightening to see the image I had lovingly carried of him in my heart become shattered and rearranged into broken and unfamiliar pieces.

I was afraid, but I was not one to give up. I pushed down my fear, and I became angry also. I witnessed Joel's shocking transformation and found myself increasing the volume of my own response. I did not deserve this kind of treatment. The caustic remarks surprised and hurt me. I replied, perhaps a bit stronger than might have been wise, "You need to calm down. We need to handle this in a more mature way." This only enraged him further.

"You mean behave more like your precious father?" he sneered. His posture became more indignant and stiff, his voice louder. "Your father has never liked me. And talk about being mature. I know he is sabotaging my job on purpose and making it more difficult for me to be successful!"

"You can't mean that!" I yelled back. "My father would never do anything like that!"

"What kind of wife are you, Mattie? Where's the support for your husband?" he jeered. "It's always Daddy this and Daddy that. Well, what about Joel? What about me? What about the vows you took to love, honor, and obey?"

I was too angry now to speak rationally myself. "When you present yourself as someone worthy of that kind of respect, you'll get it," I practically screamed. "Until then, quit accusing my father!"

"I should have known you would side with your father." His eyes had a wild look that was totally unfamiliar. I'd never seen this side of Joel to this degree before. "Daddy and Mattie!" he taunted as he threw back his chair with his body and stood with a threatening jerk. I thought for one paralyzed moment he might strike me.

The chair crashed to the floor while Joel turned with a bold movement toward me, then suddenly stopped and caught himself. He turned away with a spasmodic jerk and ignored me, then grabbed his jacket, and strode angrily out the door. It slammed violently behind him.

Shaken, my hands trembled while I tried to grasp what had just happened. I nervously cleared the table, surprised there were no broken dishes. My anger turned to despair, and I felt tears pour down my cheeks while I tried to make sense of what I had just witnessed. I went into the bathroom to splash water on my face and help my swollen eyes.

I saw my reflection in the mirror and hardly recognized myself. My blonde hair was a mussed halo around my unhappy and red-streaked blue eyes. My nose—that Blanche called "classic"—was red from sniffling, and my high cheeks were flushed on my pale skin. I eventually went to bed hurt and angry, but it took me a long time to fall asleep. Joel didn't return all night and was not home by the time I left for work the next day.

I was mystified by Joel's behavior. It made no sense to me. My boss asked if anything was wrong. I lied to him, too embarrassed to share my concerns. I managed to get through the day, but when I left work, I drove home wondering if things could ever be the same.

Joel was at home, waiting. I approached him with trepidation. He smiled ruefully and swept me into his arms. I found out how wonderful it can be to make up after an argument. We were both remorseful about our behavior, and we swore it would never happen again. We would be reasonable and not make false accusations. We loved each other dearly, and we promised to love each other forever. Peace was restored, and we were happy again.

<hr>

My eyes blinked open as memories of my husband, Joel, faded. Now I was back in this strange void. The blanket that had been a cocoon for me earlier in the day provided little help against the shivering that overtook me as I tried to shelter myself against the cold wind that shifted the boughs of the big evergreen trees until they swayed overhead like black sentinels. The sky was gray, and the light had faded to the point things were barely discernible around me.

My body had never experienced such aches and all-encompassing pains. *Where am I? What has happened? I'm worried about Joel. Is he okay? Does my dad know where to find us?* I thought I was using all my energy to push myself up, but I was still too weak to stand. Frustrated, I fell back, looked up at the trees overhead until they wavered and blurred. In this condition, I again succumbed to a comatose state and returned to more memories. Were they dreams—or were they nightmares? Which existence was real? My mind tried to sort it out, and I felt myself drifting back in time …

Chapter 5

Our renewed happiness, our promises, and remorse over our argument lasted about two months. I had hoped this episode was behind us, but the peaceful restoration of our marriage did not last. That first explosion was to become the initial example of many such arguments between us. Before this, I believed we had been companionable and in general agreement about our lives.

Now, for reasons beyond my understanding, we disagreed on an ever-widening number of subjects. We reached impasses on the subjects of our jobs, our social life, who our friends were to be, whether we were to have children or not, and so forth. I learned to my sorrow that I couldn't have a discussion with Joel in which I was able to pleasantly disagree with him.

We couldn't even agree to disagree. We couldn't compromise. I discovered to my chagrin and frustration that it was to be Joel's way or no way. Once his mind was made up, he stubbornly refused to budge. We had a big disagreement over my boss and his family. Jeff had a young son who suffered from an early childhood version of Crohn's disease. It was especially debilitating and extremely costly to treat. Jeff had four children and dreamed of college for all his children.

He made decent money at our company, and our insurance fund helped a great deal with little Ricky's disease. The insurance plan had limitations, however, as many do, so Jeff and his wife, Clarice, struggled continually to pay bills. I knew he was very sad that he was not putting money away for a college fund for any of his children, and they were still living in a cramped little house with crowded bedrooms and very small yard.

They were a wonderful family and loving parents, and I admired their dedication, so I made sure that a grant was approved through the foundation my mother's family had set up in which I received an annual endowment and another portion went to charitable causes each year. I made sure the grant was awarded from an "anonymous" donor so Jeff would never know who his benefactor was.

In an effort to be open with Joel after we had been married a while, I had explained how the foundation worked and the huge sums of money that resided for safekeeping in that foundation. I came to regret that decision to share the information because Joel became extremely critical about the large sums of money I supervised and signed off for the foundation to grant each year.

Once Joel knew all this, he insisted on knowing what grant requests had come in and what had been awarded. In the case of Jeff and his deserving family, I had told Joel it was really nice that I worked in the same office because I would be able to see if there were additional needs that might arise, and I could keep an eye on how little Ricky was faring. Joel was incensed at my "blowing" the foundation money and allowing what he termed "pathetic people like Jeff" to take advantage of me.

I could not see why he wanted me to hoard the foundation funds rather than award them. I could not understand why he did not feel the same joy I experienced when I was able to help someone in need. I began to see a selfishness in this that saddened me a great deal. We were comfortably well off, both working with good salaries, and I thought Joel would have found fulfillment and satisfaction in our lifestyle.

It wasn't just the foundation money that created issues. I found myself giving in during disagreements, against my will and often against my better judgment. This happened over and over. I was never allowed to present my point no matter how valid I thought it might be or how much I desired to persuade him to at least listen to my view. Anything other than total capitulation on my part caused a violent eruption, false accusations, and almost-hysteria on his part.

I was forced into the false position that I must always agree with him. I wanted children. He didn't. I wanted to start going to church and asked him one day, "Joel, I have heard about a captivating new preacher at a church not far from here. It seems to be a young congregation and sounds like they are having a wonderful time doing some positive and great things in the community. They have a backpack ministry, have a wonderful day care for kids, a good praise team, have a food pantry, and they have a lot of just plain fun events according to some of my friends who have started attend—"

"No way!" Joel interrupted me. "I will not go sit in some church while some dude tells me I am doomed and going to hell! Besides, all the people I've ever known who call themselves Christians have been the worst hypocrites of all! No, Mattie! Absolutely not! Don't even think about it."

"But Joel," I answered in surprise, "why not? I don't see why we can't at least go just once to find out the truth for ourselves. Your old experiences may not happen in this church. It sounds like a very welcoming and wonderful place." I pleaded softly and carefully and hoped he would see reason. I did not want to give this up. It meant a lot to me.

But Joel was adamant. "No, and that's final!" he emphasized.

How I longed for some of the loving moments of our honeymoon. Now I felt as if I were a piece of merchandise, here for appraisal, here on approval, and seldom coming up to Joel's satisfaction. How I longed for the old warm, caressing looks from my husband.

Joel began spending more and more time away from home. I spent more and more time at home alone or purposefully working late. I would hear him come in at 1:00 or 2:00 a.m. He would walk unsteadily as he weaved his way across the room. I knew then, he'd been out, probably drinking, with Freddie and Necia. Like me, he had lost weight and had begun to look unhealthy, but I was afraid to comment about it. I would lie there in bed, feigning sleep, listening as he drunkenly undressed.

This went on for months. Then Joel dropped a bombshell on me. He wanted me to quit my job and go to work for Freddie. "Why?" I asked, "I don't even know for sure what Freddie does for a living. Why would I want to work for him?"

"Contacts," Joel said as if I were stupid. "You have hundreds and hundreds of contacts that Freddie could use if you introduced him. Since he sells investments, you could put him together with some of the wealthiest clients in the area. You also are very skilled at selling people on ideas, so you and Freddie would be an amazing team." The first time in a long while Joel had given me a compliment, and it was for this! I couldn't believe it.

"I can't quit my job and leave Jeff dangling without my support!" I challenged back. "In the first place, I'm not the kind of person to desert a position, and in the second, I can't represent someone like Freddie whom I barely know! It is not an area of expertise for me, and I would feel awful if I caused someone to lose their life savings by investing with someone I don't know that well!"

Joel twisted the conversation another direction. "Is there something going on between you and Jeff at the job? Is that why you don't want to leave?" Joel's face had turned surly and suspicious, and he had completely ignored what I thought were valid reasons not to change my job.

"No! Of course not! There is nothing between us except boss and employee. Jeff is an honest and wonderful person who loves his wife and family. They have a very sick child. I can't believe you would suspect him—or me—of ever doing anything illicit like having an affair!" I was indignant and angry.

"Well, you may not think so, but Jeff is after you and I don't like it! I want you to switch jobs where you won't have to put up with his flirting and attentions," Joel said arrogantly. As I stood in shock, he paused and went on. "I don't want to discuss it further. Your boss is trying to take you away from me. You can give your two weeks' notice tomorrow. It's not like your daddy is going to cut off your allowance," he smirked. "You'll still have plenty of money coming in from good old dad—and all your other sources."

I was struck mute. I became speechless and could find no words with which to respond. I was so shocked that for the moment I could think of nothing to say in defense of my hanging on to the one tiny thing in my life that was feeding my soul—my job. True, I didn't need the money, but I did need the self-esteem. I did need to feel valued and appreciated.

Additionally, this connection to my dad was important. Couldn't he see that? I was awake for long hours that night thinking back on my honeymoon and how differently things had turned out. I wondered what had gone so wrong. When and why did things change so dramatically? Why was I so miserably unhappy? What was I going to do now? I couldn't give up my job. I could not.

Chapter 6

I had one dear friend left—one who hadn't deserted me in the last year when things had begun to change so much. She tolerated Joel for my sake but did not bother to hide the fact that she disliked him very much. I called Josie the next day and asked her to meet me for lunch.

"Please Josie, meet me at O'Rion's, say, twelve thirty?" I was practically begging. Josie must have felt my desperation because she broke another luncheon engagement in order to meet with me.

Josie was her usual buoyant self. "What's up, doc?" She barked out the hackneyed phrase with a twinkle in her eyes to belie her gruff tone as she plopped down in the booth across from me. Josie worked hard in order not to become too plump (the tendency toward being overweight ran in her family). She often despaired about this but maintained a positive attitude that one day she would conquer the problem. Her pixie-like face was surrounded by a curly cap of black hair, reminding me sometimes of a round little chickadee.

Josie's smiling face quickly fell to one of concern, however, when I looked at her mutely. It was so good to see her, tears suddenly gushed out against my will and coursed down my cheeks. I could see her shock when she appraised my thin figure. She reached across, grabbed my hand, and squeezed. Each of us searched for a tissue with our free hand, and simultaneously worked at sopping up the tears.

Suddenly we both burst out laughing at the one-handed attempts. I needed to laugh, and it felt wonderful. Our ridiculous gestures calmed me. I had always been able to laugh with my best friend Josie. Tension released, I was able to talk at length with someone I knew would honor my confidences.

I told her everything that had been going on with Joel and how unbearable my situation seemed to be. I told her about the false accusations, the wild fluctuations in personality, the change in attitude toward me. I shared it all. Even to my own ears, it sounded so fantastically unbelievable. How could we go from bliss to this—and why had it happened?

When I was done, she looked at me squarely across the table. "Why don't you divorce the creep and be done with it?" she snapped out, like my Girl Scout leader used to do. I could feel Josie's gaze penetrating my soul, and in typical open-Josie fashion, she got quickly to the crux of things.

"D-divorce?" I stammered in a wobbly voice. "I-I've never thought about divorce as an option."

"Well maybe it's time you should," she said firmly. "Maybe it's time you realize that you weren't in love with Joel at all. You were just in love with the idea of love. You wouldn't be the first girl who mistook lots of other emotions for true love."

"I had no idea you viewed my marriage to Joel this way," I said in surprise. "Why didn't you talk to me and tell me what you thought?" I asked.

"You were in no mood to hear my misgivings," she explained. "Don't you remember when I told you I did not think you were compatible, that your backgrounds were too different? You were too starry-eyed when you were getting married to listen to my reservations about Joel and whether he was right for you. Your own father couldn't talk you out of it; why would you listen to me?"

So, someone besides my father and Blanche had questioned Joel's motives in marrying me—and my wisdom in choosing him. But I was not a quitter and voiced this to Josie. She retaliated with a barbed, "Are you sure you just don't want to admit to your father that he was right?"

I wasn't ready to concede this point yet. "But divorce?" I questioned her. "It seems so final, and I'll feel such a failure. I've never truly failed at anything in my life. My dad always taught me to be a winner."

Josie was relentless. "Winning sometimes means knowing when to cut your losses, Mattie. I know a good attorney. I can get you an appointment. Do you want me to set it up?" She was tenacious and to the point when she felt she needed to be.

"Josie, I need some time to think about it. This is too sudden. I-I'll think on it and let you know, okay?" We finished our meal with a discussion about the pros and cons of staying married and trying to improve the situation or of making a clean break and ending it.

Josie's allocated time for lunch was long past. She looked at her watch regretfully, then at me. "You going to be okay, Mattie?" Her face held concern, and I know she hesitated to leave me. She grabbed both my hands and said, "You know I'm just a phone call away. Or, even better, you can escape to my place any time. I have a spare bedroom, and it's yours if you want it."

"I'll be fine, Josie. Please don't worry. You've given me a lot to hash over in my mind." We hugged each other and agreed to meet again in two weeks. I wanted that much time to think about this major decision. Josie left soon after that, and in a contemplative mood, I stayed behind to finish my coffee. When I got up to pay my check, I felt an odd sensation as if someone were watching me. I turned but saw no one.

Still, I had the eerie feeling of being watched. It wouldn't go away, and the back of my neck felt prickles of unease. The booths in the establishment were tall, which made it difficult to see who occupied the various seats. I figured I would be just as invisible to others, so I shrugged off my misgivings and the uncomfortable feeling and continued to make my way out of the restaurant.

When I arrived home, I looked up attorney names in the phone book. I remembered a female lawyer, Jane Lawrence, whom I had met at a charity ball. She was a slightly portly woman with bright blue eyes and easy facial features. Jane was friendly and outgoing. We had hit it off right away, and I liked her forthright style. I had watched her career for quite a while and noted how she was creating a very good reputation for herself, especially as a lioness for women in divorce cases.

I paced the room, back and forth, back and forth. I was indecisive and thinking about what a momentous step this would be. Finally I went to the phone and dialed the number for her office and got her receptionist. "Lawrence and Birmingham" the voice came over the line. "This is Shelly, can I help you?"

I nearly hung up but took a deep breath and asked "Hello, I was wondering if Jane Lawrence is in so I could speak to her for a few moments?"

"I'm sorry, but she is with a client right now, is it something I can help you with?" The voice was friendly, still, I paused in silence, thinking. Shelly came back and said, "Hello? Are you still there? Would you like to set up an appointment with Mrs. Lawrence?"

"Not just yet, but I would like to speak with her if possible. This is Mattie Huntington-Carter. I met her last year at the Festival of Arts Charity Ball."

"Oh yes, Mrs. Carter, she spoke highly of you after meeting you. I will give her the message. Is there a phone number I should have her use?"

I gave her the home number since I had taken the afternoon off. I did not receive a call back right away, so I assumed my request had been lost or she would return the call the next business day. I was surprised when Joel came home early that day and asked, "How did lunch go with Josie?" I didn't remember telling him about my lunch plans, but supposed I must have mentioned it earlier.

"Oh, it went fine." I smiled. "Josie is so much fun, always so upbeat." I hoped I did not look guilty. Our phone began ringing and startled both of us. Joel was nearest so he reached out and picked up the receiver.

"Hello?" he said. "Who? Oh, uh sure, here she is." Joel looked at me with a quizzical expression on his face and said, "She says she's Jane Lawrence, the attorney?"

My heart sank. What poor timing! I walked slowly to the phone and tried to recover my composure. "Hello, Jane?" I faked a smile, but even to my own ears my voice sounded wobbly. I was thinking fast. "We met last year at the Charity Ball, did you remember?" She did remember me.

"Well, we are in the midst of planning for another event this year, and we are looking for table sponsors who can guarantee us a full eight people at the table they will be sponsoring. We were hoping you would consider being one of those sponsors."

I was so happy we still had a few tables left, which gave me something to discuss in this awful predicament where Joel was standing nearby and listening to every word I spoke. I certainly could not bring up the real reason for my call to her in front of him. She was very gracious and agreed to be a table sponsor, and I eventually hung up the phone with relief.

In the next few days I would catch Joel looking at me speculatively—oddly—as if reevaluating our relationship. *He knows,* I would say to myself. *He knows I'm thinking about a divorce.* Why the possibility of his knowing should fuel such a frightened reaction within my soul I could not fathom.

I would reassure myself. *No one could possibly know my thoughts. I'm just feeling guilty for having such ideas. I'm attributing more to the situation than is there. He is looking at me differently because he's waiting for me to tell him I've resigned my job. That's all it is. That's all there is to it.*

But suddenly, unexpectedly, Joel made a turnaround. He was different. I felt it immediately. He smiled at me more. I would catch him at times when he silently stared at me with a wistful look in his eyes as if he, too, remembered better times and wished we had them back.

"I've been thinking," he said as he approached me.

"Oh?" I looked at him. We were alone at dinner—a rarity for him not to be out somewhere with his friends.

"Yes. We've slipped away from our great start and gotten lost somewhere." He scratched his head and grinned engagingly, much like the old Joel I had loved so much. "I don't know when it happened," he shrugged, "but we've lost our romance. We've become unbalanced somehow."

I started to answer him, but he held up his hand to stop me. "No Mattie, it isn't your fault. I accept the blame. I've wanted too hard for it all to be perfect, and I've allowed my job and its problems to affect our lives too much. I've forced you to put up with all my complaints and unreasonable demands." He looked at me intently as if weighing the effect his words were having. He reached across the table and took my hand and rubbed his fingers over mine so gently I almost cried.

I looked back at him, thrilled by his words, but finding them hard to believe after all the hurtful things he'd said in the past few months. I wondered if he really meant what he was saying. I wondered if I would be able to broach his continued weight loss and the pallor of his skin without his losing his temper. Neither of us was at peak health. But, in spite of questioning thoughts, I wanted more than anything to believe him. I wanted to recover the lost magic of our early days. He seemed to be able to read my mind.

"I know this may be hard to believe, Mattie, but I've done some soul-searching, and I realize that we're drifting apart, that I've hurt you. We need to do something to rekindle that flame, Mattie, and I've come up with an idea that I think will work."

"Oh?" seemed to be about as much as I could offer at this point.

"Yes. I can tell you are reluctant to believe I've made a change, Mattie, but I have. I don't blame you after the way I've behaved, but I care too much to lose you. I'm going to make things right." He continued to massage my fingers. "I've got it all planned." He gripped my hand a little tighter and looked at me keenly.

"Planned?" I asked wobbly, not sure whether to cry at the change, still unsure of this new development. I wanted it to be true, but I was fearful it would not last. I did not ask him why he thought he might "lose" me.

"Yes, Mattie—planned. I've a great idea. We'll have a second honeymoon. It's nearly our second anniversary now, and I want to recapture the wonderful times we had on our honeymoon in Europe. Remember how wonderful it was, just the two if us?" he asked, and his eyes were as sincere as I had ever seen them.

I nodded. "Yes, I remember, but that was an artificial world, Joel. We are having trouble in the real world." My doubts must have shown in my face because Joel became more insistent—and more convincing.

"Don't give up without trying, Mattie. We owe it to each other to make our marriage a go, don't we?"

I couldn't disagree with that. I nodded again, still silent. Joel went on then, like an eager young boy, the way I remembered and loved him being before all the turmoil descended on us.

"Well, I have it all figured out. This time it will be *my* treat. Our second honeymoon. It will be very different from the first. Have you ever been to Canada?"

"Well, yes," I answered hesitantly. "I've been to Quebec and Toronto. They were lovely cities."

"No, no." He shook his head impatiently. "I mean the *real* Canada, the wilds of western Ontario. Oh, Mattie, it is indescribably beautiful. I've been there before, fishing. It's remote—wild, waterfalls, eagles—and it'll be just the two of us." He was really excited.

"Well, I haven't fished since my dad took me to Wisconsin, and then there was Scout camp on Lake of the Ozarks. I was a little girl—" I began.

"I'll teach you all over again," he interrupted enthusiastically. "Besides, fishing in Canada is different from anywhere else in the world, but so much fun. You won't believe it. The fish practically jump into your lap!"

He had me laughing now, and picking up on his excitement. I joked, "I don't even need a pole?" I was smiling and he was too. It felt good.

"Well, I might concede you a fishing pole," he chuckled good-naturedly.

"What about your health?" I came right out and asked him.

"My health?" He seemed taken aback.

"Yes, I think you've lost weight, and you look a little pale lately. Do you think you need to see a doctor?"

"This trip is just the doctor I need. Yes, I've been a bit under the weather, but it is just the stress of the job and the way our marriage has been going. Believe me, you will be able to fatten me up and get my skin nice and tan again. I'm so glad you are concerned about me, Mattie, but I don't want you to worry. This trip will be great for us in many ways. It will help you too. You've also lost some weight." So, he had noticed how my clothing hung on my increasingly frail body.

"If you're sure …" I paused. How I wanted to believe everything he said.

"I'm sure." He smiled in a satisfied way as if he knew he had won me over.

Chapter 7

I was afraid this new Joel might be a temporary thing, but he maintained his cheerfulness and continued with his plans for our trip. This was a side of him I had not seen—ever. He was eager to go fishing and wanted to show it all to me. This time *he* would be the guide, the experienced one. He liked preparing me for the things we would do and see. He told me how remote the area was and how huge the expanse of water was that was dotted with mostly unoccupied islands except for the one where we would find our cabin.

There would be no telephones and no electricity except for a generator when we needed it. A fireplace and cast-iron stove would be there for heat and cooking, and there would be no air conditioning, although he explained it was seldom needed with the cool nights and moderate days. I allowed him to take the lead—to be the instructor—and he thrived in this new aspect of our relationship. I realized I should have given him more such opportunities in the past.

I felt better than I had in a long time. My appetite came back, and I felt my body renew in strength. I passed the tall hall mirror and saw a fuller, happier person. My blonde hair had a new sheen, and my complexion had improved. My blue eyes looked back at me with new hope. I decided to enlighten Josie and Daddy which, of course, meant I told Blanche too.

"Canada?" Josie and my father could have been identical twins the way each responded when I shared the idea with them. The question in each of their voices included concern. Daddy was a bit stronger.

"You're going off to Canada with that good-for-nothing …" he spluttered and stammered trying to come up with a term suitably nasty to fit his attitude toward Joel. Future Electronics had been experiencing severe drops in sales of late, and Daddy's opinion of Joel had dropped lower than ever. Thankfully, I had refrained from sharing my difficulties concerning Joel. For me to ask for time off for Joel incensed my father quite enough.

"You've gone fishing in Canada many times yourself, Daddy," I pointed out. I reminded him how I had watched his videos and learned a lot about Canada from the stories he had shared on returning home from his fishing excursions into the north land. I also reminded him of the numerous times we had been fishing together in places like Wisconsin and Minnesota—places not that much different from conditions in Ontario.

"Yes, but I know what I'm doing, and I only take experienced people with me," he rejoined, looking at me pointedly.

"Joel *is* experienced," I claimed defensively. "He's been fishing up there several times himself, and I'm not exactly a novice at being outdoors, Daddy. Remember our camping trips to Wisconsin and Minnesota? Not to mention all my Scout training?"

"It's not you I'm worried about, Mattie," he grumbled, but he held his peace and authorized the time off.

The next day I faced my friend Josie. Her reaction was the same. "Canada?" her bird-bright eyes delved into mine as if hoping to find I was joking. She listened to my story about how Joel had changed, how much fun it would be, how excited I was at this new turn in our marriage. Then finally she interrupted me. She sighed resignedly over her lunch and said bluntly, "Mattie, I think it's a mistake." When I didn't answer, she toyed with her food as if unsure about telling me something, then she squared her shoulders and plunged ahead.

"Mattie, I never wanted to spoil the stars in your eyes, but Joel is not what you imagine him to be. You've tried to fit Joel into a mold that isn't him at all. Don't go off into the wilderness with him, Mattie. He doesn't deserve all the second chances you've given him already. Think about it. Just the other day we were talking divorce, and now you are thinking about being alone with him in a remote area where anything could happen!"

When I talked to Blanche about it, my substitute grandparent just looked at me and shook her frizzy head. There was disapproval in her eyes. She said nothing in response, but her posture and the negative shake of her head told me how she felt about my new adventure. Neither Josie nor my father could deter me either, though both tried resolutely. "I have to give my marriage every chance," I said stubbornly. "I'm going."

We left early in June. We flew from the municipal airport, and I watched from the window seat as the city of the arch alongside the Mississippi River disappeared below us. Our flight took us far north into Winnipeg, Manitoba. Joel held my hand as the jet took us north, and it felt very good to have my hand in his. We rented a sport-utility vehicle at the Winnipeg airport after getting ourselves and all our gear through customs.

Soon we started our drive through the Canadian countryside. The flat farmland around Winnipeg began to change as we headed east. The terrain turned into beautiful scenery as we passed rugged rock-covered hills, deep rivers, and multichained, piercingly blue lakes. There were waterfalls everywhere. We spotted a cinnamon brown bear eating blueberries at the side of the road. I later discovered the cinnamon brown was a species of black bear somewhat rare to this area.

The air was crisp and redolent of pine and other luscious-smelling evergreens. I enjoyed the gorgeous scenery immensely and relaxed as I had not been able to do for months. We drove past the city of Kenora, then skirted around Lake of the Woods, a huge expanse of island-dotted water that seemed to go on forever. I was navigating from some maps Joel had brought along and saw nothing but blue on the map in the area south of Kenora. Such lakes!

About four hours after starting, we arrived at a floatplane base on Trout River in western Ontario. We met our pilot and the couple who owned the tourist business that catered to fishermen. They showed us where to park and promised our vehicle would be under their watchful eye. We took this opportunity to purchase our Canadian fishing licenses and filled out the paperwork so we would be legal. They provided us with a chart that listed what fish would be "keepers" and which we would have to throw back.

Next we left our vehicle as instructed, and with their help, loaded the first of our gear into the small floatplane that was bobbing in the water at the end of a wooden pier. This would be my first experience in a floatplane, and I was excited about it. Joel watched me indulgently. He had made all the arrangements, and I enjoyed how wonderful it felt to sit back and feel so cared for—so pampered.

Joel said, "I need to use their pay phone to make an international call back to the States to check in with the office." He disappeared for a long time before we were to take off. "Takes a while to get through from up here," he explained when he returned. "That's for sure, eh?" said the pilot with a northern accent that gave his heritage away.

I was happy and impressed that Joel seemed to be taking more interest in his work again. I knew there would be no telephones for the rest of our time in Canada. As a telecommunications child, I was well aware of the limitations of long distance and international calling. Joel had also warned me that we would not be near any phone service and reminded me that our cabin would be rustic but well equipped with not only a fireplace and stove for heat and cooking but also a generator for some electricity. "There will also be a two-way radio for emergencies," and he added jokingly, "which we are *not* going to have to use!"

I was a bit nervous about being so isolated, but my Girl Scout training had returned to mind to give me courage. Thus, as the time for the trip approached, I had been able to treat it as an adventure. Now here I was, as eagerly anticipating the trip as Joel seemed to be. So far it was far beyond my expectations, and Joel had been phenomenally considerate. I looked around at the beauty appreciatively and took in a deep breath of the unspoiled, fragrant air.

Joel chucked me under the chin, signaled to our pilot, and said, "Up, up, and away!"

We were quickly on our way back to the plane where we loaded the rest of our gear, and within moments we followed the pilot's directions and all the procedures to become airborne. The pilot guided the plane as the floats holding us on top of the water went skimming across the surface like two miniature speedboats. The floats performed their job well, then, when they hit just the right wave at the right speed, they released their tacky bond with the water and hung like awkward appendages as they flew along, securely attached to the aircraft.

We lifted gracefully over the treetops. I could see a magnificent view as we climbed. Miles and miles of water interspersed with islands and trees with little or no sign of habitation by man passed below us.

The flight gave little opportunity for conversation over the noise of the engine. Joel sat in front with the pilot, and I had the entire backseat to myself (along with some supplies), so I was able to observe our surroundings without interruption. Using an old Girl Scout skill, I noticed that we flew in a northeasterly direction. In slightly less than an hour, we came upon a beautifully remote section of lakes and islands. From the air, the lakes appeared to be connected—one to the other—by a stream or river and perhaps one large waterfall.

I noticed a general north/south layout with most of the lakes looking longer than they did wide. There were so many of them! They disappeared over the horizon farther than I could see from our elevation. We soon circled one of the last two lakes in the chain. Due to the high wings on our conveyance, I could peer out and see a little cabin and dock in a clearing below. We circled overhead, which gave me an eagle-eyed view while the pilot checked the wind direction. I could see him eye a wind sock that fluttered at the end of a pier below us.

Our pilot motioned to us that he was getting ready to land. He yelled over the engine to remind us to keep our seat belts fastened until we stopped. I watched in fascination as the cabin grew larger and the water came closer. The water seemed relatively calm from this altitude.

We splashed down like a flat rock skipped across the water, and then our floats became occupied once more in their pontoon function as we taxied to the dock. I saw a small cabin on shore and a boat about sixteen feet long tied to the pier, in readiness, I supposed, for our fishing.

The pilot—we had learned his name was Gene—helped us unload our gear onto the dock. Gene went into the cabin with us to show us how to use the two-way radio to contact the outfitters when we wanted to make our arrangements to be picked up for the return trip. He pointed to a folder.

"This notebook tells you how to operate the radio in case you forget my explanation," he told us. "It also shows you how to work the generator and everything else connected with the cabin." Gene and Joel unloaded some fuel for the generator and other supplies we might need for the week.

We thanked Gene for all his help and walked with him back to the floatplane where it gently wallowed on the water at the end of the small, wooden dock. We stood on the edge of the pier, Joel's arm around my waist, and watched as the plane departed. We stood, after that, just breathing the fresh pine-scented Canadian air until the plane looked smaller than a high flying eagle circling loftily above us.

We were alone.

Chapter 8

"Well, here we are," Joel said, and smiled down at me. His arm embraced me, and I smiled back in enjoyment of the affectionate gesture.

"Yes, here we are, and I'm famished! Beat you to the cabin!" I teased and tore off toward the cabin. Joel laughed out loud and quickly ran in pursuit. The cabin was rustic and made of logs with a small, screened front porch holding two rocking chairs, a sturdy wooden frame for the screening, and a front screen door with three half-cut logs in front for steps.

Inside was a kitchen/living area that held the cast-iron cook stove that used wood from a log pile outside the cabin. The flat top held a skillet and tea kettle. A fold-out couch was on the left wall, and next to it was a small table with a kerosene lamp and an electric lamp. Next to that around the corner was a comfortable chair.

A large window provided a view of the lake through the front porch. A sink with a hand pump produced fresh, clear water after a short time of flushing. Water could be heated on the stove when needed for cleanup. A small room held a galvanized tub for bathing. There was no shower, and an outhouse was located just behind the cabin.

The sink and several cabinets with dishes, utensils, and other supplies were located on the right wall not far from the stove. In the center of the room was a small dinette table with four chairs. The couch could be made into a bed, and there were two bedrooms. One of the bedrooms held a double-sized bed and things like clean bedding, towels, dish towels, and so forth that were in one of the packages the pilot had left behind. The other bedroom held two twin beds. Each bedroom had more kerosene lamps, and there were electric lights set up to run off the generator. A small refrigerator also utilized the generator.

The pilot had explained the generator was small, and we would need to refill it with gas on a regular basis. It could only support a minimum of appliances, such as the refrigerator. Gas was delivered by airplane throughout the year and left in a tank in back.

We spent several leisurely days getting to know our surroundings. Joel familiarized himself with the endless miles of shoreline as we puttered about in the fishing boat—sightseeing at first, then fishing. The small vessel was about sixteen feet long and was a red and silver craft with three wood benches running across to straddle the front, middle, and back of the boat for support and seating.

The boat was well used with several dents and scratches along the V-shaped aluminum hull, and as Gene had explained, it was designed for Canadian waters that could become covered with whitecaps and turn dangerous very quickly. The engine was a twenty-five horsepower engine mounted at the rear transom that started with a pull of the rope. An ample supply of gas was at the cabin along with a red carry-on tank that stayed in the boat and could be refilled as needed.

The weather was beautifully benevolent; the sun shone down and warmed the recently frigid land. A light jacket or sweatshirt was sufficient for warmth, and the insulated underwear stayed in the cabin. I was very happy, and Joel seemed more content and at ease than I could remember him being for a long time.

I told myself what a good decision this had been, and I thanked Joel many times for bringing me to this remote and beautiful place. We did a great deal of fishing and explored the rocky, tree-studded shoreline. Joel was particularly fascinated with a couple of extremely remote islands we found not far from the waterfall I was sure I'd seen from the air.

When it came to fishing, Joel quickly refreshed my memory and added some new skills to my casting abilities, and I proudly added to our daily catch. This enabled us to have several wonderful meals. I liked the flavor of the walleye pike, called pickerel by the Canadians.

Joel informed me the Canadians loved this particular fish also since it was succulent with few bones to worry about when properly cleaned and filleted. Joel was a little rusty in that area of cleaning fish at first, but soon he was skillfully preparing enough fish that we agreed we could take some home later to share with everyone.

I discovered that the northern pike were the most fun to catch, as it seemed to me they would shake their heads "no, no," then splash out of the water in a frenzy and fight hard against me every moment I tried to land them. These fish had large mouths full of tiny, sharp teeth that could bite right through your line if you did not have a protective steel leader section at the end to prevent this from happening.

Regardless of this, they were slippery and wily to catch and managed to get off the hook far too often for my liking. I was sure I had experienced the thrill of at least two world-record fish on my line that got away from me! I was delighted whenever I felt the tug on my line and the fight between me and the fish began. It was an exhilarating accomplishment to bring a fish to the waiting net. The flavor of the northern, when cooked, was nearly identical to that of the walleye, but we had to be more careful about the bones until Joel learned how to fillet them and eliminate bone problems. I was able to relax and enjoy life as I had not done in a long, long while.

Along about the fourth day, Joel suggested a day's length outing that would include a picnic lunch. We would go up to the waterfall and then have our picnic on a rocky point we had found on one of the islands nearby. As I was packing our lunch, I looked out the cabin window and saw Joel furtively slipping a blanket-wrapped package into the boat.

"What was that you put in the boat?" I asked when he returned to the cabin. I couldn't imagine what it was or why he was being secretive.

He looked startled for a moment, then grinned and replied, "It's a surprise for you."

"How about a clue?" I smiled.

"You'll just have to wait and see." He smiled back as he looked at me, then gently cupped my face in his hand. "You are one special lady, Mattie," he said softly. "Ready?"

I nodded. This trip was erasing so much pain, and I was happy and content. We climbed in the boat, Joel started the motor, and we were off for our day's adventure. The weather was perfect that day. I can still remember it all so clearly. The outboard motor hummed as we skimmed the small, aluminum V-shaped fishing boat across the almost-smooth, blue, mirrored lakes. The deep V cut into the water and offered a stability not found in flat-bottom craft.

There was a very slight breeze that sporadically made the surface of the lake waver back and forth a little, so the reflection of the granite rocky points and deep green hemlocks, pines, spruces, shrubs, and sage green moss rippled softly to and fro as we passed each jut and point of land.

The sky was an intense blue, the color the deepest blue forget-me-nots look in their fresh spring blooming. Cotton-white clouds gently built and bubbled their way across the sky as I searched for imaginary figures in the changing puffs of milky white. An occasional loon would dive beneath the water. It would resurface yards behind us as we passed, showing us his displeasure at our intrusion into his world.

A mama merganser, a sleek and beautiful diving duck, spotted us as we approached one of the many islands protruding into the mammoth Canadian skies. She scooted her little ducklings along the shore and tried valiantly to remain inconspicuous by herding them under an overhanging tree. Each island we passed had a unique personality. This island rose gradually from marsh and beach flat area to sharp granite walls that led steeply to a higher ridge displaying spruce sentinels spearing the sky.

Other islands rose sharply with upheaved granite cliffs breaking up from the water that led to moss-covered hillsides shaded by hemlocks, spruce, birch, poplar, and a multitude of evergreen variations. Still other islands were more welcoming with sandy beaches that slanted gently to allow a boat entrance and gently sloping granite slabs that were ideal for a shore lunch.

The island with the mama merganser had a rock shelf that protruded out into the water along with a very convenient tree that leaned out near the shelf. The shelf dropped off to a nice sandy beach, and we commented that a boat would easily slide up on the beach and could be secured by rope to the tree. It would be easy to climb out of the boat because the winds, normally coming from the west, seemed to be calm in that area as well.

We rode all the way around the island and saw some interesting rock formations on the far side. Right away I mentioned to Joel that I would like to explore those interesting granite creations. The island was about a mile in circumference and had areas where the undergrowth was so thick it would be nearly impassable. Other areas had steep, rocky cliffs covered with soft green moss and lichens.

We thought we saw blueberry bushes on the north side, but they were too far from us to be sure. The expanse of water surrounding all these islands was about twenty miles wide and connected with rivers to other similar lakes, which made the shorelines appear endless.

We continued our exploring. A short time later we saw an animal swimming. Only a round, brown head showed, somewhat indistinctly, in front of the V-shape it was cutting through the water. We watched the progress as it neared the far side of the lake toward some freshly felled trees where white edges shone brightly from a recent cut. On our approach, the brown head paused, a huge tail swung up out of the water, and *splat* went the flat of the tail against the surface of the lake.

We smiled at the indignant splash it left behind. Mr. Beaver was warning us off his possessions. I laughed from the joy of it all, and Joel laughed with me. Oh yes, it was a blissful day, and I was once again happy with my Joel, and he with me. We were mending things that had been deeply hurtful. Life felt glorious.

A little further on, we neared the far side of the lake, which was about three times longer than it was wide. The width I guessed was about eight miles across on average and, like the rest of the territory, was impressive. We arrived at an impasse to our adventurous exploring on the far side of the lake: the frothy waterfall. Huge boulders and granite slabs of rock were all jumbled into the long ravine as if tossed there by a giant's child playing tiddlywinks.

The water foamed, splashed, and swirled madly down the rocky incline toward us—a mixture of waterfall and rapids, awesome in the power displayed. It was a magnificent, noisy sight and seemed to roar at us like a hungry lion that flexed its muscles to warn us of the brute force and raw beauty displayed before us. We felt privileged to see it.

We motored as close as possible, then let the boat drift with the currents as we fished for a while in the pools and eddies formed at the side and base of the falls. We occasionally threw out the anchor when we felt we hit a good spot for fishing. We both enjoyed the thunderous noise made by the water tumbling down. We stayed safely away from the maelstrom that spelled disaster in the center. With this approach, we were able to catch enough fish for a meal, and soon Joel pointed back a short distance to the middle of the lake and called to me over the echoing falls, "Okay, it's time for our lunch, let's head for that island over there where we saw the mama merganser."

I pulled up the anchor as my Dad had taught me, while Joel started the engine. In a while we arrived at our island—the one I had wanted to explore. Joel propelled the boat onto the beach that was part of the small, sandy cove. We tied off to the tree that hung out over that large, protruding, sloping rock. On closer inspection, one end of that rock was partially covered in lush, dark green moss on the landward side in the shade.

I found the green covering to be soft and fluffy. It was over this moss I chose to spread a woolen, fleece blanket for us to share as we ate lunch. It was like a soft bed under us. "Let's take a walk before lunch," Joel said as he smiled and held out his hand. We walked around the island, generally staying close to shore. We came upon a large granite slab that protruded from the water and jutted up onto the shore then inland for about fifty yards. We walked around the base of it.

"Oh look!" I pointed. "It looks like one of those pictographs I saw in the museum once. I read about how the aboriginal people left such markings in various places in the northern areas where there were walls like this on which they could draw their stories." I examined the designs intently. I saw faint images, very faded, but definitely man-made. There were circles, arrows, and stick-figure people in differing poses. One rock face even depicted what looked like a canoe or boat. "We need to report this when we get back. It could be a significant find for archeologists."

"Oh, it's just some old scratchings on the stone by some Indian who passed by here," Joel scoffed. It could even have been done by a bored fisherman. It can't be anything important. Someone would have found it long before now."

"No, Joel, really, this could be very significant. Can't you just imagine how long ago this might have been done?"

I wanted to go back to get the camera and take a snapshot, but Joel simply looked around without the same enthusiasm and said. "Come on, Mattie. I'm getting hungry. Let's go back and get something to eat first, then if you are still in the mood, you can come back and take your snapshot, okay?"

I felt like a child who was being humored, but at least he was pleasant about it, so I dropped the subject for then, and we returned to the campsite where our boat was still tethered to the tree. When we got back, Joel busied himself and set up the portable propane stove. "What can I do to help?" I asked him.

"Absolutely nothing, princess, this is my treat," he said.

He produced some camp cookware and soon had our freshly caught fish and a can of beans sizzling. I disregarded his statement that he needed no help, and I set out plates, cups, utensils, and opened the cooler to produce some canned fruit we had chilled with our cold drinks.

This done, and while Joel was still cooking, I attempted to unsnag a few coils in the line of my fishing pole. I used my nail clippers to cut off a length of line that had become rather kinked. I was fairly proud of my efforts at rethreading and rerigging my fishing rod. I was just getting ready to show my work to Joel when I spied the mysterious blanket in the stern of the boat.

"Joel." I pretended to pout. "You still haven't shown me your surprise."

"That's right." He laughed. "Come and eat, then I'll show it to you."

"I won't be *able* to eat if you keep me in suspense much longer!" I laughingly grumbled. But I discarded the old fishing line in the weeds, stuffed the clippers in my pocket, and went over to sit next to Joel on the blanket.

I was able to eat a healthy portion of everything on my plate, since the fresh air had stimulated my appetite. Joel, for some reason, seemed less hungry and picked at his food. I found myself teasingly stealing some of his fish fillets. He watched me and smiled.

We were nearly finished eating when Joel arose and walked to the boat. He picked up the mysterious package and returned to my side. He slowly opened the blanket-shrouded item. Hesitantly, as if he were afraid I would disapprove, he pulled out from the folds a long bottle of champagne and a small gift-wrapped box.

"What is that?" I asked. "I can see the bottle is champagne, but what's in the box?"

"I've been saving this champagne for a very special occasion." He smiled secretively, seductively, ignoring my query about the box. "This *is* our second anniversary isn't it?"

I had completely forgotten the date in my enjoyment of Canada. I was thrilled Joel had remembered. It was our wedding anniversary. I assumed the box was an anniversary gift.

Joel magically pulled two fluted glasses out of the blanket, then pulled out the cork and poured some champagne from the bottle into each glass. One glass he handed to me, the other he held in his own hand.

"A toast," he said, his voice was rueful, apologetic, "to many years ahead, each happier than this last one."

"It wasn't all that bad," I chastised him. "And you've certainly made up for it this week." I held up my glass but still had my eye on that mysterious box.

"It is a very good year." He pointed at my glass and encouraged me. "Drink up!" He smiled benignly and watched me intently as I tipped the glass and swallowed half of it down. It was a good champagne—bubbly and smooth and a little sweet.

"All of it," he smilingly insisted, as I stopped at half a glass. "I have something else for you but please finish your glass first." He patted the small, wrapped package that intrigued me.

"Bully," I joked as I humored him and again lifted the glass and drank it in. It went down easily and tasted as succulent and smooth as the first. "Now you, darling." I pointed to his glass, still full of the crystalline-looking drink.

He started to lift his glass, but suddenly called out, "What's that?" Joel jumped, startled, and in the process spilled his drink all over the ground.

"Oh no! You spilled it," I mourned. I wanted to ask him what it was he had heard out there that caused him to jump in fright, but I was feeling a little dizzy. I stretched out my hand to steady myself.

"I can pour another," he assured me, then added, "but are you all right?" Joel looked at me curiously.

I was not all right. My head felt woozy. I remember thinking I must have gulped the drink down much too quickly. I put out my other arm to keep from toppling over where I sat on the blanket. I looked down at that arm as I reached for Joel to steady myself, and it looked funny, distorted, as if I had two arms. I looked across and there were two Joels staring at me. Both of them had a face that looked unusually sad, considering we were celebrating. I heard the sound of my champagne glass breaking on the rock next to me. Everything suddenly went black around me, and I descended into oblivion.

Chapter 9

I woke up in pain and confusion. Jumbled images circulated in my head. The images mixed my past and my present in a twirling movie screen full of cabins, fish, the Eiffel tower, my husband, a boat, my father, and an island. I could make no sense of those images, but they began to fade away. I struggled to stay awake and to escape the images, then very slowly, I managed to sit up.

I felt dizzy—disoriented. I ached everywhere. I could barely move. My head felt the swimming sensation one associates with ear infections. Once again I found a woozy consciousness, but this time things started to come back to me with more clarity—the second honeymoon in Canada ... the food ... the picnic ... the ancient Indian drawings. I had been on a picnic with Joel. I had been sitting on this very picnic blanket. I had drunk the champagne too quickly and fallen asleep.

But where was Joel? Why was I feeling so ill? What was wrong? Something seemed terribly amiss. I couldn't concentrate. My head and limbs felt like they weighed five times their normal amount. It took monumental effort to try to move. My eyes had trouble focusing.

Was Joel ill too? I must help him, must try to find him. I tried to move, to get up, but I felt weak and fell back on the moss-cushioned blanket. I moved in and out of consciousness. I did not know how much time had passed. Was it still the same day? I found myself lying on the ground, wrapped in the blanket.

Did I unconsciously wrap myself or has Joel been back to wrap me up? Is Joel sick too? What happened to us? Did we get food poisoning? I must find

Joel. I managed, finally, to roll over and prop myself up on my side. The world tilted around me, and I felt I would like to lie back down and sleep some more, but rather than giving in to that need, this time I steeled myself to stay partly erect.

I tried to focus my eyes. I wanted to be able to see more clearly. I compelled my lungs to breathe in deeply. My mind reluctantly commanded my body. *Inhale. Exhale. Breathe!* I told myself, *You must be strong. You must regain all your senses. You must find Joel and help him. He must be sick too.*

As I lay there half-prone, breathing hard, I managed to twist my head and look around for Joel. I didn't see him anywhere. Then I remembered something else … the boat! I looked fervently at the sandy cove where we had tied the craft to the tree. I looked away to rub the haze from my eyes, then back again incredulously. The boat had been tucked up on the shore during our picnic. Now, when I looked, I could see that the boat was gone. The tree still hung over the rock shelf, but the rope hooking the boat to the tree was gone. Impossible.

"How could it be gone?" I asked myself aloud and heard how my words sounded slurred to my own ears. I spoke aloud again. "I saw Joel tie it securely to that tree." My mind whipped through a multitude of questions. *Did it somehow come untied and drift away while I was lying insensible to the world? Does Joel know it's gone?* Again I spoke aloud to the air, "Are Joel and I marooned on this small island?" I felt more alert now, still weak, but I thought I could figure out what had happened. We had eaten something that made us both sick.

I sat a little more upright on the blanket with its edges tucked around me to think and gain my bearings. *But if we're both sick*, I wondered, *where is Joel? Did he go for help?* Then I began to notice some things that didn't make sense to me. The portable stove was gone. I looked around further. The picnic supplies had all been picked up and were gone too. The hamper, my life vest, my camera, my small purse I always carried—all were gone. They had been right here beside me.

I saw the broken glass from my drink nearby, but everything else seemed to be gone. *How? Why?* My mind churned along with my stomach, but then I thought to myself, *I know! Joel must have quickly cleaned the picnic site to get ready to go when he realized I was sick. This had to be before he also became ill—but if he's ill, where is he?*

"Where's the boat?" I mumbled this last thought aloud while my mind continued to construe what might have happened. I came up with ideas and tried to make logic out of the illogical. I continued to speak my thoughts into the silence around me, "The island is small, perhaps he wandered over to the other side while I slept, not knowing I was ill, and perhaps he thought I needed the rest. That's it! He will be back soon."

No sooner were these thoughts uttered than my mind careened on. I surmised, "Yet, if the island is that small, I should be able to walk around it and find him." It was as if I were carrying on two conversations. One was in my head and the other aloud, as I spoke into the wind. Somehow hearing my human voice comforted me.

I called "Joel! Jo—well!" I shouted as loudly as my weakened condition would allow. There was no answer. I continued to call his name on a regular interval. But I heard only—silence. Silence except for the soft *slap, slap, splash,* of the lapping water as it hit the rocky shoreline and the occasional chirp of a bird.

The evening air started to carry a chill, so I pushed myself into a more erect sitting position and wrapped the blanket closer around me. I adjusted the bandana on my head, which had slipped slightly sideways. When I did, I heard the tinkle of my nail clippers as they fell out of my pocket. I put them back in place, happy to have something familiar with me.

Next, with fortitude and desperation, I stood, but I wobbled erratically, so I found a broken branch nearby to use for support. I leaned carefully on the branch, and then, step by halting step, I began a trek around the island to find Joel. The chilly air, though it cooled my body, was refreshing to my muddled mind and allowed my head to begin to clear so I could think. I walked carefully all the way around the small island, sitting often on fallen logs or large rocks.

I passed the place of the pictographs on the granite wall. They were still there, a validation that I had been here with Joel. I continued on around the island, staying mostly to the shoreline. I guessed it must be about a mile in circumference—a small blot in that large lake. Some of the terrain was difficult for me to navigate, but I forged on as my body rebelled. At least the nausea had begun to improve.

My stomach was still somewhat queasy from so much vomiting, but it had become much less violent. My head also began to feel better. I constantly looked out at the water for signs of the boat and Joel, but I saw only the tranquil lake reflecting an early moon. I saw no signs of any human anywhere for as far as I could see. No friendly lights twinkled. I knew the lake was over twenty miles long. The remoteness was intimidating.

I finally struggled my way completely around the island, continually calling for Joel, but there was no answer and no sign of any humanity or supplies that might help me. Exhausted and weak, I trembled with fear and other feelings I was not yet ready to admit. I returned to my mossy place for a little security after my fruitless search. I wrapped the blanket ever more tightly around me and sank wearily back into the soft moss.

The mosquitoes by now had begun a set of kamikaze attacks. The blanket was my only protection against their tormenting harassment, but I also appreciated the blanket because the air was turning colder. I pulled my knees up to my chin and sat, alone, tears now flowing freely down my face, as I stared unbelievingly out at the now night-black water.

All was now dark around me. The only light came from the moon. I could see dark shapes everywhere, relieved only by the faint light offered by the celestial globe in the heavens as it moved across the clear, star-peppered sky.

The lake reflected the stars and moon. They sparkled like a silvery spider's web hanging over the black trap of dark water looming below. I heard a distant howl, the same sound made by a wolf my dad and I had heard one night in Wisconsin, then closer was the haunting, eerie cry-laugh of a loon, a cry that well matched the mood of my shattered spirit and my growing suspicions. It had been a long ordeal of a day, or had it been two? How long *had* I been unconscious? Night finally came—to me and to Canada.

Chapter 10

Fortunately, nights are short in the northern hemisphere that time of year—something, I told myself, for which I should be thankful. But I wasn't feeling thankful about much of anything the next morning as I recalled my suffering through the darkness. How I shivered and huddled in the blanket and sat all alone on the rock-strewn island with none of my usual comforts. My body was cold, achy, and miserable.

All night long I watched first the water then the deep woods behind me, fearful of every brushy, whispered movement caused by the wind in the trees. Remembering stories of bears and wolves in Canada, I had been jumpy all night. Every little movement and noise, even a twig falling, had caused me panic. I remained very still and quiet, though sometimes I leaned back on the moss in order to sleep a little, shrouded in my blanket.

I fought off hysteria and tried to be my father's daughter with the courage he had instilled in me. It would have been easy to scream, to cry, but who was there to hear me? For the first time in my life, I had no one I could call—no father who could come to my rescue. I was dependent on one person—myself. I was not sure I was up to the task. I thought to myself, *I must endure this if I am to survive. I must endure.*

At the hint of a pink dawn in the morning sky, I thought I heard airplanes or helicopters or both. I listened intently, hoping they were looking for me. Perhaps Joel went for help when he saw me unconscious. Possibly someone came by and forced Joel away at gunpoint when I was lying inert and insensible. My mind continued to invent stories. Perhaps he was free now and was sending help to search for me. But my puzzled mind continued wrestling with itself.

How could that be? I saw only my and Joel's footprints in the wet sand where the boat had been moored. No footprints of anyone else were evident. Taking another tack in my feverish hope that this would all come out right, I wondered, *Why are those planes staying so far in the distance? Why aren't they coming this way?*

Joel can direct them. Joel knows exactly where I am. If he left in the boat to get help, why isn't he sending them back here? Then my mind shifted in another direction—*but why didn't he take me in the boat with him if he really wanted to get help for me?* I knew the answer, but I did not want to know it.

The sounds of the aircraft grew fainter and fainter, moving away from me until the wind was again my only companion. I listened in vain for the aircraft to return. I prayed it was a search team and soon they would move this way. The long day dragged on and on. The sun burning down was a double-edged sword—blessing as it dissipated the mosquitoes near the sand beach, but also a danger when I felt the heat and saw my overexposed skin turn pink. I realized I needed to move to the shade of trees, but that was where mosquitos still lurked.

I tried to find a middle ground and moved to the edge of the beach where it met the first shade of the trees. The mosquitos were replaced in the heat of the day with pervasive black flies that I continually swatted away in frustration. The black-fly bites were worse than the mosquitoes and left large welts on my skin especially around my hairline and the edge of my bandana. I was hungry and thirsty, but I was so depressed and shocked and recovering from the residue of being ill. I couldn't make myself put forth any efforts to find food.

I waited. I hoped. I yearned to be rescued. I fluctuated between daydreams of miraculous rescues and a deep depression that nearly sucked the life out of me. I wanted my situation to improve, but it stayed exactly the same. Finally, after the incessant day was nearly done, I began to face what I had been unwilling to acknowledge. Reluctantly, I began to admit my suspicions, to allow them a voice in my mind.

Yes, I sneered at myself and shook my head in disgust, *you must now face the truth, Mattie.* Then I told myself bitterly, *Do not dream foolish dreams of rescue, nor hold on to your hopes any longer, for Joel knows exactly where you are. Face it Mattie, you know the ugly truth. Quit hiding from it. You are not stupid, even though you have made some stupid mistakes. Your answers are right here in front of you.*

I looked savagely over at the area where we had held our picnic. I noticed the champagne bottle was also cleverly missing. I recalled something odd about that bottle that bothered me now. I nudged my memory, thinking back … then I remembered. There had been no *pop* when Joel pulled out the cork. *Oh yes,* I finally admitted to myself, *you are exactly where Joel wants you. You've been avoiding the truth, but you cannot evade it any longer.*

I looked out over the water and talked to myself in a shattered voice, "You are a foolish, silly dreamer, Mattie. You got yourself into this predicament with your stubborn refusal to see Joel for what he was. You were warned by Josie and Blanche and your father, but you wouldn't listen. No, no, you knew better than they did. What did it get you? This loyalty to a dream, to fiction, to what you wished for. Where did it get you? None of it was real.

"You were left here to die, that's what. He drugged you, tried to murder you with some kind of poison in the champagne, then he deserted your senseless body believing you to be dead. It was a well-thought-out, evil plan." I worked myself into an angry frenzy. My voice rang out across the water and echoed back to me like laughing loons. I remembered how I had protected Joel by forbidding my father to approach him about the prenuptial agreement. I became bitter.

"Premeditated, the courts would call it," I shouted, giving vent to my wrath. "He couldn't take a chance the search planes would actually find your drugged and poisoned body and learn the real cause of your death, so he left your body here to die very conveniently, where only old bleached bones would someday be found—if ever."

I was yelling by then, my weak arm raised in a fist, venting my anger into the air. "He then directed the search over there where you heard all the airplanes—far from this spot. They will find your purse with your camera. That's why he did not want you to take a photograph of the wall drawings. How stupid of you, Mattie, not to see that. It might have been a clue to direct them to you if someone knows about those drawings. They will also find your life vest, but will assume the fishes got you. He was very clever!"

Exhausted, I sank back to the ground and bitterly meditated over these conclusions for a while. A screen had been lifted from my naive and innocent past. I was disgusted at myself. I continued my self-flagellation with more condemnation. "You're worthless, Mattie. Joel doesn't want you. He was after your mother's inheritance money, and you argued with your dad over that stupid prenuptial when he was right all along, so why don't you just go ahead—curl up and die?

"That's what Joel wants, and now you no longer want to live either. Make everyone happy. Give up, Mattie. Too bad the rest of that poisoned champagne is gone or you could just drink it up and go to sleep. No more pain. No more hurting. No more tears."

I went on in this vein of hopelessness and self-pity for some time. Then I remembered one constant in my life—my father. I knew how tortured he would be if anything happened to me. I thought of dear Blanche and knew she would be weeping and grieved. Josie, though angry at me for ignoring her advice, would miss me too and mourn greatly. Eleanor, though separated from our family would join their grief. My father would be inconsolable. I agonized that I had no way to communicate with him. I felt pangs of guilt and remorse over what he must be enduring right now. I knew he would be in one of those misdirected airplanes or helicopters searching and searching for me.

I'm so sorry, Daddy. I never meant to hurt you. This is my own fault. You were right about Joel all along. You tried to tell me. How I would like one of your bear hugs right now, Daddy. My fear, remorse, and self-pity did not last very long. I felt them gradually dissipate. They ebbed and changed and metamorphosed into a new range of feelings—frightening in their intensity.

Almost snakelike, I felt myself become gradually filled with malicious venom. I wanted to strike out hard and fast and sink my fangs into Joel and return poison for poison. I felt my eyes narrow into slits that glowed to match my coiled-up anger. I wanted to watch him suffer as he had left me to suffer. I slithered from one feeling to another, and those feelings built. I thought about what an evil thing Joel had done, and I became consumed with ferocious fury and a building desire for revenge that consumed me and burned like a raging fire in my soul.

I will not allow him to win, I claimed for myself with a powerful surge of sheer malevolence. It was almost therapeutic—the hatred. The fomenting anger gave me strength. I felt a new determination flowing through my veins. My former weakness and apathy were soon replaced with a rapacious passion to survive. I wanted to live. I wanted to retaliate. And I wanted to see Joel's face when I made it happen. I wanted to watch him go behind prison bars in the most despicable prison I could imagine. And I wanted to be on the other side of those bars watching him suffer as he had made me suffer.

I felt a renewed energy, an enormous zeal, to overcome the obstacles before me. "I will not give up," I talked aloud to the air in the unresponsive Canadian wilderness. "I will find a way out of this catastrophe. I will be strong."

My eyes glittered with resolve, and I held my fist clenched as I pronounced my terrible verdict. "Once I'm safe, then my revenge will be rapid and terrible for Joel to see. Poor inept Joel! He couldn't even do a complete job of killing me. He is going to pay for this. Oh yes, he is going to pay."

I recalled the sensation of being watched at the restaurant with Josie and then the phone call from the attorney, and I realized Joel knew he was in jeopardy of losing everything if I decided to divorce him. I had fallen for his fake change in attitude toward me. I berated myself for being so foolish and gullible. In order to get revenge I knew I had to take action.

I began to take stock of my situation. My anger turned to productive ideas. I thought about what would be necessary for me to survive. I needed shelter, warmth, food, and water. I had so little with me, but somehow between that and what I could find on the island, it would have to do. First, there was the clothing on my back, which included a blouse and sweatshirt, my jeans—with some Kleenex tissue in one pocket and my nail clippers in the other.

I wore a belt and had rugged tennis shoes on my feet along with thick, athletic socks. The warm woolen, fleece blanket was a Godsend and had already helped me survive thus far. I had on a diamond ring and gold band—my wedding rings, actually—which I looked at in disgust; two small earrings, some hair clips, and two rubber bands holding my pony-tailed blonde hair in place.

I was thankful for the long bandana scarf I had wrapped around my head and tied behind my neck. It could be used for a strainer, also to keep my head and ears warm and to protect my face, or opened out as a washcloth. The broken champagne glass pieces might be used for sawing or cutting things. My first priority had to be survival, and I was looking for items that could be my arsenal of life-saving supplies. I remembered the twisted fishing line I had discarded—one, two days ago?

Hurriedly, frantic to accumulate supplies, I searched for the line in the waning light, swatting mechanically at the onslaught of mosquitoes in the brush. Yes! I found it right where I had tossed it aside. I wrapped it into a small spool and pocketed the strong filament. It might come in handy. *Perhaps*, I wondered, *I could devise a fishing pole*. I finished my inventory and concluded that other than what little I had on me, there would be only my own ingenuity and the things I could find in the Canadian landscape to help me survive.

I was surrounded by water yet afraid to drink it. I knew I was dehydrated from all the sickness. The water looked so good, crystalline and transparently clear. I could see down to rocks lining the bottom about three feet below the surface where I stood. Nevertheless, I hesitated, remembering horror stories of impure water and dysentery. Finally, I succumbed to the thirst that had parched and burned my lips, throat, and tongue.

Then I bent over and cupped my hands, scooping up the water and taking a long drink. Suddenly, I could not get enough, and I scooped more and more to quench my thirst. Next, I splashed it on my face to rinse it clean. The water became a catharsis, giving me a new life, a focused direction, cleansing my body and my thoughts, giving me hope.

I used a corner of the blanket as a towel to dry my face and hands. As I did so, I felt all the welts on my skin from the annoying mosquitoes and pervasive black flies. My skin, when I looked at my hands and exposed areas within my sight, resembled the bubble wrap used to prevent breakage in packages. I could only imagine what my face suffered.

The darkness was by now encroaching on my second day of consciousness in the wilderness, and I did not have time or the visibility to search for food. The mosquitoes were again pursuing their vicious assault with my bruised skin as a tasty target. They dive-bombed me by pelting and pricking my skin unmercifully. I swatted at them ineffectually and realized I could now believe the stories I had read about how they could easily drive someone mad.

I started to panic but paused when I remembered my new resolve. I made myself face my situation head on. My thoughts lurked and lurched around in my mind; they bounced around like water drops on a hot skillet. *How am I going to save myself? Once again I will spend a lonely night on this remote, totally isolated, Canadian island.* I had been fortunate thus far. The weather had held, but I faced the reality that in Canada, the weather can change like quicksilver.

Given the waning light, I could not do much more, but I would get some sleep rather than spending the night in mourning and worrying about things I could not change. I determined to give my body proper rest and beat Joel at this treacherous game by being refreshed and clever in the morning.

I arranged the blanket on the moss so that it was both under me; yet, could be wrapped around me for warmth and protection from the bugs. I lay down on the soft mossy bed, wrapped the blanket snugly around me like a papoose, tied the bandana backwards so it covered my face yet allowed me to breathe through it, and surprisingly, I was able to disregard the night sounds that had so frightened me the previous evening. I slept.

Hunger and bright sunshine teased my eyelids awake the next day. I sat up on my mossy bed and looked at my surroundings. I gauged it to be midmorning already and was amazed I was still whole, unmolested by wild animals and actually somewhat rested. I looked beyond my immediate surroundings and saw how far the island was from the mainland, so my first thoughts of swimming to safety were quashed in light of my weakness. My anger returned when I remembered the missing life vest that would have helped so much with that long swim.

I had already made a cursory look in my trek around the island hoping to find wooden planks or logs washed ashore, or anything (especially food) that might be beneficial to my survival. I vaguely remembered some blueberry bushes on the south side. Nothing else major had surfaced yet, except for the possibility of making a raft—but how? I might search for some beaver cuttings later, but for now I needed to evaluate anything that might be usable as I planned for my safety.

I was interrupted in my search for survival items by a grumbling stomach. I felt stronger this morning, but my body had been severely abused, and after so much time without food, I was ravenously hungry. I had been on an unwilling fast, and I knew I would grow weaker if I did not get something to eat soon. I thought back to my scouting days and the summer camp times; some of the badges I had earned and proudly displayed to my dad, I never dreamed might someday mean life or death for me.

I would have given a year's pay to have the Scout manual with me. I knew I had forgotten much of it, but I decided to improvise and do the best I could with what I could remember. First, I went back to the place I thought held blueberries. I knew these were safe to eat. The plants were easily recognized, and I figured some early ones should be ready to pick by this time of year.

I remembered our floatplane pilot, Gene, warned us how the bears love the blueberries too. But I was not too concerned about bears at this point. I was relatively sure there were no large animals on the island since I had now walked around it twice and did not see large animal tracks or any signs to indicate their presence. I was fortunate enough to find an adequate supply of blueberries and ate my fill. I made that my breakfast. I picked extras and carried them back, using my bandana as a pouch.

Next, I decided I would have fish for lunch. This would be a bit more challenging for me to accomplish than picking berries off a bush. I searched until I found a long tree branch that would work as a fishing pole. It was not difficult to attach the remnants of my fishing line, but then I became stymied. What to use for a hook? What to use for bait?

I pulled the clips out of my hair that helped hold my long bandana in place. They were small metal clips. I tried to fashion one of them into a hook, but I was not very satisfied with my efforts, and I realized the metal bent far too easily—a fish could bend it straight. I tried adding the second clip for reinforcement and decided it would have to do for my hook. It should be strong enough to catch any small fish such as a bluegill or perch.

My father's large tackle box and his glittery assortment of lures and tackle came to mind. I took off my rings: the sparkling diamond and the simple band. I twirled them around meditatively on the end of my finger and watched the sunlight brightly reflecting back at me. I thought of all they had represented to me, and my sorrow was magnified with each shaft of light as it spun around and around in glittering splendor.

I did not last long in this mood, however, and forced my sorrow to be replaced by more practical thoughts such as getting myself fed. I would have plenty of time later to grieve as well as deal with these stronger emotions of anger and revenge as they surfaced. I took a deep breath, forced myself back to the practical necessities of saving my own life, and removed the rings. I managed to attach the sparkling diamond engagement ring to the makeshift hook I had made of the hair clips. This would be my lure, and hopefully the hooks would hold long enough to pull in the fish.

Following this, I spent nearly two hours dangling my diamond bait in the water. I threw the line out as far from shore as I could fling it, but it kept drifting back too close to shore. I diligently flung it, then dangled, then retrieved and flung it again. After a long time, nothing had happened except that my stomach was letting me know I needed to find it sustenance.

My patience was almost gone. I sat there rather apathetically and was about to give up and try to live on a blueberry diet. Then unexpectedly, a huge fish erupted out of the surface of the water in front of me and went for my artificial bait like a fast submerging torpedo. Startled, excited, and amazed, I yanked my makeshift pole back as hard as I could to snag him. His opposing weight bent my pole almost double, so I yanked again.

When I did, I felt a sudden release of pressure and then whistling past my ear, my line came sailing out of the water, far too easily. I looked, astonished, at the end of my line at a straight, now flattened, makeshift hook that was still attached. Unfortunately, nothing else was still attached. No fish. No bait. I looked back at the water where I saw the big fish splash one more time before he disappeared into the depths as quickly as he'd arrived.

My ring was gone—swallowed whole. My diamond ring was now down in the cavernous belly of some unknown big fish, and worst of all, I was still hungry. I only knew that it had been a very large fish and would have fed me for several days. I felt a fresh wave of discouragement crest and crash uncontrollably through my body.

I was filled with hopelessness as if all my optimism had been ruthlessly crushed on the rocky shore. I felt no great loss for the ring. As the symbolism in my life, I now realized it was a sham. But I knew I would miss that fish. My stomach was telling me about it already. Obviously my little hook had been defective.

I almost gave in to despair. I felt tears well, but I refused to give up. I sat and pondered the situation. Then, happily, I remembered something I'd learned in one of my elective college courses, a class I had thoroughly enjoyed—archaeology. I remembered reading and seeing photos of how they had found fish hooks made of fish bones in the digs of some Neolithic sites. I became reinvigorated and excited when I remembered how Joel had cleaned the fish from our picnic lunch and how he had discarded the remnants nearby. A short search revealed what I wanted.

I was so grateful to find bits of fish and bone intact. I was amazed at how such a small thing could bring me joy. I was soon able to fashion a hook from a sturdy fish bone with the help of my little clippers. I also utilized some pieces of our discarded fish—those pieces that weren't too deteriorated—to use for bait. I attached one of those remnants to the hook. I threw the line as far out as I could and held the pole steady. Now came the waiting. *But,* I told myself, spirits somewhat reviving, my father's inherited dry humor coming to the rescue, as I looked down at the water and saw my Huckleberry Finn image reflected, *I have plenty of time. I have nothing but time!*

I mulled over my situation from this new angle and how much time I had. I decided that, for the moment, I would likely be safe. Joel wouldn't risk returning this soon, especially if my father were anywhere around. I told myself not to worry. It would look too suspicious for him to return to Canada or take off alone without a search party after I've been declared dead, and especially if he's concocted a story about my drowning so he could claim my inheritance.

But, I felt certain he *would* eventually be back, so I settled down once more, after I calmed myself and reasoned things out while I patiently fished. My mind worried over my predicament; I sought and discarded solutions, one after another. I wrestled in my mind over each idea and tried to think of new ways out of my predicament.

I can't stay here indefinitely, and with Joel possibly coming back, I need to get away as soon as possible. Now I have a more perplexing problem: I am on an island. I'm surrounded by miles of water. I have no boat. How can I possibly escape?

My mind continued to stay busy while I fished. I devised all sorts of tortures and revenge scenarios I could use on Joel once I was rescued. The anger literally seethed out of me as I sat there calmly fishing. I was almost surprised, when I looked down, that the line didn't sizzle and chase the fish away, so strong were my feelings.

I imagined, with relish, Joel screaming and pleading for my help while I stood by and nonchalantly refused him aid. I imagined old tortures with Joel's head sticking out of the sand and ants crawling all over him while he begged me for release. Oh, I was angry … and very, very hurt. I was angry at Joel, yes, but I was also angry with myself for letting him dupe me so thoroughly. I did not like feeling gullible and naive. I had been both.

It didn't take very long before I had two nice little perch up on shore. I was disappointed that I hadn't acquired a larger fish like a walleye, or the big one that got away with my diamond bait, but I was very thankful for the perch. They looked like two gold-striped, tigereye gems lying there on the rock, only they were more precious to me at that moment than any jewel. I soon realized, however, I had another challenge. I had no way to cook the fish.

I was not inclined to eat them raw, and although sushi was a delicacy in oriental lands, it had never appealed to me and didn't now. I had no matches, no fire, no skillet or pan. I had no tools but my nail clippers and some hair clips and other fish bones, some of which were very sharp. But I was hungry *now*.

My rumbling stomach was bubbling like a dormant volcano that had revived and was about to erupt. Unmistakable pangs let me know I needed to eat—soon. I thought about this problem a bit. I didn't think rubbing two sticks together sounded like it had much chance for success. But at the moment I didn't have much else with which to work, so I spent some long and fruitless moments while I tried to work up enough friction to start a fire.

I became frustrated when nothing happened, but then the light shifted through the trees behind me and I happened to notice the broken fragments of my champagne glass sparkling reflectively off to one side while the sun shone brightly through the glass. The sunshine through the glass gave me an idea. I decided to try an experiment with that idea. I picked out several of the larger pieces and had a moment of glee as I realized I had already thwarted Joel. I was not dead.

Thus far, I was still alive, and so far Joel did not know that fact. I had an advantage. I did not have time for gloating however, so I proceeded with my plans for the glass pieces. Next, I lined up those broken shards so the sunlight was intensified and shining through the curving glass down onto a couple of pieces of tissue I had culled from my jeans pocket. I had other fuel lined up in the form of twigs and sticks just in case this method worked, and I could actually get a fire built.

I continued to work with the friction method to one side, but I also intently watched the sun method to see which one would produce smoke first. I also had larger dreams. Fire produces smoke. If I were successful in getting a fire started, perhaps I could encourage it large enough that it might attract some attention for any airborne traffic in the area. I had not seen any more search planes since that first day, but I felt I had to try every avenue. This gave me some additional hope.

I worked on friction and waited on the sun and the glass. I was tiring and about to give up and make sushi as my arms rebelled against making another shove on the two sticks I was spinning when I noticed a tiny little black spot on the tissue under the glass. I held my breath and stared at it unbelievingly, then jumped to my feet and rushed over to blow softly on it. I almost couldn't believe it when I fanned it gently with my breath and saw it erupt into a small flame.

Quickly, I put some dry twigs on the miniature flame, and breathed easier when some of them also caught fire. I moved the glass and carefully, oh so carefully, I added twigs, then larger sticks, and then still larger.

I was grateful for the beaver that had been working industriously on the island because he had left me a wonderful stockpile of wood and shavings, chips, twigs, even small logs I could use. Soon I had a bona fide campfire burning! I felt like dancing around it for joy and understood how native Indians may have felt when dancing round a campfire. I was euphoric.

I caught myself however, and abruptly reined myself in. *I mustn't get carried away,* I told myself, *I will need to keep this fire burning day and night now.* I knew it would require much vigilance to keep it alive and burning.

Once I was comfortable it would maintain a steady burn for a while, I used some of the sharp fish bones to scrape my perch and save parts I wouldn't be able to eat for future bait. How thankful I was that I had listened well to my father's fish stories and remembered the time the fish had been biting so well they used all their bait and had to cut up the smallest fish and use them for bait!

I next rinsed the edible parts of the fish in the lake, speared them on a long stick and slowly cooked them, rotating them to get all sides roasted. I held this over my fire. I felt very proud of my accomplishment when I sat back to eat the flaky, white fish.

In a little while I searched out more blueberries and had them for dessert, thinking as I did so, *it may not be the most balanced diet, but at least I won't starve.* After eating, I hesitated as I thought again about how dysentery would make me more ill, but I was extremely thirsty, so I drank more water and assured myself it was clean and pure. Next I gathered quite a bit more firewood in order to keep the fire going all night. I was also hopeful that someone might see the fire and come to investigate.

That night I lay down with the most positive attitude I had yet been able to produce. Things were still grim, yes, but they were getting better. I had survived thus far. The smoke from the fire swirled around me like filmy strips of gauze, which wonderfully deterred the pesky mosquitoes and provided some warmth to stave off the chill. My stomach was reasonably full. The sky was full of stars. I made myself avoid any thoughts of possible rain.

I wrapped myself in the warmth of the blanket and blessed the soft moss beneath me for the cushioning effect and looked up into infinity.

This entire experience had drawn me into a time of introspection. *I wonder if there is a God up there who cares about me? People say you exist, God. Blanche always goes to church and prays. Is she praying for me now? Are you there, God? Do you really care or am I just another piece of evolving amoeba like some skeptics say?* I continued with these soul-wrenching questions until I drifted into sleep.

Sometime during the night I jumped awake in a panic from a frightening and horrible nightmare. I jerked myself awake, mouth dry, heart overexcited. I was disoriented and tense. I forced myself to take a deep breath and calm myself. I noticed the fire had died down, so I added some wood to keep it burning. As I was working with the flames, I remembered the nightmare I'd just been having and why I had awakened with all my sensors on high alert.

In the dream, Joel had come back to the island to finish me off, but I had turned on him with a long stiletto knife and began chasing him with great relish through the tangled underbrush and dark woods. The limbs and branches scratched my face, but I ignored them as I pursued him. He seemed to be searching for a place to hide but could not conceal himself, so he continued to run frantically away from me. Suddenly his foot caught a loose vine and he tripped and fell to the ground in front of me.

In glee I saw Joel, silhouetted by the moon, lying at my mercy. I loomed menacingly over him with my arm raised and the long knife blade poised in my hand. I saw the knife start to plunge down. That was when I scared myself awake. It had seemed so vivid, so real. I was still shaking from the effects of it. As I remembered the dream, it almost seemed like a warning. I tried to analyze what my subconscious might be trying to tell me, if anything. Why hadn't I felt the thrill of gaining my revenge? Why hadn't I finished plunging the knife? Maybe it was Blanche's prayers warning me. Maybe it was God.

Maybe I was just overly sensitive because of all that had happened. I wasn't sure, but I kept probing with my mind. I reran the dream in my mind several times and finally decided I would worry about why I did not follow through with my revenge when I wasn't so busy trying to survive.

I did come to grips with the possibility that Joel could grow curious and return to be sure I was dead. What if he returned to get rid of my body? I had considered this earlier without a great deal of alarm, but I realized at that moment how my life was still very much in danger. Staying here where he could readily find me was not safe, and I needed to take steps to thwart this if possible.

I immediately thought about the fire acting as a beacon to light the way for anyone wishing to find me. Perhaps I should extinguish the flames that had been such a challenge to start up? But that would remove what little comfort I had been able to find for myself. It would bring mosquitoes and cold, damp air. My newfound hope and comfort dissipated, and I had another restless night.

The next morning I began searching the island more thoroughly for anything I might be able to use to help my situation. I hoped to find some old boards or wood that might have washed up in a storm along the shoreline. This was a wasted effort. I saw nothing of use at all. I did see an unusual pile of stones that had to have been made by humans. It was about four feet high and was mostly large, flat stones. It was composed of rectangle shapes about one by two feet, layered on top of each other.

I remembered hearing how the Ojibway and other northern Indians had often left these distinguishing icons behind in their travels. I seemed to recall the word *inuksuk*—perhaps from my father's descriptions. The stones were no help, but the knowledge that others had been here before was encouraging. That feeling did not last long as I continued searching fruitlessly for anything that might be useful to me.

Finally, in a discouraged frame of mind, I sat down and quietly watched my neighborhood beaver as he floated a piece of log out to his beaver lodge. I watched him for a while, depressed about my predicament. I had totally forgotten one of my initial plans to search for beaver cuttings to help me. The brown, svelte body of the beaver suddenly dived into the water and left the log floating at the surface.

Wait a minute. My mind soared, and then I became jubilant. *His logs float! Beaver logs would be better than small cuttings, but I could use the latter for fill-in pieces on a raft!* I almost shouted it aloud. I became excited at the thought of floating myself away from the island. My elation ebbed however when I began a more analytical perusal of the details I would need to work out. Could I just use one log for buoyancy and kick myself to that other shore? My mind churned. A log was not a boat, or a flat board, so part of me would be in the water if I just tried to hang on a log.

I remembered the dangers of hypothermia. The frozen lake water warms slowly in the spring in Canada, and fishermen watch the water temperature closely for optimum fishing. I had learned that the water was warmer at the surface, but much colder as it went deeper. Thus, this chilly lake water might be all right for a short dip with warm towels and clothing when coming out, but when considering a long swim, in my current very-weak condition, would I have the strength to kick from behind and hang on to a log? How would I warm up when I did come out of the water on the far shore?

In the end, I decided the lingering effects of the poison, the lack of food, the stamina I would need, and the uncertainty of the water temperature were all much higher risks than I should take at this time.

I finally decided that I would try that method if I couldn't devise anything else, but I decided I would only use it as a last resort. I'd easily won my Girl Scout swimming badge, and I had been on the swim team in college where I won awards, including first place, in several competitions for endurance swimming. Conversely, I had not done any long distance swimming for a few years, so I would definitely be rusty, and I knew this would be the test of my life, as I had guessed the distance to the closest shore to be several miles.

Even if I had wind and a strong current to help propel me, it would be an intimidating swim. Without a wet suit for protection, hypothermia could still be a problem because I did not know the water temperature. I couldn't go back to thwart Joel if I slipped off a log and died in the cold depths of the lake.

Some type of raft or floating platform would be best. I would be able to take my meager possessions like my blanket, fishing line, and fire-starting equipment with me if I could devise a raft. To make a raft or anything that would float, I would need several of Mr. Beaver's logs. That wasn't really much of a problem since he'd been very busy chopping down trees. They were scattered everywhere.

The problem was in how to find the strength to manipulate them, how to lash them together, and how to propel the logs safely across the lake. *One step at a time,* I told myself, *let's just find out if we can get several logs together first. Some of these logs are pretty large.* I proceeded to locate six nice logs, each about six to eight inches in diameter, which were not too huge for me to manage.

The beaver seemed to be gnawing down trees of all sizes but then only used the smaller upper branches and bark to create his lodge. I was thankful at this time for the beaver leftovers. With some effort, I was able to drag and roll them back to my site and place them close to the water's edge. The beaver had removed some, but not all, of the upper branches on the logs.

This proved to be helpful as I arranged the logs so that the remaining branches overlapped and, since they were more supple branches, I used them to twist around each other, braid fashion. This helped force the main logs to stick together. I was able to bend a few back then weave other branches with it. One branch ended up sticking straight up in the air, but I could still fit myself on the narrow conveyance I was calling a raft, so I left it there, thinking that branch might be helpful as a handhold.

The overlapping branches fortunately shortened the distances I would need to try to lash together. I was careful to think about the balance so it didn't get top-heavy and tip over, taking me with it. I took off my belt. It would only reach around two logs and part way around a third. I took off my shoe laces, but even tied together, they weren't much longer than the belt, and definitely not as strong.

I extended the belt with two more flexible tree branches, some vines I found, and the laces. The belt now made it all the way around three logs. My bandana came off my head to become reinforcement as I twisted it into a long rope shape and used it to reach around two logs. I was able to tie a sturdy knot at the end of the bandana.

It was a little while later when I noticed some wild rose bushes with their flat pink faces blooming. The branches were full of thorns, yet I could see they were flexible and the thorns acted almost like natural Velcro with their gripping action. I managed to stab myself a few times, but I used my clippers to cut and shape them and then I added these branches to help secure the logs. The thorns dug nicely into the logs and did not budge once attached. I just had to make note not to grab those areas or I would scratch myself.

I tried to make sure these went all the way around, top and bottom. This was time-consuming, but I continued to make steady progress and with a great deal of effort, I managed to get the tendrils securely tied all the way around the six logs. I looked at my crazy creation and worried about how well this would hold. I guessed my contraption was about a yard wide, and even though I had searched for the shortest lengths, it was still rather long at between fifteen to twenty feet to the tips.

I didn't want to think about what would happen if it started slipping apart. I was also trying to think how to stay as dry as possible. I found three more similar logs and, after shoving my craft as close to the water as possible, I laid those logs crosswise. Due to all the protrusions on the logs underneath, these last three logs stayed where I placed them and added the effect of outriggers where they hung over both sides. This made a decent platform.

I was concerned that I needed something more with which to tie the logs together since not much kept those last three very secure. The earth rotated and moved on to midday with a nice clear sky and sun directly overhead, but I hurried because I was anxious to get myself off the island. I was fearful of staying another night where I felt so vulnerable. I tried to speed up what I was doing as I found more clinging rose branches.

I ate a handful of blueberries now and then plus the rest of my leftover fish and tried to ignore my hunger pangs. In the west, the sky was beginning to darken up a bit and a breeze came up, which concerned me when I saw the water begin to ripple. I'd been blessed with good weather thus far. I didn't want to think of the problems I'd have if a storm came up. I thought again of the possibility that Joel might return and grew fearful. Nail clippers were not much of a defensive weapon, although I had been able to use them and the attached nail file in many ways during my desperate plight.

I worked feverishly and redoubled my efforts at making a craft that would hold together and get me across the lake. I thought about reinforcing my lashing work by cutting strips out of the blanket with my clippers, but the blanket was all I had for protection against cold nights and future rains. I was reluctant to cut it up. There must be another way.

It was then I remembered my ten plus yards of discarded fishing line. I stretched it out. It reached and twined around all the logs several times, which was encouraging, but as with the shoelaces, I was very worried about the strength of the monofilament line and its ability to hold the logs together. I now had both ends of my raft lashed, somewhat perilously, together. I looked down at myself. I scanned my clothing, shoes, jeans, and pockets, and I tried to think of anything else that would be useful as a strengthening agent.

I thought about removing my blue jeans and using their sturdy denim legs to help lash my precarious craft together, but I remembered from scouting that blue jeans can also be used to improvise a life jacket by tying the legs together and scooping them full of air. It seemed better to reserve the jeans in case the craft fell apart, and I needed the emergency life preserver.

I decided to take my chances with the lashing the way I now had it, with the exception of one final support. This I devised to go around the middle of my vessel. To make this support, I removed my sweatshirt and tore one thin strip off the end of my blanket leaving the main body of the blanket intact. I knotted one sweatshirt arm to one end of the strip, wrapped it around the middle of the raft and knotted the other end to the remaining arm. I remembered my scouting knots and tied it as securely as possible. I could see how this solidified the raft considerably and my spirits lifted.

After this, I felt a bit chilled with only my blouse for wind and weather protection, but I figured the sweatshirt would soon dry out on the other side of the lake, and I could still keep warm with the rest of the blanket if necessary. Of course I would be taking my fire-starting equipment. I planned ahead and hoped I could again start a small, sequestered fire once I was safely away from the island.

My next challenge was to come up with some type of paddle to help propel me and my log craft. I used a branch with a fork in it and tried to attach a piece of birch bark. Unfortunately, the bark was very fragile and kept breaking off. Pieces of it went flying off in the wind. It was then I noticed how the wind had picked up. I found a branch that had quite a bit of greenery at the end and decided it would provide some paddling assistance.

I had been so busy I had not noticed how much the weather had changed again. I looked up from my work, and it was then that I observed how much the wind had strengthened and was now whipping the water. I could see small peaks of water appear on the surface. My mind went spinning with fresh ideas along with possibilities and problems.

Perhaps, I thought, *I could use the wind to my advantage and not need a paddle that much. What if I used that upright branch on my raft, not as a handhold, but coupled with my blanket to make a sail? It just might work.* I decided it might be possible that I could even steer it a bit if I held the blanket in such a way that I could manipulate the wind. We Girl Scouts had often sailed a tiny craft during our summers in the Ozarks, so I was familiar with utilizing the wind.

But now, due to the changing weather, I had no more time for planning. I needed to make my final decision. *Well, Mattie girl, is it go or no?* It was time to face the future. I needed to make the commitment to get on this unpredictable-looking ark and depart the island. For some reason, at this critical time, I faltered. Insecurity overwhelmed me as I looked around.

I considered the dangers in staying and the dangers in going elsewhere to find safety. There had been some security here, some food, a fire for warmth. I even thought about how I could tip my raft on end and create a shelter with additional logs. I was leaving all this behind to head for a totally unknown shoreline with possibly worse hazards such as bears and wolves, or worse terrain. I could be creating a situation where I would have less chance of being found.

Unexpectedly, after all this work and focus on the goal I had just attained, I became mentally paralyzed. I could not seem to take the step to that final action of boarding my beaver-built conveyance. I knew very well I did not have much time to reach a decision, but my hands were shaking and my feet hesitated. In my heart I knew what the decision should be, but I found myself reluctant to take action.

The day had grown cooler and the light would soon fade away. I would have to spend another night here if I did not depart very soon. The wind came up stronger as if to warn me—prod me. I could see how the water was now spitting up occasional small whitecaps—a signal of more wind and stormy weather on the way. Soon the decision would be out of my hands if the water became too rough. In that case, I would not be able to take the risk, knowing the chances were higher than ever that the high wind could wreck my raft.

On the other hand, I worried that I might become more infirm from hunger or weak with illness. I deliberated hard and fought with myself, but finally I reminded myself of the people who loved me and would expect no less of me than trying to save myself. I also reminded myself of the vengeance I was going to perpetrate on the wicked Joel. I couldn't do that if I stayed here.

I took a deep breath, pulled out all my courage, and scolded myself for delaying things as I prepared to leave. I had to go, in spite of the risk; it was the only sensible choice open to me at this time, I reasoned. I pushed my fears down and forged on.

It seemed wise to eliminate all traces of my having been on this island. I figured that might help confuse Joel if he came looking for me.

I quickly did the best I could to erase any evidence of my presence. I put water on the fire using a piece of curved bark I had found, and dispersed the ashes and signs of fire. I dragged another beaver log over the remains to camouflage it and my mashed-down mossy bedding place.

I tried to make it look as unmolested by humans as possible. I put my belongings in my pocket, including the shards of glass from the champagne flute. Those pieces were now a precious life-saving tool, so I wrapped them up between several soft pieces of bark to protect me from cuts and to use for future tinder. I placed all that in my pocket with my nail clippers. The fishing line was all in use, the blanket also. Nothing was left to show I had been here.

Now it was time to leave. I would have liked to head back to the cabin and the possibility of using that radio to signal for help, so I planned to navigate in that direction if possible, but I also wanted to make shore as soon as I could because I would then be able to walk around the shoreline and eventually reach the cabin.

I knew I would not have much control in navigating the craft, but I felt getting to the lakeshore gave me a better chance than staying on the island. So, my goal was to get back to the cabin if possible, or to anywhere along the shore of the lake as a second choice. I would avoid other islands and try to head east to northeast where I thought I could find the cabin.

I tied two ends of the blanket to the upright tree branch in preparation of making a halfhearted sail, and then carefully slid my wobbly raft down the rocky incline and into the water. I quickly climbed on board with a final push before it had a chance to drift away into deep water and accidentally leave me behind. I held my stomach, my breath, and waited for disaster.

Miracle of miracles, the logs floated and didn't flip over! The lines and ties all held. I was able to sit upright and perched myself on the dry platform out of the water. I could not believe my good fortune as my contraption stayed afloat. I looked it over carefully and noticed how it held together and how it looked as if it would continue to do so.

I was overcome with joy that my clumsy handiwork was performing as I'd hoped. I grabbed the loose ends of the blanket in my hands and turned it to catch the wind. The blanket billowed beautifully, but now I paid more attention to the weather. Unnoticed by me in all my final cleaning of the evidence that showed my presence on the island, the wind had picked up with more strength and the sky had darkened on the orange horizon in front of the late afternoon sun. The strong breeze almost tugged the blanket from my hands. I had to hold on tightly, but slowly, slowly, my little makeshift raft moved out into the forboding lake and took me with it.

Chapter 11

As I edged my little craft into the water and began my progress, my perspective of the lake quickly changed. I could see cumulonimbus clouds building ominously in the western distance. Those could become a major concern if they continued on the path they were now taking.

The lake that had been so fun in the sun with a safe boat, comfortable life vests, and a companion fishing with me, now looked frightening in its enormity and isolation. It was chillingly beautiful, but I knew it could be deadly if I made even the smallest mistake. These waters were far from tropical. I knew the dangers of hypothermia in my weakened condition.

My makeshift sailboard made faltering progress. It was a cumbersome craft, but it originally kept moving in what I hoped was the right direction, which pleased me greatly. I looked back, and the island was already quite some distance away—a difficult swim should I need to try it. I was terrified that my raft was going to break apart, leaving me no choice but to attempt the swim. I held on to the blanket fiercely and forced it to allow the wind into its woolen expanse. The craft lurched awkwardly through the ever-growing waves like a milk-heavy cow heading for the barn.

"Oh, please—oh please, stay together!" I beseeched the logs as if they could hear me. "Help me reach the other side in one piece!"

I had very little control over the direction the logs were taking except in the angle by which I held the blanket. The wind was coming from slightly left as I faced the late afternoon sun—southwest, I figured.

By my calculation, I was being blown to a northeast shoreline, not far from the waterfall and north of the cabin as I remembered my bits of geography from our flight in. It would be important to keep my bearings if I were to survive this ordeal.

A dark shadow moved across the water like some primeval pterodactyl shrouding things below in darkness. It first reached long, gloomy tentacles across the end of the logs, then my legs, and then moved on to completely envelop me. The shadow brought with it a chill that caused goose bumps to rise on my arms. A threatening storm cloud encroached upon my craft by moving across the sky, where it obliterated the sun.

The accompanying wind was stronger now, and I could see whitecaps dancing all over the lake. The shoreline was coming closer, perhaps a mile away, as my raft made its clumsy way across the long expanse of water, but the storm behind me was gaining speed and momentum. I could no longer see the island behind me.

I looked back to see in terror that it had disappeared in a gray mist of descending rain. The rain showered down behind me like a curtain of cold gray metallic drops. I could see how that curtain was moving across the water; how it reached out to envelop my world, and how it was heading on a path that would soon intersect with me!

I could do nothing now but hang on, keep the blanket full with my frozen, cramped fingers, and hope I arrived on shore where I could find some shelter before the rains reached me and I became more drenched than I now was from the overspray. I watched in great anxiety as the storm continued to grow in intensity. I could see it—feel it—become more ominous with each passing moment.

The clouds now flickered occasionally with scratches of lightning that added to my fears. I looked down at all that was keeping me safe thus far—six logs, a belt, shoelaces, a piece of blanket and fishing line, and I felt something akin to panic and a deep fear like nothing I had ever experienced.

Is it strong enough? I wondered. *Can it endure the onslaught of a storm—if that storm catches me, which looks likely—before I reach shore?* The questions poured through my mind, like the rain I could see approaching from across the lake. *Am I going to make it through this alive?* I was trapped, an unwilling observer of my own fate, a captive participant in a life-or-death race between time and a storm.

A gust of cold wind grabbed my attention as it nearly ripped the blanket from my fingers. The front edge of the storm had reached me and my tipsy raft. The storm whipped the waves into clutching, curling fingers that seemed to reach for me. I gripped the blanket so tightly my fingers ached. I shifted position and held the blanket with only my left hand so I could cling to the upright branch with my other.

I had to clutch it tighter than ever in order to keep myself balanced to prevent falling off in the now pitching and rolling lake. There was no rain reaching me yet, but the wind managed to spray me with misty water as it agitated the lake. I was drenched, and I shivered from the frigid water that pelted me. I was powerless at this point to do anything other than hang on and hope to reach the shore before worse disaster struck me.

Visibility disappeared down to a small circle around me. The weather closed tightly around me now, and I knew the storm hovered over my position, on the brink of unleashing itself. I was now being thrashed as the logs hung precariously over the top of each wave, then slid dangerously down the trough to the next. The surging and swelling waves of water were becoming increasingly hazardous; yet, I had no choice but to ride it out.

I looked around me. It was as if I were inside a gigantic milkshake blender. I was tossed about at the whim of an unseen hand operating the speed of that dangerous device. I knew my life literally hung on a thread—the thread being that thin little piece of fishing line that I had so casually tossed aside, how many days ago? The difference between life and death—my life—was down to a strand of filament and whether it would snap under the strain.

I didn't think my situation could get any worse, but then I heard it: the low, rolling reverberation of thunder. The sound began softly enough; I almost didn't hear it at first, but it grew and swelled like the great crescendo of a Beethoven symphony into a colossal mushrooming roar. Electricity was in the air now, too, and the danger of lightning impressed itself immediately upon my shivering, quaking body.

A great crackling flash of light came shrieking out of the heavens and lit up my world like a momentary camera flash coming simultaneously from hundreds—no thousands—of invisible photographers. It was followed within seconds by the awful sound of crashing, shelf-rattling thunder that echoed and echoed off the water like a cannon booming.

Three seconds between flash and sound. I mentally calculated the lightning's distance away from me. I used the rough estimate of so many seconds per mile between when the flash is seen and when the sound follows. My heart felt stricken with terror. It was far too close—less than a mile away. *I didn't come all this distance and go through all this to die from a lightning strike, did I?*

The storm had no answer, but the bright flash did give me a small bit of encouragement. I could see that land was much closer. I felt the smallest expectant hope begin coursing through my blood. There seemed to be a possibility that I might yet make it to shore on my dangerous flume ride. I was very close!

Just then, as if to beat the glimmer of optimism out of my weary and exhausted body, the rain pelted down in earnest. It was a cold, cold rain, almost sleet, and it felt like continuous little sweat bee stings as it struck my face, neck, and exposed arms. My hair became sodden; every part of me was soaked through, and I shivered with cold. I knew I would not be able to hang on much longer.

My hands were becoming too numb to feel the blanket and the tree branch. Soon, I knew, if I didn't reach land, I would lose my grip and fall overboard. With the advent of rain came ever more ferocious wind as if to force me to give up. It hit me and my pitching, awkward lifeboat with angry gusts, pushing us at breakneck speed across the remaining section of lake.

I no longer held the blanket as a sail, but simply held on to it and the branch to keep from going overboard. I tried to huddle under the blanket, but that effort was almost useless. *We're almost there.* I thought in jubilation and gave animation to the raft in the joint "we." I prayed, not really knowing how and to whom I was sending my petition, but somehow it strengthened my efforts to hang on.

The next bolt of lightning turned my joy and anticipation of nearing land to appalling terror. At the apex of a wave, I saw before me the rock-strewn shoreline and great boulders waiting, like behemoth junkyard wrecking machines, to shred me and my craft to pieces as the waves crashed magnificently against them.

Just at the moment when I could see what lay ahead, my log boat rose into the air and crested on a huge wave that had been swollen into a rampaging tide by the fierce wind gusts. I could do nothing but scream in unison with the storm as I slid with my craft into a black, blank void.

Chapter 12

My senses came back to me very slowly. I drifted in and out of awareness in which I felt my surroundings for a few moments, but then surrendered again to unconsciousness. I felt cold and miserable, and my mind shifted in and out of reality. I wanted to pretend I would come to my senses and arise from my warm bed at home. I knew I should make myself wake up, but it was difficult to do so in my lethargic state.

Finally, I was able to make myself come fully aware. It was an uncomfortable position—awareness. My body felt bruised, in pain, chilled, and shock-ridden, but I was still whole and in one piece as best I could tell. I carefully wriggled my fingers. They still worked but were raw and scraped and scratched. Next, I cautiously moved my toes, then my feet, which like my hands, felt battered but in working order.

I worked my way up to my legs, and arms—testing and turning to find casualties. Everything seemed to be able to work, if a bit sluggishly, and not without pain and effort. Finally, I turned my head and tried to look around me in order to assess my situation. I could hear more than I could see in the darkness of night. Streaks of lightning finally gave me some glimpses in order to view my surroundings.

I was lying on an enormous flat rock, my log raft was broken, but most of its parts were balanced precariously beside me on the rock. I had been cast ashore by the storm like a Raggedy Ann doll. But thanks to whoever had heard my plea, I was still alive.

The bangs and bruises I had incurred caused feelings now—pains that were sharp, hurtful, jabbing; but I was able to shove aside the aches and feel gratitude that I was still present in this world, still breathing, and could feel no broken bones. I felt a splashing at my feet and was immediately reminded that I was still in imminent danger. The waves were ominously encroaching on the rock that held me. I could feel the nearness of the waves, like some liquid monsters who clawed at my legs and reached out with watery arms to pull me back into the murky depths.

While the swells spilled around me, the water pulled at me with each ebbing wave. I felt it sucking me back down into the depths. It wanted me. The storm continued to spew lightning, thunder, and rain against the rock where I had landed. It struck me that I could not have been unconscious long, though my head ached as if a blacksmith were inside pounding away with his anvil and sledge. I shivered from the cold and knew I must make myself move away from that vulnerable and dangerous spot to try and get warmer. I needed to find shelter of some kind, if that was possible.

It took great effort to move at all since I was feeling extremely weak, but I managed to force myself to sit up. I struggled and fought to stay conscious, which was difficult, because when I sat up, waves of nausea and dizziness threatened to overpower me. I refused to succumb to the enticing lure that called to me and said, *Put your head back down. Let go and fall asleep again. Slip easily down into the water—it will all be over then.*

You are not safe yet, a different, but firm, small internal voice warned me and wouldn't let me go.

I tried to disregard the first voice and listen only to the second, but it was a struggle. I looked lovingly at my homemade raft. I shook my head in awe that it had held till the end. Some pieces were, amazingly, still intact. *It got me here in one piece*, I told myself, *but now I must dismantle it and salvage what I can.* I needed the parts. I needed the logs. I needed the woolen blanket. It would warm me in spite of being wet—the only such natural fabric that would keep heat retention properties when wet. This was another valuable memory from my scouting instructions.

I began to dismember my raft with what little strength I had left. While working with the raft, I dreamed how I would go find my old summer camp leaders if I could ever get out of this unbelievably horrible adventure and give them all an enormous hug for the instructions and loving care. So far, they had kept me alive.

I moved slowly and with painstaking effort. I ached in every joint and muscle I possessed; my body fiercely rebelled at what had happened to it in this last week. I had to force each muscle to move. I began tackling the job of getting myself to safety. First, I pulled my sweatshirt, fishing line, belt, shoelaces, bandana, and everything usable off the logs. Then I tied the sweatshirt around my hips and put the other items in pockets. Next, saying a silent thank-you to the beaver who had provided them, I rolled the logs one at a time, away from the water's edge so they would be usable to me and not get washed away.

Once I had them positioned where I could retrieve them, I waited for the intermittent lightning bolts to brighten my way, then groped and felt my way deeper into the woods while I searched for shelter. Thankfully, it was not a long search. A potential refuge turned up nearby. With the help of a flash of lightning, a possible safe haven presented itself in the form of a semi-cave. I scrambled on hands and knees up a small hillside and stumbled onto what might be sufficient.

I found two large boulders about chest-high. They resembled the padded shoulders of a couple of burly football players, abutting one another. They formed a natural sheltered corner backing into the hill that would support my logs if I could manage to get at least one end of each of them up and across the top. This would create a V-shape with two sides of the rocky V coming toward me and a slanting top—if I could find the strength to get it together

I breathed with difficulty, and my body quivered from the abuse it had endured, but I dragged three of the logs into the woods one at a time. My body rebelled at this continued torture, and my muscles cried out to me, "Give up! Give up!" My endurance was nearly gone.

The inner voice stayed firm. *Go on. Stay strong, Mattie*, the voice cried to me. I refused to give in. I would not let Joel defeat me in this. I wanted to see my father again. I wanted to live. I pulled and strained and dragged my logs to the rock enclosure. One at a time I rolled, pulled, and pushed them over to the boulders. Finally, I had them in place at the base of the two mammoth rocks.

Then I was faced with another challenge. I needed to position one end of each the logs up and on top of the rocks. I wasn't sure I was still strong enough to lift them that far. Finally, by lifting one end of a smaller log and propping it part way up the rock, I was able to take one of my larger logs and in a process of lifting and shoving, I was able to slide it up using the first log as a ramp.

At that point, it teetered dangerously and threatened to fall back down on me. I took a great gulp of air and shoved with all my might. Exerting my muscles to their maximum, I slid it up, up, and across the boulders until it rested on top of them.

The second log was lighter in weight, so I was able to slide it up the rock face and across the same opening with less exertion. I shoved a third log up to join the first two and now had created a low shelter of sorts. The logs were now a base for a slanted roof. It was by no means waterproof, but, it was a beginning. At this point, I wanted to do nothing more than collapse, but I knew that would be dangerous in my almost hypothermic condition.

I forced myself to search the ground around me during intermittent lightning strikes. I looked for material I could use to increase my protection. Shivering from cold and wet, everywhere I pulled evergreen branches and boughs down and broke or twisted them off. I found twigs and smaller limbs and with the boughs, placed them across and over my new roof. Young seedlings were easiest to obtain and pulled relatively quickly out of the wet ground.

I put them, roots and all on my roof. I also scattered boughs and leaves and any moss I could find inside the shelter. It wasn't very dry, but at least I wouldn't get much wetter and my lean-to should protect me from the frigid winds that were still snarling around me.

Exhausted, aching, and miserable, I wrung out my sweatshirt and pulled it back over my head again. I was cold, so cold, and I shivered constantly. I also wrung out the woolen blanket as best I could. Next, I climbed inside my makeshift shelter, wrapped my damp woolen blanket as securely as possible around me, and collapsed in my quavering misery. I thought I would be too uncomfortable to get any rest, but it wasn't long before the woolen blanket did its magic and began warming me against the elements. My body dictated what happened next. I lost all sense of time or place and slept.

Chapter 13

My brain felt groggy, but it insisted that I needed to wake up. A noise penetrated my mind: *Someone is trying to start a tractor.* I listened in a fog and thought I definitely heard someone who tried to start a tractor. Over and over again, I heard it. *Cuh—whump, cuh—whump, whump.* But whoever owned it must have been pretty frustrated because it just wouldn't start. *Cuh—whump, cuh—whump*, again and again, the annoying noise protruded into my sleep. The sound would speed up, and I would think the engine would finally catch, but then it would stop and start all over again.

I rolled over to cover my ears with my pillow and shut out the sound, but stabbed myself on a sharp pine needle instead of a downy soft pillow. I rolled over again and instead of a ceiling I could see patches of green and brown and smaller patches of bright blue sky. My disorientation slowly faded as my memory returned. *I'm lying here*, I remembered, *stranded in Canada; but I'm still alive.* The storm had safely passed during the night and the sun was high in the sky and now warmed the earth. Steam was issuing up from my bower. Things were warming and drying out—including me.

The sounds of the tractor again intruded on my discussion with myself. It was an irritating sound and interrupted my thoughts. *How am I going to get myself rescued when I can't think for all that racket?* I mused to myself, still half asleep. My mind finally caught up with my subconscious, and I scrambled frantically to my feet, then uttered an "ouch!" when I bumped my head in the process of standing. I had banged into the low log roof of my little nest.

"Ow!" I exclaimed again, and gingerly rubbed the sore spot on my head as I hobbled out into the wooded glade that surrounded me. *Tractors are man-made machines,* I happily told myself, *which means a human is trying to start it. That also means a human is nearby who might be able to help me.* I was ecstatically happy for a few moments and listened for the sound so I could make my way to the tractor. My happiness became slightly subdued when I was met with silence.

All was again quiet around me, the only sounds were those of a light breeze moving the tree limbs in a gentle swishing way. Where was the tractor? Was there a tractor? Did I imagine it? I needed to hear it again, just once more. *Please, oh please, whoever you are—please try to start your tractor just one more time.* I thought I knew the approximate direction from which the sound had come, but I wasn't certain. I needed to hear it one more time to be sure.

I found an old, overturned tree and sat down on it, then quietly and expectantly waited. More silence. I sat like that for about fifteen minutes in the warmth of the sun. I did not move and held my breath in anticipation for long moments at a time. I listened intently. Suddenly the air vibrated with the *cuh—whump, cuh—whump* again. It wasn't quite in the direction from which I had first thought, but sound carries oddly outdoors sometimes, so perhaps I was mistaken.

I bounced joyfully off my impromptu seat and began to crash my way excitedly through the undergrowth toward the sound. I came to the general area where I thought for sure it must have been, but there was nothing. There was that silence again—and no road, no path, no tractor tracks, no tractor—only silence.

Am I going mad in this wilderness? I wondered if I was beginning to hallucinate, but then I reassured myself. *No, I am positive I heard that sound. It was someone starting a tractor, and it came from right over here somewhere.* I decided to wait again, and if I heard it just one more time, I would approach more cautiously this time. I would go quietly, stealthily, and catch them. I would find this person. *Perhaps,* I wondered, *it is someone from a logging company.* I had heard they did a lot of logging in Canada. It could be someone out checking their forests.

Once again, I found a place to sit on a fallen log and wait. I found it difficult to be patient when I was so near to my rescuer. I wanted for this ordeal to be over at last. I wanted to ride out of here on a tractor—any old clunker of a tractor, I didn't care. *Just get me out of here. Please don't leave, just try to start it one more time. I'm sure it'll start this time.* I had to wait more unendurable minutes. I sat through more lengthy silences.

I was just about to break down and cry in discouragement, when I heard that familiar sound again, *cuh—whump, cuh—whump, cuh—whump, whump, whump.* I heard it over and over with no sign of the battery winding down. I wondered why the battery hadn't failed by now. I was certainly hoping it was okay and had enough strength to get the tractor started so they could carry me out of here.

I was even ready to just ride on the hood if it meant safety and home, so I slipped quietly off my perch and began very stealthily making my way toward the tractor. I was careful not to step on any twigs or anything which could break under my foot and make a noise.

Slowly, slowly, I stepped, pointing my toes before I allowed them to land on the ground, just like Indian scouts did. Carefully I went, stepping closer and closer as the sound became louder and louder. This time I knew I was gaining on my freedom, and I trembled with excitement. I knew I was almost on top of the sound but incredibly, I still couldn't see the tractor or the man operating it. Finally, I held my breath one last time. I pulled apart two bushes and looked into a small clearing. I was as startled as the drumming grouse I saw beating his wings on the tree stump: *cuh—whump, cuh—whump, whump, whump.*

I watched a moment, frozen by surprise. I then stepped into the clearing to be sure there were no tractors, incredulous as the frightened grouse quickly flew away. I stood and looked at the empty clearing that had held all my built-up hopes and anticipation of my rescue, and I dissolved into a pathetic pile of disappointment. I plopped to the ground in misery.

I had cried before throughout this ordeal, but this time I knew such hopelessness that the tears easily passed up the cumulative total of tears for my entire life. This fresh sadness produced such a new flood that I sobbed out tears of anger, rage, sorrow, disappointment, and most of all frustration.

Finally, I stopped sobbing. I raised my head. I had to face my situation and breaking down was not going to help me. I sat up. I pulled myself together and after a few more moments, I was even able to see the humor in it.

"You didn't even latch on to the best looking meal you've seen for days, Mattie; you just let that stupid bird run off," I scolded myself aloud, half laughing and half mortified at the mistake. My lashes were still wet from my sobs when I rubbed my eyes with my fists.

The grouse had disappeared, but now that I was wise to his drumming sound, I felt that I might be able to trap or catch him or one of his friends somehow. Thus, in spite of the disappointment, I would at least be able to feed myself. I began thinking about that as I sat on the stump the grouse had been using for a drum in his mating ritual and wondered how I could accomplish catching him. As I sat there I realized that, in my anxiety to find the "tractor," I had wandered far from my overnight homemade log shanty, which held all my meager belongings.

Panic welled up as I turned around and around. I looked at the surrounding forest. It looked exactly the same in every direction and I began worrying and wondering whether I would be able to retrace my steps and find my things. It wouldn't do me any good to catch a grouse if I couldn't start a fire to cook it. My scant supplies, including my fire-starting glass and woolen blanket were still back in my very rustic lean-to. I also needed to get back near the lake again where I felt the water was safe to drink.

Don't get ridiculous and panic now, I warned myself. *You've already been impetuous one too many times this morning. Now you are sitting here stranded again*. I thought for a few moments and contemplated my position. I tried to get my bearings—to use my brain.

I knew I had headed away from the sun and the original island when I rode across the lake. The wind had been coming from my right and behind me, which meant I had been blown northeast. My lean-to was near the lake, and as I thought back, I remembered that I had walked mostly east that morning, always going toward the sun in my search for the "tractor."

So, I calculated, all I had to do is walk back toward the west and away from the early sun. I would then hit the lake and could scout north and south till I found my belongings. I had no compass, but I felt I could use the sun and maintain my bearings. I remembered that the sun in summer travels a more northerly route in its east-to-west path every day, so I tried to consider that in retracing my steps. I figured that in the mornings, as now, I should aim a little bit to the right of the sun to find due east and afternoons due west would be a little bit to the left when facing the setting sun.

As I was in an analytical mood by now, I spent some time trying to think what it was about this clearing where I scared off the grouse that struck me as something I should have noticed. I knew there was something puzzling me, something that did not seem quite right, but I could not dredge it up.

As I studied my surroundings I heard the grouse again, suddenly drumming his wings in the distance. I was chagrined as I listened and remembered my folly in believing it to be a tractor. Then as I looked down the long clearing toward the sound he was making, the answer to my puzzle popped into place and lifted my spirits considerably. This was not a natural long clearing. It was obvious as I studied it more thoroughly. I should have noticed it right away but I had been too engrossed in the grouse.

There was a sort of path, unused now, obviously, but there was a path that was well-defined by low undergrowth and an absence of trees. It was an overgrown, unused trail that had most definitely been made by man. I knew now what had bothered me. The tree stump on which I was sitting, though weather worn, had been smoothly cut off, not broken and jagged like a tree that falls naturally or has been struck by lightning. This tree stump had been cut by a saw.

The path was barely visible unless you knew what you were looking for. I rejoiced and grinned, my spirits revived. *This could be an old logging trail or a path to an old gold mine, but whatever it is, it was made by men with saws and tools to clear a trail—and I am sitting on it!*

Upon closer observation of the trees and the cleared area, my deductions became stronger. The trail appeared to be one also used by animals, who often take the path of least resistance, so that too, had helped to delineate the trail or path for me.

I could see a smaller trail and animal tracks running down the left side as I faced the cleared trail. *In a few more years, this will not show up as well because this undergrowth continues to take over.* I reached the conclusion that it had to be a logging trail because of the many stumps left behind on both sides and the obvious width in the middle that had been completely cleared, I assumed, to accommodate a wagon or a vehicle that would carry the logs.

The trail could not go much farther in the direction from which I calculated I had started, or it would end southeast of here at the lake. Thus, following this trail in the opposite direction, I surmised, should lead me back to some type of civilization eventually, or at the very least other logging trails that might have more current utilization.

A plan began to crystallize in my mind that would help me to get back to safety. I would return for my supplies near the lake, and then I would come back to this spot and begin to follow the trail, which appeared to go in a northeasterly direction.

I felt most safe in heading east because I was certain the cabin had been on the far eastern edge of the lake. I vaguely remembered seeing something from the airplane that was way in the distance north of the waterfall; something that might have been a cabin. It would have been approximately northeast of the waterfall. A line leading to it might be heading northeast, the same as this old trail.

I assumed no one would still be searching for me, at least not in the area where I now found myself. *It's up to me to get myself out of here. I have to use all my wits and stay alert.* I decided to follow the trail as the most likely method to get to safety. I knew I could stay close to the lakeshore and follow it around and eventually end up on the eastern edge of the lake close to the cabin. On the other hand, this trail was already evidence of a path to civilization and would be much easier to follow.

I picked myself up, hoped my mental calculations were valid, and began searching for a way to retrace my path back to my overnight shelter. I tried to head due south as I walked, and somewhat surprising myself, I managed to be very fortunate in backtracking quickly to my overnight haven. I began at once to prepare to leave it permanently behind.

As I planned my exit, I came up with two major concerns: food and water. Lakes seemed plentiful in this territory, so I decided to take my chances and hope that I would intercept water as I followed the trail. I tried to think of some way to carry water, but nothing came to mind at all. Food was another matter. Hunger was already crying out to me via my aching stomach. Even the leaves were beginning to look like lettuce.

I thought of several options. I could try for more fish and take the time to build a fire, then cook my catch, or I could hope to find enough wild berries or perhaps I could chance on a method of snaring an animal later in the day to help me survive as I took to the old logging trail.

Common sense told me to stay put, catch some fish, and try to regain my strength before I tackled a long trek through the woods, but my heart wanted to go *now*! I thought about the time I would lose waiting a few hours while I rigged up another pole and tried to find bait, then I thought about the time that would be spent while hoping to catch fish versus having those hours already under my belt and being well on my way.

A war developed between the urges of my stomach to get food and the urges of my heart to get to safety. I went with my heart. I took my fishing hook and line with me, also my broken bits of glass and some dry tinder in case it rained again. I tucked what I had securely in my blanket which I tied up and slung across my shoulder like a backpack. I had already relaced my shoes with those lifesaving shoelaces so I could tread through the terrain with the least risk of tripping or having a bad fall. I began walking and was able to regain the trail without too much difficulty since I had tried to leave broken limbs and marks on the way out.

I did not try to fool myself into believing this would be a certain success. I was in an extremely weakened condition and even though I felt chilly, I knew my brow was hot and feverish. I needed to find help soon. I should not be feeling this cold and achy on such a warm and sunny day. I looked at the sun. It had been steadily moving westward in the sky as I had been deciding what course of action to take. I kept walking.

It wasn't long before I realized the tennis shoes I had recently applauded were woefully inadequate for hiking in Canada. How I longed for a pair of rugged hiking boots to wear. I found a long tree limb, which I used as a walking stick to help me as I plodded along. There were frequent obstructions across the path, which I had to go around or clamber over.

These impediments caused me consternation but I reminded myself to be thankful I had found a path on which to walk. I had a goal in mind and positive steps to take. This was one more grievance I could chalk up against Joel, and I again used my burning anger toward him to push myself harder and harder.

By midafternoon I found some blueberries and practically gorged myself sick on them. They were moist and juicy and helped assuage my thirst. Yet another flashback lesson learned that fruit contains a high percentage of water. So far I had avoided any mushrooms because I did not trust my knowledge well enough to discern the poisonous variety from those that were safe to ingest.

I vaguely remembered reading that the roots of cattail plants often growing at the shallow edge of a lake were edible. There were no cattails along this trail, but I knew I would scour the next lake and look to see if these tubers were something I could pull up and eat. Wild rice would have been wonderful but it was far too early in the year for it to be usable or ripened.

That was about the extent of my knowledge regarding safe foods in the wild. The pause to eat also gave me a chance to rest my aching feet and abused muscles. I had settled in for about half an hour's rest when I thought I heard an unusual sound. It was an unfamiliar soft *wuff, wuff,* and it was nearby—much too close. I thought I caught a waft of an unusual scent in the air. It was an unpleasant odor—almost rancid—something worse than that of a wet furry dog that had been rolling in some unknown substance.

I was not certain about the odors associated with wild bears, but I definitely worried it was such a critter—one that also wanted these same blueberries. I decided not to take any chances on a large animal encounter, so I quickly made a lot of noise, jumped to my feet, and headed away from the blueberry patch and back up the trail. As I returned to my steady gait, I began to shake and shiver from the chill that was worsening. My limbs felt lethargic, but I made myself continue.

I knew, with a deep foreboding, that I was now becoming ill. Whether it was from impure water, all the abuse that had happened, or a residual effect of whatever poison Joel had mixed in my champagne, I did not know. I did know my situation was deteriorating. I forced myself to ignore the sick feeling and forged ahead. I could not give up now.

I walked a considerable distance and felt more ill with each step, but I would not give up. At one point on the trail I discovered a moose antler and found myself giggling almost hysterically as I thought about how I would have valued the flattened face as a paddle for my raft when I was escaping the island.

As I listened to my wrought-up laughter echo back at me when it bounced off the trees and rocks, I realized I was becoming more weak and ill than ever—dangerously so. I hoped I was not beginning to hallucinate or become disoriented. I tried to keep my head alert and thought, *I must stay in control of myself. I must get to safety. I must keep my mind focused and clear.*

I controlled myself as best I could once I realized that exertion from hiking and the fever consuming me were combining to make me giddy. Thus, a pattern was established. I knew I was in bad shape, yet I continually compelled myself to continue along the trail. Over and over—again and again, I said to myself until it almost became a chant, *I must survive. I must endure. I must go on.* Go on I did.

By late afternoon I was famished, achingly exhausted, and dreaming of downy-soft feather mattresses. The soft moss I had found on my original island would have been a welcome and wonderful sight to my weary eyes as I wondered if I was ever going to have a comfortable night's sleep again in my life. The trail continued to lead in a steady northeasterly direction, and I felt as if there were a slight incline rising away from the water.

I faithfully kept plodding along and looked for a place where I could camp. I scoured for a spot where I could feel at least partially protected from the weather and cold night air. The air had already turned nippy this late in the day. I kept urging myself on. I chanted to myself, go *just a little further, just a little further* when suddenly ahead of me there was a bend in the trail. I went around the bend, and I came out upon a small plateau overlooking a different lake.

Amazingly, I saw, also on the plateau, sitting back in a clearing with a beautiful view of the lake, what appeared to be an abandoned logging shack. It seemed to be intact and actually had four walls and a roof. I remember being coherent enough to think how amusing it was. *Here I am, a pampered wealthy man's daughter, thankful—no, no, ecstatic—at the sight of an old beat-up, roughly constructed, bunch of barely standing wood. Eureka! Shelter!* I staggered up, with a whoop, in spite of blistered feet, to peek inside. The door gave way easily as I turned the knob. It wobbled a bit on the hinges but opened to reveal a small one-room shack.

There was a shuttered window that opened onto the lake side. Further exploration showed an old, dilapidated, wood-burning stove inside. A metal bucket held some chunks of wood and one dry log. There were a few rusted and chipped dishes and utensils, a wooden cabinet under a small counter, a badly abused box spring but no mattress and no other furniture.

I was euphoric! Especially so, when I opened the cabinet and found an old flint and a can of matches along with a knife, a hammer and some odd bits and pieces of hardware. My exhaustion was still unbelievably overpowering. I wanted nothing more at that moment than to simply collapse on that box spring bed. But my mental outlook improved immeasurably after reaching the cabin, and my commitment to survive and endure continued to prod me.

I forced myself to go back outside to explore the surrounding area for useful objects. Outside, leaning against the cabin, was a decaying old woodpile. I found more chunks of dry wood and with shivering fingers, took some of it inside where I managed to start a fire in the stove. I dragged myself back outside for more and stockpiled extra wood on the floor and in the nearby bucket to keep it going. *I need to find myself something to eat,* I planned ahead. *Perhaps I can catch a fish and cook it.*

But first, now that I had the fire warming the shack, I succumbed to my need for a short rest. My weakness was making me dizzy. *I'll just rest for a tiny little while,* I promised myself, so I made myself as comfortable as possible on the old box spring and laid myself down to rest for what I intended to be just a few minutes. I wrapped up in my now dry woolen blanket and enjoyed the warmth of the stove and blanket on my chilled body. It felt like heaven, this simple thing—a warm bed in which to rest. I luxuriated in the warmth.

I had pushed my body to its limits, and at this point it finally gave out. I slept, deeply, as if drugged. I was inert and unaware of my surroundings. The little rest turned into a much longer time span. I felt myself slip in and out of consciousness, but I was powerless to make myself wake up. I knew by now that I was ill and infected with a dangerous sickness, one that needed a doctor's attention. I tried to open my eyes to see where I was but even that effort was more than I could accomplish. I dreamed more dreams about vengeance and payback for Joel.

I did manage to waken once and at that time I could tell it was nighttime. No light came through the cracks in the shuttered windows, and I could hear animals, wolves I guessed, howling somewhere nearby.

The heat in the room had died down and I felt as if I were frozen in place. My body shivered and quaked and made the whole bed vibrate.

Somehow I remembered the stove and woke myself enough to realize it needed tending. Agonizingly, I forced myself to roll off the box springs and literally crawl to the stove to put more wood inside. Only a few embers were still burning, but fortunately they were enough to spark to life when I dropped some more wood on the coals. The new fuel helped everything blaze to life and the black cast-iron stove door creaked as I shut it. I tried to stand and barely made it to an upright position.

Somehow I staggered across the floor and crawled back into my makeshift bed. I pulled the blanket back over and around me and fell back into and out of consciousness as my body fought to survive against this unseen assailant that was ravaging it. I became insensible to the environment around me and oblivious to time.

Burning with fever, I shivered and shook spasmodically and huddled in my blanket, trying to secure warmth to a skin that felt as if I was submerged in ice. Whenever I did manage to open my eyes, the room shifted and moved around my head like a mirage moves over a hot desert pavement. Everything was wavering and distorted and appeared unreal.

More time passed and my illness grew worse. I began to hallucinate and I could not tell night from day or how much time had passed. I knew I was very sick and delirious. I was not sure what was real or my imagination. At one time I thought I heard voices talking about me. Another time I dreamed I was being lifted and carried very gently. Next I dreamed I was being tenderly rocked.

I thought I heard the sound of water softly lapping against something and I wondered if Joel was coming back for me. I heard the sound of seagulls careening and screaming overhead, and then I dreamed I was being carried again. For a while I had the most pleasant dream of all. In that scene I was once again at home in my own soft, clean bed. It felt wonderful, so good. I slept with that positive thought for a long, long time.

Chapter 14

Sunlight came in through a clear glass window near my head. Dust motes floated in the sunbeams like little bits of shimmering fire ash. I dreamily watched them drift down. I felt comfortable and cozy. Then I remembered something: the logger's cabin didn't have a glass window. That window had been shuttered with wood. I weakly raised my head, looked around and found myself in a soft, quilt-covered bed in a small, simply furnished, white walled room.

There was a table next to the bed. On the table was a book—a Bible—also a kerosene lamp that appeared to be in working condition. My perusal of the room was interrupted by a small thud near the door that drew my attention. I looked toward the sound and encountered a tiny, round, fawn-brown face surrounded by silky strands of sable black hair.

The little face was peering at me intently. The dark eyes looked enormous in the petite face as they stared fiercely into mine. I guessed her to be about six or seven years old. She came nearer to my bed and picked up a small book from the floor, which explained the thud.

"Well, hello" I attempted, my voice cracking and weak from disuse. Fawn face took one mute glance at me as if I were Cinderella or a princess, then scampered quickly to the door and disappeared.

Soon I heard other feet approaching. There was a light knock, then a woman I guessed to be in her late forties, dressed in a simple black dress and white apron walked into the room. Her eyes were kind and held the color of forget-me-not flowers in the spring. Her dark auburn hair was pulled back into a severe bun. But her face was not severe at all. In direct opposition to her stark attire and hairdo, she had a pleasant and friendly attitude and was smiling warmly at me.

"So, our little bird was correct, you are awake." She came near me then, and felt my brow with the back of her hand as a nurse might do. It felt soothing, and she nodded her head in satisfaction as she went on to tell me, "The fever has broken. I'll return with some broth. You must be ravenous." Without waiting for a reply from me, she patted my hand, smiled again, and was gone as quickly as she had come.

In a short time the woman returned bearing a tray upon which was a bowl of broth, a half slice of what appeared to be homemade bread, and a small glass of milk. "We don't want to overdo it right at first," she told me as I wolfed the food down. "We'll see how this does, and then you may have more."

In between bites I managed to ask, "Where am I? How did I get here?"

"You are in a Mission School. A party of hunters found you in one of their hunting and trapping cabins and brought you here," she said as she smiled.

She turned at my questioning glance, and seeing the little elfin-faced girl peering around her skirts at me, smilingly introduced us. "Oh, yes." She nodded at the child. "This is Red Bird Owen. Her mother helps with our school, and Red Bird attends kindergarten here in the mornings. Afternoons she helps me while her mother works. If you need anything just let Red Bird know, and she will fetch me immediately. And by the way, my name is Beatrice Hayford. You may call me Bea—everyone does."

So, I was in a school of some sort. I wanted to ask many more questions such as how I got here—and where, exactly was "here"? And, I wondered, *Am I truly safe?* But Bea put me off when I tried to weakly whisper more questions. She told me, "I've given you the basics of your arrival, but since you have been so very ill, you need to rest, and not fret yourself by asking questions right now. Do you have someone we should try to notify that you are safely here with us?" she asked, her bright eyes looked questioningly into mine.

"N-no, no one just yet," I stammered, "I need to get better first, but—" I switched the subject, "I have a lot of questions to ask *you*." I put her off and thought about how I was going to handle questions Bea and others here would have about me.

Bea's face held questions, but she withheld them. "I will tell you all you want to know once you are more recovered, is that all right?" Bea gently removed the food tray and plumped my pillows. She was correct. I rested. Sleep came almost immediately. I ate again later that day and slept again.

The next morning I felt better but weak. Bea provided a more substantial breakfast and told me she was introducing things gradually to my poor body. She assisted me to the shower and restroom. After cleaning up and changing to a clean gown she had provided, I returned to find Bea waiting. She began to tell me more about the Mission School and the Ojibway children and the families they served. She explained more about my rescue and how two of the men from the Mission had managed to save my life when they found me unconscious in the cabin.

"I want to thank them," I told Bea.

"They will like that," she said with a smile, "but they had to go back to their hunting for a few days. You will have an opportunity when they return. Their anglicized names are Samuel and David. They may tell you their Salteaux names when you meet them." She insisted I take yet another "rest, to get your strength back." Surprising myself, I let her lead me to bed, and I was again able to sleep.

I thought I was dreaming. My father was holding me on his lap. I was very small, and he was gently stroking my hair. I felt it again … a featherlight tugging at my hair. I opened my eyes and peered directly into the intent face of Little Red Bird. She was standing on tiptoe, leaning over the bed, and stroking my blonde hair, gazing at it in rapture. I could tell she was mesmerized by the hair for some reason. When she realized I saw what she was doing, she bashfully backed away and bent her little head down and pulled her arm quickly back to her side in embarrassment.

"Do you like my hair?" I asked, amused.

"It is very pretty," she said, still not meeting my eyes.

"How would you like to help me brush it?"

She looked up immediately, her eyes shining, and nodded. I sat up on the edge of the bed, surprised at my returning strength—even my gentle attitude with her—when I was so torn emotionally on the inside. Part of me wanted to scream out, "Someone tried to murder me," and another part wanted the satisfaction of a wicked revenge, yet another part of me wanted to burrow here, wherever *here* was, and hide in safety, nurse my wounds, and think it all out.

She intrigued me, this cute Little Red Bird, and she was an innocent, so I pushed away morbid thoughts, smiled, and motioned her to climb up beside me. She clambered up on the bed with agility and stared at my golden tresses as if they were really made of that most precious of metals. We both realized at the same moment that I had no hairbrush. Without a word, she slid down on the far side of the bed, went to a drawer, and pulled out a hairbrush. She was soon on the bed and made herself busy gently brushing my hair.

"What are you learning in school?" I asked her, and hoped for more than a bashful nod.

"ABC's, one two three's, and Jesus."

"Well, I know something about all of them," I said. "Let's see how well you know your one two threes. Can you count the strokes as you brush my hair?"

"One, two, free," she mispronounced the numeral charmingly and went on, "uh … four, five, uh …"

"Six?" I prompted.

"Oh yeah … six."

"Do you know the poem that can help you count?"

"What 'pome'?" she struggled to pronounce.

"It goes like this. 'One, two, buckle your shoe. Three, four, shut the door.' Can you repeat that much?"

And so it went with us for quite some time. She soon forgot about brushing my hair and simply sat on the side of the bed and talked with me about her school. I learned that Red Bird's teacher was "Miss Meeks but she had to go home for a while, so we don' have no teacher right now."

"Oh? Why did she have to go home?"

"Somebody got sick and she had to go take care of 'em. While she's gone you could be our teacher!" Her face lit up at her own suggestion.

I knew by now this was a mission outreach for native peoples, and her idea tugged at my heart, but I was not sure I would be here that long, so I did not pursue the thought but continued to help her with her numbers. I could see she had struggled with numbers, but she really liked the numbers poem, and we made it into a game to help her remember. We were thus engrossed when Bea walked in the door with a tray for a midafternoon snack.

"Nine, ten, a big fat hen!" Red Bird laughed in glee, and I enjoyed that good laugh with her.

Bea stood in the door for a moment with an indulgent smile and waited for us to recognize her presence. Red Bird saw her first and hopped down somewhat guiltily and asked me as she did so, "Uh oh. I forgot to ask. Were you ready for a snack?"

"Your mother is looking for you, little one," Bea continued that indulgent smile and spoke to the child softly.

"Okay, bye!" Red Bird said and started for the door. Suddenly she stopped and turned back to me. "Can we do some more numbers tomorrow?" I smiled and nodded.

The precious child responded with "Yea! Bye!" and was gone.

Bea studied me in a friendly way. "I'm glad to see you're feeling better. You seem to have a way with children. We've been trying to do some special tutoring with Red Bird to help her catch up, but she won't sit still long enough for us to help her. You covered more ground with her than we've been able to do in a month. Thank you!"

"Oh, it was easy, actually. It had nothing to do with me. She's just infatuated with my blonde hair," I said offhandedly, but I was flattered, nonetheless.

"Still, you turned that interest around and made her want to learn something. That's a wonderful talent and few have it."

If you only knew what a mess I have made of my life, you would not give me such an accolade, I thought to myself, but still she left me with the warm feeling of having accomplished something good. She turned toward me and said, "Mattie, are you absolutely sure there is no one we need to try to contact on your behalf?"

I had been dreading this question and practicing my answer. Now it slipped off my tongue so glibly I almost believed it myself.

"Actually, Bea, I have no one that we could reach. Most of my family died when I was young. I have an aunt who travels and is constantly changing her address who would be very difficult to reach right now. I am pretty much on my own. We might try reaching out later if that's okay with you. For now, I would like very much if I could stay here and recuperate." Most of what I said was true, and Bea seemed satisfied with my answer but asked one more question.

"What were you doing way out here all by yourself?" she asked me.

"I was hoping to write a story about survival in the wilderness, and I felt that I should be able to write most realistically if I actually tried to travel through Canada on my own. I did not anticipate my canoe hitting a rock when I tried to navigate some rapids. I lost everything overboard and ended up with only a few things and my own wits to help me stay alive."

"Are you an author then?" she asked.

"No, I was taking a sabbatical for a year to find out if I *could* be an author. All my notes and work were swept away too." I tried to look downcast, and added, "I am really not ready to talk about all of it yet."

"Of course, you poor dear," Bea patted my hand. "Of course you will stay here as long as you need. Maybe you might find another calling. God works in mysterious ways sometimes." She smiled.

I was not ready to talk about a God who had allowed all this to happen to me, so I did not respond except to say, "Oh thank you, Bea."

After that I made fast progress in recuperating. I learned from Bea that I was on Saulteaux (Ojibway) land given to them through treaties with the Canadian government. I discovered that Bea and several others of her denomination, lived there as missionaries. They provided schooling, training for jobs, and they tried to be of Christian service to the Indians. I also discovered how I had been rescued.

Two of their mission-attending Ojibway men, the Samuel and David that Bea had told me about, had been out hunting for meat for the mission. It grew late and they decided that rather than returning to the mission, they would spend the night in the logger's cabin. Instead, they discovered me, feverish and delirious. They did not wait for morning but risked their own lives to carry and canoe me to the missionaries where Bea had taken over my care.

Bea told me the mission was not accessible by road. Supplies had to be brought in by floatplane or portaged and carried by water travel in summer. In the winter the snowmobile, or sometimes even dog sled, brought provisions by skipping from lake to lake with no roads between.

We were very isolated and far, far from my former life. Rather than causing me concern, this gave me great relief and a feeling of security. There was a generator for electricity, but since fuel had to be transported to the camp for the generator, electricity was used sparingly. There were no phones, no grocery stores, and no post offices within any close distances.

Bill Ross, another worker at the mission, operated a shortwave radio that could call for help in emergencies and that was used to order materials and things that were needed. Supplies were ordered in quantities as they must be made to last a long time. This was done to keep the expense of the floatplane deliveries to a minimum.

Most supplies or large deliveries, Bea told me, were usually brought in during winters when transportation was easier, and somewhat less expensive, by using the Big Cat machines over the ice when lakes and rivers became roads. She also told me the larger Norseman floatplanes could transport huge quantities of freight when necessary, and they could convert from water pontoons to skis in order to land in winter.

Bea informed me how they tried to stay as self-sufficient as possible simply because that was how the native Ojibway had to exist as well. They wanted to introduce technologies and assistance that the natives themselves could use, but they also wanted to work with the tribal elders in order to maintain their self-reliance as much as possible. Their Ojibway leaders were fearful of becoming too dependent on the outside world. The missionaries were careful to abide by their wishes.

Three days later, when I had begun to feel more comfortable with Bea, we took a tour of the grounds. I met David Keesik, one of the men who had rescued me. I learned that his children Sara, nine, and Kapech, eight, attended the mission school. I thanked David profusely, but he was shy and modest and said only, "Welcome. Welcome." Bea told me his wife, Mary, was out doing some planting for the family.

Many of the women, I learned, did farming for their families while the men historically took care of hunting and trapping. Bea told me this was an Indian "reserve." Thus the Canadian government also provided funds for them and protected both their land and hunting, fishing, and farming rights. The mission was here by permission of the elders of the band and was supported both by volunteer donations from the Ojibway but also from founding churches back in the United States and larger cities in Canada.

Bea took me to the home of two more students, eleven-year-old Bearhair and thirteen-year-old Wecaanimaash. Their father, Samuel Fisher, was my other hero. His attitude was even more shy and self-effacing than that of David when I thanked him for "lugging me all the way to safety here and saving my life." I was to discover a charming humility in these "First Nations" people that won my affection.

Bea continued my tour by introducing me to Bill Ross, a Canadian from Winnipeg who now lived here with his wife, Mary Rose, and their three children, Elizabeth, a bright eight-year-old, Robert, an inquisitive seven-year-old, and William Ross Jr., showing maturity and leadership already at twelve years of age.

Bill asked me if I needed him to contact anyone with his radio, but I gave him the same answer as I had given Bea. "Oh, thank you for the offer. I may take you up on it very soon. For now there is no one I can contact, and I want to recover my health before I try to leave or contact anyone."

Mary Rose Ross was a veritable cyclone. Her petite stature was very misleading because she could have led Napoleon's troops to success with her energy and drive. It was easy to see her husband and three children adored her, and when I saw the schoolchildren cluster around her as well, I knew she was an excellent teacher. Bea suggested to Mary Rose that I might be a good one to consider as a substitute in the school.

"Oh, I have already heard about her success with our Little Red Bird, so I totally concur!" Mary Rose reached out and hugged me. "Thank you so much for helping that child. Will you be here long?"

"She was very easy to help." I smiled and avoided the last question. I met many more of the people in the community, and I managed to answer questions about my unusual arrival at the mission with vague answers or I simply changed the subject with my own curiosity about this fascinating place. I found my appearance had caused quite a stir. As we walked I could see the homes and structures that made up the mission village.

I noted quite a variety of architecture in how homes were constructed. Some were very roughly built of logs and chinked with mud, moss, and even small stones to fill the gaps in the construction. Others had a more modern appearance with flat planks and boards that had been made smooth. These boards overlapped to provide fewer places for air to enter the home and to create protection from rain and storms. All had metal or brick chimneys coming up through the roof.

The land was relatively cleared up to a point and sloped down to a lovely lake where a pier jutted out into the water. Several canoes were upturned along the shore, and a few were tied to the pier and bobbed gently with the waves.

Not all homes were in the main clearing, because in the distance I could see smoke rising behind the trees from several protruding chimneys. The magnificent Canadian spruce, hemlock, pine, and other trees provided a striking backdrop with their dark green branches reaching like spears into the sky. There were homes tucked into the hillside, and there were paths leading down into the main gathering area where the school sat. It was a picturesque setting and to the southernmost side I could see a larger cleared area that appeared to be used for gardening or crops. There were several women working with implements I did not recognize.

As we walked, Bea discreetly told me more about Little Red Bird. I learned that Red Bird's father, John Crow, had only recently converted to Christianity, that before then he had been an alcoholic and sometimes an abusive spouse and parent. In the past, he had disappeared into the bush with Red Bird and her mother for long periods of time.

This, Bea explained, was the reason for Red Bird's need to catch up on her education. "She's quick to learn, but she still has trouble concentrating for very long. It's as if she expects her father to suddenly yank her away and go off into the woods again." Bea frowned. "And he might do just that. Becoming a convert can be difficult at times, and Christians are far from perfect, especially when old familiar temptations strike new, vulnerable hearts. This is not an Ojibway problem," she informed me, "but exists in every culture when people convert."

"What happens then—if he falls back into his old ways?" I asked, thinking of certain sects who shun the disobedient. "Do you kick him out permanently?" I was thinking that's what I'd like to do if he hurt precious Little Red Bird in any way.

"Oh no," she said quickly. "When Jesus was asked almost the same question by Peter who asked, 'Lord, how often shall my brother sin against me, and I forgive him? As many as seven times?" Jesus said to him, "I do not say to you seven times, but seventy times seven. "So you see, Mattie, Christians still sin even after they convert," she continued and looked at me steadily. "We are not perfect, though we try hard not to sin. The difference in our lives is that we are *forgiven*."

"Well, that explains why I've always thought so many religious people were hypocrites," I challenged. "They can go out and sin away all week, then go into a confessional on Saturday or get down on their knees anytime, and consider themselves forgiven. That doesn't sound like you're teaching people much responsibility."

Bea surprised me by agreeing with what I said. "It isn't teaching responsibility at all, presented the way you described it." She shook her head sadly, "That is one of the concepts that is sometimes difficult to convey properly to new Christians. Jesus said to the woman caught in adultery, 'Go and sin no more;' yet, He knew she would not be able to live a perfect life. The answer is in the attitude.

"The people you are describing as hypocrites, Mattie, have the flippant attitude of, 'Oh God will forgive me for this, so I can go ahead and do it.' Converts, on the other hand, who have truly repented for the past and asked God to forgive them, will not exhibit that attitude; rather, they will want to *please* God in reverence, respect, and thankfulness for His great sacrifice in forgiveness. In pleasing Him, their attitude will be one of living as good and perfect a life as they can, knowing they will make mistakes, but trying desperately to avoid them. Do you see the difference?" She looked at me keenly.

"I think so," I said slowly. I knew I had much to learn in the religion category. "But just in case, I'll be watching Red Bird's father should he need a little nudge to stay dry."

Bea laughed. "I think Red Bird has acquired a champion," she went on but shifted to a different vein while her wise eyes looked deeply into mine. "Mattie, I truly think you have a special gift in dealing with children. I've been watching you with them."

"At one time I thought I wanted to be a teacher," I responded, caught off guard, "but I changed my major to computer science and business about halfway through my degree." I added the idea as it rolled out of my mind onto my tongue. "But, it would not take much to switch that major to teaching. I could add a few classes—and," I mused softly, swayed by the attractive thought. I abruptly stopped and caught myself from this distracting direction my mind was taking as I saw Bea watch my reactions shrewdly—intently.

Careful! I scolded myself with a warning frown. I had decided to remain less forthcoming about my past and my identity to my benefactors for the time being. I didn't intend to be deceptive with them; it just happened to work out that way, and I had not corrected them when they made erroneous assumptions. I salved my guilt by thinking about how there were several reasons I felt this camouflage was justified.

First, I didn't want Joel to find me—my life was in jeopardy after all—and secondly, I needed some time to myself, now that I was safe, to sort out my life. This was an unprecedented opportunity to get to know the real me, Mattie, in a way I had never done before. I could look at myself through different eyes. To figure out what had gone so drastically wrong—and why. I also knew I had another agenda that I kept buried very deep inside, and that agenda was to plan my revenge on Joel.

After that conversation, I had to constantly remind myself, *Mattie, be careful about giving away too much information.* I had told Bea my name was Mattie Hunt. I hoped they would not have seen any news about a missing heiress named Mary Lynn Huntington, and thus put two and two together. Most likely my nickname, Mattie, had not made it into the papers, and I knew they seldom received newspapers up here in the bush.

I had concocted a story about being without any family except my Aunt Blanche (I *was* temporarily estranged wasn't I?) and how I had decided to try to live on my own in the bush in Canada for a while. They didn't need to know I had had someone with me or for how long I had planned to stay in Canada did they? I told them I had lost everything when my canoe hit a rock, overturned, and was swept away in some rapids. I *had* lost everything, hadn't I? It wasn't exactly a lie, was it? Sometimes I would find Bea looking at me speculatively but she never questioned the veracity of my story. She didn't now.

The next day Red Bird arrived with seven-year-old Kapech Keesik in tow.

"This is Kapech," she informed me.

"Yes, I met him the other day. It was his father David who helped save my life." I smiled at Kapech, whose eyes were downcast shyly.

"He wants to learn the numbers pome." Red Bird brought him closer. I was outside hanging some laundry for Bea on a clothesline strung between two trees. The sun was warm and bright that day and the last remnants of early morning fog had lifted from the lake. The air was redolent of fragrant trees.

"Can you count to ten?" I asked Kapech. He fired off the numbers quickly, but still did not make eye contact with me. I had noticed that all the Ojibway spoke English, even the elders, although they were not quite as fluent as the younger. All also spoke their native tongue and were encouraged to be bilingual by both the elders and all the teachers at the mission school.

I quickly scrutinized the items left in my laundry basket. "We are going to play a game since we are outside," I announced. "We can teach Kapech the number poem another time. Is that all right with you?" I looked at Red Bird.

"A game?" her eyes lit up.

"Yes. Would you both like to play?"

Both heads looked at each other and nodded affirmatively.

"All right here is how it works. I am going to hang up the laundry. You have to count how many pieces I hang. While I am hanging number one, you have to run around that tree over there." I pointed to a tree across the clearing "Then you have to find one pebble that you bring back to me. When I hang the next one you have to do the same only you need to bring me—how many pebbles?"

"Two!" they both shouted.

"That's right! We will put your pebbles in a row right under the things I am hanging on the line. Are you ready?"

"Yes! Yes!"

"Get set. Go!"

They scrambled off, laughing and shrieking to rush back with their pebbles. I smiled and returned to the hanging.

"That was very clever of you." Bea's voice came up behind me.

"Oh, I didn't see you there." I turned to see Bea approaching.

"That's because you were so engrossed in the little ones. I love what you did to make learning fun. I'm telling you Mattie, you really have a knack for teaching."

"Oh, I'm not sure about that, but thank you anyway." I smiled at her.

"We're short one teacher at the school," she encouraged. "Perhaps you wouldn't mind giving us a temporary hand until we find a replacement for Mrs. Meeks. She had to return to the States to care for both of her parents who were critically injured in an automobile accident. Mr. Meeks, had to go with her, of course, so we are definitely short-handed and could use the help. Mary Rose is already making plans hoping you will say yes. I hope so also."

I looked at her thoughtfully and considered the offer, but I didn't respond to the teacher shortage issue. I knew she was giving me an opening, but I wasn't sure I could help or even if I *wanted* to help. Bea went on, "Mattie this would give you a wonderful opportunity to determine if you really would enjoy a career working with children—and it would be a great help to us at the same time. We've been praying God would send us another teacher. So you're an answer to prayer."

"Not quite the answer you were expecting, I'd say." I laughed, half convinced, half hesitant. *God cannot be behind all this*, I mentally scoffed.

"God always answers prayers, and His ways are greater than our ways." She smiled pleasantly, allowing me no argument. "Can we begin using your help tomorrow?"

I thought about it for a few more moments, the analyst in me evaluating the pro and con sides of it all. Finally, I nodded, "I think I'd like that," I answered meditatively. I was growing very fond of Bea and the others at the missionary outpost. Although I did not share the belief, I couldn't help but admire their devotion to "The Lord's Work," as they called it. They really *lived* what they believed and it showed. In spite of my own disbelief, I admired their dedication and honesty and how they were helping these amazing people

The decision to help Bea with the school helped me make another decision. I simply could not put off notifying my father in some way that I was all right. I agonized over the thought of how anguished he, and dear Blanche, must be feeling at my disappearance.

I wanted to stay here a while and sort out my life, and I wanted to stay where I felt protected and safe from Joel. How to let my father know without revealing more than I wanted to the rest of the world? I certainly did not want the Canadian Mounties or the police to swarm in to me, although I might use their help later. I tossed out several ideas and discarded several.

An hour later, I found Bill Ross working alone on a broken chair from the school. I approached him and said, "Bill, you offered to send out a message for me to notify my family—which is my Aunt Blanche—that I am okay. She won't necessarily be too worried because we talked about the long times in the wilderness when I would be out of touch, but I would like to send a joke to her and my uncle that they will enjoy and it will let them know I am safe and well.

'Would that be something you could do through the radio? Could we send a message that someone would write down and mail or deliver to her? Also, I would prefer she not know where I am or where the note originated because, knowing her, she *will* decide to worry."

"That kind of thing—sending messages—is done all the time, Mattie. Sure, I'll be glad to help. Just write down what you want to send, and I can use the radio by voice or Morse code to contact someone who will help us. We may have to relay it through several operators—it all depends on weather conditions and distance. That will generally prevent my call letters from being broadcast at the end if it is relayed. You probably have a shortwave radio operator right in your own hometown and didn't know it," he smiled.

I wrote my short message "NIS-NOC-SI is alive and well. More later." I gave him Blanche's name and my father's address and hoped the message would get there and relieve both their minds. Then I went back to find Bea and determine my responsibilities with the children.

"You'll work with Mary Rose for a few days," Bea informed me, "then we'll give you some individual groups to tutor in math and reading. Mary Rose will help you understand what needs to be accomplished. I'm sure you will be a great success with the children."

The next day, I attended Mary Rose's class as her assistant. Mary Rose and her husband, my radio operator Bill, had been living among the Ojibway for about ten years. They had three children of their own who also attended the school and whom I had already met.

Mary Rose Ross was a petite little whirlwind. She had upswept dark brown hair and hazel eyes that could command unbelievable efforts from her pupils. She always wore a voluminous apron over her clothing, the pockets of which were known to produce the most enticing treats for the children.

"John," she would say in her charming, but no-nonsense, schoolmarm voice, "What country has over 50 percent of the world's fresh water supply on its surface?" John knew instantly that his treat was in jeopardy if he didn't reply "Canada!"

Mary Rose's husband, Bill, tried his best to keep up with his wife's energetic pace, but he was often left in the dust. Bill was the maintenance man. He was stocky in build, extremely jovial, and had what appeared to be a perpetual smile for everyone. He usually wore an old baseball cap on his thinning brown head of hair and would doff his cap when he saw me, his hazel eyes twinkling and creased at the corners. "Mornin', Miss Mattie!" he'd say, as if it was a tongue twister and he enjoyed rolling it off his tongue in his slight southern drawl.

Right behind him I would usually spy John Loon, who would imitate nearly every move Bill Ross made. Off would come the cap, but his head revealed a thick, lush crop of shiny black hair. "Mornin', Miss Mattie!" He would nod and traipse off behind his hero. John Loon normally wore fading jeans and a red plaid flannel shirt as he accompanied Bill on maintenance duties.

John and his wife, Sopena were childless at this point but both were a favorite with the children of the mission who could often be found doing small errands for either of them. The young couple told me they wanted to preserve their Ojibway culture and traditions, thus had chosen to stay on the reserve rather than move away to a big city as others had done. I admired their integrity and dedication.

The children here were dearly loved and treasured, so I wasn't sure about being a success with them as Bea had predicted, but I received quite a bit of attention the first day. The little girls all wanted to touch my hair—even the Ross children. The boys were more reticent but were fascinated too, I could tell.

It wasn't long before I managed to memorize their colorful names. I even learned some of the Ojibway or Anishinabe language in the process. "Aaniin" was pronounced "ah-neen" and meant a friendly "Hi" or "Hello." I put this to use as Red Bird proudly introduced me to the other children. Her proprietary attitude about our acquaintanceship amused me a great deal.

The ages of the children ranged from five or six to about fourteen. Children older than this who wanted more education were, I learned, usually sent away to government run boarding schools. This caused a sad splitting up of families that the Ojibway Indians disliked. But in most cases they had little choice in that decision. Since this was summer, our local school was only in session for a half day.

"We have to adjust our school day and school term for the Ojibway way of life," Mary Rose explained. "They still do much hunting, trapping, and harvesting of wild rice. These are major sources of income, and they expect their children to be involved to help. Our absenteeism is therefore often high, so we always offer summer school to offset what was missed during the regular school year." So, this was not the normal school year program, but was a time for catching up.

Diamond Bait

I soon became acquainted with three boys: Moosenee Keeper, an eleven-year-old, Bearhair Fisher, also eleven, and his brother James Fisher, also called Wecaanimaash, who was thirteen—one of our oldest pupils. Then there were others. I met Alice Pascal, who was ten, Sara Keesik, nine, and her brother who had played the laundry game, Kapech Keesik. Kapech was the same age as Red Bird—seven. Judas Crow, nine, came next, then Elijah Pascal, twelve, who was the brother of Alice. Lastly, were Mary Rose's three children: Elizabeth, eight; Robert, seven; and William Ross Jr., twelve.

Red Bird insisted I know everyone and with an important strut took me around the room several times while my head spun from trying to remember all the names, especially those who used their Anishinabe names as did Wecaanimaash. The children were quick to point out that Ojibway were named thus because it meant "puckered." They proudly pointed to the way their moccasins were puckered in their construction.

I continued around the room acknowledging each child and repeating their names. We ended in a corner where there were three older boys. In this last group I was introduced to John Land, twelve; James MacDonald, twelve; and Angus Mackay, thirteen; who, along with Wecaanimaash were the oldest children in the classroom. Their names struck me as an unusual mix for a tribe of Ojibway Indians, but many of the natives, I was later to discover, had adopted names from the Scots who had originally been introduced to this part of Canada in the employ of the historic Hudson Bay Company. Others used anglicized names and still others, like Wecaanimaash, preferred their Saulteaux names.

At first, I thought the children were extremely shy, and in some cases this was true, but one of many things I learned from Mary Rose was how in their culture one does not routinely make eye contact, thus my interpretation of downcast eyes as shyness was in error, when, in fact, they were being perfectly normal. Once I recognized this, we got along famously. They loved to giggle and laugh at my antics as I tried to explain things in my American Yankee jargon.

I learned many things about their amazing culture and loved to see the mothers with their babies strapped securely in their *Tihkinaakans*, which was the word for a baby board—a device created to keep their babies secure. I came to think of it as an ingenious mobile cradle. The base of the construction was a flat board. A bent arch came around the baby and cloth straps and swaddling held the baby to the board with lots of padding all around.

At first glance, it looked to be a cruel device, but the babies were extremely content when strapped in. Indeed, it was very cleverly designed as I learned when I observed in horror as one that had been leaned against a tree, toppled over—baby and all—and the arch across the front protected the baby from any injury in the fall.

The natives baked bannock, a type of bread, in a skillet over an open fire. Sometimes they used their stoves, which they often overheated. When this overheating occurred, they cleverly and simply cooled them off by opening a door or window in their home. More of their homes were constructed of logs than those of the smoothed and planed boards.

Their furnishings were few and simple, and I discovered that many of them preferred sleeping on the floor, where they rolled any bedding out of the way in the morning. They seemed to think our way of leaving a bed out in the way all day was a waste of space.

The children often offered me bannock, which was a staple in their diet, and though I always politely ate it, I never developed a taste for it. I was much happier with their offerings of colored stones and pebbles, which I saved and displayed in a small glass jar Mary Rose offered me.

As time slipped on, my days became pleasant and fulfilled. Bea insisted that I continue to stay in her spare bedroom, and she refused to accept my promise of sending her payment for food and lodging once I returned to the States. "Filling in as our substitute teacher is all the pay I want," she repeated any time I mentioned repayment.

Bea's house was a sturdy and well-built log home with a mammoth stone fireplace between the living room and kitchen. The fireplace had access from both rooms with the expansive kitchen also serving as a dining room for large gatherings. A heating stove supplemented the fireplace for keeping the cabin warm in the winter and on chilly or overcast days the rest of the year.

The young Ojibway couple, John and Sopena Loon assisted Bea with maintenance and housekeeping. Bill Ross and John Loon also worked together on major projects around the settlement. They were also fortunate in obtaining volunteer help when needed. I found an interesting mix of generosity and frugality among the Ojibway. I came to admire them greatly.

My day typically started with the smell of breakfast coming from Bea's kitchen. We used large quantities of powdered milk and had hot oatmeal or fluffy pancakes topped with maple syrup that was made each spring by all the families in the community. After breakfast I headed to the building used as a school during the week and for church on Sundays and special days. The building was small and had only two rooms.

I entered the school and noted again the low ceilings. Mary Rose had told me it was one of the older buildings, and the Ojibway had built it themselves and engineered it to fit their smaller stature. They also planned to save on construction materials and lastly, to save on the need for heat. I appreciated their ingenuity, but with my height, warned myself not to try jumping rope inside.

I prepared for the day's work at a card-table-sized desk in the front of the smaller of the two rooms. It was sometimes a challenge to stay ahead of several of the brighter children, yet encourage the slower students at the same time. I loved the children, and I loved the feeling of being useful to them. I sensed they cared for me too. I was making a contribution to their lives and they appreciated it.

The smallest things could make them smile. I thought of the children at home with rooms and rooms of expensive toys who didn't value all of them taken together as much as these little ones valued the single, small, paper airplane I taught them to make. And I wondered if our modern age couldn't learn something from their "old, but simple" ways.

The parents were wonderful too—so supportive. They wanted their children to know and appreciate the old ways, yet take advantage of new ways too. Bea told me that sometimes the young people who went away to school turned their back on their community. The Canadian government, through the Indian Affairs Department, provided schools in the large cities where they taught the youngsters a trade or skill, after which the young person often found a job in that city where he or she remained to live. Many of these Ojibway students seldom, or sometimes never, returned to their families and friends in the bush. Something, Bea shared, that often broke the hearts of doting parents.

Bea also said everyone at the mission tried to instill pride in the children about their heritage so this wouldn't happen with their students. The Ojibway were a wonderful people, and I yearned to learn more about their culture. Yes, my health had improved. In fact I was fine, and my days were having a positive effect on me.

However, nights were a different story. I would lie in my bed remembering and living over again the injustice that had been done to me. How wicked Joel had been—the evil I had not seen in him I could see clearly now. I couldn't forget the terror I had felt, alone, and deserted on that island. I would *not* forget that I was cast off and left to die from a vile poison. I had been abandoned. Each time I remembered those experiences, the memory scratched my soul anew. I ached all over and felt a renewed rage which left a searing scar on my heart.

I vowed a horrible revenge on Joel. I could not let it go. I thought about the message I had sent through Bill and hoped my father now realized I was alive and would reach out to him again. I wanted Joel to pay and pay and pay. I refused to open the Bible that lay on the table next to me. I already knew what was in it. Hadn't I heard it directly from Bea's mouth—"forgive seventy times seven"?

Well, I wasn't ready to forgive *one*, let alone seven or seventy times seven. This was one time, I felt, in which forgiveness was not necessary. So, the Bible remained unopened, though I knew Bea longed to share it with me. I remained guarded. I remained angry. I would have my vengeance. I just needed time to formulate how I would make it happen and maintain my own safety in the process. Yes, I would have my revenge.

Bea had told me her husband, Martin, worked for the Canadian government doing topology studies, mineral exploration, and some making of maps covering the wilderness areas. He was often gone months at a time employed in this work.

One day, not long after agreeing to help with the tutoring, I was in one of the two school rooms working with Red Bird on her numbers. I was beginning to get suspicious that her failure to learn was simply a ploy to spend time alone with me, as she innocently supplied me with correct answers time and again, only to look baffled when asked to answer for a test.

I looked up in some alarm when a shadow darkened the doorway, but Red Bird, instead of being frightened, jumped up and squealed, "Martin! Uncle Martin!" She ran to the front door and was scooped up in a bear hug by the tallest, gangliest man I'd seen in a long time. With a frame resembling that of Abe Lincoln, even down to the hooked nose and black hair, he was loose-limbed and awkward looking, this "Uncle Martin."

But his awkwardness was only a surface appearance as he moved smoothly into the room and deposited Red Bird back into her school room seat, then turned to me and said, "How do you do? I'm Martin Hayford, Bea's husband. You must be the new school teacher she prayed for."

"Well, not exactly." I smiled as I looked up at this six-foot-three height where his head nearly brushed the ceiling. "I'm just a temporary replacement. My name is Mattie." He peered at me as if assessing my abilities and said, "Mattie is it now? Well, Mattie my girl, maybe you can help me. I'm looking for my wife."

"Oh, well, Mr. Hayford, if you're looking for Bea, she's over at Judas Crow's cabin. Mrs. Crow is expecting a baby, and she's having some problems. Bea went over to see if she could help."

"She is, is she? Well, that's just what I would expect of Bea. She's a saint, she is, don't know how she puts up with an old codger like me."

Without giving me time to comment on this observation, he asked, "So, how do you like it here? I suppose you like it since you're still here. Are you staying?"

Without waiting for my answer he continued, "By the way, please call me Martin, not Mr. Hayford—sounds too stuffy. Now, how did you get here? I imagine you're from the Mission Board aren't you? How long have you been here? Not long from the looks of you. Got you hooked yet? They do, you know." His grin was as nonstop as his words. "You come up, just planning to stay a little while, then you stay a little longer, first thing you know, you've been here twenty years, working in the bush!

"They grow on you, these Ojibway. Ontario grows on you too. You go back home and all you can think about is the moss and the moose, the trees, rocks and water, and the wonderful friends you've made up here. Home starts lookin' mighty plain. Mighty plain. Me 'n Bea been here nigh onto twenty years now, yep—twenty years. Don't hardly seem possible. The Good Lord's been good to us. Mighty good."

Without waiting for me to answer any of his barrage of questions, and a final, "Well, nice meetin' you, Mattie. Gotta go find Bea now." he was off. He swung his gangly form through the door, and I watched in astonishment while he strode down the trail toward the Crow cabin.

"Bye, Uncle Martin!" Red Bird called out, not at all as overwhelmed as I by Bea's husband.

"Goodness!" I said to the four walls while I turned again to Red Bird to resume the work on our numbers. "He must save up all his talking when he's out in the bush alone, and then dump it out like a nonstop cement mixer when he gets back around people again!" Red Bird just giggled.

Martin Hayford enlivened our discussions at the dinner table, and Bea was glowing with happiness to have him back. The Ross family and the Pascals joined us that first night. The conversation was brisk and sometimes hilarious as Martin regaled us with tales of his exploits, wriggling his big black eyebrows in a comical way to the delight of the children.

"I have six weeks until my next assignment," he told us. "I'll have to snoop around and see what kind of mischief I can drum up while I'm here," he grinned lopsidedly.

"I can think of a few things," Mary Rose piped up, her eyes twinkling, "like fixing the leak on the schoolhouse roof, repairing the damper on the stove—"

I caught the drift of things and chimed in, "Oh yes, and the front door sags—the hinges need to be replaced—the boat dock has some rotten boards in it—"

I paused to catch my breath but needn't have worried as Bea, smiling wickedly, took up the slack saying, "Of course we also need some trees cleared to make a bigger playground for sports like softball; the back steps need reinforced; the boat needs to be pulled out so the bottom can be painted—"

She also paused for breath and was saved by the Pascal children. "We need a swing!" begged Alice. "And a climbing gym!" exclaimed Elijah. "And a sandbox!" added the youngest Ross child, Robert, with an excited look on his face.

"Yes, the children would love that," smiled the Pascal mother, Margaret.

Bill Ross added the final challenge. "If you're looking for mischief Martin, James Pascal and I could use a hand scraping and painting of all the buildings." Everyone stared in anticipation at Martin. We waited for his reaction with a collective pause.

For once Martin was silent. He stared back with the most flabbergasted expression on his face I have ever seen on anyone. He peered suspiciously around the table at all of us. He could see our angelically posed faces. Then his mouth twisted into a wry grin. A laugh started deep in his throat and came rumbling and roaring out as a hearty "hee, hee, ho, ho, ho."

The laughter bubbled and boiled forth. Soon he was shaking with humor, and tears were rolling down his face as we all joined in his contagious humor. We giggled, laughed, and guffawed. It took a while before we were once again composed. Martin was one of those people who had a good impact on everyone.

Before Martin left on his next assignment, I was amazed to note that every single job that had been requested at that meal was completed. He had a heart as big as his laugh.

The next day we were having an early supper. Bea, myself, and Martin were there, when Martin suddenly slapped at his head, "I almost forgot!" he exclaimed.

"Forgot what?" we answered in unison, both puzzled.

"Forgot to tell you, your *other* prayer's been answered."

"What other prayer?" I asked, directing the question to Bea.

Bea's face was pure sunshine as she realized the significance of Martin's comment. She exclaimed, "Hallelujah! At last we're going to have a preacher!"

"He'll be arriving on the twenty-eighth of June," Martin told us.

Bea and I looked at each other, then back at Martin. "The twenty-eighth?"

"Yep!" he said, pleased with himself.

Bea's expression mirrored mine, the shock evident when we realized the implication. Martin looked at us in bewilderment, his expression telling us he didn't understand why we weren't more jubilant about what he thought was good news—outstanding news, in fact.

"B...but, that's today!" Bea spluttered and shouted at him. Her voice nearly overrode my own excited, "This *is* the twenty-eighth, Martin!"

"It is?" he gulped guiltily with a wide-eyed stare and raised brows.

"Yes, Martin. It is!" Bea informed him indignantly. "And now you are going to have to work like a legion of angels to help us get things ready for him! I want the cabin over behind the school cleaned out pronto. That's where he'll stay. Mattie can you get some clean bedding? You know where it is in that closet off the hall?"

I nodded while Bea continued to give marching orders. "I'll hang the curtains. Martin, you go see if any of the Ross family can help us. I'll inform John and Sopena Loon we need help!" Bea was a bit of whirlwind herself when agitated.

With the help of the Ross typhoons, and the younger John and Sopena, we scrubbed, scoured, swept, wiped, dusted, washed windows, plumped bedding, brought in firewood, and worked tirelessly for the next two hours.

We had just emptied the last dirty pail of water and were looking at each other knowing how bedraggled we all must appear, when we heard the sound of an engine and spotted a tiny black speck in the air. The floatplane was arriving!

Bea signaled and we all ran like gazelles that were sprinting away from a hungry lion, each to our own assorted rooms to spruce up as much as possible before the airplane touched down.

As the floatplane scooted to a landing across the water, then taxied noisily to the dock, we were all standing sedately, waiting as if this were the most common occurrence in the world and that his room had been ready all week.

Charles La Fountain would never know what incredibly hasty preparations were made for his arrival, or how much we were physically worn down from cleaning and polishing when we first met him.

Chapter 15

I first saw Charles as he stepped confidently off the floatplane and onto our dock. He did not fit my idea of what a preacher should look like at all. His six-foot frame moved with the ease of an athlete. To me he looked too young to be a preacher. I guessed him to be about my age or slightly older. He was dressed neatly, but casually, and wore no suit or tie. The color of his shirt almost perfectly matched his eyes, an unusual shade of green, and I remember wondering briefly if his wife had picked that shirt for him. That thought made me curious enough to look, and when I did, I noticed there was no ring on his left hand.

With the exception of Bea's husband, Charles was taller than most of those gathering around the dock. He was trim, lithe, and well balanced on his feet, evidenced by his ease in moving from a wobbling floatplane, to a floating dock and then to dry land. I suppose a modeling firm or talent scout would have labeled him average in appearance, but I was immediately impressed with his carriage and demeanor that seemed to give him a type of attractiveness not found in actors or models.

He carried a small bag in his left hand and hefted it about with assurance but not cockiness. His hair in the evening sun looked to be sand-colored, and I noticed some reddish tints glinting and reflecting the light. Here was another head of hair for inspiring awe in our Little Red Bird. He strode without hesitation toward the group of us waiting his arrival at the juncture of the dock and the shore. There was certainly an interesting presence about him—a magnetism that drew me—and I believe we all felt it.

"Welcome, welcome Pastor La Fountain," boomed Martin shoving his hand out at the newcomer. "Did I pronounce it right?"

"No," laughed Charles, who then proceeded to endear himself to all of us—me included. "And I'm going to set the record straight for everyone right now. That name is too difficult for any human being to have to try to pronounce—please everyone, just call me Charles."

Bea was next, "We're so glad to have you, Pas—uh, Charles. I'm Bea Hayford, and that's my husband, Martin, you just met. Please come, meet everyone."

They shook hands and then Bea and Martin proceeded to introduce the rest of us. Charles greeted everyone individually with a handshake and friendly, "Hello, very nice to meet you." Then it was my turn to be introduced.

"Charles, this is Mattie, our other answered prayer," said Bea.

Charles hesitated, his face arrested with curiosity. "*Other* answered prayer?" He smiled at me with raised eyebrows. I noticed they were sandy brown too. But it was his eyes that were absolutely compelling.

"It's a long story," I scowled at Bea, and then smiled faintly at him. "You wouldn't want to hear it."

"Perhaps I should be the judge of that," he said, looking at me intently, "in fact, I'm certain that I *do* want to hear this story, but," he paused, "we will save it for another time, Mattie." He smiled as he used my name for the first time, almost as if he enjoyed saying it, then he firmly shook my hand with his big warm fist and looked directly into my eyes as he did so. My hand felt very secure in his grip. I felt as if he could see into my very soul and knew all about me. It was a little discomfiting.

I backed up a step and Bea moved on with him. She introduced him to the Ross, Crow, Loon and Pascal families and all the others who had come to welcome him to the mission. Word had obviously spread quickly about this exciting event. I quietly moved away and stood apart from the group as I stared out across the water for a time, while conversation floated around me. In a while, I could see I wouldn't be missed, so I turned and left for my room to face another tortuous night of dreams about Joel and my miserable past.

George, the floatplane pilot, stayed overnight with us. I watched him depart early the next morning shortly after all the gear and new supplies were finally unloaded. When I had first learned a floatplane was coming to our mission, I had been concerned that it might be flown by Gene, the pilot who had transported Joel and me. I had been prepared to avoid him if necessary, but my fears were laid to rest after Charles arrived and a different face climbed out of the cockpit. I felt an unusual melancholy as I watched the plane turn into a distant dot.

I spotted a stack of newspapers and magazines among the many piles of supplies left behind. The dates were relatively old. I noticed Bea reading through them several days later, and when she left them lying about, I tried to appear casual as I perused them one by one. With trembling fingers I held the paper as I read the article. My story was there for the world to see. "HEIRESS MISSING, PRESUMED DEAD" blazed across the page.

There was an old society page photograph of Joel and me at our wedding, but fortunately, in the photo I was turned slightly at an angle and my veil partially obscured my face. Joel's face was featured predominately. I noticed the byline on the article was a female, and I imagined how well Joel had used his charm and flattery with her. I looked at his face a long while, seeing now the insincere smile, the hard glint in his eyes that I had never noticed before. I hoped no one at the mission would look at the photo particularly closely and recognize me or think about my coincidental arrival.

The story went on about how brokenhearted Joel was, and I felt the bile rise in my throat when I read it. It sickened me. I had to quickly retire to my room with the paper. However; when I finally read the quotes from my father, his words, "I'll never give up hope," scorched my soul.

When I continued the story in the privacy of my room and read, through blurry eyes, "I won't believe my daughter is dead," I fell across the bed and used my pillow to cushion the sound of my sobs. My mind and heart were pierced with remorseful thoughts about my father. *Oh, Daddy, this isn't fair to you—but I'm not ready to come back. I'm sorry, so sorry, but I just can't.*

Yet, I could *not* leave my father in this horrible limbo. I had tried sending him one message, but what if it had failed to go through? What could I do? I tossed about all night trying to deal with my predicament. I wanted to find a solution but it kept eluding me. I didn't want Joel to find me. I also knew people often faked things in such occasions involving wealthy families in order to obtain rewards. I didn't want my father to have false hope. I wanted him to *know* I was safe, but I wanted to avoid Joel knowing or finding out, even accidentally.

I also did not want Canadian or United States police officials involved with me just yet. I needed time to think about what I wanted to do when I got back. I needed to work it all out. I wanted to stay right here for a while longer. But how was I to notify my father without Joel getting wind of it? My past life continued to haunt me.

I was restless all night. I made a scrambled and twisted pile of the bedding from my nightmarish movements on the bed. I woke early, not refreshed, but with an idea. Later that day I approached Martin Hayford with some apprehension. I made sure no one was around. I had become very fond of Martin, and he seemed to reciprocate that friendship. Martin would be a key to this plan if he agreed.

"You'll be leaving us soon," I said with a question in my voice. I remembered him informing us he would only be here six weeks till he started another surveying job.

"Yes, much as I regret leaving, the mission needs the money I earn." He smiled at me thoughtfully. "Something on your mind, Mattie?"

"Am I that transparent?" I tried joking.

"No, Mattie. I think I've just come to know you pretty well since you arrived on our doorstep, and with people you care about, you can often sense when they're troubled. Is there something I can help you with? I'd be glad to be of service, you know."

"Oh, Martin. Thank you. Yes, there is something. I've a huge favor to ask of you, and it's something that I want to remain absolutely confidential for now."

"Okay, Mattie, if I can. What is it?"

"Well, when you leave, would you take this letter with you and when you reach someplace far from here on your next assignment with the government—someplace that has a post office, would you mail this letter from there?"

I handed him an envelope marked "Personal and confidential." It was addressed to my father's office with no return address on the outside. Martin took the proffered envelope from my hands and tucked it in his shirt pocket.

"Sure, Mattie." He smiled. "That'll be easy—anything else?"

"No, but thank you Martin, it means a lot to me."

"Anytime my girl, anytime." He saluted and went back to work without asking me any additional questions.

I had agonized all night over how to reach my father without revealing my location. I wasn't ready to return. I still had some major thinking to do. I wanted to be careful with all future decisions. But I wanted my father to know I was alive and well. He needed proof that it was not a fraud or a joke or even blackmail. This would reassure him, especially if my other message had been received. The note I had finally decided to send said simply:

NIS-NOC-SI is safe.
Need time to evaluate situation.
Do not tell *anyone* about this note.
Will contact you later. NIS-NOC-SI

Our lives improved with Charles's arrival. Not only was he able to bond well with his new flock, but he put his back and shoulders into some physical labor we needed done. He wielded a hammer and a saw right along with Bill, John, James, and Martin. Many of the other Ojibway fathers pitched in too, as they were able, in repairing the school.

The first large project they decided to undertake was to draw up plans, then erect, a separate building to be used for a church. Services were temporarily being held in the school rooms, which were overflowing on Sundays—a day the Ojibway called Anamae-kiishikan, their word for Christian or church. With Red Bird's help, I was beginning to pick up some of their language.

We were all excited about seeing a new structure take shape. The men actually created their own sawmill and lumberyard utilizing the wood from nearby trees for the building. Canada was lush with trees. Spruce, pine, poplar, and birch, all grew well in the north woods. The evergreens were redolent with fragrance when the men felled them to use for the building project.

They followed good forestry procedures while also creating a protective fire break to protect the mission from that most feared event—a wild fire. The fresh wood had to be stored and dried. They were able to draw from previously dried stores of wood for current building, but they now began replacing those stacks with fresh wood that would be dried for future use. I loved the odors that emanated from that wood. Charles seemed to be everywhere at once, and I modified my description of Mary Rose to a force eight gale with Charles being a full force twelve hurricane.

I came around the corner of the school one day and saw Red Bird, her father John, and Charles all laughing and chuckling while looking at Charles's feet.

"I guess I need someone to supervise me when I dress in the morning," Charles laughed.

"You need a wife like my Alice." John Crow smiled. "She checks me all over before I go out the door."

"Yes, and she makes sure Daddy does not wear one black and one white sock!" giggled Red Bird, pointing down at the errors adorning Charles' feet.

"I see you have made friends through your mode of dress," I smiled and approached them.

"Not you too!" Charles moaned. "I am not happy with how well you have taught her the colors," he joked. "She might not have noticed one black and one white otherwise."

"Oh no, you don't!" laughed John. "I am very happy with this teacher, and so is Red Bird."

I was gratified to see how comfortable Red Bird's father, John, seemed to be with Charles. It was important that Red Bird have a stable, sober father in her life. Charles seemed to recognize this as well.

"Yes, she has a good teacher, but she also has a very good father." He complimented John, who did not reply but grunted and picked up another log with a proud posture.

One evening after dinner, I walked out and sat on the end of the dock to watch the sun set over the water. I heard soft steps behind me and then, before I could turn, felt someone sit down beside me with feet, now clad in matching socks and tennis shoes, dangling with mine above the water. It was Charles.

"Mind if I join you?" His voice was pleasant.

"Not at all," I said, but couldn't resist adding, "I see you found a way to become color-coordinated."

"Ha!" His laugh was genuine and nice to hear. "I had a little help with that. I asked Red Bird to go through all my socks and match them up. She had a ball doing it and asked if she could come back next week when my laundry is done again."

"Oh, I love that!" I smiled. "It will reinforce what she's learning in school." I hesitated. "She has been a little bit behind," I confided.

"Yes, her father, John, has shared with me about his past. He very much wants to make amends and help her catch up on her schooling. You like her a lot, don't you?" he guessed.

"Yes, I think she is precious, and I have been very worried about her father having a relapse into his old ways." I paused.

"He is in God's hands, and so is Red Bird," Charles said gently. "And it looks like God sent you here to help them."

"I don't know about that." I was embarrassed at the compliment. "But if her father, ever—"

"Like I said," he interrupted me, "they are both in God's hands. You don't have to worry."

He said it so confidently, I almost believed him.

From that day, we met often in the evenings at the end of the dock when the weather permitted. We experienced some spectacular sunsets along with some overcast and cloudy moments. We began to know more about each other.

"Tell me about your family," I encouraged the next time we met there.

"Pretty normal family," he told me. "I have two younger brothers named Kenny and Donny. Donny is two years younger than me and Kenny came along four years after Donny. My sister, Sandy, is only eighteen months older than me, but she thinks she is the backup mother to all three of us boys—she calls us "her incorrigibles." Her calling in life is to be sure we all behave properly and don't get into trouble."

I laughed. "Well you are pretty far from her reach up here." I smiled.

"Yes, and I am sure Donny and Kenny are reaping even more rules and lectures since I am not there to share them!" He joked, but I could tell he loved and missed his sister a great deal.

"What about your parents?" I was curious.

"My mother holds our family together. She cares for children taken from their parents for a variety of reasons. We've always had a lot of children in our home, some of them very troubled. Mom has a special way with them, and yet she has also managed to motivate the rest of us to do well in school and to make something of our lives. She is also an amazing cook!"

"Getting a little lonesome for home cooking are we?" I teased. Food at the mission was plentiful but could become a bit monotonous at times.

"I don't want to even think about her homemade apple pie!" he moaned and rubbed his stomach.

"What about your father?" I asked. "Was he in the picture? I imagine your mom could have used some support with all those children in the house."

"My dad is an incredible man. If more dads were like him, we wouldn't have so many problems with kids today."

"How so?"

"He is an electrician by trade, so he does that business as a self-employed contractor where he is on call twenty-four hours a day—at least it seemed that way to us kids growing up. But get this: he also had a part-time job as the pastor of a small church near our home. He had to work to support us, and the church was too small to give him much in the way of salary.

"Still he was always over at the church fixing something, repairing something, or working on his sermon for the next Sunday. In addition to that, he and my mom were always doing something for the kids who landed on our doorstep. They make a great team."

I thought of my own childhood and how differently I had been raised. I loved my father, but Charles made his home sound wonderful too.

"Did everyone get along?" I asked, thinking of the lack of conflict in my home.

"Oh, most of the time, but there were quarrels occasionally and our parents would have to step in and intercede. It was a bit rough when I was living at home and going to the Christian seminary in Winona Lake. My brothers did not understand why I couldn't drop everything and go to their games or play with them as much as I used to."

"Was it that intense?"

"It was a challenge, but what made it difficult was that I had to work a job while attending in order to pay my tuition and books. My parents pitched in to help monetarily, but they had three other children who would need an education as well, and there was only so much to go around."

"What kind of job did you do?"

"I tried working for my dad, but the hours he really needed help were in a conflict with the hours I needed to be in class, so I finally found a job at a factory working on an assembly line. I worked from midnight to 8 a.m., then I got off work, cleaned up, and went straight to classes where I tried to stay awake until midafternoon, then I headed home and studied, did homework, and crashed until it was time to get up and go back to work."

"I can see why you didn't have much time for your brothers."

"Fortunately I only did that five days a week. I did get weekends off."

"But you made it."

"I made it."

I learned much more about Charles's childhood, his brothers, sister, and loving large family. He had shared with me how, after seminary, he had been at a local church, helping it grow for a few years when he felt the call to preach in Canada. Now he was here, and it was obvious he loved it.

Though our friendship was growing very strong, I had been much less forthcoming about my childhood and life. I usually described it in generalities and evaded most personal questions. This evening, however, he asked a question I could easily answer.

"How do you enjoy working with the children?"

"Oh, I love it!" I enthused. "They are so eager to learn and so rewarding to teach. They seem to appreciate everything we do."

"Red Bird seems to have developed a great attachment to you," he commented with a sideways glance at me. We were seated as usual in our favorite spot, the end of the dock with a view of the lake.

"She's a very special little girl, and she's had a difficult time. I've wanted to thank you."

"Thank me?" he questioned in a puzzled voice. "Why?"

"You've made a great impression on John Owen, Red Bird's father. He's been much better since you've arrived. When he's better, Red Bird and her mother, Mary, fare better too."

"I see," he said slowly, and I knew he did see and would redouble his efforts with John. His next comment, however, was unexpected and threw me off balance.

"When you leave, Red Bird is going to have a really hard time."

So he guessed I was planning to leave, though I had never expressed that possibility to anyone; nor had I pointed out that this was all temporary for me. I said nothing in response—I couldn't. We watched the rest of the sunset in a silence tinged with sadness.

That night I woke drenched in sweat, my fear palpable in the dark room. I had been dreaming again. In the dream, Joel began by searching for me. He suspected I was not dead, and he was coming after me. This time the dream took the same twist. As he began searching, I found a way, in the dream, to retaliate and attempt to kill Joel. I tricked him like he tricked me. I made him fall. I had a sharp shard of glass, and I was determined to stab him but he scrambled away in fear. I began to chase him with the glass weapon.

I felt adrenaline and euphoria surge through my body as I was about to gain my long-awaited revenge. It seemed so real. I woke in such a frightened state that I was sure the loud thumping of my heart would wake everyone. I could feel the vibration and trembling loudly to my ears and my breathing was harsh, my mouth dry with panic. I didn't recognize the Mattie in the dream. Yet I understood her desire for reprisal. In spite of my certainty that I must have woken everyone when I jerked awake, the house stayed silent. I was totally awake now, restless, and I couldn't go back to sleep.

I threw on some clothes, more of my borrowed wardrobe, and I walked down to the one place that soothed me: the dock. A faint, soft pink light was in the sky from the impending dawn, and it helped me see well enough to find my way. It was beautiful. A distant loon called to its mate, and the sound reverberated across the water in a melancholy warble. I stood in the cool morning air and thought about how different Joel and my old life had been—still was—from the people and the life here at the mission and how happy I was when working with the children.

"Can't sleep?" I involuntarily jumped, but I didn't need to turn to recognize Charles's voice nor to sense his nearness at my shoulder. "Sorry, I did not intend to frighten you," his voice carried to me with concern.

"It's all right." I relaxed. "I had a nightmare." I surprised myself by admitting.

"Want to talk about it?" he probed, his masculine voice gentle and near to my ear.

"Not yet. Maybe someday," I evaded and paused. "—But Charles?" I had remembered something from my other life that Freddie had said. Maybe Charles would know why it had always bothered me.

"Yes?"

"God is supposed to be loving and forgiving, right?"

"That's His nature," he said and I turned to see him nod. "So, yes, that's right."

"Well, how could He keep anyone out of heaven then? If He really loves everybody, then He will let everybody in, right?"

"It isn't quite that simple. You are correct in that God loves and forgives, Mattie, but you must remember that He is also *just*, or some would say, fair."

"So?"

"Let me explain it this way. Since you like working with children, let's suppose you wanted to have a big party in one room at the school, okay?"

"Okay—a big party. So?"

"Let's also say you have worked extremely hard to clean the room all up; it is sparkling in fact. You have provided all kinds of food and entertainment and wonderful things for the children to do. You are really looking forward to having all the children there because you love them dearly. In fact, you have invited them all to come."

"Sort of like God has fixed up heaven with all the streets of gold and so forth, huh?" I guessed.

"We don't know for sure what heaven will be like," he smiled and continued, "but we know it will be a place of joy for us. However, you are getting the picture I'm trying so inadequately to paint. Thank you for listening. There are many who do not search for truth as you are doing."

He didn't give me time to acknowledge the compliment but continued with, "Now, Mattie, suppose the only thing you said to the children you had invited to your big event—your party—was that they had to clean up and prepare to get in the front door and come to the party. That's all. Just be clean and come in."

"That's not too hard. I would definitely want them cleaned up before I let them in the door, especially if I had everything as sparkling and as nice as you had said."

"Okay, then, you can understand how the children—all of them, know your rules—'Be clean. Use front door.' Now suppose a few of the children spy a mud puddle on the way to the party."

"Uh, oh—is this the temptation part?"

"You catch on quickly, Mattie." I could feel his words like a benediction. "Now, suppose the temptation is too much for some of them, and they jump and play in the mud until they are covered. They are dripping with the gooey stuff. They are a mess! But the other children stay clean and show up at your door.

"Some of the remaining muddy children also realize they've broken the rule, so they run back home and get cleaned again, and they also show up at your front door. In this group, the children are all clean. Are you going to let these children in?"

"Yes, of course. They obeyed the rules, and I want them to come in and enjoy the party." By now I sensed where he was headed with this analogy but I wanted to hear the rest of it.

"You let the clean ones in." He smiled at me. "Of course. Now, suppose the remaining muddy, dripping children don't want to go home and clean up. They decide to come knocking at the back door and expect you to let them in anyway. They say that if you love them you will let them in.

"It's true. You really *do* love those kids. You really want them to come to the party. Is it fair to let them in when they've broken the rule by their own free will? When they deliberately disobeyed you? Was it *your* choice or *their* choice at this point?"

"No, I really can't let them in at this point. I see what you mean by just and fair. This is amazing. I never looked at it this way before."

"If you turn them away, does it mean you don't love them?"

"Absolutely not! In fact, I will be heartbroken about them, but it was their choice, not mine. Oh Charles, I see why you are going to be such a good preacher. You've explained something to me that has puzzled and disturbed me for a long time. Thank you!" I turned to go back inside.

But he didn't let me go. His voice arrested me when he asked softly, "Are you clean or muddy, Mattie?"

I stopped and turned back, my interest caught. "What do you mean?"

"I mean, I can't let you walk away from this conversation without asking you to consider what you need to do to get *yourself* into heaven someday. I'm planning to be there, and I'd like to know that you will be there too."

"Well, I've lived a good life, if that's what you mean. I haven't robbed anyone or killed anyone or done anything really bad."

"Are you perfect?"

"Don't be silly! No one's perfect!"

"God is. And that's what you need to be able to share His heaven with Him. You need to be perfectly clean."

"Goodness! Then no one can get in, Charles, because no one is perfect!"

"Let's go back to our story." He looked intently into my eyes, and I felt a shiver at his sincerity. "Let's return to the example of your party, Mattie, and maybe I can explain it. Suppose all the muddy children at the back door had some way to get clean. Would you then let them in also?"

"Of course!"

"Suppose there was someone perfectly clean and pure who was willing to make a sacrifice for all the children who were now sorry they got muddy, and let's say that same someone was willing to take all the mud off them and onto his own person, just so the children could still go to the party. Keep in mind, he would only do this for those who were sorry for their mistakes, those who repented of the wrongdoing and were going to try not to do it again."

"If such a person exists, the children are pretty fortunate." I responded.

"That person does exist, Mattie. His name is Jesus Christ."

"I know some things about Christ, but I've never been taught a lot about Him. I always wondered about this salvation thing the TV preachers talk about."

"Well, this Jesus Christ is actually one with God. He died for you and me and anyone who wants to share a beautiful relationship with Him in heaven. You can have this, Mattie. All that is required of you is to ask God for forgiveness of sins in your life and to believe in Jesus, to accept Him into your life."

But I now came to a stumbling block. I was not ready for such a decision. I heard and mostly understood what he was saying, but there were so many things he didn't know about me and so much I had to learn. It was not so simple for me. There was also the matter of Joel, and the revenge I was planning. I was touched by what he said, but I was also resistant to it.

Charles was wise. He knew not to press me, but from that evening on, I could see a hopeful expectancy in his face whenever he looked at me. He never said so, but in addition to his hopes for my soul to attend God's party, I believed he might be starting to care for me as more than a friend. It was something I thought I saw in his expression—the way his eyes changed when he saw me. And I was beginning to care greatly for him—too much so. Guilt would consume me sometimes when we sat watching the sunset.

My mind would be in turmoil thinking and rethinking: *I am not free to care for him. It is wrong to encourage him, yet he is so kind, so wise, and so good for me. He is wonderfully different from Joel. I need all that very desperately in my life right now. I'm coming to rely on him. I do not want either of us to be hurt. I should end this immediately.*

But I could not find the will-power to end it or to rebuff him. He had come to be a significant support in my life. I needed someone who admired and encouraged me. I had been unselfish for so long with Joel.

Now I decided to be selfish. I took the affection and considerate care he gave me.

My conscience would cry out to me, *but this is not being fair to Charles.* My soul would cry back, *but I need him!* Back and forth my mind would tumble, and all the while I was allowing myself to feel nurtured and loved by his actions. And all the while I continued to plan my revenge on Joel. I became a conflicted person. I selfishly continued to allow Charles to seek me out, justifying it as best I could, knowing Charles would treat me differently if he knew of my marriage to Joel.

I knew he was more honorable than me. I told myself I needed this because of all the injustice I had suffered, but I knew in my heart that I was not being the kind of principled person Charles deserved. One evening when I went to the dock I saw a canoe tied there. I sat in my customary place and waited. When Charles arrived he said, "Ready?"

"Ready for what?"

"A canoe ride." He smiled.

"I don't think so." I shivered.

"You don't strike me as a fearful person, so what's wrong?"

"Nothing."

"If nothing is wrong, then hop in and let's go. I've something I want to show you."

I shook my head.

"I won't let anything happen to you, Mattie," he said gently.

"I know. It's just—"

"Just what?"

"I—I'm not feeling all that well. I think I'll go to bed early tonight," I lied.

I could feel his eyes follow me as I made my way back to the cabin and security. I yearned to take him up on his offer, but anything to do with being out on that water brought back all the terror of my experience on that island and the raft.

Meanwhile Charles continued his work with the Ojibway. He trained the men how to become spiritual leaders in their church and community.

"I'm working myself right out of a job!" he sometimes laughed, but we all knew the natives were determined to keep Charles there for as long as he was willing to stay.

I continued to work at the school as I soaked up the love and adoration of the children. I knew they too would be disappointed should I return to my home in St. Louis. I tried to pretend nothing would change, and we could all continue as we had been.

Charles preached wonderful sermons. They were full of anecdotes and stories that often touched my heart. I could see the rapt attention the congregation gave him, and I felt privileged to know Charles. I was learning many things about the life of Jesus along with many biblical principles. But, I clung to my hatred of Joel and my overwhelming desire for revenge. The Bible beside my bed remained unopened.

It was an education just hearing the Bible stories Mary Rose and Bea read to the children. I'd attended some summer Bible schools as a youngster, and had made occasional visits to church and Sunday school with Blanche, but it was as if I were hearing all this for the first time. Bea had a flannel board that entranced me almost as much as the children.

We would all moan together when she would say, "All right, that's all the time we have for today. We'll finish the story of Jesus and the loaves and fishes tomorrow."

I learned it all as if through a child's eyes. I watched the effect it had on Red Bird and the others, and at the same time I felt the effect that was beginning to dawn within me.

Chapter 16

We decided to take the children on a picnic as a reward for their hard studies. All available boats and canoes were commandeered for our excursion across the lake. We were going to be landing at a clearing near a waterfall the students had described to me.

"You'll like it, Miss Mattie," the children informed me.

"That's where I found the pretty red stone you have in your jar," Red Bird told me proudly, "right by the waterfall!" She was bouncing with enthusiasm. I was less enthusiastic but told myself I must have the courage to participate.

Charles, James Keesik, Bill Ross, and John Owen would accompany us, each in charge of one boatload. Martin was gone on one of his government assignments, so he would miss the fun. I was to ride with Charles. The older boys would share a canoe they managed themselves. Each boat, even the canoes, had a small motor attached. Our boat, being the larger, carried most of the picnic supplies.

The day that was, according to my students, "taking forever to get here" finally arrived and the children chattered excitedly as they boarded. Nearly everything that we were to take with us had been loaded into the boats. No one had noticed how I lingered behind on shore, nor my reluctance to take my place in the watercraft. All the children were soon positioned aboard the boats and were safely situated in their seats. Finally, it was my turn to climb into the boat. I could delay no longer. I had determined to get over my fear and had decided to go on the picnic, therefore I could not understand the strange feeling of reluctance that came over me.

This was not one adversary trying to kill me, but a large group of people who cared about me. Charles extended his hand to help me aboard, but I hesitated and looked down. My feet seemed unable to move, and I looked across at Charles wondering if I would be able to empower my legs. I thought perhaps I should try to beg off. My mouth went bone dry when I thought about climbing onto that boat.

Charles, always intuitive, was sensitive to my feelings, "Is something wrong, Mattie?" he asked, concern in his voice.

Garnering my courage, I finally breathed deeply, took his hand, forced my legs to move and stepped in, saying as I did so, one more lie to Charles, "No, no, everything's all right."

"You're sure?" he appeared skeptical.

"Sure," I mumbled insincerely and sat down quickly to appease the sick feeling in the pit of my stomach. I couldn't make myself tell him how I had suddenly been overwhelmed by memories—how I remembered my experiences on the water—the crashing waves, the fears of dying, almost drowning in the storm, the poisoning. Suddenly, all of it surfaced again, and the memories overpowered and frightened me.

The boat in which we were riding was so like the one Joel and I had used for fishing. The smells and sounds of the water—the beautiful day—brought it all back to me so vividly. I relived every single moment of my ordeal with Joel. My mind told me it was over, that I was safe now, but it was hard to believe. We moved easily across the lake. The boat left a gentle trail behind us. Everyone else was laughing, comfortable. I sat rigidly in the boat and fought down my panic as we glided smoothly across the serene face of the water.

I could feel Charles's eyes on me and I turned to meet his gaze. He looked at me intently with those probing eyes and after a second or two, smiled at me encouragingly. I surprised myself with my ability to smile back. The connection between us seemed strong, but I tried to tell myself it was just a friendly reassurance I was feeling. Inexplicably, however, from that moment on, I felt calmly comforted. His strength and support enabled me to forget the nightmare while it dissipated like the mist on the lake when the sun begins to lift it off. My squeamishness finally disappeared, and I was able to sit back at last to relax and enjoy the ride and the beautiful day.

It *was* a gorgeous day—mild and warm. The lake reflected milky-white clouds, their splendor intensified in the mirrored view against the sharp, blue bird colors of the expansive sky. Around the rim of the lake were also reflected the rocky ledges of the Canadian Shield and towering green spires of the various strains of evergreen trees—the pines, firs, spruces, hemlocks, and cedars that were plentiful in this part of Ontario. The trees offered a natural dark sage green frame for the panorama as it unfolded before us.

The children began to sing songs as we traveled. Their youthful voices echoed delightfully across the water like a Gregorian chant rebounds off the hills of some distant monastery. Little Red Bird's hand crept into mine and she smiled up at me as I joined in their song.

We eventually neared an area where the lake narrowed and we turned down a wide channel that shortly tapered, tightened, and became an enchanting river. We skimmed pleasantly along and could see more and more wildlife due to the proximity of the shores on either side. We watched a family of otters as they propelled themselves gleefully, and skidded, one by one, pell-mell down a large incline into the water on a well-used slide of packed earth. At another bend in the river, we overtook a majestic animal, a mammoth moose, that raised his head to watch us like some regal guard about to call the alarm that his wilderness was under attack by intruders.

We went a mile or so further and the river became more rapid, our ride a little less smooth. Then as we came around another bend, we could see a mist in the distance and what appeared to be steam rising from a point that dropped off beyond our visibility. It looked like the end of the world to me; but, before our boats could be siphoned off by the rapids into the nothingness that loomed straight ahead, our adept captain,

Charles, veered sharply to the right. He maneuvered us carefully and aimed our craft toward a cluster of large boulders to the side of the river.

When I was certain he was mistaken in this direction and was just about to cry, "Charles! Look out!" he surprised me. Just as I thought he was heading us into the danger of crashing straight into the giant boulders, he contrived to steer us, cleverly, right through the middle of the rock-strewn water. I was amazed, as we progressed, to find the boulders spaced just enough of a distance apart to allow our boats to pass through a small, almost invisible, opening. We traversed this narrow channel between the boulders and came out into a pleasant surprise—a beautiful little, quiet cove that had as its prime advantage a wonderfully sandy beach.

"Our friends," Charles told me, "the Ojibway Indians, have generously shared their secret place with us." He grinned like a little boy, "I've been practicing the maneuvering it takes to get in here," Charles informed me. "John Owen has been teaching me." I felt very hopeful then about Red Bird's father, and was so thankful he felt this bond with us.

There was no pier or dock in the cove of course, so we drove straight for shore and beached the boats, where their hulls scraped lightly as they touched the soft, moist sand. One occupant from each of our watercraft jumped ashore to secure the bowline, and we soon disembarked. Everyone pitched in to unload our picnic supplies. Red Bird's mother, Mary, came along to help for the day. She joined Mary Rose and me to prepare some of the activities we had planned for the outing and soon happy chatter ensued.

One of those activities included a planned hike to the waterfall, which I could hear in the distance. One of the children informed me that a path led to the waterfall. She pointed across the cove where I could see a break in the trees heading toward what they told me was a steep incline. I could hear the waterfall roaring and knew, based on the magnitude of the sound generated, that it would be a powerful sight.

Another planned activity was to spend some time collecting various plants and rocks for the children to identify. We decided to save the waterfall hike for after lunch when everyone would be drowsy and looking for a change of pace.

We began by playing games. The adults joined in, to the amusement and hilarity of the children. We watched Charles, his leg strapped to little Judas Crow while they attempted to coordinate their feet as they took clumsy steps in the three-legged race. Their antics had us all fatigued and holding our stomachs from so much laughter.

Charles was so good with the children. I felt my heart catch when I saw him tumble about and roughhouse with them. I was thinking I had never known a man quite like Charles when he glanced over at me and grinned while he disentangled himself from Judas. I watched and smiled as the children clamored for more attention and climbed all over him. It was obvious he was enjoying himself.

Lunch was a nice break after all the frivolity. Moosenee and Bearhair presented a little skit from the Bible, after which Charles offered the blessing for the food. The exercise had worked up appetites; thus, the meal disappeared as fast as food given to a nest of hungry baby eagles.

After we had cleaned and straightened things from lunch, we prepared to take our hike to see the waterfall that we could hear as a constant thrumming sound in the distance. John Owen was to be our guide. We began walking single file on a barely discernible path through the forest. The moss was thick and lush, the trees closed around us like a hushed cathedral.

The sky was only occasionally visible as if it were stitched of tiny blue patchwork pieces sewn by some mighty seamstress into the all-encompassing forest green quilt over our heads. Charles and I brought up the rear and fell slightly behind as I stopped to appreciate our surroundings. I felt safe and secure with this group in my life.

"It's hard to imagine all this thick, almost tropical, vegetation as it must look covered with snow in the winter," I said, sharing my thoughts and shaking my head wonderingly at Charles.

"As it will be a few months from now," he agreed quietly.

Our thoughts and attitudes, it seemed to me, often ran in a similar pattern. I could see the knowledge in his eyes that my talk of winter gave him pause too. Where would either of us be this next winter? What would each of us be doing?

I sensed that we each knew and recognized this time as a special moment; one to store away in the mind's catalog of pleasant memories. I believed I saw in Charles's face the same thoughts I was having: a cognizance that these were temporary times, fleeting days that were evaporating far too rapidly. We must savor his day. We stood silently beside each other for a few moments. He turned toward me.

"The others are disappearing." I pointed out in a whisper, spellbound by his eyes.

"We must catch up to them," he said and nodded, but did not move his feet. We stood very closely together; our eyes locked in unspoken meanings.

One of the children shrieked in the distance, and the moment was broken much as a thrown pebble breaks the surface of a quiet pond. We did not speak or act upon our impulses but instead resumed our walk and followed the trail down a slope as the terrain changed from tall trees to low bushy shrubs. We could hear the adults and children ahead of us calling out to one another as they reached the destination. They were looking for rock and plant specimens, I could tell, for I heard them shouting back and forth, sometimes wrangling over who found something first.

As Charles and I drew nearer, I could feel a vibration in the ground accompanied by a constant noise over the children's squeals and laughter. A noise that sounded almost like trucks and cars rumbling along a superhighway grew louder as we approached; yet, I knew there were no highways or vehicles within hundreds of miles.

We turned, laughed together along the way at the crookedness of the steep downhill path and came around yet another bend in the trail. The path opened in front of us like a curtain that was slowly pulled back from a stage. The sound was much louder now. There was one additional slight bend in the trail and then I could see it.

The waterfall in all its virulent energy was displayed before me. The turbulent water spilled over gargantuan boulders in a frenzy while it frothed and foamed in its need to reach the bottom. I recognized it instantly. Frozen in place, I looked in horror and fear and watched in astonishment while it tumbled before me. It was the same waterfall where I had fished at the base with Joel.

I remembered now, how Joel and I had come upon it from the downstream side. Today, with this group, we had arrived from the upstream angle, which had left me vulnerable and unsuspecting. I stood now, unable to move my limbs, horrified at what it represented and what came crashing into my memory. It all rushed back into my mind again. Everything I had repressed was there—the memories, the paralyzing terror, the pain and fear for my life. I wanted to run, but I could not. My chest felt constricted. I could only breathe in shallow gasps as I felt the panic of my remembered experience overtaking me. I dimly heard a voice.

"Mattie! Mattie, what is it?" Charles called me. I felt powerless to move or to answer the voice that seemed far away. I was reliving the excruciating pain of Joel's betrayal all over again. Torn between then and now, my hand went to my ring finger. The diamond ring was gone. I remembered anew why it was missing. The pain was staggering.

Then, I felt a hand pulling my arm. It tugged me back to the present. The disembodied but comforting voice led me to a large, flat boulder. "Here, Mattie, come over here. Sit down for a minute." The same remote voice put an arm around my shoulders and asked, "Are you ill? Mattie, answer me!" The voice materialized into Charles. He hovered in concern, "What's wrong?"

I sat down, my hand over my mouth to keep the terror within, the scream contained. I didn't want to frighten the children. I didn't answer him. I couldn't.

We sat this way, silently, away from the others for a time. Charles gave me time to compose myself and waited patiently. He let me know he was there, but he did not pressure me to talk. It was the best thing he could do.

"I hate him for this," I finally said aloud, as I took several deep gulping breaths. My heart was still racing and the pain in my soul felt acute. I felt as if someone had thrust a hundred barbed hooks through a tender part of my soul and was pulling them out, one by one.

There was a silence from Charles as if he were gathering his thoughts. My words hung in the air between us like weighted balloons that could not rise any further than a few feet. Charles shifted his weight, then very slowly, thoughtfully, he began to speak to me.

"Hate is a very strong word, Mattie," he paused. "You must feel very deeply about something to use the word *hate* as you just did."

"Yes," I responded without looking at him. "There is someone I have learned to hate. I will *never* be able to forgive him."

"Never?"

"No, never!" I shuddered.

There was a long silence, then, "Who do you think your lack of forgiveness will hurt most, Mattie—him or you?"

"You think I should forgive something that happened to me that is so vile I can't sleep at night?"

Another long pause came with this revelation, and then I heard his voice say, "It isn't that *I* think you should forgive, Mattie, though for your own sake I do believe you should. More importantly, it's that God commands it of us. Matthew 6 verses 14 and 15 say, 'For if you forgive men when they sin against you, your heavenly Father will also forgive you. But if you do not forgive men their sins, your Father will not forgive your sins.' And yes, you must forgive even though you can't sleep at night. In fact, I dare to say you will *only* begin to sleep well at night again when you *do* forgive."

I turned to him in disbelief, my voice scornful, "That's easy for you to say, Charles, but what if something horrifying happened to you? Let's say, for example, some ax murderer came in one night and murdered everyone in your family—your mother, father, the wonderful brothers and sister you've told me about—would you still feel the same way?"

"Bea and Martin did," he answered simply, while he patted my shoulder, "and I hope I would be able to do the same though I know it would be difficult."

"What do you mean, Bea and Martin did?" I asked, puzzled and instantly distracted from memories of my own hurtful wounds.

"You don't know how they lost their only two children?" he asked me.

"They had children?" I asked in astonishment.

"Yes, they had two lively, healthy and, I'm told, wonderful children: a boy and a girl," Charles assured me.

I shook my head, "I had always assumed they couldn't have children of their own and worked with the Ojibway as a substitute."

"You are partially correct. They work with the Ojibway as a substitute, but first, before they came here, they had two children of their own."

"What happened to those children?"

Charles seemed to consider whether he should answer but sighed and settled into the tale. "It was a terrible tragedy," he said. "Bea and Martin were a long time in recovering from it. It happens they were on a family vacation. With them on that vacation was their son, Tad, five years old, and daughter, Becky, who had just turned seven." Charles hesitated and appeared to be taking great pains with how he couched his words to me.

"My parents and I knew the Hayfords very well. The children were bright and inquisitive. Everyone loved them. They seemed like the perfect family. It was spring. They were traveling through Georgia on their way to Florida where they had reserved a vacation cottage on the beach. They wanted a very early start that morning because they were all so excited to reach their destination. They were out on the road not long after dawn. It had rained overnight and the streets were slippery."

I could visualize the scene while Charles described it. "So? What happened then?"

"Martin was driving and had pulled out of their motel and down the street a few blocks to access the main highway. A stoplight turned red in front of them, and Martin stopped for it. Unfortunately, the drunken driver just behind them, who had been out all night drinking, did not stop. In a stupor, while traveling at high speed, he drove his car into the rear end of their vehicle."

Charles looked at me in concern. "The children were in the backseat—closest to the impact. Both children died from that crash."

"Oh, no!" I was appalled at this news. "Oh how horrible! Bea has never spoken a word to me about this. How can she be so cheerful all the time? Was the driver arrested?" I had many questions, but first I wanted my pound of flesh. Sweet, stoic Bea had never once referred to her tragic loss.

"Actually, it turns out the driver had been arrested numerous times. He was habitually drunk, but he had always managed to find a smart lawyer who got him off with a slap on the hand and release from jail. Unfortunately, he was out on the street again and the Hayford children were the casualties. Betsy died instantly, while little Tad lingered for agonizing days. Finally, he slipped away too.

"Bea, who was recovering from her own severe injuries, and Martin, who sustained only minor injuries from the crash, stayed with Tad when his little body ceased to struggle. In addition to all this grief, Bea suffered from internal injuries that resulted in her inability to have any more children."

"Poor Bea—and Martin too, I had no idea."

"Yes. Their children died, and they both lived."

"The driver of the other car-what happened to him?" I wanted revenge on their behalf.

"Was hospitalized and later recovered from all his injuries, some of which were severe. I was away in college during all this, but my mother said the courage and faith of Bea and Martin became an inspiration to everyone in town."

"Weren't they devastated? How did they continue to function? I can't imagine their pain."

"Well, get this. They actually visited the man who had killed children while he was recuperating in the hospital. He had some bad injuries so he was there for quite a while."

"Did they tell him how they hated him and what an evil person he was?"

"On the contrary; they showed no ill-will at all."

"Unbelievable. Didn't they scream and yell at him? I think I would have had a difficult time controlling my temper if I were in their shoes."

"Actually, my mom told me they marched into that hospital and tried to save his soul. They told him how badly he needed Jesus in his life."

"Impossible! Didn't they care at all that their children were dead and that he was the cause of it?"

"Oh yes, of course they cared. They cared and grieved deeply, more than we will most likely ever know, but when you are a Christian, Mattie, you have resources and guidance and wisdom to provide strength to you—a strength that the world can never understand."

"How could anyone possibly have that much strength? I can't believe, much as I like Martin and Bea, they were able to deal that gently with the man responsible for their children's deaths."

"With God 'all things are possible' Mattie. They knew their children were safely in heaven, the best of all possible places. They had confidence they would see them again someday when they join them there. They also knew God commands us to forgive others their trespasses."

"But how could they feel any forgiveness at all? What if it just won't come? Not only that, their story is not quite the same as my ax murderer scenario," I argued.

"No, not quite the same, but if you wait for forgiveness to come to you, or for your feelings to change from some other influence than your choice, you'll have a long wait. No." He shook his head. "Forgiveness isn't an emotion, Mattie; it is simply a choice—an action from a decision consciously made. You decide you will forgive, even when the feelings inside you may contradict that choice at the time you make it. It is not easy, but we have to decide to obey God. We must take the steps necessary for our own healing. It is amazing. Once we make the decision, in spite of our negative feelings, we soon find that not long after taking these steps, the feelings are changed too."

"You think that's how Bea and Martin did it?"

"I'm certain of it. Hate and an unforgiving spirit don't hurt the one at whom it's directed. It hurts the one who is carrying the negative baggage around. Hate festers in one's spirit and grows nasty like a stagnant pool of water. Soon it is full of algae, bugs, and rotting plants. Eventually, the water becomes unfit to drink. Then it begins to clog up so it can no longer flow freely. Hate does that to your soul.

"Forgiveness, on the other hand, though difficult at first, is like pouring that same pool of water down a channel to a cleansing stream where there are bubbling rapids and tumbling waterfalls to mix it with oxygen and purify it. It doesn't take long before all the old nastiness in the water is completely gone. It becomes pristine again, and we can take a very satisfying drink from it."

"You make it sound easy, Charles."

"I don't mean to imply that being a Christian is easy. It's not. In fact, sometimes it is extremely difficult. However, it is always what is best for us in the long term. You must have faith in God—let Him be the ultimate judge. Let His wisdom be your guide. Learn to do as He commands then develop a desire to please Him with your life, and you will find a satisfaction beyond anything material this earth can offer."

"That was a very impassioned speech, Charles."

He grinned lopsidedly, "I feel very impassioned about the subject."

I wasn't sure if he meant me or God—or maybe both. Not long after this, I was able to rejoin the group, and we finished the day very well. We sang more songs as we boated back to the mission. I was thoughtful as we returned. I had much to think about, and I could feel a battle between two factions in my soul.

One side of my mind was being pulled toward Bea's seventy times seven, along with Charles's just and fair God. The other part of me was pulling just as fervently in an opposite direction—urging me to nurture my hate for Joel and go on with my plans for revenge. I also had tremendous guilt about withholding information that I thought might make a difference in my relationship with those I had learned to love.

I observed Bea more closely after that day. She had become a puzzle to me, and I wanted to take her apart and inspect her, find out how she could function so contentedly with the way life had treated her. It was not an act. She was genuinely happy. I could see no bitterness in Martin or Bea, and it seemed an impossibility to be so serene—an act perhaps—but I discovered it was real. They were content—I was not.

Not long after this incident, Charles tried once again to encourage me on an evening canoe ride. "No, Charles," I said as I slipped breathlessly into my usual spot on the dock beside him. I stared at the canoe tied neatly to the pier nearby.

"You need to conquer your fear, Mattie," he counseled me. "Besides, don't you remember I have something I want you to see?"

"You know this is part of a bad experience," I pointed out. "Remember what happened when I gave in and took that canoe ride with you to the waterfall?"

"All the more reason to get back on the horse," he persisted. "Besides, I promised you I would not let any harm come to you. You trust me don't you?"

"Yes, but I don't trust *me*." I sighed. "I admit it. I am afraid now. I never used to be afraid of anything to do with the water. Now it haunts me."

"You need to replace that fear with little steps of good memories, Mattie. This, I promise you, will be a very good memory. It will help you. I won't let any harm come to you. Please?"

He was hard to resist. He said no more, just stared at me and waited patiently. Finally I sighed and said, "Okay, but if I panic and tip that thing over, you're gonna get very wet!"

"It won't happen." He smiled. "That's because I trust *you* more than you trust yourself. Now, wait till I get in and get positioned, then you just step off the dock and sit right there." He pointed to the forward seat in the canoe and smiled encouragingly again. "You don't even have to paddle, just sit back and relax and ride. I will do all the work. Just look how calm that water is this evening,"

I did as he said and climbed into the narrow craft and faced forward. I gripped both sides as if I were hanging over the edge of a skyscraper. My back was stiff, and I felt the old familiar fear start to roil in my stomach.

"Don't be afraid, Mattie." His voice consoled me as he pushed away from the pier. "Try to relax. I'm right here behind you. You are going to love what I want to show you. Think about that. Think about the beauty of the trees reflecting along the edge of the lake. Think about that beautiful eagle soaring over there on the right—isn't he majestic?"

His voice was calming, and he continued to talk to me, helping me to relax and see the things around us. He dipped the paddle rhythmically in the water and talked in a cadence to match. It was almost hypnotic. I could feel the tension leaving my body. A soft breeze caressed my face, and tendrils of hair blew around my features and tickled my neck. It was a perfect evening, and I began to relax and appreciate it.

Charles continued to paddle. Each soft splash propelled us along the edge of the lake as he continued his monologue. "The Ojibway see so much more than we do with our big boats and noisy motors," he informed me. "This is the best way to get truly close to the things God has created. Notice how quietly we slip through the water?" he asked me.

I nodded. It was amazing how undisturbed things were even as we moved through the water. We slipped silently past beautiful terrain on our way to Charles's destination. We rounded a rock-strewn point and came upon a moose. She dipped her antlerless head into the lake for a drink then lifted her elegant head as if catching a scent of us. Without a sound, and belying her huge size, she slipped back into the underbrush and disappeared instantly from sight. I thought I had spotted a small shadow next to her but could not be sure if it was a young calf. We floated quietly past the spot where she had reentered the forest.

"A bonus," Charles said softly. "But not what we are after. We are almost there, Mattie. Be very quiet."

I held my breath as his paddle slowed. We drifted quietly and came around a protruding tree branch that hung out over the water. More branches dripped along the edge providing a privacy screen of sorts for what lie just beyond. I caught a peek through a break in the leaves and was immediately entranced. Charles stilled the canoe at the edge of the dangling branches, where we remained in relative obscurity and watched.

The young otters played with abandon. Their black bodies gleamed with moisture as they slid down the watery playground to the lake. A natural slide was created by a small waterfall between two moss covered hillsides. It appeared to be a mama and babies who were having such fun. Zip, splash, slide, and then climb they went. They scampered back up the mossy sections where their feet could easily grasp the soft green lichen in order to climb.

Once they reached the top, they would shake the droplets of water off and scoot pell-mell down the waterfall and splash, *kerplunk*, into the pool of water at the bottom. I was frozen and mesmerized by their antics. Their fur was wet and shiny. The slide was mostly mud with a small amount of water from an offshoot of the main flow that supplied the majority of the waterfall. The mud attached itself to their fur but was cleaned off with each foamy splash at the bottom. They seemed never to tire of this game. Sometimes they rolled with each other and tumbled together to the bottom. Sometimes they skidded sideways and other times they went topsy-turvey.

It was an incredible show, and I viewed it in fascination. We watched together for about ten minutes when suddenly the high-pitched whistling shriek of an overhead eagle brought the antics to an end. At that sound, all the otters dashed immediately into the water. They disappeared like cotton candy when it touches your tongue, and we were left to see only a trickling waterfall where boundless activity had just taken place.

"Ooh. Thank you, Charles," I whispered.

"I had nothing to do with that," he answered. "I was an observer, just like you. It does remind me though of what a wonderful God we have who created all this for us to enjoy. Did you enjoy it?"

"You have to ask?" I smiled. "It was wonderful. Thank you." I looked down at my hands. They were now relaxed in my lap and no longer clenching the sides of the boat. "Thank you for helping me get back on the watery horse too." I laughed.

Charles laughed with gusto, his white smile contrasted with his now darkened skin from days working in the long sun. He looked at me as if I might melt and disappear, then began to paddle the canoe in a return path along the shore toward our camp.

We saw one other extraordinary thing on the way as we slipped along the edge: a family of mergansers perched on a long log that stretched out into the water. They were all females and their flame-red topknots looked gloriously on fire as the setting sun touched them with an additional orange burst of color. Their white breasts were tinged with the peachy sunset too. Miraculously they did not panic or fly away but stayed in place, which gave us a good view of their beauty as we quietly floated past them.

"Wow," was all I could say.

"I agree with that," chimed in Charles after we were well past them.

During the next few days I thought more about Bea and Martin and things Charles had said to me. I decided to capitulate a little. Perhaps I could read this book—this Bible they were all so sure about, to see if I could puzzle it all out. What was their secret to this contentedness with life? That night I began my search. It was waiting there, residing next to my bed, in the prominent place where it had always been, every night since I had arrived.

I opened the book I had been resisting for all this time. I was in the privacy of my room when I first delved into the mysteries I hoped I might find solved within these pages. Since I had fallen in love with the stories about Jesus the children had been taught on the flannel board, I determined I would go to the part of the Bible that told about Jesus and His life. I knew enough to turn to the New Testament. Each night, from that time on, I took the Bible from the nightstand next to my bed and began reading. I would fall asleep reading it.

Our work resumed. The sanctuary for the church was nearly completed, and a date for a dedication ceremony had been planned for August 17. My trip with Joel had begun the end of May. It was now early August. The community seemed elated they were finally to have a real church. They were delighted to have a building where they could have their services. Everyone pitched in and worked hard to meet the dedication deadline.

In the midst of all this activity, John Owen and his family came up missing. "He's done this before," said Bea, when I became frantic about the welfare of Red Bird and her mother, Mary, "so don't fret. He'll bring them back. They'll be all right. We must trust God."

I was growing weary of all this God talk. I was angry all over again. If God was to be trusted, then how could He allow this to happen now, when everything seemed to be going so right for Red Bird's family? I was also going to give John Owen a piece of my mind when he returned. I kept remembering that little face and those intent eyes of Red Bird's when I had first awoken here in this sanctuary. I had grown to love her.

Charles, who had invested much time and energy in John Owen, agreed with Bea. I wanted to send out a search party but Bea said (and Charles agreed), "We wouldn't know where to begin searching. They are familiar with this country and know how to fend for themselves. They will be all right. We must trust God." I couldn't help myself. I stared, accusingly, without speaking, at Charles.

Charles reciprocated and looked at me pointedly when I kept muttering about John Owen "falling off the wagon" in rather detrimental terms. But Charles didn't allow me an inch of anger. "We must all agree to pray for them," he said. I held my tongue but pouted for a while after that. Bea and Charles, to my disgust, continued to be serene about this disturbing situation.

Reluctantly, when I realized there was nothing in my power I could do to help my little friend, I succumbed to my worries and decided to try every avenue to help my loyal little admirer. Thus, in desperation, I too, turned to prayer. It was an awkward prayer; a request from someone who was not comfortable with talking to God, but it was from my heart.

I sat at the edge of the dock. My feet dangled over the water. I could see the dark reflection of trees along the shoreline. It rippled and wavered before me. I closed my eyes and the words came out in a whisper, "God, please let this turn out all right for Little Red Bird and her family. Please, please bring her back safely." I opened my eyes. I don't know what I expected, but nothing had changed. The scenery before me still showed trees reflected in the softly moving waters.

I felt a thump, thump of footsteps nearing then there was a thud on the dock as Charles plopped down beside me. "They'll be all right," he assured me. Somehow he knew Red Bird was in my thoughts. He added softly, "Things are often not what they seem. We must not judge John too harshly. It is not our place to be his judge."

I was torn. I admired how Charles, Bea, and everyone at the mission approached life. I wanted to emulate their serenity and strength and trust, yet the vengeful side of me wanted to strangle John Owen, and my mind kept trying to put him in the same category with Joel: people I would never forgive.

So, the battle within me raged on—but the dark side started to win whenever I thought of Little Red Bird out in the wilderness somewhere, away from her friends, her school, and her home. Away from me, who, I now admitted to myself, loved her very much.

The day of the dedication approached. Little Red Bird, sadly, was going to miss all the festivities. A special meal was being prepared. The children had been preparing skits and songs to perform for the church on the big day. The seats were finished and ready, the pulpit was almost completed, the structure was now weatherproof and the heating was functional.

Still, there was no sign of John Owen and his family. I looked toward their cabin first thing every morning when I awoke. I hoped I might see movement or smoke coming out the chimney. I continued to see nothing. It was as if they had vanished from our lives forever. I ached to see Little Red Bird again. I resolved to remain unforgiving.

Chapter 17

The day of the dedication dawned with a cheerful, bright sun and brilliant blue sky. A hint of the crisp fall weather, which was just around the corner, was felt in the nippy air that morning. I wore the sweater Bea gave me to keep the chill off my shoulders. It was the same soft blue of the sky, and Bea told me, "It matches your eyes."

The service was an inspiration to all of us. The children were flawless in their recitations and songs. The skit Mary Rose had them perform was comical, yet poignant too. Then Charles began speaking. A hush fell on the congregation, and we gave him our rapt attention. It was as if every word were being channeled directly from the heavens through Charles and straight into my heart where it pierced my armor. His words made me start to see things in a new and better light.

I sat riveted, and listened. During those moments I came to the understanding that God was asking me to make a choice, here and now. I was to choose Him and forgiveness or I was to choose revenge; but, I realized I could not have both in my life at the same time. Charles made his plea to the congregation, "Won't you come forward to publicly acknowledge Jesus as your Savior?"

It was addressed at large, but I knew the words he spoke were for me. I heard him clearly, yet I could not make myself move from my seat. It was as if there were two magnets tearing me apart. One pulled at me and urged me forward to become a Christian; the other magnetic thrust mesmerized me and told me to stay in my place. Indecision racked my mind. I sat as if paralyzed. My heart wanted to go forward, but my mind kept me seated.

The congregation sang softly, "Just as I Am," and I wanted nothing more at that moment than for the torture to end. I wanted both, but I felt as if I was being forced to choose, and I simply couldn't do it. I sat motionless and ambivalent. No one else had risen or gone forward either, and I did not want to make a spectacle of myself. I wondered if others were as torn as I was.

Suddenly, there was a commotion in the main aisle to the side and behind me. A whoosh of cool air came through the room. The audience stirred and turned in their seats to see what was causing the disturbance. I turned too. My eyes fastened on a scene that will always remain emblazoned in my memories.

I saw our missing John Owen stride—very erect and in control—down the aisle of the church. He marched with a big smile on his face to the front of the building. I saw an astounding sight when I looked behind the clear-eyed, totally sober John Owen, for behind him walked his proud wife, Mary. I watched in stupefaction as my little smiling sunbeam Red Bird walked—almost strutted—down the aisle behind John, with her mother. Mary and Red Bird carried a large package between them to the front of the church.

Mystified, we all watched as the trio approached Charles who stood behind a small handmade podium. It was obvious Charles was as surprised as the rest of us.

"What's the meaning of this, John?" he asked quietly, but gently. His face carried an almost comical puzzled look on it.

John, who seemed unfazed at the question, just smiled in reassurance toward Charles, assisted his wife and Red Bird to stand beside him, and then turned to face us.

"You all know what my life was like before I became a Christian," he said. Heads nodded. Faces held curiosity but no censure. He went on. "I admit it. I was a drunk; an alcoholic. I can't tell you how much it has changed my life to get the demons of drink out of it. My wife loves me more than ever, my daughter is proud of me again. I can hold my head up. My life is greatly improved and I know it is better for my family. I have only been able to do this with the help of God and the prayers of you, good people."

Here, he paused, and as he did so, I remembered my feeble attempts to pray for Red Bird and her family as I sat at the dock. John looked out at all of us with a direct, sober gaze, then gave Charles a quick glance where he stood beside the podium before he continued his story.

"When I heard about our church being dedicated today, I wanted to do something special for the occasion." Here he turned to Mary and Red Bird. "You may have wondered where we disappeared to, but we wanted this to be a surprise," he smiled at Red Bird and said, "didn't we?" She nodded shyly.

Red Bird knew it was her cue to speak. "My family went by canoe and sometimes walking, and sometimes we carried the canoe. We went all the way down to the City of Red Lake." The congregation gave a collective murmur of "ooh" and "aah" at this news. Undaunted, Red Bird continued her saga. "We picked up something in Red Lake we had specially ordered for this day. It was very f ... f"—here she stumbled over the word and looked to her mother who smiled and supplied the word for her: "fragile."

Red Bird went on, "Yes, fragile, and we had to carry it carefully to get it back in one piece."

Here all three members of the family focused on the mysterious package they had gone to such extreme efforts to bring to us. They carefully unwrapped, then removed, the plain brown paper. They soon had unveiled a small, but beautifully detailed stained glass window for the church. It was a gorgeous work of art—a composite of all things Christian. In the center and extending to all edges was a cross.

Red Bird explained it to us. "This cross is red glass to remind us of His blood shed for us." Four corner sections were created by the division of the cross and its leaded borders. Red Bird pointed to a white dove with wings spread made of an opalescent white glass. The area had a soft transparent blue background and was located in the top left corner. "This is how the Holy Spirit is, always waiting to visit and live in us." Next, she pointed to the lower, more elongated left space with a light green background. The symbol was created from light tan and brown glass with fingers separated by lead work. "These are two hands lifted in prayer to remind us always to pray."

I remembered my feeble prayers and Bea and Charles's steadfast trust and saw the result with my own eyes. I nodded as Red Bird continued her explanation of the exquisite piece. "Now …" She stepped to the other side and switched places with her father who was helping to hold the piece up for us. "In this corner we have a long white lily with green leaves. It is pure white because Jesus is pure and because we can be pure too. It will remind us our sins are forgiven and we must forgive others."

The lily was created from the same opalescent glowing glass as the dove. The graceful green leaves were made of dark and light shades of transparent green glass. The background behind the lily was a lovely contrasting blue.

"Now, the last corner, Red Bird," prompted her father.

"Okay." She grinned straight at me and my heart lurched. "This corner is a fish, but it is not any old fish. It is one of our fighting fish we all catch in Canada. This fish tells us we must be fishing for others as Jesus wanted us to, but we must fight hard to make it happen so we do not get lazy in doing this." The fish was a beautiful piece of glass: grey swirled with green and salmon pink colors. It was a striking design, poised in an arch as if erupting from the water. The background was a soft blue-green with a white splash designated just at the tail of the fish.

John held the piece up high so the light could gleam through it. There was a unified "oooh" of appreciation from the congregation as we all looked upon the lovely, thoughtful gift. How precious. I felt tears scorch the corners of my eyes. I could see that Charles, like me, felt extremely moved by this generous gesture.

John Owen spoke again. "We want to give this gift in respect to God. Also, my family wants to dedicate our lives to God today."

Charles smiled down at them and paused. I watched his eyes as they moved straight across the lectern, and searched the room until they connected with me. It felt as if two flaming arrows had been shot across the pews to my own eyes. The message was piercingly clear. *See Mattie, God has answered our prayers, far beyond what we could have expected. It's just like I told you. You also must trust Him now. Today is the day for you to choose. This is the right thing to do. Come out of the mud puddles, let Jesus save and cleanse you. Choose God, Mattie!*

Charles nodded down at the Owen family and said, "Let us sing 'Just as I Am' one more time. Anyone who wants to join this family in trusting Jesus and dedicating your life to God, please come forward now."

The congregation began singing, and then in a spontaneous move, one by one, they began leaving their seats. They continued to sing, but moved forward as if drawn by an irresistible force to the front of the church. Inexplicably, I felt myself also rising, rising and floating as if being lifted by invisible hands. I felt as if I went forward weightlessly, effortlessly. Hands reached out to me, and I joined the others, and soon I felt myself cry out with them. A great release took hold of me, and I found myself weeping along with many others.

I unleashed all my pent-up emotions. I felt surrounded by a warm aura of love and approval. I hugged Bea, who was there too; next I gave a hug to Mary Rose and Mary Owen. I found myself on my knees beside that precious child, Red Bird. My arms went around her, and she shyly returned that hug while I wept for joy. From my kneeling position my eyes were drawn toward Charles. I could see him beaming on all of us. His face appeared brilliant.

Charles looked up at the roof as if in a private conversation, then he turned that dazzling smile on me like a spotlight while tears streamed silently down his face. I felt purified and so completely healed from the blackness that had surrounded me. The energy of forgiveness surrounded me like a warm electric blanket. It was unlike anything I had ever experienced in my life. My first thoughts were of my father and how I wished he could have this same happiness.

Euphoria surrounded our little church that day. We were so happy to have the Owen family back and to know our fears—at least mine—had been for naught. I remembered how often Bea had told me, "Cast all your cares on Him," and knew now from personal experience just how right she was. A wonderful feeling of having done the right thing, of taking the first steps to mend my life pervaded me. My steps were lighter, my smile felt brighter. "I choose God," I said to myself over and over.

After the service had ended and almost everyone had departed, Bea and Charles and I were straightening things in the church. Bea and Charles spent some time counseling me. I realized I was in the care of good and wise people. "You are an infant," they said. "You must keep reading and learning in order to become a mature Christian. It does not happen overnight."

"There will be setbacks," Charles warned.

"And times of temptation," Bea added.

"When that happens, you must read your Bible. You need to remember that you are a Christian and now under the protection of Jesus and a league of angels." Charles, I knew, was remembering our conversation by the waterfall and preparing me to deal with it.

"You can always call on other Christians to pray with you, to give you support and help. We will be here for you always." Bea smiled and with a hug, added, "I can't wait to tell Martin about this. It's so wonderful."

Bea and I walked back to Bea's home, and I remained in a glow of well-being it is difficult to describe. As happy as I was, however, a momentary twinge of sadness swept over me in the midst of this joy, for I knew I must now tell them my story—all of it. I also knew that in the telling of that story, my position here would change. My relationships and friendships would be greatly altered—perhaps negatively.

Though I had not directly lied to them, I had lived a lie. I had allowed them to make assumptions about me that were not true. I had deceived them all about who I was. I knew this, yet I also knew an enormous burden was now removed from my life. I returned to my room and bid Bea good night and allowed my gratefulness to shine through as I said, "Thank you so much, Bea, for caring and instructing me."

"You are like one of my own children, Mattie. I am so happy for you … and you are very welcome!"

That night following Red Bird's return was the first night in a long time when I did not have nightmares. I slept a long, restful sleep and woke feeling refreshed and reborn. After that, life continued but the changes I felt taking place in me amazed me. My new attitude was a source of delight to me. I began to realize that the events that had occurred in my life had all been choices based on a life without God. I knew that finally I had made the most right choice of my life. I did not believe mere coincidence had sent me here to this mission.

Looking back, I could now see God's guidance had been drawing me to Him all along. That guidance explained why I had arrived in this place. The future was still unclear to me, but I knew now it would be far better and easier for me to deal with that future from my Christian perspective. Now I yearned to read and pray, so I spent many hours learning more about Christ and I hungrily devoured my Bible. Charles and Bea both smiled indulgently at my eagerness, remembering I suppose, how excited most new Christians are about their rebirth. They recognized how I might feel as if the experience had never happened to anyone else before me.

The following Wednesday, we took the children to the new church where we were going to be starting a weekly children's worship in the more spacious building. Charles came in just prior to the time we were to begin while I was ushering several other youngsters to their seats. I looked over at Charles and observed him as he swept a small, giggling child into the air, and thought, *What a wonderful father he would make.*

But I knew that even God couldn't fix the fact that I was already married. "You have a husband, Mattie," I reminded myself sternly. "Charles deserves the most wonderful girl in the world. And that is not you. No, that person is not you and that's that." I knew then that I needed to take some difficult actions, one of which was going to be forgiving Joel, and the other leaving this place and people I had come to love.

Chapter 18

I prayed about how to tell them my story. Should I tell Bea and ask her to tell Charles? Should I tell Charles and let him tell the others? *Could* I find the courage to tell Charles? I thought often about telling Charles, alone, at a time when we were sitting out at the end of the dock. I rejected that idea. Selfishly, I did not want to ruin what would be the most precious memories I would take from here. I wanted those times when we sat there together, laughing, talking, enjoying each other, to be inviolate.

I realized now how precious those times were to me, and I knew, too, just how much of myself I would be leaving behind. Yes, I was now reconciled to the fact I would be leaving this place, and a big part of my heart would be severed when that happened. I knew I would have to go back to face my old life. I hoped my friends here might see my side of the story and forgive rather than condemn my actions with them. I was risking that beautiful community I felt we all shared together should I share my past, but in my heart I knew the right thing to do was to return to my old life.

The days now passed like quickly eaten spoons of ice cream and melted as fast as that treat dissolves on one's tongue. Autumn was reaching in to color our lives and was anticipated by a new bite in the air. I stretched the hours left to me like a greedy child. Finally, the morning after a bitter frost left ice crusted everywhere, even decorating the edges of the lake, I could delay no longer.

I gathered my courage. I selected a date, a time, a place, and asked Bea, Mary Rose Ross, Bill Ross, John Crow, Alice Crow, the Pascals, the Loons, and Charles to come meet me in the school room as I had something important to tell them. I sat at the little table where I had worked so many hours with my students and waited for their arrival. I looked around the room with fondness. Nostalgia swept through me when I remembered it all. My audience arrived en masse right after dinner as I had asked. I was very nervous.

"I have something to tell you," I began with a catch in my voice. "It is about my life before I came here."

I could see their loving, kind, interested faces before me, and I nearly fled the room in fear of losing their approval, but I knew what had to be. I went on. "My name is not Mattie Hunt. My name is Mary Lynne Huntington-Carter. Mattie is a nickname my father gave me when I was a little girl. My parents were—are very wealthy people. The recent newspapers even called me an heiress." I could see I had their full attention now. I was not able to look at Charles as I told most of my story. I was fearful of disapproval or—worse.

I spent the next hour giving them all the details. I told them about my marriage to Joel and his ultimate betrayal. I described the poisoning. I explained the horror I had endured—the storm—and how I had nearly died in the rampaging water. I told them why the waterfall had affected and shocked me so much. Finally, as I described the end of my ordeal, how my feet had bled, how the lack of food had felt—the illness, and how I had ended up alone in the logging shack, I glanced at Charles. For perhaps the first time, I could not tell what he was thinking. His face was almost unreadable, his expression fixed on me as he gave me his attention. He appeared to be struggling with some strong emotion, but I could not recognize what it was.

The room was silent as I finished. They all stared at me. I knew my story was amazing. It still astounded me, and I had actually lived it.

"I have come to love all of you very much," I said, and tears welled in my eyes. "I hope you will forgive me for deceiving you about my past."

"Forgive *you!*" boomed Bill, who stood in agitation. "I want to find this Joel character and beat him to a pulp!" This outburst from our gentle Bill brought laughter to all of us and set the tone for the rest of the evening. They had many questions for me, and I produced the newspaper articles for them and showed them who I was. We talked about how much my father must have missed me, and we decided that our radio would be used to get word to my father that I was alive and well.

I would no longer need the secret code word having sent two prior missives to assure my father. Bill suggested that we might even be able to set up a direct communication through a ham operator in St. Louis so my dad and I could talk for a few moments and in order to make arrangements for him to come and retrieve me. "I do have to go home and straighten out my life," I pointed out to them. "I hope you all understand." I turned to say something to Charles, but he was gone from the room.

My heart felt a sharp and devastating loss. I seemed to be the only one who noticed his disappearance from the little schoolroom, so I turned quickly back to the others and tried to hide the tears that threatened. "I hope you can help me plan a course of action."

I pulled myself together as much as I could while we continued to discuss the situation in which I found myself. We agreed that I would need to be careful. My life was still in danger. Nothing had changed in that regard. I should not place myself in jeopardy, but I must return and straighten out the situation as best I could. My frequent glances toward the door were unfruitful. Charles did not return.

"What about the police or the Canadian Mounties?" asked John Crow. "Do we need to contact them?"

"Police on both sides of the border were involved in the original searches, according to what it says in these newspapers," said Mary Rose, setting the old newspapers aside. "They also should be told that you are safe."

"I think it would be wisest to let her father notify the officials since we don't know if Joel is still in the area, living in her apartment, or if he took her money and ran," said Bea. "For that reason, I say no contact with the police unless her father suggests it. The poor man has been through enough. He will have some ideas on protecting Mattie, I'm sure."

The consensus was that I should place myself under my father's protection, and then do what was necessary to eliminate the temptation for Joel to kill me for my money. "It isn't likely that he will do anything more, once it is known what has happened already," Bill said. "But I think you should do what you can to eliminate the temptation entirely."

Bea and Mary Rose agreed. They all hugged me fiercely and assured me that I was forgiven for misleading them; and, more importantly, that they still loved me. No one but me seemed to notice the continued absence of Charles. I, on the other hand, was acutely aware of his disappearance.

He remained invisible. I did not see Charles in any of our usual meeting places, or anywhere at all, for that matter. This continued the entire next day. He remained out of my sight the day after that as well. Otherwise, life settled back into the old routine. Meanwhile, a radio message about me and my safety was relayed to my father with a warning not to share this information with anyone else. A time was scheduled quickly after that for me to talk directly to my father.

When that time finally came, I started the long overdue conversation with, "Daddy?" as my voice quavered.

"Oh, Mattie, is that you? Are you all right? Talk to me!"

"I am just fine now, Daddy. These wonderful people saved my life. I will explain it all when I can see you in person. When can you come and get me?"

"I will be there tomorrow if someone can give me directions to your location," he promised.

"I will let you talk with Bill Ross, Daddy. He can tell you where we are and how to get here." I paused, and then added, "I love you, Daddy. I am so happy to hear your voice. Here is Bill."

"I love you too, sweetheart," my father's normally strong voice cracked. "Bill Ross is it?"

I handed the microphone back to Bill. "Yes, sir, this is Bill Ross."

The two of them talked. Instructions were communicated, and arrangements were made. If all things worked out, Mitchell Huntington would arrive by floatplane the very next day. Knowing my father, I was quite sure this difficult task of crossing international borders, obtaining a floatplane and a pilot, and finding me, would happen without fail.

The change in my life was now activated. Everyone at the mission was excited about this arrival, especially me. I longed to be in my father's warm embrace again. It was a bittersweet feeling because my future looked as if a piece of me would be missing.

In all this time, I still had not seen Charles. I went—and waited, but he did not even appear at our customary meeting spot at the dock in the evening. I missed his companionship greatly, but I did not find fault with him for avoiding me. He was an honorable man and I had misled him, or at the least had held back information that might have made a difference. I was afraid to admit to myself how much I was going to miss him.

Finally, that very evening after the early morning contact with my father, I went out to sit on the dock one last time, despairing of ever seeing Charles again. As I sat there and watched the sunset, I realized I needed his personal forgiveness very much. I was in a melancholy and lonely mood as I gazed across the water. I knew my future was going to be very difficult. I felt wrenched in half at leaving this beautiful place and the people who had come to mean so much to me.

"We will send you a photo of the snow," Charles said and he quietly dropped his athletic frame lightly into place next to me.

I noticed he had said the corporate "we" not "I" and understood what he was telling me.

"Yes," I said softly. "I would like that very much. Thank you."

"Red Bird will miss you. We will all miss you," he replied, still using the blanket "we."

"Am I forgiven then?" I squeaked out from a painful place inside me.

"You have to ask that?" he said tersely, and before I could respond, he went on, his voice calm and thoughtful. "Of course you are forgiven. I certainly understand the ordeal you've been through and why you would wish to keep your identity secret. Besides, even if I were angry—which I am not—I could never stay angry with you, Mattie. You know I wish you the most happiness."

"You do?"

"Yes. I wish it very much."

"Thank you. That means a lot to me, Charles." I paused. "I don't know what it will be like when I return to the States," I pondered with my head averted. "In many ways I am very frightened. My father will want to kill Joel, or at the very least put the authorities in charge of arresting him." I tried to memorize the current moments, here at the dock. I wanted to savor the smells, the sights, the nearness of ... I would not allow myself to continue that thought.

"And you?" the voice at my shoulder prompted me.

"I think you know very well that I've spent many hours planning a rather evil revenge on Joel. I was going to hate him forever."

"And now?"

"And now, thanks to you, I've become a Christian."

"You make it sound like a punishment." He laughed softly. My heart ached and I tried to memorize the sound of his laughter to take with me.

"If so, it has been a very wonderful punishment," I said earnestly and carefully while I looked out at the glistening water. "I will find it very difficult to forgive Joel. I have already told God I am going to try, but I do not know how it will be for me when I finally face him—if he can be found. My father did not tell me if he is still in St. Louis or long gone."

"Forgiving him will be separate from having the authorities arrest him. You understand that don't you?" Charles voice sounded protective.

"Yes, I understand. You have been an excellent teacher, and I will miss these times with you, Charles. They have meant a great deal to me." I needed to see him, so I turned to face him this last time. "You have been an unbelievably good friend."

He too, was staring at the water, his profile strong against the waning light. He sensed my stare and slowly turned to look at me. His eyes penetrated mine with unspoken meanings. His steady hazel gaze stayed strong and unwavering, and he answered me with, "You've been a good friend too, Mattie. Please keep in touch with us through Bea will you? Everyone will want to know things are going well for you."

He paused as if about to say something more then changed his mind and said instead, "Remember, you will always be in our prayers." He touched me lightly on the shoulder, so lightly I almost mistook it for the breeze, then he jumped to his feet and looked down at me with an expression I could not read on his face—was it pain? I could not tell.

"God bless, Mattie."

"God bless you also, Charles." I felt an odd sense of relief that he had not said "good-bye." And he was gone.

The next day was a whirlwind of activity. I was so anxious to see my father again it was hard to contain myself. I kept doing the same little tasks, like straightening the pillows, and smoothing the quilt on the bed, then wiping down the kitchen counter and sweeping the floor, repeatedly in nervous agitation. I suspect Bea laughed at how often I needed to check the clock in anticipation of the arrival of the plane. At last, the agonizingly slow clock chimed the time the plane should be arriving. Bea, me and nearly everyone, except Charles, gathered at the dock when the floatplane finally arrived and touched down out in the lake.

The big Norseman floatplane from Red Lake taxied slowly up to where we stood. I thought it would never get up to the dock. A tie-down was quickly attached, and the boat/plane was pulled up snug to the pier. The propellers were still turning when the door was flung open and out jumped not only my father, but also Eleanor!

I was surprised at first to see my stepmother reunited and arriving with my father, but when I saw them arm in arm, I was ecstatic to see them both. All my past reservations disappeared. I flung my arms around each of them in turn. I cried and kissed them on the cheek, then hugged them each again. My father had giant-sized tears in his eyes and brushed them briskly away, like the no-nonsense man he pretended to be. Eleanor let her tears fall unashamedly.

"But Eleanor, what are you doing here?" I asked. Then, realizing how that sounded, I blushed and began stammering, "Not that I'm not happy to see you, I am I am—it's just that—"

"It's okay, Mattie, I understand." She smiled at me. "It's just that—I." she turned to my father helplessly.

"Mattie, I have so many things to tell you," my father explained hurriedly, "One of which, I hope you will approve, is that Eleanor and I are remarried."

"Married?" I laughed. "But this is wonderful! I'm so happy for you both." I loved the whole idea. It felt so right this time.

My father looked relieved, and Eleanor clasped my hand in hers lovingly. She smiled at me, then turned to my father and said, "See Mitch, I told you there was nothing to worry about. I knew Mattie would be happy for us."

I squeezed her hand back and kissed her again, fondly, on the cheek. "You are absolutely right about that," I said. "It's some of the best news you could bring me." I paused, and then decided it was time to put my new Christianity into practice. I would try to tell the truth. "You'll never know, Eleanor," I confided, "just how much I missed you when you left. I'm so sorry I never told you."

"Well, we're going to make up for all that when we get back, aren't we?" She smiled, ever the gracious lady I had come to know. "We all make mistakes. Now that God has given us a second chance, I don't want to muff it." The three of us smiled in agreement.

"We had to practically tie Blanche down to keep her from coming with us," said my dad, "but she is getting older, and I was afraid the excitement of the trip and her joy at seeing you all at the same time, would be too much for her."

"I convinced her that we needed someone to get everything ready for your homecoming, so she's probably turned the house inside out by now." Eleanor smiled. "And, her other requirement was that I had to promise to get you home by the fastest possible means."

Suddenly, I realized that everyone in our mission, all the adults and children, were standing patiently, listening to every word, while they waited to meet my family.

"Oh, goodness, forgive my manners! Daddy, Eleanor, I want you to meet everyone. Oh, Daddy, you can't believe how wonderful they have all been to me! They saved my life and so much more," I gushed.

Introductions were made all around, and of course, I had to give them a tour and an explanation of what all we did there. They fell in love with Little Red Bird who presented Eleanor with some of her precious pebbles.

We walked around the school building and toward the church when we encountered Charles doing repair work on some of the school benches. He quickly stopped and smiled up at us as we encouraged him to walk over and show us his new church.

"Charles has made tremendous inroads since he's been here," I bubbled proudly. "He's not afraid to pitch in and get his elbows dirty, as you can see." I laughingly pointed to the grease he had just acquired on his bench project. Charles just smiled, not at all embarrassed, brushed off his sleeves, and proceeded to give us a tour of the church. He was not as relaxed around me as was his normal bearing, but he was gracious and friendly to both Eleanor and my father.

I began explaining the symbolism behind the stained glass window, and I could feel Charles's eyes on me, but when I turned toward him, he quickly turned his gaze on my father. I could tell my father was impressed with him. Eleanor liked him too. We all walked closer to better examine the stained glass window from the Owen family, now prominently displayed and installed in the wall where the sun could shine through and send beams of color into the sanctuary.

As we shared the story of their journey through the treacherous bush country to deliver their precious gift, Charles seemed to relax around me a little more. I was aching inside at losing that sense of closeness we had shared during my time here. Eventually, Charles excused himself to "attend to some of my other duties," and as he left, one quick, last look was made between us. I could see the contemplation in each of their faces as my father and Eleanor exchanged glances. They looked at me searchingly but it was more than I could stand.

"Come," I said firmly, "let's return to Bea's home to pick up my belongings." They didn't challenge me, but I could see the speculation sparkling in both their eyes. Their unasked questions remained unanswered, and all too soon it was time for us to depart. Everyone gathered at the dock to see us off.

"Don't forget to write!" commanded Bea.

"I'll write often," I promised.

"We'll write back," Mary Rose pledged.

Red Bird presented me a small booklet decorated with native dried flowers. In the book she had written down all her numbers. They were in exact order and written to perfection.

We hugged and kissed, then said good-bye. There were tears in many eyes, including mine, and promises to write often. A mood of melancholy swept over me, and I fancied I could sense it also in many of the friends I would leave behind here.

Finally, we were on board the aircraft, and the pilot was about to taxi away. Once I was aboard and in my seat, I glanced out the window for one last look. As I did so, I saw Charles standing behind Bea, with his eyes focused on my face. For one brief flash of time, I thought I saw an expression of deep pain flare in his eyes. That look changed so quickly that I thought I must have imagined it, because it was gone as soon as it appeared.

Charles waved along with everyone else. I waved and they all waved back, but it was now a blur through my misty tears. We taxied out on the water and in a little while, the craft, clumsy in the water, transformed into a graceful bird as we lifted away from the lake. We became airborne and headed for home.

Chapter 19

After lifting us into the air over the mission, our floatplane took us south. The noise of the engine and the placement of the seats precluded conversation. I appreciated the time alone with my reminiscences. I was thoughtful as I watched the emerald green and topaz blue bejeweled Province of Ontario glitter beneath our wings. How could such gorgeous country house such danger? I had seen it placid and safe. I had seen it turn almost instantly into a life-threatening wall of raging water. Yet, I had grown to love it—and respect it.

We flew into Red Lake, Ontario, and then slid to a watery landing on their vast lake where a hundred years ago the voyageurs of the Hudson Bay Company plied their fur trapping trade and where much of that atmosphere still exists. Our craft taxied up to a shoreline where a cozy little city nestled against the hills. We could see that the citizens of Red Lake owned a spectacular view that looked out over the water.

My ever competent and industrious father had arranged for us to transfer to a small private jet that would depart from the Red Lake airport. Red Lake not only had the water for a floatplane airport, but it also had a land-based airport built on top of one of the city's beautiful hills. From here, the jet would provide a way to get us back home to St. Louis with a minimum of fuss at the US Customs office, since I no longer had a passport to show. My father, as always, accomplished what seemed to be impossible.

A waiting crew quickly shifted our gear to the jet, and we were soon airborne. It was on that flight when I finally told my father and

Eleanor the entire saga and the ordeal I had been through because of Joel. I could see my father clench and unclench his fist as I went through all that had happened to me. His eyes glistened when I explained how I used my Scout training and rings to form the diamond bait and feed myself.

They extolled my ingenuity. Daddy controlled his anger when I talked about the storm and how I had made it across the lake only to be thrown ashore by the raging waves. Eleanor's eyes were sympathetic pools. I knew he had every right to say, "I told you so," but my father had no recriminations to offer me.

I ended my story with, "One positive aspect of all this, is the time I spent at the mission with the Ojibway Indians and the missionaries. I have a wonderful new outlook on life because of my experiences and living with those people in Canada." I stopped and looked across at both Eleanor and then my father. I plunged ahead, unsure of their response. "Daddy, Eleanor—I want both of you to know: I've committed my life to Christ." I don't know what I was expecting, but it wasn't silence. I repeated myself. "I became a Christian while in Canada."

"You *what?*" My father sounded stunned.

I tensed, having expected a reaction but not what sounded like disapproval. I quickly defended myself, "I realize now that my life was somewhat shallow before all this happened. It wasn't a bad life, but it held no meaning. Daddy, I don't want to go back to that same existence. I hope you will understand. I want to do something with my life from now on." I looked at my father with hope. "I have found something wonderful, Daddy. I hope you will let me tell you about it because I want it for you too."

Rather than the disapproval I was expecting, my father and Eleanor suddenly looked at each other with something like wonder surfacing on both their faces.

"This is incredible!" my father said.

"It's just marvelous!" Eleanor enthused at almost the same time, her eyes brilliant. I watched them look at one another, and then they burst out laughing. I frowned, puzzled at their odd behavior, certain they were now making fun of me.

"Oh, darling, we're not laughing at you." Eleanor chuckled as she saw my face. She rose and quickly hugged me and then clutched my hands. "But at the circumstances." She looked at my father with a grin and said, "You tell her, Mitch."

"Tell me what?"

"I guess I'd better start at the beginning," Daddy said, settling back in his seat, a satisfied look on his face. "Mattie, when you disappeared, my world tumbled down about me. I realized that nothing I had gained all these years by being so involved in my work meant anything at all to me when I considered the loss of you and your love," he sighed and looked fondly at Eleanor, "and the love of others in my life. I was devastated at the thought of losing you. You knew Eleanor and I had amicably divorced and yet still remained friends?"

I nodded.

"Well, when the news hit all the newspapers about you, and the FBI came to interview me, I called Eleanor." He smiled at Eleanor.

"I was devastated that you were missing." Eleanor shuddered.

"She came over right away and stayed here by my side, lending her support. I couldn't have made it through the ordeal of not knowing whether you were alive or dead, without Eleanor." He patted her hand. "When things looked their very darkest, when they found your belongings but not you, I nearly went crazy. Eleanor wouldn't let me give up, nor give in to despair. She made me pray for your safety."

Eleanor picked up the story. "I guess I should interject some facts for you, Mattie. This probably seems rather incredible to you, but knowing the Lord, we should expect nothing less than the incredible. After your dad and I divorced, I went through rough times and soul-searching, but I found no answers. A couple of years ago a friend encouraged me to go to her church one Sunday. I went, and I went again, then again. Soon it was a regular thing and before long I found myself, like you, becoming a Christian." She smiled into my eyes. I smiled back with a silent prayer of thankfulness as she continued.

"It made such a difference in my life, Mattie, just as you are saying it has for you. I felt that the major mistake I had made in my past was in divorcing Mitch. I started praying God would give me an opportunity to renew my vows with your father and to make things right. I had always loved both you and your father; but I had been too impatient to allow both of you to develop in your feelings for me.

"At any rate, I was distraught, along with your father over your alleged drowning in Canada. I just couldn't let Mitch give up. Call it intuition, call it God speaking to my heart, but I felt that we should not give up hope that you would be found safely."

Dad resumed the story. "Eleanor practically picked me up and carried me to church with her. But once there, I realized it was exactly where I belonged. Her faith that God would deliver you safely was so strong, that I began to believe too. She was right." He chuckled. "Here you are!"

Eleanor laughed—a wonderful tinkling sound—that warmed my heart. She continued their story. "I trusted the Lord, Mattie, but your father left out the part where we both went forward to dedicate our lives to God, and then the very special part where we asked our preacher to marry us again!" I loved the way they kept looking at each other. My father was committed to make this work, I could tell. I loved the way Eleanor was glowing.

My father took up their story. "It was right after the dedication we made, Mattie, that we received your code letter. When I saw 'Nis-noc-si' and knew you were still alive and okay …" He faltered as tears welled up in his grey-blue eyes and threatened to pour down the wrinkles now sprinkled around the edges. Eleanor patted his hand while he composed himself and went on.

"That note from you was inspired, Mattie, and—and an answer to my prayers. I'll never forget how—" My stalwart father struggled with the strong emotions filling his face and groped blindly for Eleanor who grasped his hand. All three of us became too touched to speak. My faith was strengthened through their story. I could see the hand of God moving wisely to bring us into His fold.

Eleanor struggled with us but gained her composure first and continued to tell me about their experiences. "When we were on the way to pick you up, your father and I were praying that we would be able to introduce you to the Christian way of life. That we would be allowed to show you the ways we had learned and lead you to the Father we had come to honor and love. That's why we were laughing. God had already answered our prayers before we even prayed them!"

I remembered my former worries over Little Red Bird, and I remembered how God had been in control of that situation all along. I knew firsthand what she was talking about. I was beginning to understand most vividly how we had a God who was concerned with every detail of our lives and in whom we could trust every aspect of our lives. My father became more serious.

"There's still the matter of how to deal with Joel. Can I assume, Mattie, you'll come home and stay with us where you'll be safe? There's also the matter of notifying the authorities. We want to approach this very wisely and carefully."

"Yes," I said and nodded, "home. That's exactly where I want to go." I thought a few moments and said a silent prayer for strength, and then broached the difficult subject. I asked, "What did Joel tell you when he came back without me, Daddy?"

"First he called from Canada saying your boat had capsized and that he had tried in vain to dive and find you, but you never surfaced. Supposedly the water was too murky for him to find you."

"The boat capsized on a bright, sunny day with smooth water? Did anyone question that?"

"Yes, I did. I had checked with the authorities regarding the weather conditions that were as you said. When I challenged Joel about this, he said you had a big fish on your fishing rod and were fighting it, that you stood up and you were drawn off-balance by the fish, which caused the boat to tip over and take you with it. He claimed that he fell into the water as well and was able to swim to shore."

"All lies." I couldn't keep the bitterness from showing.

"I flew there immediately and arranged for a massive air and water search for you. We searched a long time and scoured the area Joel pointed out. The overturned boat and some of your belongings were eventually found, but no sign of you ever turned up. It was agonizing, especially since I suspected Joel was not being truthful about all of it."

"I heard the air search, Daddy, but it was far from the island where Joel left me." I remembered how helpless I had felt when I could not notify the planes where to find me.

"I'm so sorry you had to go through this, Mattie." Regret and guilt filled my father's voice.

"It wasn't your fault. I insisted on marrying him, remember? But that is enough about the past, daddy. Have you had contact with Joel since all this happened, Daddy?"

"Mattie, do you remember the documents I had you sign right before you and Joel married? You didn't pay much attention to them at the time, except for the prenuptial papers that were also in that stack. Those are the ones you made me promise not to approach Joel about, remember?"

"I do remember. George had me sign some about the trust fund I inherited from my mother, which I did, then I found out you had also added a prenuptial agreement, and I became so angry. I remember I made you promise not to tell Joel about it or make him sign it."

"I complied with your wishes about the prenup," my father spoke softly, "but those other papers you signed were also to further protect your inheritance."

"I didn't pay much attention to them," I recalled.

"That's right. Well, Mattie, those documents were carefully crafted by George. He told you before you signed them that they would protect the inheritance you received from your mother, yet would let you use as much of it as you needed, when you needed it. You brushed them off in your hurry to convince us to give your marriage our blessing, remember?"

"I do remember being more focused on marrying Joel. That's right. How stupid I w—"

"There is no need for remorse over past mistakes," my father interrupted me gently. "But what I am trying to tell you is that those other documents, in effect, stated that it would allow you, and no one else, not even me, to touch the money in that trust. They stated that if anything happened to you, and you had no children, everything would go to charity."

"Oh."

"They had your signature, and George and I both witnessed the documents."

"I see."

"When Joel discovered that those documents existed and that the majority of your money would be held in a trust and given to charity rather than to him, he nearly went crazy. He stormed out of my attorney's office and slammed the door so hard the wall shook. He disappeared after that, Mattie. He took your car, your furniture, anything he could turn into a quick dollar and sold it off. He never showed up at work again, which was very good because I was planning to have him fired for nonperformance.

"I haven't seen him since—not that I've searched very hard." He leaned forward, hands on his knees and looked at me earnestly. "Mattie, I need your forgiveness. I knew you didn't fully understand those documents I had you sign. You were too anxious to marry Joel. If he had known about them, you would have been far safer. Mattie, I'm so sorry. I'd have given him every cent you and I both have if it meant keeping you safe."

"I know that. You were protecting me. I understand. So you have not seen Joel since then?"

"No, but we did receive a challenge and a lawsuit from an attorney who claims to represent Joel. This attorney has threatened to prove in court that Joel should inherit it all. That has gone nowhere thus far, and our strategy was to prolong things and drag it out as long as possible and hope his attorney would quit once Joel's funds to pay his fees ran out. We predicted that once this attorney realized there would be little or no chance of attorney's fees from winning the case, he would quit pursuing it. Thus far, your funds have remained safely inviolate. Now that we can show you are alive, it will all revert to you again."

So, Joel had discovered to his dismay he would have been better off keeping me alive! What a twist of fate! Or was it God working again? I could see the agony and remorse in my father's eyes. "No, no, Daddy. I won't allow you to feel badly about this. I made the choice to marry Joel, not you. In fact, you need to remember how hard you tried to talk me out of the wedding with Joel. You have no blame here at all. None. I won't have it.

"Think about it, Daddy, our marriage was just awful. It was all a farce. He never really loved me or none of this would have happened. If Joel had known the only way to get control of my money was for me to hand it over and change your document, he would have made my life more miserable than it was. His feelings were all a sham. This way, I found out his true feelings, and I learned a lot about myself as well. It is better this way."

"Mattie, I want to thank you for agreeing to come home with us. I do believe you will be safer at home with Eleanor and me. I've already taken extra precautions for your security. If Joel discovers you are still alive, he will know that you can access your own money. He may then try something to force you to give it over to him since you are still legally married. I need some time to confer with our lawyers about what is best to do in this situation. Would you agree to stay within the confines of home for a while until we get this sorted out?"

"Yes, I agree to this. It sounds like the best way to handle things for now."

"You need to think about filing a complaint and having him arrested, Mattie. What he did to you is inexcusable and should be punished by the authorities. You need to remember that we are also bound by the laws of the land in which we live as well as those of Canada where the crime actually happened. Everything he did against you was illegal. You need to be thinking about prosecution."

"I will."

"I think we all need to pray about this situation with Joel," suggested Eleanor. "It seems to be beyond our human control and we need not only our lawyers' advice, but the wisdom that comes from God as well."

Daddy and I both looked at the beautiful, wise, woman sitting with us on the plane and said, almost simultaneously, "You are absolutely right."

It was wonderful being home. Blanche smothered me with food and attention from the moment I stepped through the door. My old room looked as though I had never left it. Blanche was standing nearby as I carefully lifted out the Bible Bea had given me and placed it reverently on the nightstand next to my bed. She looked at me questioningly. "You readin' that Good Book, Mattie?"

"Yes, Blanche, I am. And you are right, it is a *good* Book."

"Hallelujah! My prayers are answered," she beamed, and then hugged me fiercely. "I've been praying for this family since I first came here and finally, finally it's all happening." She put her hands on her hips and tried unsuccessfully to glower at me, "And it's high time!"

I laughed at her and hugged her back.

"I hope it doesn't take as long for *my* prayer to get answered," I said mysteriously.

"What prayer is that?" she questioned me.

"The one in which I ask for some of Blanche's homemade noodles at dinnertime!" I grinned at this loyal and lovable surrogate grandma.

"Just you wait, missy. See what you get for dinner!" she countered.

I walked over and planted a big kiss on her cheek. And thus we settled back into being a family again, and I was enveloped back into the household as if I had never left it. My first call was to Josie. She was at the house in what seemed like two seconds.

"You looking for a speeding ticket?" I teased her as I hugged my dear friend fiercely.

"I would gladly pay it to have you back!" She hugged me till I thought my ribs would crack.

We had a wonderful visit, and I spent a long time telling her about what I now called my adventure. I scurried quickly through the bad parts and spent most of my time sharing with her my newfound faith and the wonderful things the mission was doing with the Ojibway. Of course, I shared my love for all of them, and she was captivated by everything I told her about Little Red Bird. She decided to start a support group that would send supplies and help to the mission, and I thanked her for that help.

Josie did not let me avoid talk about Joel for long, and soon had all the details and the entire story out of me. We took our friendship back up just like it had never had a separation. She was a staunch friend, and I treasured her more than ever.

We did contact the authorities in Canada and the United States. I was interviewed about the ordeal and gave them as much information as possible. They began a search for Joel but warned me that it could take years to find him and that this could be a difficult case to prosecute even though they were certain I was telling the truth. It would boil down to my word against his word.

"A confession, when we find him, would be the best way to work this," said one agent. "Meantime, we will do our best to see if we can find the guy," added his partner.

Life took on a certain routine after that. I attended church with Eleanor and my father and occasionally Josie or Blanche, who were members at another church. We would sometimes attend with them, and they with us. Fall weather was nearly over now, the dark skeletons had shed most of their leaves, and snow was starting to be mentioned on the weather reports for our area.

I found that Eleanor was very active in several charitable endeavors. One project included assistance to a small inner-city church that was struggling to meet the needs of their members. There were a large number of families with young children who needed tutoring. I began spending much of my time working with these children. Many of them were about the same age as Little Red Bird. I would remember her fondly with nostalgia and wonder how she was faring back in Canada and if they were having a lot of snow. Many of these children, like Red Bird, had alcoholic or abusive or absent parents.

I became acquainted with the pastor and his wife who lived in a small home behind the inner-city church. They had the same zeal as Bea, Martin, and the others. The wife's name was Margaret, and everyone called her husband, Mark, "Pastor Lewis." I learned they had two children, both away at Christian colleges. I liked them both for their dedication to the students.

One day I was working with Roberto, a charming little six-year-old boy who was behind the others in his schoolwork, when Margaret Lewis approached with a tall stranger in tow.

"Mattie, I'd like you to meet Douglas Culbertson," she said.

I found myself looking up at a friendly face where two bright hazel eyes peered out at me from under bushy brown eyebrows. The same texture of bush had created the moustache that protruded somewhat haphazardly above a smiling pair of lips. A similar mop of sienna brown adorned his head and spilled down over his ears in spiked tufts—to the dismay, I am sure, of any neat and tidy barber.

He stuck out his hand with a friendly smile. "Call me Doug," he said.

I found my hand enveloped in a warm, large paw where it seemed to nestle quite securely. "Hello, Doug. My name is Mattie Huntington." I reciprocated the smile.

Margaret said, "Doug is a local doctor, Mattie. He's been in practice here for a couple of years. He's volunteered to provide free medical services to our children. I told him you work with the children a lot and could fill him in on any potential physical problems that may need his help."

"I'll be coming in one day a week to examine the children and offer medical advice to their parents. I hope to educate some of the parents in things they can do to prevent illness in their homes." He winked at me with a friendly grin and went on with, "In fact, I may find a need to come over more often than that, now that I've met Mattie."

"Now Doug, don't go trying to impress Mattie with your blarney," said Margaret, "she's far too sensible."

Doug and I became quite good friends. I liked the way he genuinely cared about the people in the community. The children loved him too. He had an engaging way with them and quickly gained their trust and confidence. We developed the habit of sitting over a cup of coffee after he'd seen all his patients on his weekly visits. We talked about the children, and I pointed out things I had noticed while working with them. Doug was open and friendly, and I found myself telling him about my disastrous marriage and my experiences in Canada.

"What an incredible story!" He shook his head in wonderment and went on, "Since you didn't wear a wedding ring, I had assumed you were single, like me. Now I know your ring is inside some fish!"

We laughed together, and it was nice to find something in the ordeal that was now laughable. As I found more opportunities to be able to laugh and joke about some of my experiences, I realized I had developed in the areas of maturity and inner confidence. It felt good to know I was making improvements in myself. "It's a little hard to believe, I know," I told him, "but that's exactly how my ring disappeared. I haven't felt very married since it happened, and I have no knowledge of the whereabouts of my husband, so I simply haven't bothered to wear another ring."

"You have no clue as to where he is?"

"No. The police have been hunting him for quite a while, and we did hire a private detective to go in search of Joel just last week," I informed him soberly, "but so far he has turned up nothing on Joel's whereabouts."

"What will you do when he is found? Have him arrested?"

"I honestly don't know. I'm taking it one day at a time and trying my hardest to trust in God. I pray it will all work out and that I will know the right thing to do when—and if—we find Joel."

I continued to have pleasant chats with Doug on his visits, and my work with the children continued to make good progress. I was surprised to look out my window one morning and realize that the winter season had arrived. The leaves were long gone from the trees, and the wind had turned chilly. It was very near Christmas, and we still had received no information that would lead us to Joel. I received a letter from Bea. My hands trembled as I opened it. I read:

Dear Mattie,

We received your early Christmas gift. Everyone here is shouting "Hallelujah," and now we can sing it too, thanks to you and the lovely, wonderful, exquisite piano! Can I find enough adjectives to describe it? No! Can we ever thank you enough for this lovely donation to our church? No! The only thing we would like better would be if our Mattie were here to play it for us. Red Bird has decided she will learn to play the piano, "so I can show Miss Mattie when she comes back," she says.

Our weather has turned cold and we have had plenty of snow. The lake is now frozen. It's solid enough for snow machines to traverse and bring our supplies, which is how we received delivery of your lovely gift. We received another package too, one ordered by Charles as a surprise, for the school to use. It's a new Polaroid camera with an ample supply of instant film. Charles wanted you to have a picture of Canada in the snow. I've included some of our first attempts for you. Charles has become quite proficient in the use of cross-country snow skis and seems to be tramping about someplace new nearly every day. He has encouraged some new attendance at our church during his ski travels.

Mattie, I can never thank you enough for the generous gifts from you and your father. Please tell your friend Josie that her school supplies have been welcomed too.

Dear Mattie, your generous gifts have made it possible for my husband, Martin, to retire from his government job and devote all his time to our mission. We've always needed his monetary support in order to keep going, and though I missed him desperately when he was gone, it was one of the only ways we knew to keep us in the black on our funding. Thank you so much for your generosity and the fund you've set up to help our cause as an ongoing endowment. You've made an old woman very happy.

Love, Bea.

Enclosed were several snapshots. I smiled back at Red Bird's big grin with a gap where one of her teeth had fallen out. She was proudly holding the tooth out toward me as if it were a trophy she had won in a tooth-pulling contest. I admired the snapshot of our mission taken from the dock. Smoke was pouring out all the chimneys, and snow appeared, piled up in huge drifts all around the buildings. The massive, towering evergreens in the background were laden with snow too, their branches bent under the weight. It was inviting. It was beautiful. It brought a pang to my heart.

I looked for a long time at a snapshot of Charles. It was obviously taken when he was unaware he was being photographed. He was in a bent position and stood near the school. A light from the nearby window shone down on his head like a beacon, where his dusky silhouette was in the process of fastening his skis. I didn't think he had on enough protection from the cold. I wanted to write and tell him to bundle up more warmly. I wanted to tell him to be careful and not to have an injury while on the skis, but I had no right to tell him anything at all.

I carefully took the photos and handled them gently. A few days later, I framed each photo and stood them, one by one, on my vanity where I could see them on waking and as the last thing before I went to sleep each night.

Every night I prayed to God and asked Him to bless the mission and all the people in it. I prayed for Red Bird, her parents, Bea and Martin, Mary Rose and Bill and their family. I always ended by asking God to send a special woman into Charles's life; I asked Him to bless them both, and to bless Charles's ministry.

One day Doug called with an invitation. "I've acquired some tickets," he said, "I thought perhaps you'd like to go with me. It's *The Nutcracker*." Then quickly, before I could voice any objections, "Mattie, I know what you are thinking ... you're a married woman, but how long has it been since you've had a fun night out with no strings attached? I know there can be nothing between us in your current situation, but I want to go with you—just as your friend. You can even invite Eleanor, or how about Blanche? They can be our chaperones!"

He had me laughing now, and since Blanche hadn't been out in a long while either, I took him up on his invitation and invited her along. The three of us had a wonderful time. Doug was at his most entertaining and soon had Blanche captivated. We went to a small café after the performance and had gooey chocolate éclairs, with decadent hot chocolate and paired it with wonderful conversation.

We all three agreed on our biblical principles, but had very different political views. We had a rousing debate about a bill currently presented to our state legislators for a vote. Finally, Blanche looked at the Mickey Mouse watch on her wrist and pointed at the time. Doug delivered us to our front door where he managed to be a dashing prince charming and claimed he had two Cinderella's in tow. He left in a flourish of gestures and bowed backwards down the sidewalk as he went, where he nearly fell when he slipped on a stretch of icy pavement. Blanche and I closed the door on that scene and collapsed in laughter. It was so wonderful to laugh again.

"He's a wonderful man," said Blanche.

"Yes, he is," I agreed.

"He says no strings attached? He just wants to be your friend?"

"Yes, that's what he says."

"I think you must be careful, Mattie," she mused. "He looks like someone who already has heartstrings attached to you. He may be telling himself he is just a friend, but he is halfway in love with you already."

"But I'm still a married woman!"

"Exactly," Blanche agreed.

The next day at dinner, I asked my father and Eleanor what they would think about my returning to school to get my teaching credentials.

"I don't think it will take much, maybe a year, to complete the education courses I will need," I told them. "I've already checked out several colleges, and many of my credits will transfer to the education degree program. The university nearest us offers night and weekend courses too."

"I think it's a wonderful idea," my father said with a smile.

"Oh, Mattie," Eleanor joined in, "I've seen you with those children. I believe it is your true calling. How can we help?"

"Well, I'm out of the habit of studying." I laughed. "I may need some coaching in order to pass my exams."

"Count on us!" Eleanor's eyes were shining approval.

I returned to school the second semester, right after the Christmas break. I continued to tutor the children, but I had to cut back to two days a week. I still saw Doug, but less frequently than before. We still had our coffee occasionally, and our friendship grew stronger, but I was careful to keep it at that level—friendship. Doug seemed to accept this gracefully, but sometimes I would catch a wistful look in his eye that caused me concern. I could not deny that it was flattering and that I was attracted to him, but there were too many unresolved issues in my life for me to allow it to go beyond friendship.

I received my master's degree almost exactly a year later at the midterm. I was now qualified to teach school. I had decided to concentrate on elementary education. I loved working with the smaller children, and they seemed to like me as well. Their minds were like little sponges to me, and I wanted to have an impact on their absorbing the best things for little minds to soak up for future use.

Life seemed almost normal, but underneath all this we were all still disturbed because there had been no news of Joel. What was to keep him from returning and wreaking havoc or stalking me? Now that I knew what he would do for money, it continued to be an underlying concern. I had put off contacting an attorney to file for divorce because I had been so busy with my education, and I was not sure how one divorced someone when you could not serve papers on them.

I did not have time to pursue that avenue, and I procrastinated taking this final step for some reason I could not even explain to myself. I became somewhat reconciled to living in a limbo-like existence, but there was always an undercurrent of concern in my life. It was as if Joel had never existed before or since coming to St. Louis. Why couldn't our detective find him? It was perplexing and unsettling.

More than a year had passed since my days at the mission. I still corresponded regularly with Bea, who was ecstatic about my going into elementary education. She wrote a nice letter when she heard my news.

"I always knew you had a talent in that area," she wrote. "I know your students will love you, and you will be good for them. Things are about the same here. The Pascal family had another child, a girl. You will never guess what they named her! You should feel honored, dear. They named her Mattie, after you. So, you see, you are still missed here. Oh, and in regard to your question about Charles. He is fine. He tried growing a moustache this fall 'to keep his upper lip warm through our cold winter' but we teased him so unmercifully about having a pastor who looked like a villain that he shaved it off!"

Meanwhile, in St. Louis, Pastor Mark and Margaret Lewis had decided to start up a K–6 private Christian elementary school near their grounds. A building next to their church had become available for sale. It was ideal for a school and would require only a minimum of modification. Doug partnered with me, and we initiated several large fund-raising projects to help acquire money for start-up along with other funds needed to purchase the building. Everyone at the church worked long and hard that entire spring, but soon we had the building remodeling well underway and I had a job offer to teach first grade for the school term starting in the coming fall.

We congratulated ourselves when we reached our goal and saw the building purchased with help from generous donors, including my father. I surreptitiously added some funds to this pot of money and was thrilled to see the joy on the Lewis faces when their dream came to fruition.

We were in the middle of the renovations needed for the new school when my father dropped his bombshell. The three of us—Eleanor, my father, and me—were at home having dinner and had been discussing the progress of our project. We were talking about what colors would be most effective on the interior walls of the school. I extolled the virtues of bright primary colors, but Eleanor thought natural, earth-tones would be better. Neither Eleanor nor I had noticed the unusual silence from my father who normally would have teased us about painting the walls camouflage and purple or some such nonsense.

"Mattie, I have some news for you." My father interrupted our discussion and looked at me keenly.

"Oh, what is that?"

"We've found Joel."

Chapter 20

The drive to Chicago on I-55 with my father and Eleanor took place with very little discussion between us, but the tension in the car was like a living, writhing broken electrical power line. What was there to say after all? I was going with them by my side. We would confront Joel. We followed the instructions we'd been given, and after about four hours of driving we arrived and pulled up in the parking lot of an older building in a somewhat depressing neighborhood. There were some signs of revitalization, but the area was not what one would call luxurious. The building was distinguished from its neighbors by being in slightly better maintenance, cleaner, and with an impressive architectural style.

"Detective Mattson will meet us there," my father had informed us tersely. "I want to be certain there are no chances for any mishaps even though the detective informs me we will not be under any danger from violence."

We walked into a cavernous entry that echoed the sounds of our footsteps like the rebounding, eerie sounds heard when underground with the stalactites and stalagmites in Mammoth cave. We followed signs and made our way to a dark mahogany desk that was shiny but slightly scuffed at the bottom from the contact of hundreds, perhaps thousands, of shoes.

"We're here to see Joel Carter," my father said in his authoritative voice to the elderly woman wearing a volunteer badge, who stood behind the desk and a sign that said "Information."

"One moment, please" she said, and began fumbling through a stack of cards she had in a small file in front of her. She paused about halfway through the stack. "Here he is." She looked up at us, curiosity bright in her eyes. "He never gets visitors, you know. Now he's had two visits in one day. Someone named Mattson is up there already."

I wondered if her volunteer leader knew she was volunteering too much information to people. When we didn't indulge her curiosity by responding and remained silent, she looked at the card grudgingly. "You need Room 325. Go up two flights and down the hall to your right."

I could feel her inquisitive eyes follow us to the elevator. We punched the buttons and rode to the third floor in silence. The doors slid open to a somber, but clean hallway. We followed it down to an intersecting hall that held some nice but slightly faded art prints, where we then turned to the right. None of us spoke as we walked through the halls before us. The antiseptic odor was overwhelming in some areas without good air handling, but we passed a friendly nurse who smiled and directed us on. There were muffled sounds of cries of pain coming from behind some doors, but others spilled out laughter, and we could see the occasional bright bouquet of flowers as we passed.

It was a busy place, a mixture of misery and hopeful healing. A doctor passed us and walked to a nurse's station we could see at the end of the hall. We heard the clatter of a stainless steel utensil as it clanged against something metal, and then the aromas of fresh luncheon plates as they were delivered. The combination of it all contributed to the general atmosphere of a lower class, but striving-hard-to-be-good, health care facility.

We arrived at 325. Detective Mattson was just outside, waiting for us. The door was slightly ajar. We heard no sounds coming from within the room. All three of us exchanged anxious glances. The detective said, "You should not approach the bed or touch him. Otherwise, you should be fine." he nodded his okay. Eleanor clasped my hand as I took a deep breath. We stepped into Joel's hospital room.

This emaciated thing with the sunken, hollow eyes lying on the bed could not be Joel. The circles around his eyes were so dark as to make his brown eyes look like giant pools of shadowed mud in his gaunt face. The skin hung from his arms like lightweight, almost sheer, fabric suspended from a drapery rod. There were machines, and tubes and more tubes connected to his body, giving him sustenance, pacing his life for him.

There must be some mistake. My mind fought to make sense of what I saw before me. This could not be Joel. The being on the mattress looked at me as I went to stand at the foot of the bed. A railing around the bed kept us from getting too close. I wondered if he had something contagious to the touch. "Mattie?" he squawked. "Is that you? Am I dreaming?"

I found myself rearranging my thoughts and dreams of putting him in his place. Then I became angrier than ever. Was I going to be cheated of my revenge? I remembered my promise to try and forgive, but this was awful. How could I forgive not only the near-death of myself but the ruination of the life before me? My carefully rehearsed speech dissolved like butter on hot pancakes. "Yes, Joel, it's me, Mattie."

"You're real? You're alive?" His voice was almost a whisper.

"Yes, I made it out alive, Joel," and then the bitterness came out between my clenched teeth, "no thanks to you."

"Ha!" he almost snorted, and seemed to gain more strength in his voice. "I underestimated you. I always underestimated you, Mattie. Did you come to inflict your revenge? You're a little late. It's already been done for you." He held up a spindly arm and pointed witch-like fingers at me. "As you can see, I'm dying Mattie. Isn't that a joke? I'm dying." He sounded hateful, resentful.

I said nothing and stared at this wreck of a human being. Long moments passed as we simply looked at each other. Finally he seemed to soften. "Actually, Mattie, I'm glad you're alive. I feel so terrible about what I did to you. I never meant to hurt you at first."

"You never wanted to hurt me!" I said, astounded. "Then what was it that happened to me? Did I imagine it all?" I couldn't keep the rancor out of my voice.

"No, no, you don't understand."

"You are right, Joel, I don't understand. I don't see how there is any possible explanation other than that you tried to kill me, so," I paused, "why don't you make me understand? Can you just clear it up how you could leave me for dead and still lie here and say you never meant to hurt me?" In spite of his obvious illness, I felt no sympathy for him at all. Again my anger surged against him. You would think I might have found it easy to forgive him with his announcement that he was dying, but quite the reverse happened. He was getting out of this too easily. He needed to suffer. Death was a reprieve. I felt cheated and hostile.

"Yes," my father spoke up for the first time. "We would certainly like to hear what you have to say for yourself, Joel." His face looked like steel, and I could tell he was holding his emotions in check.

The story Joel then told us, the *true* story of his childhood and his life, was an incredible tale. It turned out that Joel's "friend" Necia was actually his older sister. Joel's "friend" Freddie was Necia's husband! I listened in shock as Joel's story unfolded. *How could I have lived with this man and known so little about him?* Evidently Joel and Necia had been adopted by new, loving parents when they were young.

Joel had been happy with these parents and had learned to love them at first, but Necia had never accepted them, and her strong influence caused Joel to grow to feel the same resentments. Since Necia was the only constant in his life, Joel allowed himself to be led by her whims although he felt none of the animosity toward his adoptive parents that Necia spewed out.

The children were never told what happened to their real parents because it had been a "closed" adoption. When Necia became a seventeen-year-old rebellious teenager and Joel was but thirteen, their life took another turn. She met and became infatuated with Freddie, a twenty-two-year-old drug dealer.

From that point on, according to Joel, Necia became incorrigible. After a bad fight with their parents over her association with Freddie, Necia finally ran away from home to marry Freddie.

But Necia was not happy to make the break with these adoptive parents just for herself. She came back and managed to convince Joel to run away from home with her when he was only fourteen years old. Joel was far too easy to influence and thus he left behind the only real chance he had for a normal, decent life and followed Necia.

Freddie was a very bad influence on Necia, and consequently Joel. Soon brother and sister began helping Freddie distribute his drugs by providing them to schools, as well as fast crowds at country clubs and college campuses. Joel's education from that point on was what he picked up from the street or from Freddie. They were able, with Freddie's help, to elude all searches from their frantic parents, who had put out a nationwide hunt for them. They moved to another town in another state and changed their names.

"So none of that story about how your mother was killed by your father was true?" I accused Joel. "And of course you, poor innocent Joel, had nothing to do with any of it, and it is all Necia and Freddie's fault. You were just their stooge!" I could not keep the venom out of my voice as I added, "Is that right?"

Joel had the decency to look contrite and tried to explain. "Necia was the only one who was always there. I cared about our adoptive parents, but Necia was much stronger than me psychologically, and I was completely under her thumb for as long as I could remember. You are right. I should have talked to them and stood up to Necia," he admitted. But in the next breath he was back to blaming Necia. "I don't know why she couldn't accept them. It would have made a big difference if she had."

"Right, poor, poor Joel," I sneered. "So what happened when you and Necia and Freddie moved away, then?" I asked, still not sure if this story were true or not. His veracity had proven to be untrustworthy in the past.

"It got worse," he said. Joel then told us that things deteriorated when Freddie began to give both Necia and Joel small doses of drugs "so you can mellow out," and thus he tied them ever more firmly to his side and kept the brother and sister under his control. Under Freddie's tutelage, Joel cleverly learned how to insinuate himself with people.

During their years of plying the drugs, Freddie taught and educated Joel in how to be a charming con artist. The jobs Joel had told me about were nonexistent or, as in the case of our country club, temporary covers for his real job—that of being a drug dealer. Their targets for the drugs were young teenagers and even preteens. They focused on this age group because they could encourage them to become hooked on the drugs most easily. Thus, the innocent youngsters would become dependent on them to supply the high to which they would become addicted.

I choked down my distaste as I realized I had been in complete ignorance of this other side of Joel's life. My father had sensed it. He had been right.

It turned out that Necia and Joel were not so firmly addicted at first because Freddie wanted them able to function for his purposes, so he simply gave them low-level drugs. After my marriage to Joel, which again, according to the poor whining tale of Joel's, had been a scheme of Freddie's for the purpose of gaining access to my wealth, the drugs were stepped up in strength.

At that time, Freddie, for some reason of his own, perhaps fearing that I might begin to initiate some control over the two siblings, moved them onto harder drugs. As Joel related the history of his life, I remembered back to the time period he was discussing. That time was exactly when I began noticing personality changes in Joel and a complete alienation toward me. Of course Joel still did not accept his own responsibility in all this.

"So you are blaming everyone but yourself, even though you participated in all of it!" I almost shouted but tried to be conscious of the hospital walls and other patients. "Everything is their fault even though you participated to the extent that you—yes *you*—Joel tried to kill me." I was finding it harder and harder to keep my promise to God about forgiveness. This all seemed so incredibly unforgivable.

So, Freddie the master manipulator had stayed in control because the brother and sister needed the drugs more and more and became addicted. My money and Joel's salary had been providing the access to the drugs. I remembered also, Joel's change in health I had noticed about the same time all this happened and how I had questioned it. Could the drugs be the reason he was now dying?

"So why did you say you had a change of heart and wanted to take me to Canada?" I interrupted his story, already suspecting the answer.

"Necia had a friend waiting tables in the restaurant that day you met with your friend Josie. He knew who you were and overheard you discussing our marriage, and Josie encouraging you to leave. We couldn't have that. Then I answered the phone call from the attorney that night. We added two and two, and knew you could be serious about leaving me."

So, they knew then, that I might decide to divorce Joel. I had promised Josie I would think about it. All three knew that could be an end to my money—and probably Joel's fancy new job. Both our marriage and that job were excellent covers for a team of drug dealers. That's when Freddie hatched the plan to dispose of me in Canada.

"So, you never wanted to go to Canada until Freddie suggested it?"

"I argued with him about it Mattie, but he threatened to cut off my drug supply or turn me in to the cops if I didn't go along with his scheme. Of course, Necia was applying unbearable pressure too. She didn't want to go against Freddie. By now we realized Freddie was very dangerous to cross. Necia, of course, didn't want to lose her connection to the drugs that were a habit of necessity to her now too.

I know it's no consolation to you Mattie, but I came up with the most painless way to end your life I could think of," Joel told me, his mouth grim. I could not resist a bark of sarcastic laughter, "Oh, gee, thank you so much, Joel. I hope you don't expect me to be grateful!"

He went on with the information we were having difficulty digesting. "Much as you will find this hard to believe, I did care for you a great deal, Mattie. If I had not gone on to the hard drugs, I think there might have been hope for us. But when you have an addiction, as I did, nothing will stand in the way of it. Not even love for another person. It is all-consuming. It is a curse." He flinched and finished his story with a bitter sigh while his head fell back against the pillow.

Poor, weak, weak Joel could not evoke any sympathy from me at all. He finished his revolting tale. Even now he was whining and blaming others, like his sister, for his poor choices and actions in life. I could see by their grim faces that my father and Eleanor spared him very little sympathy. All my thoughts and dreams of revenge, arrest, and separation went out the window. He was dying after all. But that did not mean I had to forgive him. I would not be cheated of this now that I saw a different situation from the one I had planned. I did make one concession in that direction.

"Oh, Joel, why didn't you tell me all this? I would have gotten you some help."

"You couldn't have helped me, Mattie," he said fatalistically, "I was already infected."

"What do you mean?" I was genuinely puzzled.

"Oh Mattie, you're still such an innocent. The needles, Mattie, the needles for the drugs. I picked up AIDS from a bad needle. *That's* why I'm dying. *That's* why I'm in this private room instead of a ward even though I'm a charity patient. Oh, yes, by the way, I went through all our checking and savings and sold off everything I could and tried to get more from your father. I know you still have a fortune, but good old dad managed to stop me.

"Now, unless you decide to pitch in something, or the hospital comes after you for my care since we are not divorced, I am out of funds. For a while though, after you 'died' I had fun and had a good time with my friends. Then, about the same time your father stopped me, I found that I have AIDS. Comical isn't it? I have always been the life of the party." Now I am isolated because the other patients in the ward accidentally found out and had such a fit, the hospital had to move me here to a private room. None of them, including the staff, want to catch it. They say they know enough now to keep others from getting it, but I can see the fear in their eyes when they come in this room. Especially in the aides who drop off the meals. They practically throw the tray on the table."

You have AIDS?" I shuddered involuntarily and stepped back, remembering Detective Mattson's admonishment not to go near or touch Joel. AIDS had received a lot of publicity, most of it negative, but I did recall that it was not quite as contagious as first thought. That did not stop me from piling up another brick in my anger against Joel.

Dear Lord, this is worse and more difficult than I ever imagined it could be. You can't really expect me to forgive all this can you? I quickly looked at my father who was shuttering his face closed on a look of abhorrence and fear. Eleanor had the same reaction I could tell, but we all recovered quickly and went on with our conversation.

"Yes, I am infected with AIDS. You got your revenge didn't you, Mattie?"

"You said the other patients found out 'accidentally' about the AIDS." I ignored his question. "Didn't the hospital have to warn them you had such a deadly disease?" I was still doing most of the talking for our threesome.

"No. In fact, it's illegal for them to break the confidentiality between a patient and the doctor. That's why you could walk in here like you did and not know I have AIDS or that I'm dying."

We left soon after that. Detective Mattson confirmed much of what Joel had told us when we met with him afterward. We discussed pressing charges with the detective, but decided we needed a little more time to evaluate the wisdom of that, particularly in light of the negative and unwanted publicity that would ensue. Before we started home, he informed us they were still trying to apprehend Freddie and Necia, who would be considered accomplices. He would stay in touch with us.

We talked about Joel and his life on the drive back to St. Louis. All three of us were subdued. It seemed such a waste. And every bit of it stemmed from selfishness, ungratefulness, and rebellion—all of which led to their giving drugs total control of their lives. Why couldn't people see this horrible end when they were starting down that path? What kind of self-destructiveness made them take that path in the first place? What made someone like Joel, who had been given a great opportunity in life to have two adoptive parents love and rear him like their own—what would make him reject them and choose instead this horrible ending for himself and his sister? We had no answers

"I don't want to bring up this most difficult subject, but I feel I must," said Eleanor as we neared home with a glance at my father's rigid profile. "Mattie, we must get you in to a doctor to be certain you have not been infected as well. It sounds as if he was possibly infected with the AIDS virus long before he took you to Canada." Her voice cracked.

"Yes, I agree," said my father, his voice choked also. "Chances are you're okay. We don't want to alarm you," I saw the look that passed between him and Eleanor as he said this, "but it would be good to get yourself checked out immediately so we can all rest easy. Let's be sure, sweetie, okay?"

I remembered Sir Walter Scott and his famous, "Oh what a tangled web we weave, when first we practice to deceive," and thought to myself, *oh, how right you were, Mr. Scott!* How many repercussions there were from Joel's actions—and from my own.

I would have one more testing of my newfound faith. I wrote to Bea. "By the time you receive this I will know, but as of this writing I do not know if I have been infected by Joel with the AIDS virus. This is a time of great testing for me. I pray I will be able to accept whatever is in my future. Please continue to keep me in your prayers. I am finding forgiveness very difficult."I also told Bea about the entire experience with Joel and what had happened. I shared with her my new difficulty in following through with my promise to God for forgiveness.I wrote, "Bea, I looked at this wretched person in that hospital bed and I felt no forgiveness or sympathy at all. I was actually sorry to see that he did not seem to be in any pain! How does one forgive not only a murder attempt, but my possible infection with this horrid disease, when I cannot evoke even one small feeling of sympathy for him? He made these choices and brought this all on himself! Oh Bea, this is the most difficult thing of my life—even more difficult than surviving the murder attempt!"

Eleanor set up an appointment with our family doctor, and though I was an adult, went in with me "for moral support" she said. I saw an instant's panic in the doctor's eyes when we told him of the possibility of AIDS. I had some understanding of how a leper in biblical times might have felt as I went through the process of being tested. Everyone was extremely cautious with plastic gloves, needles, and any paraphernalia needed. I also understood how the doctor and his staff might feel, for it is a horrible disease and no one wanted to take any risks that might cause them to acquire the disease too.

Eleanor and I later commented about how we could almost feel them give out a physical sigh of relief when we walked out of their offices. We would have the results in less than a week they told us.

I think I loved Eleanor more at that time than I ever thought possible, when, in spite of everything that had occurred recently, she took me in her arms and hugged me. She told me, her voice fierce, as we left the doctor's office, "No matter what happens, Mattie, I'll stay with you. I love you, sweetheart. Don't let it get you down."

"I need to call Josie, too" I said, knowing my friend would be concerned. I dialed Josie's number and explained the situation. She cried bitterly when I told her it was possible I had been infected.

"Will this never end, Mattie?" she had asked in anguish.

"I have learned to trust God in all things, even as difficult as this," I told her over the phone. "My biggest problem right now is not so much concern for me, but how that is affecting my decision to forgive all this. I am not sure I can do it now. I saw perfect examples of how we should always trust Him when I was in Canada, but now I am truly struggling with this whole issue in spite of the lessons I learned at the mission," I told her.

"Mattie, you know I will be praying for God's wisdom and your safety," Josie said.

"Don't come over for a while until I know the answer. I don't want to infect anyone else."

"I go to church, but I still wish I could have the kind of faith that always trusts Him," she had answered me with a sniffle.

"We'll work on that together," I told her. "You'll see."

The time of waiting was pure torture. I tried to isolate myself from everyone, in the fear that if I did have the virus I might expose the ones I loved. I devoured everything I could read about the disease and learned more about how people could, and could not, become infected with Aids. After my research was finished, I relaxed a little about the possibility of infecting others, but I still kept to my home, waiting for the results. Waiting—a very small word that can encompass so much.

My father was having his own battles. He had been fighting his hatred for Joel in his new Christian walk, and now this new threat to me had given him a whole new battleground he had to conquer. I could see how despicable he thought Joel was to have brought this new curse into our lives. He and Eleanor left the house for several talks with our pastor, gaining his advice on how to deal with anger—and righteous anger—and how to differentiate the two.

"Easier said, than done," my father shared with us at dinner one evening. "Wanting revenge is an almost automatic reaction to a situation like we've all been through. But ultimately we become just like our adversary and we sink to that level, if we allow revenge to eat us up. However, it is extremely difficult not to find yourself praying for that revenge to take place. I find it is even more difficult knowing he is going to escape punishment or revenge with death. It makes it too easy for him and more difficult for me."

"So, it is a conundrum," added Eleanor.

"Yes, like a labyrinth with no exit," he replied.

Blanche, who had been informed of the entire situation, called me to the telephone exactly one week after I'd been in for my tests. "It's Dr. Miller's office," she said, and her hands trembled as she handed me the phone. "They want you to come in," her voice matched her hands and wavered. Blanche showed her concern on her face.

I took the call and took the earliest appointment available. They said they could not tell me anything over the phone, which caused an ominous sinking sensation in the pit of my stomach. I hung up and mentally noted the hours before I would get an answer. I could see Blanche from the corner of my eyes as she went off to get Eleanor while I finished the call.

Eleanor went with me the next day. The staff ushered both of us into a waiting room right away as if they knew I was facing something dreadful.

"Mattie?" Doc Miller entered the room with his white coat flapping behind him. "I had my staff get you in here quickly because I knew how important these results would be to you." I held my breath and looked over at Eleanor who was stiff and motionless. I could hear my own heartbeat pumping in my ear.

"Mattie," he went on and seemed to take an interminable time to get out the words, while my world swam by. "You are okay. You are not—I repeat—you are *not* infected with the AIDS virus."

I dropped my purse off my lap, burst into tears, and then rushed into Eleanor's arms. She said "Dr. Miller, thank you! Thank you!" Then she hugged me again and said, "Oh praise the Lord! Thank you so much doctor."

Doc Miller just stood with a beatific smile on his face and the glint of a tear in his eye and said, "I'm pretty happy about these results also, I must tell you. It made my day." Then our old family doctor surprised us when he walked up and wrapped his arms tightly around both of us. We left his office as if someone had attached helium balloons to our bodies.

"Oh dear!" exclaimed Eleanor. "We've got to call Mitch right away!" We had nearly forgotten how anxious my father would be for the news in all the excitement.

"We're close to his office," I pointed out, "let's run over and tell him."

"Yes, let's do that!"

My father was as overjoyed as we were and insisted on taking us to "the best lunch we've ever had, even if it is just burgers and fries." His eyes crinkled with his big smile.

I called Josie with the good news. "Remember that faith in God?" I started the phone conversation.

"Yes," her voice was hesitant—waiting.

"He answered our prayers. I am not infected, Josie." She began crying over the phone. Such a loyal friend is rare. "I am so grateful to God for you, Josie" I told her before hanging up.

"This calls for a celebration!" my father told us that evening over the dinner table. He was in jaunty spirits. "How about I pick up some tickets, and we take a little excursion to—oh, I don't know—anywhere. What about a cruise to the Bahamas? Hawaii? How would you like a cruise to Alaska? You name it, Mattie, and it's yours."

Eleanor and I looked at one another, then back at my father. He was quick on the uptake. "Okay. What gives, you two? Did I make a faux pas? Don't you want a trip to celebrate, Mattie?" He was so happy. I could see the new lines of strain in his face, but his smile was erasing them. I did not want to cause him concern, but …

"It's not that, Daddy. I appreciate the offer, really I do. In fact, I may take you up on it in the very near future, but first there's something else I'd like to do, and you may not like it. Eleanor and I have been discussing it this afternoon."

He looked at each of us in turn. How could I ask this of him? Yet I felt it was the right thing to do. I wanted his face to stay happy, young, and free of worry. But I also felt a compulsion to finalize some things with Joel.

"I suppose, Mattie." My parent smiled. "You don't think I've been through enough turmoil and testing the last couple of years, so you're about to dream up something new for me eh?" He smiled. but there was a slight edge of concern to his voice.

I did not want to add to this concern and I suppose Eleanor sensed that. "Please hear her out, Mitch," Eleanor urged. "She has it worked out, and I think you will see that she has a point."

"Yes, well, something like that," I stammered.

"Well, go ahead. Spit it out. What won't I like?" He was trying his best to be gentle, patient, and understanding, but he also had a strong parent gene that was already in resistance mode.

"I want to take an apartment somewhere near Joel's hospital so I can visit him every day for what little time he has left." There—I'd said it.

"You what?" my father shouted. "Are you crazy? You just found out you're free of infection, so you want to go into an environment where you can possibly get AIDS after all? And from a man who tried to *murder* you?" His face was getting red, "No! Mattie this isn't fair ... Haven't you—all of us—been through enough?" He struck the table with his fist for emphasis, "No Mattie! I can't stand the thought of putting you at risk again."

"But Daddy ..."

With a softer voice, he touched me and I felt my heart soften, "Mattie, Mattie, have a care for me. Please?" He looked wounded and heartsick.

Then I touched him a little. "Dad, you know I love you more than anything, but—Joel is not a Christian."

"So? Send him a preacher. I'll pay for his costs. Besides that has been Joel's choice."

"Is it his choice. Daddy? Is it really? Has anyone ever spent the time to tell him what it means to be a Christian? Do you think anyone has ever read the Bible to him?"

"His adoptive parents probably did, and it didn't take," he grumbled.

"Hasn't God protected me thus far?"

"You shall not put the Lord your God to the test," he quoted Deuteronomy.

"Who desires all men to be saved and to come to the knowledge of the truth," I quoted 1 Timothy.

"and do not throw your pearls before swine," he quoted Matthew 7:6.

"The Lord is not slow about his promise as some count slowness, but is forbearing toward you, not wishing that any should perish, but that all should reach repentance." I quoted 2 Peter 3:9

Eleanor stepped in. "This could go on all night," she said, "And I have a couple of my own, including 2 Timothy 1:7: 'for God did not give us a spirit of timidity but a spirit of power and love and self-control.'" She smiled and added, "I have a compromise I would like to propose."

"I don't see how we can come to any sort of agreement on this. I'm violently opposed to the whole ridiculous idea," my father groused.

I looked at the father who was so dear to me, who only wanted what he saw as best for me, and said a silent prayer that I would do and say the right thing. I held up my hand and said, "Wait. Before we discuss this any further, I want you to know that I am not going to do this unless I have your blessing, Dad. I went against your wisdom when I married Joel, and that got us into this whole mess to begin with. I'm not going to make the same mistake again. I may have reasons for what I want to do, but unless Eleanor has a good compromise worked out, and we can both live with it, I will not do it. Okay?"

"Ok." He seemed somewhat mollified.

"Now, what do you have in mind, Eleanor?" I asked.

Her suggestion meant the three of us went together to Dr. Jorgenson's clinic. He spent a great deal of time explaining to my father that I was not in danger by being in the same room with Joel. "AIDS can be contracted through body fluids," he said, "It is not an airborne virus. Mattie would have to have an open sore, for example, which would then have to be contaminated through contact with blood or fluid from an open sore on the AIDS patient, in order for it to be transferred to her body." He looked at us over the rim of his glasses. "You cannot get AIDS from being in the same room."

He went on to explain that Joel would likely die of a pulmonary infection. Most AIDS patients contract pneumonia, he told us, and their immune systems cannot fight it off, so their weakened bodies succumb to the battle. Joel, it turned out, was in more danger of my bringing an airborne virus into his room, which would kill him, than I was of contracting AIDS from him.

This did not satisfy my father. He continued to be against the whole idea. He brought up other issues of safety including the fact that Freddie and Necia were still at large and that I was likely still in danger from them. I was still married to Joel, thus they would see this opportunity to try to get to my money since both of them were presumably unaware of the protective paperwork my dad's lawyers had worked up prior to my marriage to Joel.

Finally he agreed to the compromise when he presented a list of requests in which he asked me to take some extreme precautions for my safety. I was to touch nothing in the room at any time. I was to wear plastic gloves at all times when I was in the room, in case I forgot the "don't touch" rule. There was a list of safety items for my health.

He followed these ideas with a final stipulation. I nearly rebelled at this last requirement, but in the end, I compromised. As Eleanor pointed out to me, my father had to make more difficult concessions than I. His final request was for a bodyguard to be with me on each visit. The bodyguard would sit quietly in a corner, or outside the door, but he would be there in case I needed help of any kind.

"Actually," my father admitted, "I have used him before. When you first returned, Mattie, I had him keep surveillance on you when you left the house since we had no idea where Joel was or if he might try to kidnap you or try something else." He looked a bit shamefaced and said, "You didn't know he was even there, did you? That's how good he is at his job." He saw my face and said quickly, "I'm sorry, Mattie. I just couldn't take any chances. I hope you will forgive me for not telling you, but I didn't want you to carry that additional worry. You had been through so much already." He sighed, "Ted is very good at his job. I think you will like him. He helped Detective Mattson a great deal when we were trying to find Joel."

I could not chastise my father for loving and protecting me. "It's okay. I understand why you felt you had to have me watched."

"But back to these hospital visits. Do you promise me you'll abide by all this I have asked of you, Mattie?" Daddy said firmly and looked me squarely in the face.

I didn't see how I could possibly need a bodyguard in light of Joel being in the weakened condition we had found him, but I could see that my father meant business. "I promise, Dad," I answered solemnly, and meant it.

None of us thought at the time to question the whereabouts of Joel's sister and brother-in-law, Necia and Freddie. They were assumed to be alive, out there in the world somewhere, but according to Detective Mattson they had not been seen for a long time and did not visit Joel. So, our concerns were of the immediate dangers that might exist in my plan to see and visit Joel.

Doug was nearly as disturbed as my father had been when he heard my plan. "Mattie, you owe him nothing, *nothing*. Why would you waste your time on that scum? He's proven over and over that he's beyond redemption. You're going overboard with your Christianity. We can't save the world. Yes, we should forgive others, but you've already done that.

"Now, you need to move on. What you are doing here at this school is important. It's necessary work. We need you here! Would you trade the souls of all these children you are helping for one unredeemable person? Where did you pick up this attitude that you need to become a martyr?" I had never seen my calm, implacable, witty Doug become so distraught. I silently prayed for guidance. I also knew I had to come to terms with the forgiveness I had yet to offer Joel.

"Doug, I learned the type of Christian I want to be by the wonderful example of some people I knew at the mission in Canada. I think they would be encouraging me to do this for Joel."

"Not if they thought you were risking your life! I think you're wasting your time, Mattie. He's too far gone to want to hear anything from the Bible. Let someone else do it."

"Doug, there *is* no one else."

Chapter 21

My father sent someone to meet me one afternoon at home. His name was Ted Slaymaker and he introduced himself to me and then informed me he would be my bodyguard. He was in his forties with thinning brown hair and merry hazel eyes. He appeared to be a former weightlifter that had fallen on times of paunch from less lifting of weights and more lifting of food to his mouth. He was good humored, however, and joked about how well his last name of Slaymaker fit his occupation. Though stocky, he appeared to maintain sufficient physical fitness that I felt assured and safe in his bulky presence.

Blanche became quite enthused about him, and I relaxed when I realized she had been very concerned as well as my father and Eleanor. We had several meetings with Ted, during which we filled him in on the entire story of the attempt on my life. My father had given him bits and pieces before, but now felt that Ted should know every detail so he would be aware of all angles.

My father pointed out to Ted that "now there seems to be little real danger to Mattie, I don't want to make a mistake in judgment this late in the game. I don't want to take any chances that Joel still might try something foolish, so I want your presence there to guarantee her safety."

"I never guarantee anyone's safety," smiled Ted, which took the edge off his statement, "There are too many unknowns in this world for that. But I will tell you I've never lost a client yet!" He paused somewhat dramatically and said, "Except the ones who didn't pay me!" His joke caused him to laugh so hard his paunch was moved to jiggle a bit.

We all laughed and relaxed. I felt loved and protected, and I knew my father was relieved that we had acquired the services of Ted, who downplayed his bodyguard abilities. I, however, knew my father would only hire the very best and most qualified person, so I was not fooled by his modesty.

In Chicago, near the hospital, Ted found two small, furnished apartments for rent next door to each other, "so I can be handy if you need me," he said. It was agreed between us that Ted would meet me every day right after lunch and drive me to see Joel. I would spend as much time as I liked there at the hospital, reading or talking to Joel. Ted would stay nearby, on a chair just inside the door, and then he would escort me back to the apartment. Mornings we kept open for errands, correspondence, or miscellaneous things as the mood struck us. The transition was not difficult. We soon melded into a routine.

At first, Joel was sarcastic and bitter about my being there; yet, he did not refuse me entrance. "Here is Miss Goody Two-Shoes again," he'd snarl when I walked in the door, or "Here's Saint Mattie—with her watchdog." Ted calmly ignored his comments and took up his post in as comfortable a chair as one can find in a hospital room. I also did my best to ignore the sarcasm and stuck to my mission.

I think sometimes my presence reminded Joel of the things he had done wrong in his life. And, like most of us, he didn't want to be reminded. "What are you trying to prove by coming here, Mattie?" he'd say, and turn his head away from me. "Go away and play with your rich friends. I don't need you. I don't want you here."

Yet, he didn't go that final step to ask the hospital to have me refused entry or to have them evict me. I felt that was significant, so I persisted. I knew that by being there, I was demonstrating forgiveness, even if I still railed against the evil thing he had done. I remembered Bea and Charles telling me this was how God helped us to forgive others. Going through the actions that made up forgiveness would eventually work that feeling in my own heart they had told me. I was following their instructions.

I ignored Joel's petulant attitude and said things like, "I'm doing nothing more than reading to you. It's a book you've never heard before. I think you should hear it." Then I began to read about the life of Jesus, starting with the four Gospels. He would lie with his back to me. He tried to ignore me, but I kept reading aloud. I used my study Bible, and frequently I would go ahead and read aloud some of the explanatory paragraphs referring to certain passages.

Sometimes I would read from *The Living Bible* that had been the brainstorm of a professor who lived in Winona Lake, Indiana. I told Joel how this man had translated the Bible on his daily train trips to work in Illinois because he felt it would be more relevant to his own children. It may have been my imagination, but Joel seemed to be attentive when I read from this version.

After about a week of this, I began to see a slight change in my reception. There was a different look in Joel's eyes when I walked in the door. He tried to hide it from me, but I sensed it with gladness in my heart. The wariness was still there, the feigned indifference, but it was mixed with a guarded look of eagerness now. That eagerness was a fact that he tried unsuccessfully to hide from me. I knew he was starting to look forward to my visits. That he didn't have to protect himself from my deserting him. He began to trust that I would return.

The monotony of hospital life was helpful to my purposes, and I knew my visits would be a welcome break for Joel. I continued to read to him and sometimes explain more about the passages I had read. Finally an eventful day came when my patient gave up pretending disinterest, and he would lie back and listen avidly, all his attention on what I was saying to him.

Then came the day I hailed secretly as a great success. On that day, Joel actually spoke up and asked me a question about a passage I had just read to him from John, chapter 14 verses 2-3: "In my Father's house there are many rooms; if it were not so, would I have told you that I go to prepare a place for you? And when I go and prepare a place for you, I will come again and will take you to myself, that where I am you may be also."

"So does that mean everyone is going to heaven?" Joel asked me expectantly. "That's what it sounds like."

I knew God had prepared me for this question and mentally thanked Charles for his beautiful explanation of the children and the birthday party. "No, Joel, God is a loving God and He wants all of us to join Him in the beautiful place He has prepared, but—and this is important—we additionally must remember that He is also a just and fair God." I went on to explain the clean and dirty children and their attempt to get into the birthday party. I explained how we must be clean through the sacrifice of Jesus Christ. Joel listened attentively, and I felt a little shift in his attitude from that point on.

Things progressed more quickly after that hurdle, and I sensed a new spirit in Joel's room. It was much less oppressive. Soon, we were quite often having a lively dialogue about this or that aspect of the Bible and what it meant to be a Christian. So, eventually, Joel came to the point that he looked forward to my visits. A day came when he actually thanked me for coming. I praised God and congratulated myself on our progress.

One day Ted and I arrived a little earlier than usual. As we were pulling into the parking lot, I noticed a figure hurrying away from the hospital. It was a woman who looked to be very "down and out," judging from her unkempt appearance. Her clothes were bedraggled, her hair a mess; a strap from her shoe was loose and flapped as she walked. She looked homeless except that the typical grocery cart was not in evidence with her worldly belongings.

There was something faintly familiar about her, so I mentioned that fact to Ted. "I wonder if I know that woman," I told him as we got out of the car, "she looks familiar to me."

"Where?" he barked, and turned instantly. Ted lived up to his reputation for his occupation because his body quickly tensed. I could tell he was immediately alert.

"There. She's just going around that corner." I pointed.

But she was gone before Ted could see her, and I soon discounted the possibility of seeing anyone I knew in such a neighborhood of Chicago and so far from my home in St. Louis.

"I must have imagined it," I said. "I apologize. I'm sure it was nothing."

"Maybe so," Ted remained noncommittal.

We arrived for our normal appointment time at the hospital, but Joel seemed restless that day as we worked on our lessons (as I now called the visits). We were reviewing the Old Testament and the time when God handed down what is now the Hebrew Bible to Moses. Joel was not his usual inquisitive self. He seemed inattentive and withdrawn. Ted in the corner had repositioned his chair that day as well. Things seemed a little off.

Finally I put down my books. "Is something the matter?" I asked Joel point-blank. "You seem preoccupied today."

He looked startled for a moment, then, he smiled that old, engaging smile. "No, no, Mattie, everything is okay. Please don't stop."

I was not convinced, but I continued with the discussion, and soon we were back in the groove of things, and Joel was excited about what he was learning again. He now practically inhaled everything he could about the Bible and the life of Jesus. His questions were incessant and intelligent, and I marveled at how much he was learning. I sometimes felt a pang when I realized what potential he had and how much his life and learning had been thwarted by his sister's influence and his own bad choices. It was a shame no one had encouraged him. But he was changing, I could see it.

From then on, every day we worked, we dug, and we scoured the Bible. I brought in writings and books by some of the great people in the church, and he devoured those in the times I was not there. He particularly liked C. S. Lewis's book *Mere Christianity*, and even more special to him was *The Screwtape Letters* that I had casually left behind for him to read.

"I can really identify with this," he told me after reading *The Screwtape Letters*. He went on to inform me of things I already knew, but I allowed him the excitement of being the discoverer. He told me that "Mr. Lewis was very astute. He seems to know all the temptations and misfortunes that befall us human beings.

"And writing it from Satan's viewpoint, exposing his guile and his ploys, was a very clever approach. The Uncle Screwtape who is the devil writes these letters to his nephew, Wormwood, on how to make humans stumble. It gives you a totally captivating view of how easily sometimes we are taken in," he ended thoughtfully. "A couple of things he wrote really struck me."

"Such as?"

"Pilate was merciful till it became risky."

"Yes, that fits most of us doesn't it? Another one you liked?"

"The surest way to tempt a man is to make him think that he has twenty-four hours a day that belong to him."

"Ah, yes, I remember that too. Very good. Any others?"

"One to the effect that a moderated religion is as good for the devil as no religion at all—and more amusing."

His heart was changing. I could see it happening to Joel before my eyes. He was growing in his knowledge. He was learning to love the Lord. I could see the yearning in his eyes to be reborn. But as yet, he did not have the courage to broach the subject with me.

One day he opened up a little more and said, "You know, Mattie, I've never asked how you made it out of that wilderness where I left you, mostly because I didn't want to deal with the guilt and with knowing more about the pain I caused you. If you want to tell me about it now, I'll listen." And because I thought he needed to hear it, I spared no details. The agony of the stomach pains, the nausea, the vomiting, the fear, nearly starving, being ill and delirious, almost drowning. I told him all about it. I spared nothing in the tale.

When I was done with the memories, he looked at me wonderingly. "You are a courageous woman, Mattie. I'm glad you made it out all right.

I'd like to see everyone you described at the mission, especially Little Red Bird; she sounds enchanting. But most of all, I am so sorry for what I did to you. You must hate me and I don't blame you.

"Actually," I corrected him, "I don't hate you at all and I forgave you a long time ago. Bea and Charles both helped me deal with that. They said sometimes we may not feel it inside, but we should go through the motions until the forgiveness comes." I was surprised to find this was true. It was a liberating feeling. So gradually I had not noticed, my own heart had been forgiving Joel. I no longer had this almost maniacal lust for revenge. I did not tell him how they had also said forgiveness does not mean letting people out of the consequences of their actions. I could see some of the consequences Joel was paying with my own eyes.

"They all sound like wonderful people," he went on wistfully. "And Charles? He sounds like a very good pastor."

"They are—he is."

I could feel Joel's eyes on me as we discussed my friends in Canada. He was thoughtful for a few minutes, then he surprised me again. "Thank you for forgiving me, Mattie. I know I don't deserve it, but it means a lot to me," he blurted out awkwardly.

"You need to ask God for forgiveness, too, Joel."

"Yes, I know," he paused, "before it is too late."

I nodded, and looked at his almost translucent skin, and I knew there wouldn't be much more time.

A day or so later, Ted and I were shopping at a small local market near the hospital in the morning right before the time we usually visited with Joel. I had picked up some fruit when I felt the oddest sensation. It was as if someone or something was observing me. I turned quickly to see who might be behind me, but I saw only Ted thumbing through some magazines. I shook off the feeling and went about my business, but when we reached the parking lot after making our purchases, the same eerie feeling returned. I looked around and could see nothing that looked unusual anywhere.

Suddenly, an old sedan, which was on its last legs, smoke pouring out the exhaust, roared past and swerved toward me at an excessively fast speed. I jumped back in an automatic reflex and watched the car miss me by inches. I heard the wheels squeal as it drove rapidly out of the parking lot. I glimpsed a wan face behind the wheel, and although she wore sunglasses and had on a scarf to cover her hair, I felt the uncanny sensation that I was familiar with this person. It was the same woman I had seen leaving the hospital. She was my "homeless without a cart" memory.

I felt ridiculous expressing such feelings with nothing more to go on than eerie sensations, so I decided to laugh it off. "Just got her driver's license I guess!" I joked with Ted, who stood beside me. His sunglasses hid his expression, but he did not disagree with me. I would not tell Ted about my concerns until I had something more concrete than intuition to go on. I laughed myself out if it. *You've been watching too many TV mysteries. There's nothing sinister going on here*, I told myself.

I wrote my father, and Bea and Pastor Mark and Josie and Doug Culbertson about my progress with Joel. I told them the end was drawing nearer and that I was encouraged about the changes I had seen in Joel. They all wrote back in encouraging ways, even Doug, who still felt I was being foolhardy with my life.

I became very optimistic and felt God had worked in both my life as well as Joel's. I knew He had helped us both to grow in a way never before possible during our married life.

"You know, Mattie," Joel said to me one day, "I wish I could make it up to my adoptive parents somehow. I realize now that I threw away something special when I made the choice to leave with Necia."

"Why don't you write to them, Joel?" I suggested.

"And tell them what? That I now have AIDS? Don't you think that will be welcome news for them?" he said, some of his old sarcasm returned, if lightly.

"Maybe you aren't giving them enough credit for being able to love you," I answered.

"They're better off thinking I'm dead," he said glumly.

I dropped the subject and planned to bring it up again later, but fate, as is often the case, intervened and changed my plans.

About a week after that conversation regarding his adoptive parents, Ted and I walked into Joel's room at our usual time. As we entered the room, we knew something about it was not as usual. I looked at Joel. He was lying propped up on his bed as he normally was, but this time his face was not eager and happy to see me. Joel's eyes held panic as I had never seen it and when they met mine, he communicated a direct warning to my soul.

We quickly saw the reason for his horror as we looked at the other occupant who was waiting for us in his room. Hovering over Joel on the far side of his bed, her hand holding a gun, whose barrel now pointed directly at me, was the woman I had thought looked familiar. It was the same woman I had seen on the two previous occasions, but now, on close inspection I realized why I thought she looked familiar. Standing before me was Necia, but it was a very different Necia. No wonder I had not recognized her!

Her eyes were glazed and red-rimmed. She was thin and gaunt. Ragged and dirty clothing hung on her once beautiful figure like brown shreds of moss drape on dying trees in the swamps of the south. Her nails, once immaculately groomed and polished, were now dirty and broken and matched her unkempt appearance. She had made an effort to put on some makeup, but the glaring red lipstick was a discordant smear on her pallid face, and the turquoise eye shadow only accented the haunted look in her eyes. I barely recognized her, but she instantly knew me.

"Well, well, Mattie must be part cat," she began to talk with a hoarse voice I could barely recognize while she continued to wave the silver revolver at me. I knew from having seen and fired similar weapons in my father's gun collection, that this was a deadly gun, the opening too large for a .22 caliber. *Most likely a .357—something large and dangerous.* My mind scrambled to make sense of things as I looked down the barrel and hoped it wasn't going to be my last mental activity. Necia continued her almost incoherent rambling, "She seems to have nine lives, hmmm? Isn't that right, Joel?"

"Necia, I told you, leave Mattie out of this," a worried Joel protested weakly from the bed.

"Why should I leave her out of this? It's all her fault that we don't have any money," she whined. "I think she should make it up to us, don't you, Joel?"

"No, I don't think Mattie has anything to make up to us, Necia. I want you to put that gun down and let us help you," Joel said with a firmness I knew he could not be feeling. Nevertheless, I was happy to see him standing up to her.

This seemed to infuriate her further. "What's she been saying to you? Why has she been here? Have you gone soft on her, little brother? I should have known you would. I could see it coming before. You were starting to fall for her, weren't you? You tried to talk us out of killing her last time too. Can't you see she's got all the money I need? I told you the last time I was in here that I needed money, and now that she was visiting you, you could persuade her to part with a little of it. But no, you didn't want to ask it of ..." her mouth curled contemptuously, "sweet little Mattie.

"You had your chance, Joel. I gave you an option. Since you wouldn't do it the easy way, I'll have to take matters into my own hands. Her daddy will jump at the chance to pay me off and keep his little darling safe." The gun wobbled as she pointed it around the room. It was as if she focused only on me and did not realize Ted, who had become very quiet and still, was in the room also. He and I were now joint spectators in an unreal tragedy. A drama acted out in front of us with the hospital room as a stage.

"Necia, this is insane. You can't get away with it in the first place, and I won't let you do it in the second." Joel's voice was sounding stronger.

As Joel spoke, I could see with my peripheral vision how Ted was carefully moving, little by little further into the room. I knew I needed to keep Necia distracted for him to be able to take action and perhaps divert this potential disaster. I took a deep breath, said a silent prayer, and joined in, like an actor entering the scene of a stage play. I jumped into the conversation.

"So, Necia, hiding behind your little brother as usual? You thought you were very clever didn't you? But look at you now. You're a wreck, your brother's dying, and all you care about is yourself and money. Have you no shame?"

"Our little kitty has fangs now, it seems. Is that how you got off that island, using your fangs, or did someone come and rescue you? Joel botched that job up too, didn't he? He deserves to die after messing our lives up like he did with you. I told him the other day when I found out you were still alive that he shouldn't have given you food before he had you take the poison. It must've weakened the effect."

That made sense, and it was something I hadn't thought of before now. I knew very little of poisons and their effects. I had asked my doctor, who guessed it might have been arsenic, digitalis, or deadly nightshade. I made a mental note to ask Joel what poison had been used, if we both made it safely out of this situation. My gaze shifted back to that gun. I knew I had to keep her attention focused on me, so I talked to her.

"Poison or food or not, I am still alive and I'll die before you see one cent of my money, Necia. I don't know why Joel is offering to get help for you. Your condition seems beyond help—" My voice became a harsh rasp, and my feelings of disgust must have shown, "Besides which," I said sarcastically, after a shocked pause reverberated around the room, "I can see by your comments you have a lot of concern for your brother. How touching, you callous, wicked woman. You're one of the reasons Joel is in the condition he is, don't you see that?"

"Joel has made his own choices. I didn't make him do anything!" she blustered edgily. Her eyes were witch-like with menace. Her face was contorted into a demonic glare.

Trying to evoke feelings for her brother didn't seem to be working, so I tried another tack. "You must be a real joy to be around, Necia. Is that why I don't see any sign of Freddie? Couldn't he stand the sight of you anymore?"

I must have hit a nerve with that missile. I saw her flinch as she became infuriated at my mention of Freddie. "Leave Freddie out of this!" she screamed at me.

I saw Ted gain some ground—casually he slid his hand to where I knew he kept his Glock, so I decided to push back a little harder on the same topic that seemed to distract her: Freddie. I was hoping to give Ted an opportunity to overpower and disarm her.

I looked over at Joel and saw him look back at me intently. His eyes beseeched me. When he saw me make eye contact with him, he spoke up, "I tried to keep her away from you, Mattie. I didn't want this to happen. I thought I would be dead soon ..." he didn't finish the sentence, but we all knew what he meant.

"Shut up, Joel!" Necia cried out. "And just because you've gone soft on her," nodding her head in my direction, "doesn't mean little Necia has." She aimed the gun more firmly at my chest. I tried to block out the image of my father grieving at my funeral.

I resorted to a discussion about Freddie again, "Where's Freddie, Necia? I don't see him. Doesn't he want you around anymore?"

"I told you. Leave Freddie out of this!" she screamed, her eyes wild.

Ted gained additional ground—one small step, then two.

I pursued it again. "But I don't want to leave Freddie out of this." I smiled sarcastically. "You used to be so tight with Freddie. I don't see him fluttering around you anymore, and no wonder—look at you. What happened, Necia? Did he find someone younger and prettier?"

"No!" she screamed again. "Freddie loves me! He's always loved me!" She appeared to go berserk, while I wondered where in the world the hospital security people were. Couldn't they hear all the commotion? Necia shifted her face into a feral snarl. "I'll kill you for saying that! I'll kill you!"

I could see her thumb move up to the hammer on the revolver. I had miscalculated and pushed her over the edge.

She yelled it again, and we could hear feet running down the hospital hall as she screamed at the top of her lungs, "I'll kill you!" Her sanity, already wavering, moved over the border and became full-blown insanity in just one breath. She swung her arm around the room while we all inhaled and stood motionless.

In one instant of time, her eyes crazed and she swung her arm back and leveled the gun straight at me. I heard the hammer click back as she prepared to fire. Her finger began to squeeze the trigger tighter. I looked into the raw passion in her glazed eyes and knew I was going to die in the next second. I prepared to meet God.

"No!" screamed Joel, simultaneously throwing his body. He catapulted himself across the line of fire from where he lay and where Necia stood at the far side of the bed. He lunged from the waist toward Necia, as she pulled the trigger. The report from the gun deafened me while the roar reverberated and echoed through the hospital halls.

A second shot, equally noisy came belching from Ted's gun within a fraction of a second of the first. Ted's shot felled Necia. She crumpled to the floor, her long scrawny fingers pulled at the sheets as her body disappeared behind the bed.

Ted lowered his gun. I could see his big shoulders give a nervous shudder, and his upper lip shook as he looked over at me. He walked over to retrieve the gun from where Necia had dropped it as she fell, saying as he did so, "You okay, Mattie?"

"I—I think so," I stammered, while I trembled and could not believe I was still standing, alive and unharmed. "How could she miss at such close range?" I looked down in shock at my untouched body, but I was intact.

"She didn't miss."

"What do you mean? I'm alive aren't I?"

"I mean Joel took the bullet meant for you. He saved your life by pushing himself in front of the gun at the last moment. He deflected the bullet meant for you."

I looked at the unmoving, crumpled heap on the bed and saw the crimson stain spreading across the white sheets like a scarlet sash. "Joel! Oh, God in heaven, No! Joel!"

The funeral was held on a muggy Tuesday.

We had successfully managed to avoid publicity on my return from Canada, but this time the throngs of reporters would not be denied. They invaded our lives like hungry hyenas after fresh, raw meat. They were an unwanted presence that constantly undulated like an unceasing tide; as one group of reporters left, another wave arrived. Their questions were rude, harassing, and went on and on. They constantly murmured innuendoes and searched out scandal; like pigs rooting in the mud for some small remnant of a nut, their eyes and noses and telescopic lenses pried into our most personal lives.

The accuracy of their reporting matched their courtesy and politeness: It was nonexistent. I was portrayed as a high-living, party-going, jet-setter who had caused Joel to become a drug addict in his despondency over my disappearance. His sister, in anger with me for ruining Joel's life, had tried to take my life. The conjectures continued to be dreamed up, endlessly, it seemed. Very little of it came close to reality.

The news media were incensed that I would not reveal where I had disappeared when I was presumed dead. I did not want my friends in Canada to come under their surveillance and scrutiny or to have their lives disrupted. So my silence meant they assumed I was protecting someone, possibly a lover I had somewhere, which again, contributed to Joel's despondency and then his dependency on drugs. So, according to them, Joel and Necia's deaths were my fault. I was persecuted beyond belief by the press corps. They would not leave me alone. The media hounds were present en masse at Joel's funeral.

The day of his funeral was an overcast day with rain brooding in the air, and the clouds prepared to unleash themselves of their watery burden at any moment. My skin felt clammy, my clothing stuck to my body and weighed me down with humidity, which matched my despondent mood. We were at the graveside. I had asked my friends, Pastor Mark and Margaret Lewis to come in and say a few words for the service. I warned them in advance about the onslaught to expect from the press.

As the service proceeded, I prayed silently about Joel, asking God, "Why?" I couldn't understand why his life had ended when it did. I felt he had been so close to accepting Christ. Combined with the guilt I had about pushing Necia too hard, which I felt caused Joel's life to end prematurely, my spirits were very low.

My conscience kept telling me, "Your actions cost the time that Joel might have needed to make his decision for Christ." I cried in sorrow as they lowered Joel's body in the ground. I cried for the Joel who might have been, the Joel I had been allowed to glimpse only briefly near the end, the Joel I had been unable to help. The press, of course scoffed at what they called my crocodile tears. Eleanor and my father protected me from their flying questions as we exited from the grave site.

The heavens upended their torrential buckets of rain upon the crowds as we left. My mood matched the weather. Later we quietly buried Necia next to her brother. Ted told us the police were at both funerals, hoping that Freddie might appear. They very much wanted to end his drug ring. It seems they were acutely aware of his activities and had been hoping for some time to put him behind bars. I could have told them he was probably hiding somewhere; that he never really cared for either Necia or Joel. He had only used them for his own ends. He proved me right because he never showed up at either funeral. Their search for him widened.

I wrote to Bea:

> Dear Bea,
>   This has been a terribly difficult time for me, dear Bea. You may have had the news up there by now, so you'll know what they're saying. I'm burdened with guilt

and I'm being crucified and misunderstood by the news media. The latter doesn't bother me all that much except for the difficulties it has made for both my father and Eleanor. Neither of them deserves all the anguish they've had to go through. The reporters have been ruthless and I no longer know how to deal with them.

The bigger question for me is—why did God allow all this to happen? You've always told me, "His ways are greater than our ways," and usually I can see that. This time it makes no rhyme or reason, and I don't understand. I feel simply awful about pushing Necia so hard that she wanted to kill me. Joel saved my life, Bea, but I couldn't help him save his soul. It is torturing me!

Pastor Mark tried to counsel me. My father and Eleanor tried their best to pull me out of my depression. Doug plied me with his cheerful disposition and positive outlook. Josie called me every day and told me I was not to blame for any of it, but my misery persevered. It was amazing how I had gone through such an ordeal only to be defeated when total victory was at my fingertips. How I longed for a quiet talk with Charles at the end of our dock. I knew he had wisdom far beyond his years and would understand my feelings very well.

I received a letter back from Bea:

Dear Mattie,

You must not scourge yourself over this situation with Joel. You obeyed God's commands in every way. You have no blame in this matter and must not blame yourself. In a way, by blaming yourself, you are taking God's place as our judge and we are not to do that. Do you understand what I am saying? If God does not blame you, and I know He does not, based on my knowledge of the Bible, then what right do you have to lay blame on

> yourself? Do not set yourself higher than God, Mattie, for that *will* be a grievous sin!
>
> One other thought, Mattie. How do you presume to know the condition of Joel's heart when he died? How do you know he had not asked God's pardon? How do you know he is not in heaven right now? I think you must take the high road, trust God with Joel's soul, and quit blaming yourself!
>
> As to the media spotlight, I think it will all die down very soon. There will be something else that will draw the attention of the ravening news wolves. You are in a wonderful position to understand what Christ went through when He was so violently treated and totally misunderstood. It is not a pleasant experience. You will learn from it not to be so quick to judge and condemn others—not that you were doing this—but this will give you another perspective from having been on this end of a situation. Remember: "In everything give God thanks."

Dear, wonderful Bea. She gently chided me and didn't sympathize with me, but she was right. I didn't know Joel's heart. I knew he had been changing. I knew God had been working in him. I must trust God with it. Bea's letter helped me go on with my life. I decided to ignore the press as much as possible, and I went back to work at our inner-city mission where I helped to prepare for the coming fall term at the new school in the building we were renovating. Bea was right, the notoriety and attention did wane, and rather quickly. A diplomat's daughter, overseas, was kidnapped one day, and the press went off in search of another sensational story. I was moved a few pages back and then soon disappeared from the radar altogether.

I began seeing more and more of Doug. He was a pleasant companion and a wonderful man. My family liked him very much too. My life made it back to a semblance of normalcy. I was able to reconcile myself somewhat to the way things had turned out with Joel. I looked back sometimes in wonder and could see God's hand at work in many ways throughout my life.

My father and Eleanor settled in; my father more relaxed and happy than I had ever seen him in my life. Eleanor was contented too, and I was so happy for both of them. My ordeals were over now. We could get on about the business of living a normal life again. My AIDS tests continued to show no sign of infection. We were growing confident that it would stay that way when the doctor told me I did not need to return for any additional tests.

It was nearing September, almost time for school to start, when my bodyguard, Ted Slaymaker made an unexpected appearance at our home one evening. My father had thanked Ted repeatedly for my deliverance and protection, but Ted had said, simply, "Joel saved her, I didn't." He refused to take any credit, and told us he'd been shaken by such a close call. The hours he'd spent listening in the hospital had had an impact on him too.

"They've arrested Freddie," he told us briskly. "He'll be spending a lot of time behind bars where he belongs."

"Where did they find him?" I asked.

"They used the information you and I gave them, Mattie, about how he worked the playgrounds and schools. The techniques he used, and all the information we got from Joel helped them. They set up surveillance around his likely target areas and sure enough, he eventually showed up. It revolts me—a creep like that picking on little kids! I hope they throw the book at him," Ted shook his head disgustedly. "I sometimes wonder if Joel had never met him …"

"Yes," I said sadly, "sometimes I wonder too."

"So." Ted smiled, shrugging off our melancholy with a Bogart flair. "Our case is closed, kid."

"Finished," I smiled back in a game we had played during our days at the hospital.

"Ka-put."

"Sealed."

"Wound up."

"Done."

"I give up," he said with a laugh.

"Thank goodness!" grinned Eleanor.

"Amen to that!" said my father cheerfully.

Ted turned to go. "Oh, I almost forgot!" He slapped his head and pulled an envelope out of his pocket. "This is for you, Mattie."

I reached out and slowly took the envelope from his hand. "What is it?" I turned it over and recognized Joel's haphazard scrawl on the outside.

"It's a letter to you from Joel. The police had to keep it as part of their investigation, but now that the case is truly closed, and the police have arrested Freddie as well, they felt you should have it. It's written to you."

"Thank you," I said, and turned it over in my hands. I wondered if what was inside would add to my wounded heart.

Later that evening as I prepared for bed, I picked Joel's letter up from my dresser where I had placed it earlier. I read:

> Dear Mattie:
>
> It is now late in the wee hours of the night. The hospital is quiet, but I can't sleep. You and Ted left a little while ago, and you will never know how much I hated to see you leave. Your visits have come to mean the world, and much more, to me. I see things now I never saw before, thanks to you. I look at life from a different viewpoint. I've become quite voracious in reading my Bible, and it has made such a difference in how I feel about dying.
>
> At first I argued with myself when you started coming to see me. *She's after something,* I thought. *She's waiting until I get vulnerable then "zap" it'll be time for revenge* I told myself. But night after night, day after day,

you came to read to me and talk with me about being a Christian, and slowly, slowly, I could feel myself being drawn to believe as you do. You truly believe in what you are telling me. You love the Lord so much it shines in your beautiful eyes when you speak of Him.

Mattie, I don't deserve what you have done for me. You have returned love for evil and because of you I was forced to learn what it was that could make a person have that kind of commitment and love in her life. There will be a special place in heaven for you, I know. And Mattie, this is something I'm writing down for you because in Luke, the Bible says we should acknowledge Jesus before men, so I'm acknowledging this before you.

Tonight when you left, I prayed the sinner's prayer you left for me. I opened my heart and asked God for forgiveness, and then I asked Him into my heart. Mattie, it was as if I could see the glory of heaven already! Such a weight was lifted from me and I felt such peace! For the first time I can face my approaching death with a calm acceptance, knowing Jesus has "gone to prepare a place for me."

I know it will make you very happy to hear that I plan to be in heaven too. I want to be where you are, of course, but more importantly, I want to be where our Lord is. I wanted to write this all down right away because I wanted to be sure that you know your efforts have borne fruit. My health is so unpredictable that tomorrow I might not be able to tell you all about it. If that happens, you'll be reading this instead. Mattie, through all this I've learned I love you very much. I'm so, so, sorry about all the anguish I've brought into your life.

And now, onto a subject you will not wish to discuss with me: Charles. Mattie dear, deny it if you will, but you are in love with Charles. I may not have been much of a husband in our marriage, but in these last few weeks I've come to understand you very well. I can now tell when you're happy or sad or upset or angry. You've become very sad, Mattie. I can see the wistful look in your eyes sometimes, when you are telling me about your experiences after you were rescued in Ontario, and I suspect this wistful look has to do with a certain person you are missing who now lives at that selfsame mission.

Yes, you've told me all about the mission in Canada, but you were really telling me about a very special person named Charles. You revealed far more of your feelings than you realized as you talked of everything that happened to you up there. Your face has a kind of glow when you mention his name that I now wish I had been able to put on it during our time together. But it was not meant to be. I wasted my chances, and they are gone. Now I want you to be happy.

You must not let pride or other foolish emotions to get in your way, Mattie. I think Charles loves you too. I can tell from the things you've told me and from his care of you. You mustn't let this slip away from you. You told me once that you prayed every night for God to send a special woman into Charles's life. Well, He already has, and that woman is you, Mattie.

When I die, and we know that is going to be very soon, please fulfill this dying man's last request and go to Charles. It is where you belong. I know it is where God now wants you.

Thank you for the privilege I had of loving you, Mattie. I'm sorry I didn't recognize it sooner for the honor it is.

Love, Joel

Chapter 22

One year later ...

It was a beautiful, glorious fall, and was late afternoon in Canada. But, now that I had arrived, I wondered if perhaps I had made a dreadful mistake, for as I looked around, I did not see him anywhere on the grounds. *Perhaps he is no longer here.* Bea had not mentioned him for several letters; was it possible he had taken another assignment somewhere else? Most of the buildings seemed to be quiet for the evening; no one appeared to be around anywhere.

I had not notified anyone that I would be arriving today. I did hear some rather noisy activity over at the school, which might explain why no one came out when I arrived. Somehow my arrival seemed to have gone unnoticed. I had sent the floatplane pilot on his way, and even that noise had not drawn any spectators.

Was this all a mistake? My heart filled with fear as a sense of despair and sadness started to creep in, but I tried to shake it off and remember the Scriptures about not having a "spirit of fear." *Am I wrong in thinking there might be a place for me here?* I turned around from my search and walked in melancholy meditation back down to the dock on the shore of the lake.

I sat and dangled my feet over the water as I had so many times in the past. I was reminded of how we used to do this together. I watched the panorama in the changing sky, and my soul became more and more discouraged, but I tried to retain my faith and courage. The sun was setting before my eyes and beautiful patterns of vibrant color ebbed and flowed over the sky and water, touching my heart with their beauty, as always.

Then, as twilight came slipping into this wild and beautiful north country, I saw a movement way out on the lake, a silvery reflection of water splashing. I peered more intently and my heart felt a flicker of hope as the rhythmic splash and ripple of the water drew nearer. Now I could make out a solitary figure in a canoe. It paddled across the serene water toward the dock—toward me.

I stood and became a silhouette on the dock against the evening sky. I could tell when he looked ahead and saw me standing there. He hesitated in his systematic strokes of the paddle as the canoe drew near. He allowed it to glide silently with the paddle poised in his hands while he stared at me, his gaze riveted in my direction. He shook his head as if seeing a mirage, then shook it again in disbelief, and then he remained motionless for one more heartbeat. The canoe began to drift aimlessly. I felt the penetration of his gaze like two missiles locked on my own two eyes.

He broke the moment and looked heavenward for a time as if in prayer. Next I saw him dip the paddle in the water again, more surely than before, firmly now, faster and faster. On he came, quickly now. My heart was beating in syncopation with the paddle—strong and fast. He was looking at me intently, closer and closer. Finally, he arrived at where I stood, and the canoe glided silently, swiftly to the dock. He tied off the canoe, and then jumped easily and lightly onto the dock next to me. A smile lighted his face like a thousand candles, and he wrapped me in a warm embrace.

Epilogue

My son, Charles Jr., came to us with an incredible tale at dinner this evening. He told the story in front of his two little sisters who looked at his shining face in awe. I smiled around the table at our three beautiful children as he told the tale, but my eyes caught those of my beloved husband in silent communication as it ended.

Charles Jr. heard the story from two of his Ojibway friends. It seems there is now a rumor floating among the Ojibway Indians about an old chief who was fishing one day not long ago.

The chief caught an enormous fish and was very proud of his good catch. But when he split the fish open for his dinner, he found a beautiful diamond ring.

The story is spreading like wildfire among the natives, who are wondering what kind of person would use diamond bait to catch a fish. No one is sure if the story is true, or if it is just the great imagination of an old Indian.

Printed in the United States
By Bookmasters